THE JUNO LETTERS

BOOK #1 - THE JUNO LETTERS

Gulliver —
Hope you enjoy
the read as much as I
enjoyed the play.

L.W. HEWITT

L.W. HEWITT

DEDICATION

The Juno Letters is dedicated to my mother, Bonnie Hewitt. She was my inspiration, my muse. You gave a gift to your family that can only be repaid by passing it along to others. We miss you, Mom.

DISCLAIMER AND CREDITS

This is a work of fiction. Although the context of the novel is based on known events, license has been taken to fit the story. The characters and situations are creations of the author's imagination. Any resemblance to persons or historical events is strictly circumstantial. Technical information where not attributed is either freely available from public sources or imaginary.

Cover design:

Tatiana Vila, Vila Design
http://www.viladesign.net

Cover Photograph

Infantrymen in a Landing Craft Assault (LCA) going ashore from H.M.C.S. PRINCE HENRY off the Normandy beachhead, France, 6 June 1944.
Photographer: Dennis Sullivan
Canada. Dept. of National Defence, Library and Archives Canada; PA-132790

Back Cover Photograph
Infantrymen of The Royal Winnipeg Rifles in Landing Craft Assault (LCAs) en route to land at Courseulles-sur-Mer, France, 6 June 1944.
Photographer: Unknown
Canada. Dept. of National Defence, Library and Archives Canada; PA-132650

CONTENTS

THE LETTERS

*Hostile armies may face each other for years, striving for the victory
which is decided in a single day.*
— *Sun Tzu*

Present Day

A small package was left by a delivery service on the front porch. I
take my morning coffee at a downtown café so I was not at home
when it was delivered. I call the café my "office" - a small table next
to a giant wood stove in a former "Gentlemen's Club" - a prohibition
term for pub - that serves as the pool hall, bar, and restaurant for a
small historic hotel called The Olympic Club. This is where I like to
begin my day.

Today was quiet. My waitress brought me coffee in one of the
"old cups," reserved for regulars like myself. The manager had
decided to spruce up the place by playing classical music (a good
thing) and changing to large teacups for coffee (not so good). They
were clumsy to hold and the coffee cooled too quickly. When the

regulars revolted by bringing their own coffee cups, he relented and kept a small supply of the old cups for us troublemakers.

I finished some routine work - checked my email, reviewed some client notes, and chatted briefly with one of the customers about the massive urinals in the men's room. These things resemble a porcelain coffin standing on end and are plumbed with ancient copper pipes with pressure valves attached, circa 1920 or so. There is a window in the door so people can take pictures without having to enter (another good thing if you have an aversion to infectious diseases). Centralia, Washington is likely the only town where a men's room is the main tourist attraction.

After coffee I took a short walk around the corner to the bank and paid the mortgage, then drove to the local grocery to select something for dinner, then home. The package was waiting for me on the front steps. It was nondescript, irregularly shaped - a bundle wrapped in plain brown paper. The return address caught my attention - the writing was in French.

Courseulles-sur-Mer

I had never heard of Courseulles-sur-Mer, and knew no one in France for that matter. I had travelled to Europe only once, to Germany to visit my daughter and two grandsons. I have an interest in World War II history and worked in a family visit with trips to Munich, Berchtesgaden, and Berlin. I've never been to France.

I sat the package on my desk and went to pour myself a cup of coffee. When I sat down, I first typed "Courseulles" into my browser's search field. The first return link piqued my curiosity.

COURSEULLES-SUR-MER Calvados - 18 km north of Caen … In Courseulles-sur-Mer the Germans had fortified the mouth of the river Seulles. On 6 June 1944, …

June 6, 1944. D-Day. The Invasion of Europe. I clicked on the link and read the first paragraph ...

> In Courseulles-sur-Mer the Germans had fortified the mouth of the river Seulles. On 6 June 1944, at 7:45 a.m. the amphibious tanks of the 1st Hussars were launched in the ocean three kilometers from the coast; many of them sank because of the hard swell. Those that succeeded in reaching the sand of the beach immediately opened fire on the German positions. They enabled the 7th Brigade to liberate Courseulles-sur-Mer in a few hours. By the evening of 6 June, 21,500 men and 3,200 vehicles had landed on Juno Beach.

As an American I have often heard the stories and watched movies of the D-Day assaults on Omaha Beach and Point du Hoc by the American army. Admittedly, even though I was an amateur historian of World War II, I had spent little time studying the action on the other landing beaches. Just what connection was there between this package and the Canadian assault on Juno Beach?

I cut the tape holding the paper package together. It consisted of two bundles of old letters tied by coarse twine. Several of the envelopes had been opened and the letters appeared to have been recently read and refolded. There was a cover letter enclosed, and a name in the first paragraph immediately caught my attention. Henry Anderson. And further down, a date - 1918.

Henry W. Anderson, the Reverend H.W. Anderson, was my grandfather. He had served in France in WWI, and later served as an army chaplain in the Pacific during WWII. He retired with the rank of lieutenant colonel. Grandpa "Andy" had been the chaplain of the Veterans Administration hospital in Vancouver, Washington when I was a small boy. My family used to take the train from

Tacoma to Vancouver to visit. He and "Nana" Lucile lived in the old Fort Vancouver Officer's Row - vintage Victorian homes that housed the post's officers.

The cover letter was in English.

To: Monsieur Lawrence Hewitt

Centralia, Washington USA

Dear M. Hewitt,

Recently our city demolished a small cottage on the outskirts of Courseulles-sur-Mer. The construction company found a metal container with these letters inside.

One set of letters is addressed to Henry W. Anderson in Tacoma, Washington. The other set contains letters written by the same Henry Anderson from several addresses in both the United States and overseas. The time frame is 1922 - 1944. I must apologize for opening and reading several letters, but we were trying to identity their owner.

We discovered through U.S. Army records there was a Henry Anderson stationed in Tours, France, in 1918. A further search of public records indicated he had a daughter named Bonnie who married John Hewitt of Tacoma, Washington. They had a son named Lawrence. Records indicate both John and Bonnie are deceased, but we traced a Lawrence Hewitt who had lived in Tacoma to Centralia, Washington, and surmised this may be the correct family.

The Juno Letters

If these are the letters meant for your grandfather, please accept them with our compliments. If not, please return them to me. It is our desire to see they are forwarded to the correct party.

Yours sincerely,

M. Frédéric Pouille

Mayor, Courseulles-sur-Mer, France

I placed the letter aside and cut the twine binding the groups of letters. The first group was written in French by "Andy" Anderson to "Antoine." The dates covered a span of some twenty years, the last one dated 1942.

The second group, also in French, was addressed from "Antoine" to Henry W. Anderson. They were sealed, except for a few opened by the city, but never posted. There was no indication as to Antoine's last name and no return address.

All the envelopes were old and yellowed, obviously from the same period. I carefully slit them open with a pocketknife and removed the letters, organizing them by date. I examined the latest one first. It was from Antoine, but the writing was shaky and uncertain.

I opened the French - English translator on my computer and typed in small pieces of the text. Although the translation was a little clumsy, eventually the meaning of the letter came through. It read,

– 11 –

6 Jun 1944

My Dear Andy,

This will be my last letter, for I will die this day, I am certain of it. I wish only to be remembered as a patriot, but that cannot be.

Pray for me. You are my only friend.

Antoine

CHAPTER 1 - THE GREAT WAR

The world plunged headlong into war with banners flying, bands playing, and giant armies poised to vanquish traditional enemies in a matter of months. It was called The Great War. It would last four agonizing and murderous years, and change the lives of its children - and their children's children - forever.

The bow crashed into the trough of the giant wave with a shudder. Confined below decks, the company of soldiers suffered through the cold and damp air, fouled by the rancid smell of vomit. Private Henry W. Anderson wrote in his journal,

> Jan 16, 1918 Wed
> Conditions rotten beyond words.
> Air damp and cold.
> Feeding fishes.

The RMS Carpathia, famous for rescuing the survivors of the Titanic disaster in 1912, served as a transport between America and England, ferrying troops for the Great War raging in Europe.

The year is 1918. The first leg of the trip to Halifax was cold and rough. Despite the ship's size, 541 feet overall and 64 feet in beam, it was tossed violently in the rough seas.

Arriving finally after three days, the great liner anchored at the head of Halifax harbor awaiting the other vessels that would form a convoy to Glasgow, Scotland. The weather cleared somewhat, and on January 19, the day after making port, the soldiers were allowed on deck.

"Nice to get a bit of fresh air, eh, Andy?"

Lee Gray was from Chicago, just eighty miles as the crow flies from Andy's family hometown of Rockford, Illinois, and had befriended the 21 year old Henry "Andy" Anderson of Santa Cruz while struggling to keep the passage rations down in the rough seas. The two young American recruits strolled the deck together, their first time at sea.

"I cannot imagine what the trip across to England will be like after that," Andy replied, happy to breath the clean harbor air and stretch his legs on deck. "Will you look at that!"

While the European war seemed remote, there was ample evidence of the conflict even here on the coast of Canada. A massive explosion had rocked this port in Nova Scotia just over a month before when the munitions ship Mont-Blanc filled with 3000 tons of explosives bound for the war and the Belgian relief ship Imo collided. A fire started and after the crew abandoned ship, the Mont-Blanc exploded, laying waste to two and a half square miles of the city in a mostly working-class section. Two thousand were killed, and more than six thousand wounded.

The men stared in silence at the giant debris field that once had been a part of the town.

For a young man from Rockford, this had already been the trip of a lifetime. Rockford was located northwest of Chicago, and had been populated by industrious Swedish and Irish immigrants. Among them was Lars Johan Anderson of Harnesta village, Munktorp Parish, Wästmanland, Sweden. The son of Lars Anders made his living repairing shoes in his own repair business and running the village's commercial scales.

Andy Anderson had left home and moved to the San Francisco Bay area in April 1917 just three days before President Wilson declared war on Imperial Germany. His parents visited him in California, and so liked the area that by July his father had sold his business and moved west to San Jose. Andy's mother Karolina, sister Ruby, and brother Sam followed by mid-September.

The letters were all written in Andy's schooled style, but in French. Certain phrases that I could understand caught my eye. It would take a while to piece all this together, especially using my computer translator. My first thought - who was Antoine?

I remember my mother telling me Grandpa Andy had served in France during World War I, but no one in the family really knew what he had done or where he had been. My mother had compiled a comprehensive family history that included extensive genealogy and family scrapbooks, organized by family name on both my maternal and paternal sides. I would start there.

The histories were stored in boxes in the attic. After rummaging around in the dust I managed to pull out several boxes filled with binders, some with photos and letters and another marked "Anderson, Hewitt, Kelso, and Greene; Genealogy, History." The Hewitt line was the least known, the genealogy records stopping with an adoption. The Greene line was the longest, stretching as I remembered multiple generations before the Revolutionary War. My father's mother was a Greene, and Nathaniel Greene, a friend of George Washington's and a famous general in our Revolutionary War, was a direct ancestor. The Kelso line was Irish.

On my Mother's side I was Swedish and English, an Anderson on one side and a Bond on the other. My Grandpa Andy's parents had immigrated to America in the Northern European migrations of the late 19th century, and had settled in the Midwest. There was nothing even remotely close to an Antoine, on either my grandfather's or grandmother's side. I found nothing in the genealogy or the photo and letter binders either that gave me a clue who Antoine could be.

"Did you check the old box on the closet shelf?" my wife asked. I wasn't exactly sure what she meant, but on looking further I found an old wooden box with a keyed lock on the front. Inside was a lift out shelf, and a separate compartment in the lid. It contained some old buttons, an old Boy Scout badge, and other little mementoes. Nothing of relevance to my current search, but I found my attention wandering as I carefully touched these precious little objects my mother had so carefully saved.

Lifting the shelf out, I found some old books and what appeared to be journals. There were old maps of Paris and Tours, France. Beneath these, I hit pay dirt. There was an old journal stamped with the title, "A Soldier's Diary." It was my Grandpa Andy's personal diary from World War I.

I carefully opened the first page, and read,

> Nov 28, 1917
> Quit job at Fageol Motors.
> Enlisted 660 Market St.

Young Andy had taken his first job at the American Can Company in San Francisco, but soon moved to a position at Fageol Motors, a manufacturer of farm equipment and an ill-fated luxury car that cost $12,000 in 1920 dollars.

His job there was short lived. On November 28 he quit and enlisted in the Army, just 26 days after the first American casualties of the Great War with the grand idea of adventure "over there." Andy had attended a private vocational school as a boy where he learned drafting and the use of machining tools, so he was given a position in the Engineering corps.

As he bade goodbye to his family, his father Lars Anderson gave him a gold cross with a simple inscription, "To Henry from Father."

"The pastor of the church blessed it before God. It will bring you luck," he solemnly said. Andy was moved to tears - his father never wore nor approved of jewelry.

Andy made a special point of writing to family and friends often, as was the custom of the day. He also diligently recorded each day's events in his journal.

On December 12, 1917, after a quick orientation at Ft. McDowell on Angel Island near San Francisco, Andy boarded the Pacific Limited San Francisco. After stops in Ogden, Omaha, and Chicago, he finally detrained at Fort Devens, Massachusetts where he bunked in barracks 688. After less than a month of training, he was off to New York where he boarded the RMS Carpathia for Europe.

By the following day six other transports and two escort cruisers had joined the Carpathia. The small flotilla left Halifax harbor for the open Atlantic. The rough seas continued, but in a few days they had crossed over into the warmer waters of the Gulf Stream and the cold weather began to moderate, allowing for some fresh air time on deck. Six days out of Halifax, while Andy was taking a late morning nap below decks, the monotony of the cruise was shaken.

"Andy! Get up, man!" Lee shouted to be heard above the pounding engine drone in the steerage compartment. "The cruisers have made contact!"

He burst out of the narrow bunk. The cruisers were sounding the shrill alarm of general quarters. They sped off, boilers belching heavy black smoke, to the fringe of the convoy to the south.

The British had been convoying materials and supplies across the Atlantic in the face of the German submarine threat since the outbreak of the war, some fours years before. A tactic often used by the U-boat commander was to shadow an innocent neutral vessel. When the escorts raced off to inspect, leaving the convoy vulnerable, they would sneak in for a kill. Over the years tactics had improved, and losses reduced. One of the escorts challenged the target, an unidentified steamer, while the second steamed ahead-full in a picket line around the convoy, alert to the possibility of an unseen attack.

U-boats usually attacked at night, so this was likely a false alarm. But the potential threat was taken seriously. The ship's alarm sounded.

"All hands on deck. Life jackets required. This is not a drill. Repeat, this is not a drill."

The two friends scrambled quickly out of steerage to the deck, life jackets in tow, clumsily pulling them on in the process.

"Submarines?" Lee sounded out loud, excited.

"I hope not," Andy shouted back, as they hit the deck railing.

"Get to your stations!" the unit commander screamed, running down the deck. He was a nervous fellow, so the boys below decks liked to joke, and was what Andy would later write in his journal, "a bit of a spectacle, all things considered."

The escort cruiser cut quickly in between the Carpathia and the SS Mary Catherine, closing off a wide opening at the front of the convoy, then cut back across to race down the length of the transports again. In the rough seas the spray from the bow crashing into the sea was frightening.

"Can you imagine being on that thing?" Lee gasped. "I'd be feedin' the fish all day."

At the end of an hour, with all the troops crowded together, the call of "All Clear" was given. The life preservers disappeared quickly, and for a while things settled down. At least until Capt.

Nervous Nellie, the "bit of a spectacle" unit commander, got all fired up.

"Not good enough," he would say, again and again. The unit repeated the "on deck" drill all afternoon. "No, not good enough. Again!," and they would trod back below decks, only to scramble once again topsides.

"I can't take much more of this nonsense," a small, wiry recruit standing next to the two friends remarked, under his breath. And for some unexplained reason, by the next day Capt. Nervous Nellie was "green to the gills," and confined to sickbay.

Andy wrote in his journal,

> Jan 28 Mon
> Fine day. On deck. Convoy meets us.
> Changed course.

The Carpathia arrived in Glasgow on the afternoon of January 29 with no further excitement, nine days out of Halifax. The recruits boarded a train to Carlyle and reached their destination, Camp Winnall Down.

The camp was both a staging area for troops traveling to France and a rest area for the battle weary. The unit was kept sequestered from troops recovering from front line action for the next several days. Drills and orientation followed, but it was a very short time to prepare for a trip to the front. They left the camp on February 3, and boarded the steamer Mona's Queen at Southampton, quickly leaving port bound for Le Havre.

A seaman treated the boys to the heroic story of the "Queen Number 2" as the crew called her, the second in the line of steamers of the Isle of Man Steam Packet Company line to bear the name, Mona's Queen. The side paddle steamer had come under attack in the English Channel on February 6, 1916. In trying to run clear of an approaching torpedo, the captain ran over the top of the partially submerged U-boat, the left side paddle wheel crashing into the conning tower. In the melee that followed, the captain tried to retire his crippled ship only to watch in amazement as the U-boat disappeared. The ship's exploits as a sub-killer were the stuff of ever increasing grandeur as the crew told and retold the ship's exploits to the recruits heading to the front.

"I'd be a lot happier if she had a blumin' gun on her foredeck," Private Gray grumbled, only to be chastised by Andy Anderson for his language.

"No need for swearing," he would constantly remind him. Although a son of a Swedish immigrant, Anderson was a staunch Baptist - not a Lutheran. He insulated himself from the rough language of many of his fellow soldiers, and was constantly reminding his friend Lee of the sin of blasphemy.

"You're a bit of a pain, Andy," he would come back, but the two remained close friends throughout the voyage.

They were glad to finally be on French soil, away from the threat of German U-boats or surface raiders. The unit formed on the quay at the port of Le Havre and marched to Rest Camp #2 a few kilometers outside of the city. After a short night's rest in bivouac, they boarded another train.

"I feel like meat going to the slaughter," Lee groused as they rattled their way through the French countryside. They had been loaded into open boxcars, unlike the passenger trains in England and America. It was cold and damp, with little chance to rest. Andy tried to get some sleep by stretching out across the wooden floor, but awoke just before midnight. In the distance he could see the lights of Paris, but the train bypassed the City of Light heading south. He tried to sleep again, but had little success.

Trains were assigned various priorities for track time, and a boxcar load of raw recruits heading for a depot detachment behind the front lines was about as low a priority as you could get. Soldiers called the boxcar a "hom forty" from the load capacity stenciled on the side - 40 men (hommes) or 8 horses (chaveaux). It moved at a maddeningly slow pace, spending long, cold hours idled on sidings, averaging about two and a half kilometers an hour between points. So by the next day they were still heading south through the countryside.

They passed groups of German prisoners on work details. Conditions in prisoner of war camps were often deplorable - muddy, wet, and miserable. Work in the country was preferable to life in the camps, and so much better than life in the trenches.

Finally, they arrived at Blois in south central France and marched six kilometers to another rest camp where, for the first time since leaving San Francisco, they had a chance to rest. For the next six days Andy was assigned light details, and tried to keep busy.

The engineering headquarters was located in Tours, a short distance away. Tours was the point of intersection of railroads coming from the ports of Brest, Bordeaux, and St. Nazaire. Tours was the headquarters for the Services of Supply (SOS). This meant it was both a busy yet generally safe place to serve out the war. Andy had been recruited as a draftsman.

Map making was critical to the war effort, and one of the duties a devout Baptist could do and not violate his vows of nonviolence. Andy had to wait for a special waiver from the War Department to avoid trench assignments, but this was waiting for him when he arrived in Tours on February 12.

Andy was barracked in an old stable along with other members of the 447th Depot Detachment Engineers, glad to be safely away from the front, and glad to be settled in place at last.

Two days later, on February 14th, he was ordered to Paris.

CHAPTER 2 - THE SPRING OFFENSIVE

If you order your men to roll up their buff-coats, and make forced marches
without halting day or night, covering double the usual distance at a
stretch, doing a hundred Li in order to wrest an advantage, the leaders
of all your three divisions will fall into the hands of the enemy.
— *Sun Tzu*

Present Day

The journal documented Andy's experiences beginning with his
enlistment, training, and eventual transport overseas as a part of the
American Expeditionary Force (AEF) in 1917. I was surprised to
read that after a brief station in Paris, where he experienced some
enemy bombardments, Andy had spent most of the war in the
central part of France, at the headquarters company in Tours. Like
most of the soldiers in an army, he was a part of logistics and supply.
These were the critical functions of an army in the field, even if not
filled with drama.

The entries were fairly cryptic, short, and to the point.

> Mar 26 (1918), Tue
> Not much doing during day.
> Made payroll.

> Apr 24 (1918), Wed
> Worked on colored maps

> Jul 19 (1918), Fri
> Fair. Letter from Smalley.
> French lesson.

To put these into perspective, I created a timeline of activities associated with the Great War beginning in 1917 when America declared war on the Central Powers. Against these benchmarks I plotted out significant entries in the diary, such as when Andy arrived in certain cities, when he experienced bombardments, when he worked on certain projects, etc. Slowly a pattern began to emerge that helped expose the daily life of a soldier in a support detachment as war unfolded all around.

———⟳———

Paris, 1918

The Sainte-Anne Hotel was located on Rue Sainte-Anne a few blocks from the Paris Opera House - the heart of the old city. The major avenues spoked out from the Opera House and led to the Champs Élysées in one direction, the Eiffel Tower in another, and the Louvre and Notre Dame in yet another. Troops reported to the headquarters company at the Sainte-Anne when ordered to Paris, then transferred to locations throughout the city, usually hotels taken over by the AEF. Andy Anderson wrote, "Almost missed the train" on the day, he reported in. He ended up sleeping on the floor with a couple dozen others.

The next day he reported to Lieutenant Richardson at the Hotel Mediterranée about a thirty minute walk from the Sainte-Anne. That night he slept in a real bed at the Alexandria Hotel.

Paris seemed a long way from the front, but the city was the target of air raids, mostly from Zeppelins. There was plenty of work to do, and between shifts Andy had a chance to sightsee. Over the next month there were intermittent air raid scares, and as February turned to March the death toll among civilians began to climb.

March 23 was a fair morning and Andy was at work early helping to create signs. The bombardment began at 7:20 am.

"Anderson, let's get in the shelter. It's another Zeppelin."

The commanding officer was unconcerned. The Zeppelin was capable of only limited attacks, and they lacked the mobility to catch anyone off guard, especially once the first bombs fell. It was great sport watching them place their bombs, only to be shot at by the fighters. Drama in the sky, but not too much risk on the ground.

But the explosions continued, regularly.

"Every fifteen minutes, Captain," came the report back from the spotter. "And there's no Zeppelin in sight." Where were these explosions coming from? A new high altitude Zeppelin? The Germans had used rail mounted mortars and cannon before, but the front was a long way out of range, some 70 miles, or 150 km.

Still the explosions came - 21 in all. They continued unabated the next day. A single shell hit the roof of the St-Gervais-et-St-Protais Church, collapsing the entire roof onto the congregation hearing the Good Friday services. A total of 88 people were killed and 68 were wounded. A shell had landed near the Cathedral of Notre Dame. Something new had entered the war, and the people of Paris were in a panic. The press fueled the hysteria with wild speculation about a new wonder weapon.

The military took little time once the continuous bombardment began in triangulating the location of the attacks, some 75 miles northeast of Paris. Examination of the fragments revealed the explosions were from shells, not bombs, which ruled out an air attack. It would be a few days before air reconnaissance was able to confirm the existence of a new cannon - called the Kaiser Wilhelm Geschütz - that could shoot a massive projectile over 75 miles, and rain death on Paris beyond the range of defensive artillery.

What later became known as the "Paris Gun" shot the very first man-made object into the stratosphere, some 25 miles high. While it created panic among the civilian population, the army quickly mobilized to attack the giant cannon. The Paris Gun took a crew of 80 to operate, and consumed so many resources it would prove to be valuable only as a weapon of terror. The gun had fired between 320 and 367 shells, but only killed 250 people, wounded over 600, and damaged property. However, it ushered in a new face of war - random civilian casualties from long-range weapons.

Andy contemplated his situation. He had joined the army with a waiver that, because of his religious beliefs, granted him the status of a non-belligerent. That is how he ended up in the headquarters company. Now the fighting could be taken anywhere, and his assignment in Paris grew increasingly dangerous.

What kind of people are these Germans? he thought. War between armies was confusing enough, but to wage a war of terror against helpless civilians? These Germans are less than human, he convinced himself.

The bombardment signaled the beginning of a new offensive. On March 21, 1918, the German army launched a series of attacks along the Western Front. The objective was to throw the weight of some fifty additional divisions freed up by the collapse of the Eastern Front at the British and French forces along the Somme before the overwhelming supply of men and material from the Americans could be brought to bear. German storm troopers advanced quickly, carrying few provisions and ammunition, scavenging off the enemy as they continued forward. They attempted to outflank the British and force an armistice on terms favorable to Germany. News from the front was carefully censored, but rumors circulated wildly.

He was relieved when he finally received orders to return to Tours. He boarded the train and bid farewell to an increasingly dangerous Paris on April 6.

That day a junior officer in the AEF communications headquarters in Brest read a memo from the American hospital administrator.

> There has been a sudden increase in cases of influenza reported in hospital. We are currently experiencing a shortage of personnel to meet this unexpected outbreak. In the past three days, 120 patients have been admitted from bivouacs throughout the region, with 15 fatalities. The staff anticipates at least that many more fatalities within 36 hours. Requests for hospital transfers for influenza will be denied at this time due to a lack of beds. It is critical that field units take immediate steps to curtail exposure.

The officer stamped the memo CENSORED, and passed it to his company clerk for filing. The information about the spreading influenza outbreak would not spread to the front line units. The flu, however, would not be censored so easily.

———— ∞∞∞ ————

Present Day

There were thirty-two letters. They were dated but not addressed, with many references to things that were cryptic, almost as if in code, that blurred the meaning. It was difficult to place these in context to help unravel their meaning and relevance to my grandfather.

Why had these been saved, presumably by Antoine, and buried - not mailed? What was the nature of the relationship between Andy and Antoine? It seemed clear from the first letter their relationship was intimate and robust - odd considering Andy was in the Pacific during the Second War. Who was Antoine and where did he and Andy create such a personal relationship?

And that last letter, the one that spoke of Antoine dying "this day." The desperation and futility of those words - sent to my grandfather - had some meaning, some deeper sense behind them. This was no casual friendship. The letters created more questions than they answered.

I turned to the community college in town for help. The comptroller, Jim Anderson, is a business contact of mine, so I phoned and asked him to arrange a visit with the college's French professor, Dr. Suzanne Tauscher. I needed to get an accurate translation of the letters from someone versed in the nuances of the language - something the computer translator was unable to do. She agreed to meet with me the following afternoon.

"Bonjour, Monsieur Hewitt," she cheerfully stood and offered me her handshake as I entered her office.

"Bonjour, madame. Comment allez-vous?"

"Ah, je suis bien, monsieur. Your French pronunciation is very good. Have you been to France?"

"No, I'm afraid not. Just two years of French in high school, but that was a long time ago!"

"Perhaps you will have the opportunity someday. Now, I understand you have some interesting letters," she responded. "And please, just call me Suzanne."

I handed her the letters. She glanced quickly at them and raised her eyebrows inquisitively in my direction.

"Where did you get these?" she asked, her academic curiosity piqued.

"They were sent to me from a small village on the French coast by the mayor, intended for my grandfather originally when they were written in the period from 1922 - 1944."

"Yes, through the German occupation. And you said these were interesting … Mon Dieu, that is an understatement!"

"What do they say?"

"Well, your grandfather's correspondence to Antoine is like hearing one side of a phone call. One has to read between the lines to try to discover the origin of the conversation. Was your grandfather fluent in French?"

"I have no idea. That's something that never came up before, and I was surprised to say the least."

"The letters from Antoine are more direct, but they lack a context. Especially a location. I am afraid some are very difficult to read. The letters are faded, and some are stained. They could be scanned and enhanced, and would be easier to translate."

She continued to browse through them, then looked up with excitement on her face.

"I have an idea. This will take some time to scan, enhance, and translate, especially given that some of the language use is a little clumsy, as I might expect. Would you let me turn these into a class assignment? I could form teams to do the translations. Our graphics department could scan and enhance them as a part of a class project as well."

I could sense a growing excitement over this, and decided it would be useful to bring in others to help in the daunting detective case before me.

"I would agree to that."

"We would, of course, make an agreement protecting your copyright on these, and defining the terms of use, to protect your originals. I would like to have the history department look these over, too, once they are translated, if that is agreeable."

"I'm game. I have a lot of work to do to track down just who this Antoine is, and being able to offload this part, and have other eyes look at them, will be a big help, I am sure."

"OK. I will have to get approval from the department, but that is just a formality. The agreement will take some time - bureaucracy, you know. But in the meantime, I can simply give you a receipt for the letters to scan them. We will have no right to use them until our agreement is signed, but we can get started on the scanning right away.

"I'd like to arrange a meeting between you and Professor Douglas from the history department. I am certain he will be interested in partnering on this project. He may have some insight into helping you locate your elusive Antoine - which would be a big help to know before we tackle the letters in earnest. I could plan to have the letters delivered to him after they are scanned if that would be acceptable.

"Here, let me give you his contact information. I might suggest you email a copy of the translated 'D-Day' letter with a synopsis of what you know - and what you do not know - before your meeting."

I left her office with a renewed sense of purpose and optimism.

Northern France, 1918

"C'est le renégat." The French private spat on the ground at the feet of a young soldier dressed in a tattered German infantry uniform. "This is the turncoat."

The soldier stood in line with other German prisoners bound for a forestry work crew. Prisoners were collected at Abbeville on the channel coast before being sent to England for internment or assigned to forced labor. Captain Lejeune had received orders to provide French-speaking POWs for active service in various support depots behind the lines. The report of a young Frenchman in German uniform who had been beaten severely by his French captors and sent to hospital caught his attention.

"Bring him to my tent," he commanded curtly, and strode off. The prisoner was jerked out of line and prodded at bayonet-point toward the commander's tent. He prepared for another violent beating, so was surprised when the captain ordered him to take a seat. "Asseyez-vous."

The young soldier sat uneasily on a simple wooden stool in the corner. Sitting in the presence of a French officer could mean a rifle butt across the side of the head, or worse, so he was decidedly nervous. The officer had a paper on his small desk, but the prisoner dared not look at it. He kept his eyes fixed straight ahead, a prisoner's defensive stare.

"You speak French?" The captain demanded.

"Oui, Capitaine, I am French," but he offered no further information. The captain prepared to take notes.

"You are in German uniform. I could have you shot. Explain yourself." The captain did not look up from his paper.

"I am from a small village near Château-Salins in the Alsace."

The French captain looked up. Germany had annexed the Alsace-Lorraine region of eastern France on the German border after the War of 1870. The French-speaking minority had been allowed to immigrate to France by German authorities, but a small population of French descent remained. By the start of the current war less than 20% of the region's inhabitants were French. They spoke French as their mother language, a situation tolerated by the Imperial German government. Although some limited autonomy was granted the region in 1911, it was still considered a Reichsland, or Imperial Province, called Elsass-Lothringen by the German government.

At the outbreak of the Great War the able-bodied men throughout Germany were conscripted into the army, by force if necessary. He was sixteen when the local military authorities arrived in his small village and swept up all the young men, forcing them onto horse-drawn carts at gunpoint. The prisoner's older brother, Lucien, age 19, had resisted. He was captured and shot in the village square as an example.

The French were escorted to staging areas where open boxcars were waiting to transport them to an army base for training. They were then shipped to the Eastern Front to fight against Russia. The collapse of Russia in late December 1917 freed 50 divisions for the fight in France.

He was captured in the Flanders sector in April 1918 when the so-called Ludendorf, or Spring Offensive, stalled. He had been knocked unconscious during an artillery barrage near the town of Arras and had awakened in a squalid prisoner encampment under the command of the French. As a Frenchman, a renégate, he was subjected to occasional beatings that were generally tolerated until he ended up in hospital.

The captain knew of the conscripts from the annexed territories, but had little sympathy for those fighting against their home country. Even if they had no choice. "They should have preferred to be shot," he would say when confronting a prisoner of French descent. But he had his orders. The influenza was killing as many soldiers as the fighting, and manpower was short. POWs could do nonessential work, releasing able-bodied men for the front. He despised the renégates, but was ordered to put them to work.

It was with a mix of relief and anxiety the prisoner from the Alsace boarded a train along with a ragged mix of other prisoners bound for an undisclosed location in France. In the trenches the German commanders had spread rumors of unspeakable crimes and violence against prisoners in England to create a fear of surrender or capture.

The train rattled along at a maddeningly slow pace. The boxcar with prisoners spent more time on railroad sidings than on the main tracks. By nightfall the second day it was passing Paris, apparently heading south. The weather that spring had been cold and wet, and the prisoners huddled close together with no blankets to warm them.

"This is better than the trenches," he told himself, shivering in the chill of the open train car. He had been fed a consistent diet of warm food, and had clean water to drink instead of the vile swill reclaimed from the bottom of the trenches. He was lucky to be alive.

The train finally jerked to a stop and the car doors were opened for the first time since boarding. The prisoners were ordered out of the rancid-smelling car, and forced to stand at attention in a sloppy rain. The prisoner looked up, surprised to see an American flag hanging on the flagpole next to the marshaling yard instead of the French Tricolor.

He knew they were near Tours in central France from the buildings he had seen through the slatted sides of the boxcar and the names of the train depots they passed through. Marched to a crude barracks, the prisoners were deloused, forced to take a cold shower, and dressed in rude woolen clothing of a POW. He ate a meal of oatmeal and bread and took his evening sleep on a hard wooden bunk with no ticking.

He was assigned to a work detail cleaning the mess at the depot headquarters in Tours. The day was long, the work dirty and hard, but he could steal bits of fat and uneaten bread from the officers' mess with no recriminations. Soon he began to recover his strength and weight. Despite the hard working conditions, he was content to live out the rest of the war far from the trenches.

CHAPTER 3 - TOURS

An army without its baggage train is lost; without provisions it is lost;
without bases of supply it is lost.
— Sun Tzu

The encampment at Tours was an odd assortment of tents and commandeered buildings that housed the headquarters unit of the 447th Depot Detachment Engineers. Its primary mission was twofold - to support the forestry division that logged French forests for the lumber required to maintain the war effort, and to provide the Second Aviation Instruction Center located at the nearby airport with supplies, logistics, and maps.

Andy Anderson was bivouacked in an old stable along with about a dozen other enlisted men. In early spring it was cold and damp, but some of the more creative soldiers rigged scrap lumber and old tarps to provide extra shelter from the incessant rainfall. Compared to life in the trenches, this was paradise.

Andy bunked next to Roy Freeland, born in Albany, Oregon but lately from Minneapolis, who worked in supply - a useful friend to have when it came time to scrounge up some meager creature comforts. Private Freeland was an anomaly of sorts. At age 40 he was more the age of his contemporaries' fathers. They used this to their collective advantage, for he was accustomed to a few more creature comforts than the "young-uns" as he would call them, and was not above creatively procuring certain additional comforts for the barracks.

A hastily constructed wooden shed served as the enlisted men's mess. At promptly 06:00 hours a line of soldiers would file in through the opened door for morning mess - usually oatmeal and bread, local cheese, and coffee. During that cold spring the kitchen fires warmed the room, and helped drive away the aches and pains of the lumpy straw mattresses masquerading as beds.

The soldiers would shuffle along the serving line as the slop was doled out by dour looking privates, and occasionally a nondescript soldier with PRISONER stenciled on his rough tunic serving time for some sort of disorderly conduct, usually drinking and fighting. A devout Baptist, Andy was unaccustomed the to rough demeanor of many of the young recruits and conscripts, and he stuck close to his older friend Roy.

The men regularly stretched their morning meal out as long as they could, preferring to stay in the warm mess hall instead of heading off to their various assignments. It was here, in the mess, where Andy saw his first German.

Present Day

The rest of my mother's genealogy binders offered no additional answers. I returned to the attic and began pulling out more boxes, working my way toward the back - back in time, back to my mother's stored personal things. I found several boxes marked with the label, "Working Files" and hauled them down to my study. Inside were more binders marked "Hewitt, Martin, Greene, Meade Work Book,"

"Bond, Dickason Workbook," and what I was looking for, "Anderson Work Book."

The box had been unopened for about fifteen years. Inside were copies of several documents I had already seen - family trees written in long hand, a photocopy of the Lars Anders family bible where my mother began her genealogy research, and photocopies of various family pictures.

Lars Anders' transcribed memories were here, typed on thin onion skin paper by one of my mother's cousins some time back, as well as early memoirs from Grandpa Andy and some unknown relatives.

There were two faded yellow pages that had been removed from a standard contact notebook, tabbed "A." The writing was in Andy's script, and entitled:

Schools Attended from Sept 15, 1915 to …

and here the headline stopped. Below this in a broad ornate script was written:

H.W. Anderson
Missionary Institute
Nyack, N.Y.
Sept. 15, 1915 to May 15, 1916.

This was the first time I had ever seen any reference to Grandpa Andy and early training for the clergy. It was not mentioned in any memoirs or histories anywhere in the family material. Two of his brothers had been engineers, David and Lawrence. David had passed away in 1969, but a newspaper clipping reported that in 1982 he had been nominated for the Automotive Hall of Fame for his early work on internal combustion engines. In his diary Andy wrote he had applied for engineering school in the army. However, here was the first instance of his interest in the clergy, which became his lifelong mission. Below this was a chronology of places where he studied including the first listing after his return from war:

Berkeley Baptist Divinity School
Berkeley, Calif
Aug 15, 1919 to May 1, 1920

From 1922 through 1926 he listed nine different student pastorates in California, Oregon, then Missouri, where my mother was born in 1925. They were followed by a listing in Ohio before returning to California in 1931. Andy was an associate pastor at Bethany Baptist Church in Los Angeles in 1934 and 1935.

I remember Grandpa Andy talking fondly of the days during the Great Depression when he worked with the "CCC boys" as he called them. Here is where he became a full-fledged chaplain for the first time in the Civilian Conservation Corps in the Medford District (Oregon), making his home in Roseburg. When the Second World War broke out, he was activated from reserve duty in 1941, serving in New Guinea, Manila, and "P I," presumably the Pacific Islands.

After the war he continued as a chaplain with the Veterans Administration, and in 1955 took a post in Vancouver. This marked my first recollections of Grandpa Andy.

No one knew that he had wanted to study engineering.

P64335

It was stenciled across the back of his tunic in faded black letters. He unobtrusively shuffled through the mess, cleaning up after the American soldiers who liked to deliberately sabotage their eating area just to watch him clean after them. Occasionally one would offer a jeering comment or two, but nothing compared to the outright hostility reaped on P64335 by the occasional French soldier.

Although a soldier in the German army, P64335 spoke perfect French and a clumsy, rough form of English he was slowly learning from the Americans. He understood more of the English than he let on. When he wanted to avoid the abuse aimed at his direction he pretended not to understand, and he could turn away generally taking the insults in stride.

"Hey, Hymie, get over here and take care of that mess." A soldier with corporal stripes and a scar on his cheek sneered at the POW who was assigned to mess duty. Andy chafed at the slur, meant both as a slam against the enemy and Jews at the same time. P64335 simply ignored the insulting slang and set about cleaning the tables.

"Dirty Hun bastard," he sneered. "They should shoot all of them."

P64335 did not seem much like the image Andy had built in his mind of the German soldier. After the bombardments in Paris, and hearing about the atrocities committed throughout the Belgian countryside as the German army took what they needed to survive from the land, he too had imagined the Germans to be heartless brutes. This quiet, unassuming prisoner, near his own age, certainly did not fit the popular mold the soldiers created of their enemy.

Andy kept his distance, however. There were clear orders that prevented any of the German prisoners from interacting with the enlisted men. Officers generally refused to lower themselves to even address one of the POWS, unless it was to shout an order for this or that. They were treated as barely human, more like slaves. Under the Geneva Convention prisoners could be required to work while in captivity but they could not be used in areas to directly promote the war effort, such as munitions factories. Officers were exempt. Companies of POWs routinely worked in the lumber camps, the coalfields, and in construction throughout the countryside. In an increasingly crowded prisoner of war system, it was common for a large contingent of prisoners to build their own internment camp.

Most of the prisoners taken by American troops were transported back to the states to select POW camps. Many more, those taken by the British, were interred in Britain where they were generally well treated, while still doing routine work patrols. In France, those who seemed relatively harmless could be posted to various headquarter companies. Hospitals often used POWs as "body snatchers," slang for stretcher-bearers.

Andy's life in France was mostly mundane. He filled his time with walks, lectures, and sightseeing. He later recalled writing to his brother, Lawrence:

> My biggest enemy is boredom. We hear reports
> from the front, such as they are, and see trainloads of
> troops and supplies passing through, and troops
> returning from the front. No one talks of it. It is
> like the war does not really exist, and we are playing
> at children's games.
>
> There are no bombardments here. I have learned
> when I am busiest, especially making maps, we can
> expect some major action. When the action begins, I
> have nothing to do but take walks and visit with my
> friends here. I have applied for advanced training at
> Engineer school.

The letter was censored and never delivered.

Andy was a regular at camp church services. The pastor often spoke about the lack of morality that afflicts soldiers. Those who at home would display the finest manners and considerations would, far from home, defile the local women and sink under the repressive weight of alcohol, he would scold his congregation. Andy saw such behavior all around him, but was determined to insulate himself from foul talk and actions as best he could. He chose friends selectively.

"I bought a map," he explained, "and it has all the monuments of Tours." He spread the map distributed by the YMCA out across the mess table for his friends, George Asprooth and Roy Freeland. Major attractions were drawn in relief style to encourage soldiers to visit.

"We are here, just up the river from the city. We can easily walk to here, and here, and even this far." As he spoke, he drew small circles with his finger around the drawing of a cathedral, a museum, and one of the chateaus not commandeered by army operations.

"What's this?" Roy asked. The men began to cross-reference the location in the map legend.

"La Cathédrale Saint-Gatien," came a response from the next table.

They looked over at P64335 cleaning the table, such a common sight they would scarcely have taken notice. None was accustomed to being addressed.

"What did you say, Fritz?" Roy spat out.

"It is a cathedral, a very good one," P64335 replied in halting English. He turned his back and moved away from the three, expecting more cursing. He was used to such behavior, and gave it no mind but to stay clear. P64335 was surprised himself he even responded. He moved quickly out of conversation range.

"Now how would he know?" Roy wondered aloud. "I didn't think they let the Fritzies out."

"Watch yourself, Roy," George warned him teasingly, "them Fritzies'll draw you in and try to sell you somethin' they stole. Get yerself in some heap o' trouble."

Fraternization was strictly forbidden. German spies were active in and around headquarter units. An analysis of routine traffic could uncover useful intelligence. No piece of information was too small, too insignificant, to be of value.

Andy watched P64335 shuffle off toward the kitchen. He had never met a German before, at least not one of the enemy. During the recent bombardments in Paris he developed an image of the hideous Hun, mustache and spiked helmet, laying waste to the Low Countries, raping the women, killing little children. The propaganda machines of the Entente powers played on those excesses of war that did occur in creating an image of the vicious Boche. Reports from the recently repatriated areas of Belgium and northern France simply reinforced these stereotypes.

P64335 did not fit the stereotype. He was small of stature, and Andy would describe him as skinny, likely from years of poor diet at the front. He was clean-shaven, albeit somewhat disheveled. His POW uniform was nondescript, his demeanor subservient and subdued. He walked with a shuffle so as not to draw attention to himself. He did not seem like the evil spawn of Satan as he had been so carefully portrayed. He never made eye contact. As a mess worker, Andy saw him most every day, but until now had paid little heed.

The Americans made plans to meet up with a couple of young ladies from the nearby village and visit the Benedictine Abbey L'Eglise Saint-Julien on the banks of the River Loire that formed the city limits. Andy, however, suggested La Cathédrale Saint-Gatien further towards the city center.

"What? And walk into some kind of Boche trap? Why do you suppose that Fritzie mentioned it? Come on, Andy. Don't fall for that," George reprimanded him. The matter was closed. The boys finished mess and headed outside.

"I'll get hold o' the girls, and we'll meet up in front of the Escadrille," George offered with a grin. "It's what I do best!," and he strode off with what Andy could describe only as a swagger. The two remaining friends ambled back toward their barracks.

Tours buzzed with activity on this Saturday afternoon. It was a rare weekend day without a work duty and the young soldiers were eager to get out of the depot and into town. Most of the young soldiers went south and east towards the seedier parts of town with the clubs and bawdy restaurants. This was a dangerous place, patrolled by French police looking to enforce army camp justice on the young recruits. Fights were common, as were invitations for a night of pleasure, and possibly a crack across the skull and a stolen wallet for the trouble.

For many of these soldiers this was the first time away from small town America, from the moderating influence of family, community, and church. The average AEF doughboy was illiterate, from family farms, naive, and restless for action. Most of the American infantry soldiers passing through had not yet been to the front, and were boasting of the action to come. For the "Tommies" that filled the bars that afternoon, veterans of the mud and blood of the trenches, there was little patience for these arrogant "Yanks" and their untried boasts.

Andy and Roy had made a pass through the red sector as their commander called it shortly after they arrived in Tours weeks ago - Roy "riding shotgun" as he put it for the naive Swede from Rockford, keeping him out of trouble.

"This is a place of sin," Andy warned him, hesitantly. He knew he was over his head and leaned on Roy as a protector. Something about the vileness of the drunkenness and debauchery attracted him, like the proverbial moth to a flame, but not for the same reasons it attracted the rowdy soldiers. He could feel something pulling at him, drawing him forward when his instincts told him to flee.

"They'se a dangerous lot when drunk, that's to be sure," Roy simply answered. "But who can blame 'em, from where they've been."

"You don't plan to join them, do you?" he cautiously asked.

Roy just let out a deep, bawdy laugh.

"Not me, Andy. No, sir. I've had my fill o' that kinda life. The missus now, she'd have my hide tanned and stretched if she even heard I was on this here street, let me tell ya," he laughed.

This was Freeland's second stint in the army. As a young lad he enlisted to fight the Spanish and served in a rifle company in Cuba. He had been surrounded by heavy fighting, but he had to admit to Andy, "Never got no chance to even fire a shot. Don't tell no one." He was hoping to see some action in this war, and earn a promotion, and better pay.

Roy Freeland had two children, a girl of ten and a boy, fourteen. When his son was afflicted with polio Roy gave up drinking, concentrating on providing for his family. With work scarce, and doctors calling for more treatments, he rejoined the army. Being so far away was Hell for him, but he was at least able to send some money to his family back home.

They passed the camp chaplain, talking to a small group of young soldiers loitering in front of one of the noisy bars that looked too young to be even out of knickerbockers let alone in uniform. Andy watched as the chaplain led them off in the other direction, gently reprimanding them, but insisting nonetheless. He slowly began to understand what he was feeling, standing in the muddy street of this den of sin.

On this fine Saturday, however, they headed south and west, along the riverfront, toward the city center - the "civilized" part of Tours, with its giant cathedral, hotels, and beautiful medieval architecture. Andy stopped and bought post cards with scenes from the town lithographed in brilliant colors to send home to his sister, Ruby.

Massive bridges spanned the Loire, stretching across islands in the river channel. Barge traffic moved slowly down river as they walked along the quay, stopping to look at the odd assortment of vessels tied alongside. At the Rue Jules Simon they turned away from the river, meandering along the broad avenue, until they finally came across George, a sour look on his face.

"No luck today, boys. Sorry," he gave them the bad news. "Les mademoiselles n'est pas ici."

Just as well. Money was short, payday a week away yet, and the boys always spent just a little too much when accompanied by the mademoiselles they had met at the church. They took in the museum, although Andy managed to steer the trio back to camp the long way, passing the giant cathedral the POW had mentioned, just to prove a point.

It rained hard that night. Just as well, for he was sequestered at his duty station all the next day, despite it being Sunday. Andy would write in his journal simply,

> Apr 23, Tue
> Worked on Maps.

CHAPTER 4 - THE ARMISTICE

A million guns spewed death until the last toll of the bell, then fell silent.
At first the quiet was terrifying. Then in the distance, a single voice
called out, "It's over!" The cheers, quiet at first, grew into a thunderous roar,
forgetting the horror and carnage that lay around them in all directions.
Oh, to be the last to die by the very last bullet.

Present Day

The binder contained miscellaneous information, and in a sealed plastic bag in the back I discovered the original Anders photos that had been photocopied for other parts of the histories.

I examined the rest of the genealogies hoping to find some sort of reference to "Antoine." The only thing related to any French connection was a story attributed to Andy that his great grandfather, Lars Hurtig, had come from France as a drummer boy in the army of Prince Bernadotte around 1750. In the family bible, the names Balsta, Bläck, and Gleuck are also listed.

I did some checking online. Gleuck was German, originating in Bavaria. Bläck was an early Anglo-Saxon name, and a search on Balsta was inconclusive. The relationship - if any - to a French lineage was unclear.

I almost missed the envelope. It was punched with holes and set in the binder marked "To check" in my mother's handwriting, sandwiched between some unused genealogy templates and some background information on the Anders family. Inside were some old photos of locations, presumably in the Anders family village in Sweden, and some letters from what appeared to be miscellaneous cousins.

One letter was still in an old yellowed blank envelope, with her handwriting, "Who is this?"

I opened the letter inside and began to translate.

> 8 Apr 1941
> Dear Andy,
>
> The Boche are back and life here is very dangerous. They came with their administrators and police and have occupied the towns. We have been issued identity papers which we must carry everywhere.
>
> I sent Marianne and Ariéle away to safety.
>
> A friend will post this from England. What we do post is opened and read.
>
> I wear the gold cross you gave to me always. It helps me remember our friendship, and the talks we have had together.
>
> I will still try to write. I do not know when I can post a letter again.
>
> Antoine

I poured a cup of coffee and sat back at my desk with the letter laying open in front of me. The tone of the letter was informal, as if the two wrote often. Yet it was obvious this was something Andy meant to save above the others, above letters from family and friends. By the tone I presumed Andy knew who Marianne and Ariéle were - most likely his family. This letter and the "Antoine" who wrote it were important to him.

The last line kept drifting through my thoughts.

> I do not know when I can post a letter again.

The original envelope with a possible address was lost. By piecing together the scattered bits of information from the stack of letters that arrived from Courseulles, I was able to make some extrapolations.

France fell to Germany in late June 1940. He refers to the system of German administration in occupied France, but mentions no specific location. It would have taken some time for German administration to establish itself throughout France, which places the period for "Antoine" sending away his presumed wife and daughter likely in the late winter or early spring of 1941 - what he referred to as "the winter past."

The big question - where would a young, naive Midwestern Baptist Swede meet and become friends with a French man? I made notes as I continued to think out loud.

This letter connects Antoine and Andy as more than acquaintances. It confirms the detective work done by the city clerk in Courseulles that this was the correct "Andy" as they thought.

This was going to be a challenge, but the puzzle intrigued me. First things first - I looked up the village of Courseulles-sur-Mer again on the Internet to get a feel of where this puzzle started.

I sent an email to the Office of the Mayor by using the link on the commune administration home page and confirmed that yes, they had found the correct Anderson. I explained I had a corresponding letter from the mysterious "Antoine" then asked the obvious question - who was Antoine?

There is a nine-hour time difference between Washington State and France, so I did not expect a prompt reply. Instead I began to research the area and its history during this period. What immediately struck me was a fact that bound me irretrievably to that final, desperate letter that opened this search: Courseulles-sur-Mer was dead center of the Canadian invasion beach on D-Day, June 6, 1944 - code named Juno.

This was the historical context for the letters. But this was all about World War II - some twenty-six years after Grandpa Andy's service in France. How did Antoine and World War I fit with the letters?

--- ∞ ---

France 1918

It was late May. The Spring Offensive launched with such success by the Germans had stalled. Analysis after the war showed they had committed substantial reserve resources to the initial assaults without adequate preparations for resupply. Although large sections of Allied ground was captured, and large numbers of prisoners taken, the offensive appeared to have no clear objective. The Germans failed to exploit their advantage strategically, and the allies counterattacked and recovered much of the lost ground.

Both German and Allied forces had been hard hit by the influenza pandemic. The press referred to the outbreak as the Spanish Flu, mostly because initial news reported widespread outbreaks and high fatality rates in Spain. Reports of the flu at the front were systematically censored to prevent panic. The large numbers of dead soldiers were simply listed among the even larger numbers of those killed in action. High concentrations of soldiers in miserable conditions, combined with poor sanitation and rations, contributed to the spread of the disease in Europe. German manpower was waning from both combat and influenza, forcing the army to act while it still had the manpower to attack.

German generals tried again. In what would later be called the Third Battle of the Aisne, the German army launched Operation

Blücher-Yorck on May 26. The British had concentrated infantry units along the trenches bordering the German retreat positions, contrary to orders from French General Petain, convinced the Boche was reeling and ready to collapse. The German attack caught the British completely by surprise. It began with a concentrated artillery barrage by over 4000 guns British intelligence had insisted the Germans did not have. After a gas attack against the Allied trenches, the Germans advanced.

They smashed through the badly disrupted defenses and rushed forward toward Paris in a diversionary attack meant to draw units from the northern front to defend the capital. The Germans then launched a flanking action in the north meant to destroy the French army before the manpower weight of the AEF could be brought finally to bear. The French general staff, in a panic, implored the American General Pershing to release the American troops to their command, but he refused. Pershing would retain American control of the AEF at all costs.

The Germans advanced within 56 kilometers of Paris by June 3. That is where the offensive stalled, beset by supply shortages, fatigue, lack of reserves, and heavy casualties. Pershing's troops, under his personal command, flooded into the breach and despite being untested in battle inflicted heavy losses on the Germans in the Battles of Chateau-Thierry and Belleau Wood.

The German advance halted at the Marne.

"Would you look at that!" George cried out over the raucous rattling of the locomotive. "They's full o' darkies!"

He and Andy had gone down to the tracks to watch the troop trains bringing exhausted troops, wounded, and prisoners back from the front - dangerously close to Paris, according to the situation map

Andy had been working on, and about which he had been sworn to secrecy.

The French had large numbers of troops drawn from their extended empire, and these included blacks from African colonies. Unlike in America, blacks in France were considered a part of the empire and had all the same rights and privileges of European French. Most of the blacks Andy had seen were in French uniform, but the sight of black civilians in village restaurants and cafés was a surprise to him, which he kept to himself.

These soldiers, however, were not French, although they fought under French authority. From the situation analysis briefings Andy had attended as part of his map duties he knew these black soldiers were American. He would not have believed such a thing in the states, but in this world everything seemed upside down from what he was raised to believe.

They were called American Buffalo Soldiers, a name first used by Native Americans on the western frontier. The 92nd and 93rd Infantry Divisions were the first Americans to fight in France, but they were detached from the AEF and fought under French command. Neither the British nor American command would permit black soldiers to fight in this stage of the battle. It would not be until late in November that the black units would come under American command.

As the train cars passed, they saw the small flag tacked on the side of the troop car, an American flag. It was used to help sort out the cars in the marshaling yards, and soldiers in the rear were accustomed to seeing the British flag and French Tricolor on boxcars filled with returning troops. This was the first time they had seen an American flag. And the cars were full of Negro troops. The unit flag, a Blue buffalo, fluttered in the wind from the back of the car as it passed.

"I'll be damned," George said out loud, not even caring if Andy scolded him again about his swearing. Even Andy let the language pass. It unsettled him, this train of death and pain. He did not believe himself to be prejudiced - the thought would not have crossed the mind of a decent young man from the Midwest. Such a sight was simply such an aberration, so removed from his experience, that he was left to question many things. He was a man of devout upbringing, and knew all men were God's creation. God's teachings seemed at odds with those of Rockford, Illinois, circa 1918.

The next six cars were medical transports. Inside were troops wounded in battle, or suffering from influenza, what the soldiers would call "the grippe." Where flu symptoms were mild, soldiers were required to remain at the front, further infecting those around them. Those diagnosed as severely ill were sent on crowded trains to even more crowded field hospitals, spreading the deadly virus. Troop and supply movements around the world ensured the flu virus would quickly spread worldwide, not just at the front. It would kill people the likes of which the world had never witnessed.

The last two cars carried the dead.

Back in his barracks later that night, he slept fitfully. Images of pain and death washed through his semiconscious mind as he drifted into and out of sleep. The vision of the enemy, juxtaposed with the image of the German prisoner. American soldiers, supposedly virtuous and clean, fouled by sin, slander, and blasphemy. Women from the village, wholesome and pious, while women in the bistros and bars, wanton and sinful, taking up with willing farm boy soldiers breaking their vows to wives and sweethearts from home. Soldiers of all colors fighting together, drinking together, talking strange languages. Nothing fit together as he had learned as a small boy. Temptations were everywhere, intermixed with images of war, death, and destruction.

This is insanity. How can God turn His back on such excess? How can the rules that seemed so simple and clear dissolve into the fog of this war? What was real? What was right? With so much death - this terrible war, and this plague killing so many. How can a man survive this confusing place? Is this the apocalypse? Are we bringing down the wrath of God by this folly?

Have I contributed to this madness? Have I turned my back on God, too? Am I meant to learn more than just how to make maps to help men kill other men? Did He send me here to find another purpose?

This challenged him to face his God in ways he had never before considered. He would not fall asleep until he made a commitment to his God that would change his life forever.

───── ∞ ─────

"What's your name?"

P64335 cautiously looked up from wiping off the table. He ignored the question. He knew better than to engage a soldier in a conversation. It would end in trouble for him in any event. He turned his back and continued to clean.

"Where are you from? Do you understand?"

What does he want? He is just a private. I need not answer him. Leave me alone, American. He continued to clean.

Andy took a different tack.

"I am finished. Will you clean off this table for me?"

P64335 moved over cautiously and began to clear the dishes. If he refused to acknowledge this direct request he would face trouble from the mess captain. He felt he was walking into a trap.

"You do understand English," Andy replied. "So, what's your name?"

"What do you care, American?" he spat. He finished clearing the dishes and began to wipe down the table.

"I don't mean anything by it. I'm just curious, that's all."

Andy had come to mess early to avoid George and Roy. He knew he would have a better chance at success alone. P64335 figured he could dismiss this conversation only by replying.

"Bouchard," he cautiously replied, not without a little sneer in his voice.

"Bouchard. Do you have a given name?"

Bouchard muttered something under his breath Andy did not understand, but knew was in French. Not German.

"You speak French instead of German?"

That was one step too far. The hackles on the back of his neck bristled with indignation he would normally have kept to himself.

"I am French!" he declared, glaring at the American. He finished quickly and pushed the cleaning cart away to the kitchen as fast as he could without drawing too much unwanted attention.

Andy sat and thought about the encounter. French? In a German POW tunic? What is this all about? He was determined to find out.

The next morning, Bouchard P64335 kept his distance from the small group of American soldiers. Later that afternoon while returning from lunch, as Andy passed by a small work party grooming the officer's mess grounds, he spied Bouchard P64335 among the workers. He returned to the mess and brought back something wrapped in a plain brown napkin. As he passed the work crew at the officer's mess, he thrust the package quickly, unseen, into Bouchard P64335's hands - too quickly to be seen by the guards and too abruptly to be refused. Bouchard P64335 simply glanced back at him as he walked briskly away. He stuffed the package in his pocket for the time being. Later, in the marginal privacy of his barracks, he carefully unwrapped the napkin, revealing a piece of biscuit cake inside.

Andy repeated the ruse for several days, either leaving something wrapped up on his plate as Bouchard P64335 was cleaning, or clandestinely passing it to him on work duty. If he had been caught, he would likely have received a stern reprimand.

After a week of these clandestine bribes, Bouchard P64335 passed behind Private Andy Anderson during a morning's mess, and simply stated, "Antoine. Antoine Bouchard."

———— ∞∞∞ ————

The next day Antoine Bouchard was replaced in mess by an American private - obviously not too happy at the assignment.

"Didn't you hear? Them Fritzies are all under wraps for a while," he growled when questioned. "Got us cooks doin' KP, doin' the work o' the Fritzies, can you believe it? Ain't fit for no 'merican, let me tell ya."

The soldiers looked at each other, knowing what this meant. Something big was happening, something at the front. All POWs were held under guard. Had the German army broken through the lines? Were they headed toward Paris? Trains began running all hours of the night, ferrying fresh troops north and east, bringing home the tired and wounded. And the dead. Unlike the other allies, American war dead were generally shipped home, something that elicited contempt from the British and French common soldiers. "Too good to be planted here?" they would jeer. "Gotta go home to momma!" Such comments often resulted in fistfights and a night in the brig.

On September 26 Andy received the news his application for Engineers school had been dismissed. There was no time for such things now, he was told, although it would be weeks before he knew why. September 26 was the start of the Meuse-Argonne offensive, the final thrust of what would be called the Hundred-Days Offensive. Andy was shuffled among commanding officers during the hectic days in the supply depot, although his work had been largely completed by the start of the offensive.

Little information came in from the front, save for meager briefings at the camp YMCA in the evening. The soldiers listened attentively to these briefings. When they were finished, Private E.R. Nelson of the 2nd Air Depot, also stationed at Tours, expressed his opinion to Andy and a group of friends who attended the talks together.

"What a bunch of bully!" he laughed. Bully referred to the imaginative byproducts served as "meat" in British "Bully Tins" that made up field rations. It was not complimentary.

They all had a good laugh, but were glad to be in support and not at the front. He had not seen Antoine Bouchard again in the camp mess, although occasionally he would be seen among various outside work parties, always under guard.

The Hundred Days Offensive continued full force, and in October news arrived that Bulgaria had signed an armistice and quit the Central Powers. By month's end Turkey followed, then Austria. Germany was reeling from battlefield defeats and political isolation, a lack of manpower, and a crippled economy.

Anderson wrote in his diary,

> November 7
> War's Over!
> Germany Signs Armistice
> Rumor

November 10
Kaiser abdicates

November 11
Armistice signed!
Big celebration in Tours
Bands and parades

By the time the fighting had stopped, the influenza outbreak had peaked. Records are incomplete, but before the flu mutated into less virulent strains and efforts to treat it became more successful, it would kill between 20 to 60 million people worldwide. Later reports estimated the death toll at nearly 100 million.

———❦———

CHAPTER 5 - REPATRIATION

When the tide of battle turned, the victims became the oppressors as they have since all time began. The only true victims were the silent ones who disappeared into the night and fog of war.

Present Day

Two days later I received a reply from Madame Lesperance at the commune of Courseulles. The email was fairly short and to the point.

Merci, M. Hewitt.

His Honor Mayor Pouille appreciates your confirmation of the receipt of the letters.

He extends his regrets, however, that we do not know who Antoine is. We would be pleased to assist you in any way, but a check of our records has yielded no such person in Courseulles during this period.

Not a good beginning.

I had reached a dead end. Neither the village of Courseulles-sur-Mer nor the department of Calvados had any record of an "Antoine" that shed light on the letters.

I sat and puzzled over the dilemma at my table in the Olympic Club making notes on the back of the children's coloring page in longhand. I drew a rudimentary timeline of the key locations in the diary, each forming a box connected by lines to show the chronology. It began with Andy arriving in France, being stationed in Paris, his transfer to Tours, subsequent duty station changes, and ending with his locations described on his return trip to California. Inside each box I decided to add the number of days spent in each location. A picture emerged I had not considered when I started.

Andy spent the longest amount of time in Tours. 378 days. If he met "Antoine" and developed a personal relationship over time, it would make sense it likely occurred in Tours. It was a place to start.

This was no small task. What would be the trigger that could reveal the relationship between one American and one Frenchman in such a large city? If there were a key anywhere, it would be in the letters.

Dr. Tauscher from the college had given me a text file with the letter translations, and the originals were safely put away. On a separate page I drew a grid and tried to create a chronology out of the letters, with few dates to guide me.

The "Boche" seemed obvious. The series of events and a sense of desperation and resolve in the letters revolve around the German occupation of France in 1940, and especially Normandy. That letter chronicles the arrival of the German army. The letter that would be the last one in the chronology was also obvious. The others were more problematic being the backside of the written conversation - my grandfather's replies to Antoine's original correspondence - and letters to Andy that were never posted. I circled key words and phrases, looking for answers through the span of over seventy years.

I knew I needed help to unravel this mystery.

———— ∞ ————

Tours, 1919

The Armistice changed life in Tours. Bouchard was not under constant guard any longer, although his movements were still regulated. He was assigned to regular work details in and around

camp besides morning mess hall duties. He often found himself
cleaning at the Engineers division where Anderson was stationed.

The two began to slowly, carefully, build what could be called a
friendship in those early days. When George learned Bouchard was
French instead of German, he called him the "Fritzie-Froggy" in the
derisive manner soldiers have of referring to their enemies in slang.
It caused an irreparable rift between him and Anderson, and the two
drifted apart. When George received orders home, Andy did not
bother to see him off.

As winter turned cold life in camp became dull and routine. The
opportunity to develop their friendship grew, albeit slowly.
Although Bouchard was restricted to the camp, he could attend
regular church services as long as he was not on work duty, and he
attended alone.

He had spent most of the last four years alone with little news
from his home. The Red Cross occasionally had been able to pass
letters from prisoners' families during the war, but as the location of
specific prisoners was a closely guarded secret the process was slow
and cumbersome. Every letter was opened and read at least twice,
and return correspondence was scrutinized even further. Even
though the fighting had ceased, and lapses of procedure became
increasingly common, letters were rare. Those that did make it
through the administrative morass were still censored. Bouchard
was surprised to find a letter waiting for him when he finished his
morning shift. He sat on his bed and opened it anxiously.

The letter was from his cousin Rachelle, the daughter of his
mother's sister, who had immigrated to Strasbourg during the war.

14 Dec 1918
My dear Antoine,

There are terrible rumors the French want to rid
Strasbourg of all who have German roots.

They are forcing some Germans from their homes. It
is said soon they will be forcing merchants and
workers out to make way for the French moving
here. More come everyday.

The people are close to hysterical.

In the market they shout jeers at us even as I protest
we are French. A man threw horse manure at me
and screamed I should leave. Justin was cut badly on
his forehead by a rock thrown by another.

I pray for a relief from this terror, and for your safe
return.

Rachelle

He tucked the letter away beneath his crude bed. His mind raced
with worry and concern. He thought of Rachelle, and wondered
just what would come of his last remaining family. He had to get out
of that bare room for some air or he would suffocate.

He stepped outside and walked off through the damp late winter
mist that hung in the air, heading for the small canteen at the edge of
the depot - just within his "freedom" boundary. He had no money,
but could draw a hot cup of coffee nonetheless.

Antoine was sitting in the canteen by himself when Andy and Roy
walked in. They took their seats at opposite ends of the long table.
Antoine did not acknowledge the two soldiers. There were still

unspoken barriers between them, at least in public places like the canteen.

In private, he could talk freely with Andy. They spoke of their homes, of the beauty of the Alsace as well as of California and Illinois. Antoine encouraged Anderson to take French lessons, and would often grill him over language. Anderson in turn helped him with his English.

Antoine would not talk of his experiences at the front. Whenever the conversation drifted toward current events, he would become agitated and pull away. Andy was a compassionate observer of people, and could feel the pain his friend felt. He tried to stay clear of those conversations. The mistrust dividing these two from such different backgrounds faded with time even if the society around them forbade it. It is much harder to hate a man when you look straight into his eyes when you speak, Andy thought.

Andy had seen so many things that shook his foundation values to the core. He had seen black American soldiers shed their red blood for a country that denied them, and yet watched as they joked and jostled with the French soldiers as equals. He had seen Turks and Indians in strange costumed uniforms as well as drab khakis strolling through town, welcomed by strangers. He had watched in amazement as French civilians turned out in the streets at the news of the armistice with bottles of wine to share spontaneously with anyone in uniform, regardless of their nationality. Young women openly hugged and kissed any soldier in uniform, white, brown, or black, on that joyous day.

His own countrymen, from the land of freedom, denied equal footing to these men who shed their blood in this far off place. The locals were simply glad to be free of the horror of the war. Just who was free, and who was still in chains? In this place, where violence had been routine for so long, he had learned so many lessons of tolerance. He wondered just how he would feel towards the life he would return to in America.

Bouchard rose and left the canteen. He did not look at Andy. For the troubled young American, it felt like the stab of a bayonet.

— ∞∞∞ —

"Professor Douglas? Larry Hewitt. I phoned you last week and you asked me to stop by your office ... ."

"Oh, yes, Mr. Hewitt. I have been expecting you. Please, come in and have a seat ... let's see ... where are my notes ... OK, here they are. I am sorry, but you caught me a little disorganized."

I had arranged the meeting with Professor Terrance Douglas as Suzanne Tauscher suggested, and had emailed him both a copy of the "D-Day" and "Boche" letters along with a list of knowns and unknowns. I had phoned him for an appointment, but he insisted I simply drop by during office hours at my convenience. In the meantime, he would begin to do some background research to help me.

"I'm sorry, professor. If there is a better time ... ."

"No, no, this is fine! Just fine! Quite a puzzle you have here, Mr. Hewitt. Let me ask you first, do you have any experience with pure historical research?"

"No, not really. A have an interest in history, and a Master's degree in business. I did a lot of research for my degree. I just have not had much reason to delve this deep before, and it is harder than business research."

"Yes, quite so. Using peer-reviewed sources is one thing. You can leverage someone's research to your advantage, and build on another's foundation. Using original source material is something else. It is quite the inexact science. I am sending you a link to an article I want you to read that will help you in your search. It's about applying the physics Principle of Uncertainty to sociology. Your letters, they contain several seemingly inexplicable contradictions, don't you agree?"

"That's why I contacted you, professor. They do not make much sense."

"Ah, my dear Hewitt, but they do. They do! Because they made sense at the time they were written by the men who wrote them! That is the key. Your job is to find just what that sense was, in the reality of the writers! Just because it is unknown to us now does not mean it was not real! Every phrase, indeed every word, has a reality. If not, it would not have been written, do you agree?"

"OK, I can agree with that."

"Good. That is the foundation. Now, if you had been able to read that article on the Uncertainty Principal first, you would have had a toolset at your disposal to help you with the next big step. In this case, a giant step backwards."

The professor was quite eager to share his discoveries with me, but took an even greater delight in lecturing me on methodology. For my part, I was grateful for better ways to help unravel this puzzle, even if it meant a very long visit.

"The Uncertainty Principal tells us if you look closely at the micro-elements of a set of actions, the larger context becomes diffused because the very action of observation changes the outcome. And vice versa. Just like in quantum physics, where the principal was first postulated. To measure the speed of an atomic particle you have to change its mass; to measure its mass, you have to change its speed. The very act of observation changes the result, and you cannot therefore know both properties at the same time.

"To understand the context within which your letters were written, you need to step away from the details and take a broad view. You must, in actuality, discount the accuracy of the details.

Both context and detail cannot be known simultaneously. And do not trust the micro elements.

"Have you ever played the parlor game where someone runs into a room, acts out a scene for the others, then just as quickly runs out? If there are eight people observing the mini-play, and they immediately record what they just witnessed, you will receive eight different accounts of the same event. Sometimes the details of what we search for are unintentionally misleading."

The professor was making sense in a broad view, I supposed, but I was uncertain how all this was going to help. He pulled a stack of letter copies with scribbles and notations all over them as he continued.

"Let's begin by breaking the first letter down by phrases. 'the Boche are back.' Boche is a very negative term, implying a form of racial prejudice or bias. I am sure you figured that out. But 'back' … back from what? You say these were written somewhere on the French coast? The Germans did not occupy the coast in the first war, nor the War of 1870 for that matter. So how could they be 'back?' Were they really even 'back' or did your Antoine mean something else?

"Perhaps the Germans were 'back' in your Antoine's world, his own personal perspective, as opposed to back in some geopolitical sense. That would imply they started by intruding into his world once before."

"The 'discharge papers' is what throws me," I interjected. "If he were discharged from the French army, perhaps it simply meant he was fighting the Germans?"

"I do not think so. As an American, you would think the name "Antoine" was French, so therefore he would have been a French soldier. I do not think so. His discharge papers were sent to Strasbourg. That would be a key that would have limited meaning outside of a very narrow context, which shrinks the universe of possibilities significantly."

"I'm afraid I don't follow."

"Official papers would be sent to the district of record for anyone with a civil matter that was resolved, what I call a 'civil signature.' The administrative capital of his home district - much like a county auditor here - would have to be Strasbourg, the district capital of the Alsace region bordered by the Rhine."

"OK, but I checked. Strasbourg sounds German, but it is in France."

"Now it is, yes. But in 1914 it was under German control. It was taken by the Germans in the Franco-Prussian War - what we call the War of 1870. Over the nearly fifty years that followed, most of the region became dominated by German culture. They did, however, tolerate the Franco subculture. As a result, there was a substantial minority population of ethnic French who spoke the language and lived a local variation, or dialect if you will, of French culture.

"As a Frenchman in German-controlled Alsace he would have been subject to conscription in the German army in 1914. Some 370,000 Alsatians were rounded up and in many cases forced to serve the German Imperial Army. They were usually sent to the Russian front. They were considered too unreliable to fight in the west against their fellow Frenchmen."

"OK, so we are supposing he was a German soldier, in Tours, discharged and sent home."

"No. Not quite."

I groaned inside. This was getting convoluted. The professor sensed my confusion.

"Look, Mr. Hewitt ... May I call you Larry?"

"Yes, please."

"Good. By the time this is over we will be quite familiar with one another, I can assure you," he offered with a slight air of whimsy.

"Consider this. You are an American. You were raised believing the story in your school history books that America is a 'melting pot,' under the presumption it somehow made this country different. Yet the truth is that compared to Europe, our culture is and always has been relatively homogenous. On the continent, wars have been fought over such trivialities as dialect differences let alone national interests. There are hundreds of subcultures, and mixes of people from many countries, all jumbled up. The Great War was fought over conflicts between such subdivisions.

"Nothing is what it seems to an outsider," he continued. "Your Antoine was French, I am sure. He served in the German army, I presume. And not by choice, most likely, which places him geographically in Strasbourg, and politically in the Alsace-Lorraine, one of the most hotly contested regions in Europe.

"But you say he met, or likely met, your grandfather in Tours. Tours was behind the lines. It was a rail crossroads, a supply and air depot. It was far from the front. Antoine would not have been dischargeable at Tours if he were a German soldier, especially not in 1919. As a German soldier, after the armistice, he would have been quickly demobilized and sent home, not anywhere inside France proper, and certainly not with an official civil signature. There were simply too many soldiers scattered over too great an area - an area where civil order and process had long since been disrupted.

"However, if he were a POW, that would be a completely different story. First, his location and activities would have been closely monitored and recorded. He would not have been repatriated in 1918 and simply sent home. Most prisoners were not allowed home until late 1919 or even 1920 - long after the ratification of the Treaty of Versailles."

The details that comprised his logic seemed to contradict the essence of his so-called broad contextual view, and I told him so.

"Ah, my friend. That is the point! The universe of human interaction is inextricably bound together with contradictions! You are familiar with popular conspiracy theories, are you not? They take on a life of their own because it is very easy, and convenient, to draw causal relationships backward in time. Looking back, you see everything as connected because they DID occur in sequence, however chaotically. Looking forward, can you predict any outcome with such causal certainty? Of course not.

"It is not the intricate details that matter, but the scenery within which they might have occurred. Build the scenery, and you will know where to look for the detail. Hold onto nothing that resembles a preconception. That is the contradiction you must reconcile to locate this Antoine.

"Remember, the clues and solutions to your puzzle will be scattered to the four winds. Your missing puzzle piece could be the solution someone else is seeking. So publish your results as soon as you can, and let others who are also searching help you, and you them."

France, 1918

Antoine could occasionally retrieve a newspaper left by one of the officers and get caught up on current events. Now that the war was over, security was relaxed even more than the usual carelessness of soldiers away from the front. He was always eager to receive news from his homeland in the Alsace region. The little news he could get was unsettling.

French troops had entered the Alsace-Lorraine in December 1918 just as President Wilson arrived in Versailles for the peace conference. The story of the French repatriation of his homeland was big news, igniting a frenzy of nationalism and fueling Deutschfeindlichkeit, an anti-German paranoia. It would not take long for reprisals to begin against the minority German population in the Alsace region as citizen was pitted against citizen in a frenzy of racial purity propaganda by French central authorities.

The French government began a vicious policy of Épuration, or purification, shortly after the hostilities ceased. The objective was to eliminate any semblance of German culture, influence, and language from the region that for hundreds of years had been a mixture of German-Franco influences and cultures. While "high" German and formal French were used in official business and taught in schools, the populace spoke a mix of dialects influenced by both cultures.

For the Germans in the area, it simply meant expulsion. The news shortly after the armistice told the story.

> Dec 23. Germans Ordered to Leave the Alsace. The central government announced today that persons of German descent would be repatriated to German soil, effective immediately. Holders of B, C, and D identify cards must return to their native Germany.

Antoine had heard only bits and pieces about the identity cards during the active days of fighting. Rumors the French would enforce language-based categories on citizens of the region would occasionally filter in through various sources. Holders of the "A" card had privileged rights in the region. This card identified them as legitimate French-speaking natives, and conveyed certain privileges, among them a favorable exchange rate on German marks and other Allied currency. All others exchanged currency they could no longer use at great cost.

Antoine received another letter from Rachelle. The censors had blacked out parts, but he could manage the meaning.

> 18 Jan 1919
> My dear Antoine,
>
> They have taken our home. The government moved in with terrible restrictions and classified us as German. My identity card is class "D" which puts us at great risk. We have been forced across the river into Gehl, but there is nowhere to live and no work. We are despised by the Germans just as much.
>
> Justin is ill now, and very weak. We have no medicine.
>
> Please, my dear cousin, if you are soon released, do not try to go home.
>
> Rachelle

The system was confused and complicated, so much so that the tone of the news articles began to change as the year 1919 progressed. By late spring even the liberal Parisian press began to charge the system was corrupt and unworkable.

On April 22, 1919, the French paper "La Nacionale" carried a blistering attack on the excesses of the civil authorities in carrying out the policies of ethnic purification.

> A woman of mixed parentage, a widow of the war whose husband was forced at gunpoint to fight for the German army in the east, was ordered to vacate her home with her three children. Each traveller was permitted 30 kilo of baggage, 2 days rations, and a maximum of 2000 marks. Gold, coin, or French or Allied money of any kind was forbidden. French

authorities promptly confiscated all additional
property. The family left Metz and crossed into
Germany at Strasbourg, destitute and homeless.

Are they better off in Germany? A land so devastated
by war that even persons of property are starving?"

The story ended with the publication of an anonymous letter sent
to a civil servant in Metz, smuggled out by a sympathetic worker,
and forwarded to the newspaper. It carried an ominous warning.

Something terrible will happen which will result in
war, for the humiliation you are inflicting on these
people will leave them gripped by a secret,
implacable and wrathful anger, which will avenge
itself in an indescribable manner.

Over 90,000 Germans were forced to leave their homes in the
Alsace-Lorraine region between 1918 and 1921. Antoine Bouchard
would receive no further letters from his cousin Rachelle. She had
been forced east into Germany at war's end, and simply dissolved
into the refugee chaos that is the ultimate spectacle of this most
terrible invention of man.

———— ❧ ————

April 1919

Andy left the paymaster's office where he collected his allotment,
and dutifully recorded his monthly pay in his diary's pay log. He had
earned corporal stripes by now, and his pay had been raised to a
whopping $19.30 per month.

Today there would be none of the usual grousing over the pay.
Instead, Andy hurried through camp heading for the back of the mess
hall. He burst excitedly through the back door into the kitchen.

"Antoine!" He was breathing hard, as much in excitement as winded by the long run. "Antoine, I have orders. I get to go home!"

The news was greeted with a stunned silence, immediately felt by both. Going home. Antoine was losing the only friend he had here. This was good news, nonetheless. Years of sacrifice and witness to horror had steeled him toward displaying his emotions too openly.

"Andy. When do you leave?"

"Today! I just cleared payroll, and I am on the train today!"

The orders were brief.

> Prepare for transport to embarkation port immediately.
> Leaving 18:30 hours.

"I don't know where I am headed right away, but I am going home."

Home. Antoine knew this was his friend's most fervent wish. Home was where he could never return.

"Look, I have some things here I will not need. Take them. A jacket, these mud boots. The scarf. I will not need them in California."

Andy and Antoine had talked of California often. It seemed a magical place, of hills and warm winds, with fruits and vegetables year 'round. And the wine - not as good as from Alsace, he would tease Andy, who knew little of wine or other spirits.

"You can write to me, and when you get out of here and go home we can remain friends," the excited Andy blurted out. Antoine smiled carefully, looking around to see they were not being watched. Now was not the time to talk of the repression in his homeland, or his fear of never seeing the Alsace again. It was a time of joy, a time to remember. He gave Andy a hug and kissed him on the cheek as he would if he were home, a move that startled the reserved Swede.

"Yes, I will write you. All of this will end one day, and I will find a new home, too. The world is becoming a smaller place. Perhaps there will be a time we see each other again." He knew that would be unlikely, but he would not dampen his friend's enthusiasm at heading home.

Andy left him his small stash of personal items, then quickly scribbled an address on the back of a post card he had planned to send home before he had received his orders.

"This is my parent's home. That is where I am headed. Write me here, and I will return a letter. When you get out of here, we will stay in touch. I promise."

He then removed the gold cross that always hung around his neck, a gift from his father when he left California for France. It was inscribed with characteristic simplicity, "To Henry from Father."

"My father said it was blessed by the pastor of our church for luck. I pray He blesses you with the same good fortune He has blessed me."

With that, and a firm grasp, Andy was off. He had little time to complete his processing before heading to the train. His head was spinning, thoughts of home, of family, seeing Lawrence, Ruby, Sam, his mother and father, of never seeing his friend Antoine again. What a strange thing war is, he thought. It brings the strangest of fellows together and just as quickly flings them apart. Memories are left hanging in the air like a morning mist that refuses to rise.

Antoine could not see him off. Such was the lot of a prisoner even when the war was over.

Andy boarded the train, and a few hours later was bivouacked in temporary quarters in Aignan. It was a miserable place, full of mud, cold tents, and little to do. April turned to May, and the air began to warm, and green began to return to the ravaged land, if only as the irritable thistle. The land would heal, somehow, as it has always done, despite man's incessant folly.

—⚬⚬⚬—

The company was called to parade formation on May 3. Orders were to "spit and polish" which meant someone important was coming to do something completely unimportant. After standing for an hour, a group of officers arrived. General Pershing himself inspected the company, although it made little impression on young Andy at the time. It was something in later years he could recall, although it is likely it made a greater impression on him than it did on the general.

He wrote in his diary,

> May 6, Tue
> Left 'Agony' at 10 am on 'doughboy Pullman'.
> Stop over at Tours, arrived Le Mans 11:00 pm.

For twelve days he had little to do but walk through town. He wrote a few letters home, but mostly waited, and waited more. He finally left on the last train leg of his French journey, and arrived in the seaport of Brest on May 18.

Two days later Andy was marching through the streets of Brest in formation, preparing to board the S.S. Finland. He endured eleven days at sea jammed four deep in canvas bunks, a parade through Newport News, and Pullman cars to Fort Grant, a luxury compared to the rude transport of army life in France. Fort Grant was near his hometown, Rockford, Illinois, and Andy visited his brother Lawrence, other family, and friends. Finally, he was bound for the coast.

He wrote his final diary entry on June 18.

> This Way Out!
> Discharged!
> Never again!

Present Day

"Now, to continue. The letter to your Grandfather was sent to the states, was it not?"

"Yes. In late 1919."

"Headquarters units often used German POWs for manual labor - in lumber camps, rock quarries, hospitals, mess halls, garden tending - any form of menial labor not directly connected with armaments manufacture and the like could have been filled with forced prison labor. I predict Antoine was a prisoner working somewhere near where your grandfather was stationed, somewhere they would have met."

"OK, that gives a place to look, but how would he have been here instead of the Eastern Front if the Germans mistrusted their French conscripts so?"

"That's not such a stretch. By the time the war was in its bloody fourth year, the early conscripted units would have been chopped up badly, subjected to resupply and breakups, and scattered all over the Eastern Front. When Russia dropped out of the war following the Bolshevik Revolution, those troops would have been sent west. They would have been scattered even more. The original ethnic basis for their unit formation would have long ago been turned inside out.

"So, where are we? We have made some long distance extrapolations, and conjured up a story where Antoine was a

Frenchman living in the Alsace region, swept up by the Germans at the start of the war, sent east, and then ended up on the Western Front late in the war. He ended up a prisoner, and was assigned to menial labor at or near the 447th Depot Detachment HQ Company at Tours, where through some unknown series of events he met your grandfather."

"But how and why did he end up on the French coast, and his records in Strasbourg?"

"That's the easy part, as long as you retain that broad, fuzzy contextual focus - meaning as long as you don't mind being completely wrong. At war's end, the French moved quickly to take back the Alsace-Lorraine, even before the Versailles Treaty was written let alone ratified. The area had been deeply infused with German culture, and the French wanted the 'dirty Boche' out.

"Under administrative control from central authorities they first introduced a system of identity cards that basically forced all Germans, and anyone else the locals didn't like, to be formally removed - 'purified,' as they called it, épuration - in the first of the great 20th Century ethnic cleansings in Europe. This failed, and was replaced by a witch-hunt type tribunal, which also failed. The economy collapsed, the labor pool was decimated, shops and business seized. It was total chaos.

"Your Antoine likely would not have returned to Strasbourg in fear for his safety. Any family he had there would likely have been expelled, since he had served in the German army. His discharge records, however, would have been forwarded to the department records office, which was in Strasbourg."

"But discharged-why would he be allowed to remain in France if he was a German POW? Wouldn't he have been sent back to Germany?"

"Ah, my friend. Again, nothing is ever that simple. Especially in France. To counteract the disaster of the German expulsion policies, the Entente powers, and especially President Wilson, insisted Germans who came from the Alsace-Lorraine region could be repatriated as French citizens. This was incorporated as Article 79 of the Treaty of Versailles. Our wonderful sense of fair play, don't you know."

"So Antoine became a French citizen ... again?"

"We'll, technically he had not been one. He was now, more than likely. According to my research, over 80% of those that applied for nationalization were accepted. He probably chose not to return to the Alsace region, which was still seething with anti-German hysteria despite Wilson's best intentions. Or perhaps he did return but was forced to leave. But he could have easily assimilated into the French countryside, fully conversant in French, which would have been his native language and culture."

"Wow, what a lot of suppositions."

"Yes, but you now have some specific places to search in original records sources if you choose to. This narrows your search tremendously ... or it is all supposition and complete fiction. Such is the Uncertainty Principal at work."

"OK, but to the last question. How would the Germans know he was in France?"

"This is all speculation of course, but look at what is probable. When Hitler's armies occupied France, the Gestapo would have scoured civil records looking for German citizens. A fundamental concept of Germany in 1914 and 1940 was that if you were German by birth or custom, you were German for life. And of course, under the Nazis, as long as you were not Jewish. Antoine would have been too old for active duty at this stage of the war, but not too old to serve as a spy, or an informant more likely."

"But how did they find him in France, especially since he would have spoken perfect French?"

"His accent and habits would stand out as different from the locals. He could be viewed with suspicion. Someone probably reported him, possibly for some completely unrelated personal issue. A supposition, yes - but probable. By eliminating these probables, you may just get lucky and find a connection. All you need is one - one known and verifiable fact."

"Great," I signed. "Where to start?"

"The tone of the letters is personal, which implies Antoine and Andy already had a special relationship. Uncover that first. Despite the allure of the June 6 letter and its historic implications, don't be mislead by the 1940 time frame at this juncture. It is like two parallel train tracks through time - each will have its own reality, but the connection will come from the older track to the later one - not the other way around.

"Limit your research to finding Antoine in 1918. I would start with military and civil records in Tours. If Antoine existed there at all there has to be a record somewhere. Let the whispers in the wind show you the connection."

Antoine Bouchard wrote the first of his letters to his friend Andy, who had left Tours for his point of embarkation just three weeks prior.

10 May 1919
My friend,

There is still no news on when I may be released.
Work continues, although I am no longer under
constant guard. My freedoms have increased,
however I must return to my barracks by nightfall. I
have been dreaming of my return home, but I fear
this may not be possible.

The newspapers have been telling of anti-German
atrocities in the Alsace. My only family has been
forced to leave, their property taken. They are
accused of conspiracy. I have made inquiries about
obtaining an identity card, but my inquiries have
been ignored.

There are stories of a commission that decides the
fate of anyone suspected of having German
influences. For now I am safe, as long as I remain a
prisoner. What an irony.

I hope your return home was a safe one. I will write
and tell you of my condition.

Antoine

The letter arrived in San Jose in September 1919, three months
after Andy Anderson was discharged from active duty.

The American captain looked up from his desk as Antoine Bouchard
was escorted into the office by one of the camp's designated prison
guards.

"That will be all, corporal," he replied briskly. The dismissal was curious, for Bouchard had never been allowed in the presence of an officer without escort, a common security procedure.

"Remain standing," he barked. Bouchard stood uneasily and carefully eyed the captain who remained expressionless.

"Antoine Bouchard. P64335. You are hereby formally released from custody, under General Order S2332, dated March 15, 1920. You will report to the Red Cross station in camp for processing. Dismissed." The captain did not even look up from his desk.

With that, Antoine Bouchard stepped out of the captain's office and into the light drizzle of the morning for the first time without a guard, without constraints. It was bewildering.

The Red Cross station was at the far side of the camp. As Bouchard walked briskly through the muddy streets, he could feel the eyes watching him uneasily, or so he imagined. As he stepped into the Red Cross tent the first friendly face he had seen since his friend Andy had left camp for America met him.

"There are papers here for you, Private," the pretty young clerk in a gray apron explained. Her British accent was strangely melodic. He had not been referred to as "private" since he had been taken prisoner. He was not quite sure just who she was speaking to.

"So where are you headed?" she asked sweetly but naively.

"I do not know. My home was the Alsace, but I fear I will be forced to Germany if I return."

"Oh, but haven't you been told? You are now a French citizen. Your papers have been authorized by the French Government."

"A citizen? How can this be?"

"It is in the peace treaty. It says so right here: 'All persons from the Alsace-Lorraine region who can trace their ancestry to France are to be nationalized pursuant to Article 79 of the Treaty of Versailles.'

This letter states, 'this applies to Antoine Bouchard, held as POW P64335 at 447th Depot Detachment Engineers, Tours'. That is you!" The young woman's enthusiasm was in stark contrast to the drab room surrounding them.

Bouchard signed his release and naturalization forms, and pocketed a small amount of francs provided by the Red Cross. His travel orders allowed him passage to Strasbourg, the capital of the Alsace-Lorraine district, by train leaving Tours that afternoon. He still could not return home for there was no home, and no family, to return to.

The Red Cross clerk deposited the signed naturalization papers in a mail packet and dropped it into a bin marked "Strasbourg."

Within the hour he stood on the platform as the train wheezed and puffed steam, preparing to depart. In the hectic maze of soldiers and civilians that filled the station Antoine Bouchard was simply just another anonymous soul traveling to only God knew where. He was invisible.

He breathed deep. For the first time in a long time, he did not look over his shoulder to see who was watching him. That felt like freedom, the closest thing to freedom he had known these past six violent years.

The train left Tours station, hissing steam and belching black smoke as it headed east towards the border regions and Strasbourg.

Bouchard watched it pull away, then strode off the platform and into the streets of Tours.

CHAPTER 6 - BRITTANY

*The countryside was healing from the ravages of war - from the bombs,
the trenches, the mud, and the neglect of fields robbed of its tenders.
Villages were ghostly still. The soft blur of color slowly returning to
the land was mostly the prickly illusion of the thistle.*

Present Day

My search had entered its third excruciating month. I spent the next
several weeks tracking down the unit archives of the 447th DDE HQ
Company and all associated units in Tours and Paris. Because of the
age of the archives, most of them were not digitized, certainly not
available through electronic means. I would have to go back to the
traditional research methods, back to "the stacks" as we called them
in college years ago. It would be tedious, boring, and more than
likely unsuccessful.

The archives of the French authorities were even more difficult to
locate let alone examine. I had taken French in high school - some
forty-five years ago! My French was conversational only, and not
very good at that.

While the French who worked in traditional tourist or business
areas generally could speak better English than I could French,
researching document archives was something else entirely. My
phone calls yielded little results.

The search for Antoine began to consume me. I spent hours
every day searching out obscure references, following dead ends,
and compiling background information on the periods of the Great
War - but nothing to tie any of this to the elusive Antoine. He was a
ghost in my dreams, a phantom that plagued my thoughts and toyed
with my emotions.

My client work began to suffer, but I did not care. Antoine was important to my grandfather, so he became important to me. He had eluded my mother's search, but I was determined he would not elude me. I felt an obligation, a spiritual connection to my grandfather through the letters. I often reinforced my resolve by promising out loud to Grandpa Andy that I would find Antoine. I was getting desperate, running out of ideas.

Researching obscure information on the Internet is often like the punch line of the old joke, "Why are you looking over there? ... The light's better." There are numerous tricks to take advantage of the better light. One is to key back through directories in an Internet address from a document you discover to find what may be stored online but not directly referenced in links. It is a process called "scavenging" by technology types. It is frustratingly slow, but can yield interesting if not relevant information.

I found such a source on the website of the International Red Cross (ICRC) in Geneva. I had searched for "World War I prisoner of war records" and found a brochure in PDF format on the ICRC website and downloaded it. It was entitled "The International Prisoners of War Agency; The ICRC in World War I." While it contained some interesting yet brief background information, it gave me directory access to mountains of electronic documents in the bowels of the server at the Red Cross, directories not protected by a permissions block that would have prohibited directory access. I began another painstaking search.

One seldom finds exactly what one seeks. This is Research Law # 1 - of my own creation. However, each properly researched and cited paper, as opposed to brochures created for popular distribution, contains citations, references, and reading lists that formed the basis of another writers' research - the basis for peer review.

In one of the numerous documents I scavenged from the ICRC site, I found a reference to an obscure information repository in the capital of the Somme department at Amiens, France. The Somme was the northern theater of the Great War, and the scene of many of the critical battles of World War I. Information in the repository was used by the writer of an obscure paper entitled "Methods for Cross Referencing Prisoner Chargeback Payments in WWI French Administration, 1919." The paper listed the information's location within the general administrative records of the department's financial archives.

Further research revealed the hint of a point of leverage. It was customary for the French to charge for the services of POWs assigned to various tasks, whether in support of a private company - like the owner of a rock quarry - or a POW assigned to an American unit, perhaps. These charges are sometimes referred to as "chargebacks" or "transfer payments."

Official records between what are the functional equivalents of states, the French departments, tend to have similar organizational structures. Their methodologies are prescribed by the central government, their location and structure common. If there were identifiable financial transactions for transfer payments between organizations for POW expenses in Amiens, then there was a likelihood such a record exists in Tours for the Indre-et-Loire department (DPT I-L).

A dozen phone calls later and I was frustrated to the point of exasperation. Neither the telephone nor the Internet was going to help me any further.

⎯⎯

France, 1920

Bouchard roamed west from Tours, staying away from the rails and main roads, seeking out muddy countryside tracks and small villages where he could remain invisible. Although he had proper identity papers, nearly six years of the war and postwar captivity filled him with mistrust. There were so many displaced soldiers and civilians wandering all over France that even with his odd dialect he could slip away through the countryside unnoticed.

He eventually wandered into a small crossroads commune of Peucel. The village was quiet, almost deserted. A mangy dog tied to a fence near a ramshackle cottage barked at him. A few pigs rooted through what seemed like abandoned gardens. Along the muddy track leading into the village was a small church. In the cemetery he saw an old priest, bent over, tending a fresh grave. He rose up slowly, painfully, by leaning on a long staff.

"I have little food, my son," he apologized, "but what there is I am happy to share."

"Where are the people of the village?" Bouchard asked. He had seen no one save for the old priest. Fields were left untended, the small square in the village center unkempt.

"The young men were taken by the army when they came of age. None have returned. Many more died of the pestilence. I have two villagers who passed on to God yesterday, and I have not the strength to bury them. Perhaps God has sent you to help relieve them of their earthly suffering."

Antoine agreed to dig their graves for the old priest himself was weak with the grippe.

"You may stay in any of the empty cottages. The fields were barely planted and there are few left to work them. Some villagers just left, to where only God knows. He has sent you to me to tend to the dead. I am sure He knows your heart is good. Stay here and rest awhile. You can help me glean the fields for the winter, lest we both starve."

Bouchard holed up in Peucel for the winter. There were fish in a nearby reservoir, frogs in the grasses along the banks, and the fields gave up a paltry supply grain, enough to survive. He managed to catch the free pigs, and gave one to an old woman who kept the skinny dog on a leash. The old priest would come by and break bread now and again, and bring the last of the church wine to help ward off the cold. Bouchard attended mass out of respect for the old priest, although he was the only one there. The old woman was too enfeebled to get to church, so the priest would see her on his solitary rounds through the empty village. As winter slowly loosened its grip and the wretched road turned to mud, both the old woman and the priest had left to join their God.

The auditorium was filled about half-full which for this small college was a large crowd. I was taken a little by surprise at the sight and the excitement that buzzed in the room. Suzanne excitedly bustled about, introducing me to the faculty members who filed into the room, notebooks and e-tablets in hand - including Professor Douglas.

"We are ready. Could I ask you to give a brief introduction, explaining how you received the letters and who your grandfather was? I will take it from there. Sorry to put you on the spot," she added with a wry smile.

"OK, but you asked for it. I'm not exactly shy in public," I laughed.

She walked briskly to the podium and turned to address the crowd.

"Good afternoon, students, faculty, and friends. I must say when we first started this project, I certainly did not expect it to become of such interest to so many. I am grateful to all of you for coming today.

"I would first like to introduce the owner of the letters, a local businessman from Centralia, Mr. Larry Hewitt, who will give us a brief introduction. Larry ... ."

"Thank you, Professor Tauscher. Well, I wasn't prepared for such a gathering, but I'll do my best. I received a package in the mail from a small village on the Normandy coast of France called Courseulles-sur-Mer. The letters had been discovered in a metal box buried in a small cottage being torn down. A cover letter from the mayor of the town indicated they believed they had been meant for my grandfather, H. W. 'Andy' Anderson.

"Grandpa Andy had been a soldier in France with the American Expeditionary Force. I have been researching his journal, and discovered he spent part of the war in Paris - he was there during the German spring offensive of 1918 and the bombardments of Paris. He spent the majority of his time at a supply depot in the center of France, in Tours. He rotated home in April 1919, and his diary entries stopped. Sometime during this period, I believe he met the mysterious 'Antoine.'

"Andy Anderson became a chaplain, worked for the Civilian Conservation Corps during the Depression, and was recalled to duty during World War II. However, he served in the Pacific, and as far as I can tell he never returned to Europe until the late 1970's as a tourist - long after the last of the letters was written. At this time, I do not know who Antoine was, or what connection there may be between the two of them. I have started to try to track this connection down, but this is all I really know at this point. Suzanne ... ."

"Thank you, Larry. OK. There are two groups of letters. One group are from the Reverend Anderson to 'Antoine' - in French, although as many of you have all seen, the French was a little … creative."

A small chuckle rippled through the crowd of students who had worked on translating.

"The second group are from Antoine to Anderson, although they were never mailed. The French in these is native, although there are some dialectical issues we had to deal with because of the region of origin.

"We're going to go through the letters one at a time. After scanning the originals and subjecting them to electronic enhancements, my advanced French class split into teams and each created their own translation. We then compared and reconciled the differences, and I personally approved each version you see today.

"Professor Douglas from the history department has graciously agreed to provide a bit of historical context behind the time each letter was written. We will have a thorough discussion afterwards, so please hold your comments and questions until then. Can we have the lights, please?"

Professor Tauscher displayed the letters one by one. For each letter, Professor Douglas gave a brief description of what was happening in and around occupied France.

"At this stage," he concluded, "we do not yet know who Antoine is, or how he is connected with Chaplain Anderson - who, if you recall, is back in the U.S. Army and serving in the Pacific."

"OK, you have all seen the letters. Comments, or questions?"

Students in the auditorium nervously began to raise questions and concerns, prompting Professor Douglas to reach out in a loud, animated voice to elicit more interaction. He was a big man, perhaps 6' 4" or so, and carried himself just as large, with a loud booming voice and a sharp, challenging intellect. He would accept no half-baked opinions or questions.

"Could this just be a hoax, professor?" asked one student, sitting near the back.

"Certainly, that would be something you would want to verify. You look at the paper, at the ink, the context in which the letters were found. All these are important considerations, but fairly easy to verify."

"These letters," another asked. "They are mostly mundane, except for the last ones. I don't get the point. We can read about all of this time in books and on the Internet."

"You can read what someone else thinks happened, but these people wrote about what was happening in their lives at the moment it happened. They did not have the advantage of hindsight. In the early letters, they cannot know what is about to be unleashed across Europe. As we read through them, feel the terror build, feel the tension, then try to imagine what was happening to prompt each line, each word."

"But Professor, I mean, really, why would anyone write a letter they did not intend to mail, and then bury it along with all these others? I don't get it."

"Of course you don't!" He boomed, bounding off the stage onto the floor, waving his arms dramatically. "Because here you are so safe, with your Blackberries and iPhones, exercising your little thumbs," he chided as he worked his thumbs in a mock-texting manner.

"You do not have to worry about the secret Centralia police crashing down your door in the middle of the night and hauling you away to a concentration camp in Pe Ell. You don't have to worry your classmate is selling information on your sexual escapades to the police who are planning to round up all of you 'undesirables' and ship you off to some place in Asotin County to die in a work camp. And your campus security does not carry submachine guns and haul away instructors like me who question authority." His rant became more animated with every example.

"You live in a safe community with a tolerant government built of laws, despite your narcissistic complaining. All this we are reading laced in between the writing of the letters - this DID happen! And not in some long lost time, but in the time of your fathers and grandfathers! There are people still alive who wore the black skulls head of the Gestapo, who ran the extermination camps, who jumped out of planes to parachute into flooded fields to liberate France, or somehow managed to survive the withering machine gun fire as they stormed the beaches on D-Day!"

He turned and pointed back to the last letter, still on the screen, and boomed out, "The anguish, fear, and resignation of that letter is all too real! This is what people felt and experienced every day as the world collapsed in chaos all around them! This is the stuff of history, ladies and gentlemen. Not Wikipedia or About.com!"

<hr />

France, 1921

On a morning as cold and still as empty Peucel village, after he washed the wet earth of the cemetery from his hands, Antoine Bouchard headed out on the road again. He had enough bread to last a few days, some dried potatoes, the last slab of bacon from the pig, and two bottles of the old priest's wine. By October he was wandering among the marshes and fields of the Brittany coast, doing odd jobs for food and a night out of the rain in a farmer's shed.

"We need some wood chopped, for the kitchen. You can stay with the gardener." The estate manager of the chateau was a rough and dour sort, but here was warm food and a pile of straw to sleep on. He had walked to the coastal plains of Brittany, seeking work, perhaps on one of the fishing boats that plied the waters of Biscay Bay. He received a cold reception from the villagers. His accent was neither Parisian nor Breton. He was not to be trusted.

But the chateau needed a constant supply of firewood, and Bouchard was young and strong. So many men had been lost to war that a struggling seaport needed a supply of labor. He would soon find hard work could overcome even the most suspicious of Breton minds.

Work was plentiful though it paid little. He worked for food, for a roof, and to forget. Forget the war, forget Alsace, forget captivity. Forget everything of his past life.

He would not forget his friend in America.

> 28 Oct 1921
> My dear Andy,
>
> It has been too long since I have been able to write. For this I am sorry. I am settled in a shed on the grounds of a magnificent chateau on the coast in Brittany. I chop wood for the chateau, and do what I can.
>
> I am well, and I hope this letter finds you so. Write to me, and tell me of life in California.
>
> The chateau manager, M. Garant, glared at me when I asked him to receive my letters, but he is not as disagreeable as he appears.
>
> I wait for your reply.

Antoine

The address on the envelope read:

Chateau Domaine de Kerbastic
56520 Guidel - Morbihan
Bretagne Sud, France

———∞∞∞———

The economy flight to Paris seemed like flying in a telephone booth, so I went ahead and splurged on my train ticket. Standing at the ticket counter in the Gare Montparnasse, one of Paris' six main train stations, I weighed my options: Paris to Tours aboard a high-speed train, the Train à Grande Vitesse (TGV); Nonstop, 1 hour 12 minutes; Economy, 56 E, Luxury ,141 E. Luxury it was.

I had landed in Paris two days earlier and taken a cab from Charles De Gaulle Airport to a hotel in downtown, near the Opera House, where I met my daughter who joined me from Germany. I planned a few days in Paris to see the sights - my first time in country. I also brought my grandfather's diary and planned to visit the hotels where he stayed and the places he visited.

The first was the Opera House, and Avenue de l' Opéra - the broad avenue Andy often mentioned where he strolled through the downtown core as a poor soldier in Paris. At the Opera House I asked my daughter to take my picture at the exact spot where Adolf Hitler had been photographed on the steps when he made his infamous visit immediately after the occupation of Paris in 1940.

The Hotel Sainte-Anne was just a few blocks away, so we strolled down the avenue until we reached a narrow side street off to the left, the Rue Sainte-Anne. A few blocks away I saw the sign on the side of the hotel and entered the lobby. The clerk, however, rather rudely insisted I was in the wrong place. "Le Fireman's, Le Firemans," she exclaimed in a combination of French and broken English, and pointed down the street. The St. Anne Hotel had been located about a block and a half from this location that was now called the Louvre Sainte-Anne. The original hotel location is a fire station, which explained the "Le Fireman's."

A tour bus offered the easiest way to get around downtown Paris, and it stopped along a prescribed route at all the places one might wish to visit - the Opera House, the Louvre, Notre Dame, and the Eiffel Tower among many others. Busses arrived at the drop off points every few minutes and made moving about the downtown core very easy. At the Trocadero, I stood on the exact spot where Hitler had been photographed in his famous Eiffel Tower photo with Albert Speer and his favorite sculptor, Arno Breker, and recreated this photo as well.

After a visit to the Louvre, where I left my daughter to browse the collections, I trudged off for a rather long walk to find the Méditerranée Hotel where Andy stayed most of the time he was in Paris. Like most of the Parisian hotels, it was a small "store front" hotel sandwiched among the historic buildings, but charming and elegant. The clerk was far more obliging than at the Louvre Sainte-Anne.

After saying good-bye to my daughter, I took the tour shuttle back to my hotel for my bags and had lunch. I then walked the short distance to Gare Montparnasse to board the TGV to Tours. I relaxed in comfort as the French countryside rolled by, reviewing my notes and preparing for my upcoming visit to the document archives.

Promptly on time, the TGV rolled into Tours-Saint-Pierre-des-Corps on the outskirts of Tours, across the canal from the city center. It serves as a hub for rail service radiating throughout France and is why Tours was such an ideal location for a headquarters unit.

Now a modern city and rail system, the rail yards would have looked very different in 1918. The Gare Orleans in Tours, the train depot in the city core, is an end-of-the line station where trains do not pass through, so would not be as suitable for the rapid movement of men and materials for the war effort.

My hotel was located near the records hall in the city proper, but given the sunny weather and beautiful scenery, I chose to walk from the station into Tours instead of taking a cab. I crossed over the canal and walked the kilometer into the heart of the city, imagining walking in Andy's footsteps. After settling into the hotel, I spent the afternoon leisurely exploring Tours, enjoying the beautiful sunny weather, and locating all the places listed in Andy's diary. After a relaxing dinner in a corner bistro with a bottle of local wine, I returned to the hotel to prepare for my day tomorrow in the records section.

The Prefecture was a short distance away, and I met my contact at precisely 8:00 a.m.

"Bonjour," I called out cheerily.

"Ah, bonjour Monsieur Hewitt. I have been expecting you." The chief clerk at the records section, Monsieur Duprés, was an elderly gentleman with thick glasses who spoke very good English and had previously agreed to grant me access to the records. I could not remove anything from the records section, of course, but there were photocopy machines, and I was allowed to scan materials and copy them if needed for a fee. To protect the record assets, the chief clerk carefully monitored everything.

"I am not so sure you will find what you seek. I have worked here for over 30 years and cannot recall records such as you described. But perhaps you will uncover something to help you in your search."

He led me into a small anteroom off the main records library where I could set up my computer and portable scanner and work in private. "As we discussed, please do not copy or scan anything until I have recorded the documents. Some may be confidential, though I doubt any such problems will arise from records as old as those you are seeking."

"I understand. What I am looking for is very specific, and I do not need to copy much I am sure. We shall see."

"Please call upon me if you need any assistance," and he walked me into the archives and gave me a general look around to understand the structure.

"As you can see, this diagram reveals the general areas, although the information is of course in French. Can you translate these?"

"The labels are fairly self-explanatory, and I have a translator on my computer that can help."

"Very well. Again, call on me if I can be of assistance." M. Duprés returned to his desk at the entrance to the section.

I was alone among hundreds of shelves, file cabinets, tall movable ladders, and small working desks - it looked like something out of an Indiana Jones movie.

Inside the archives time stood still. Nothing stirred, and in the first eight hours not a soul came in to disturb me. The sound of traffic outside was the only indication there was life at all around me. I was still nowhere nearer my objective. When the office closed for the night, I was politely invited to return the following day.

Day two was the same. Dusty shelves gave way to thousands upon thousands of records, all in French of course, and difficult to read. After a while, however, the patterns of language became more familiar, and I was able to skim over large sections of information more efficiently. Again, my efforts yielded no results. At dinner that night, in the bistro on the corner near my hotel, I wondered just what I should do next. I was going nowhere.

On day three I had uncovered a series of cards in long trays that contained indexes to financial records back hundreds of years. The cards could not be removed from their trays, so I meticulously recorded the information of a series of cards from 1919 and went back to my working area next to the stacks and began to slowly, patiently, unravel the language barrier to see if any of these could be of help. By noon I was spent, emotionally and physically. I cleaned up and began to pack my computer away.

"Monsieur?" Her voice was very soft and muffled among the massive archive building.

"Oui," I responded. I looked up and saw the young assistant clerk walk in with a wooden box of ledger cards in her arms.

"Monsieur, je m'áppelle Cherié Honorée. I am a clerk in this section. When I first came to work here I helped the public works department of the city locate records for a prisoner compound built near Tours-Saint-Pierre-des-Corps. I remember there were a series of requisitions issued to pay for materials used to build the compound, but there were no such payments for labor. This would be very unusual, for labor in the accounting system used back then would have been the first entry on a ledger.

"These are the ledgers kept for the expenses of that compound. Perhaps they may be of help to you. M. Duprés has asked me to help you today to go through these."

There were several hundred ledgers, recording a multitude of expenses for Compound P223, a prisoner barracks built by the POWs themselves as such bivouacs often were. That explained the lack of labor expenditures. Going through the expense reports was tedious, and seemed hopeless.

"Monsieur, pardon," the young clerk interrupted. "What was the name again of the army unit you were searching for?"

"The 447th Depot Detachment Engineers, AEF."

"Perhaps you should look at this," and she placed a faded ledger on the table in front of me. Near the bottom of the ledger was an entry, barely legible with age and yellowing of the ledger stock. It read,

> 14/6/19
> P64335, transfer receipt, 447 DDE
> 85 fr

447 DDE-447th Depot Detachment Engineers! Grandpa Andy's outfit. On June 14, 1919, a transfer fee of 85 francs, or approximately $16.40, was paid by the 447 DDE to the Department of Indre-et-Loire.

"What is this, P64335?"

"Why, monsieur, that would be the prisoner number for the person in this transfer."

My pulse began to quicken. Here was the first concrete clue connecting anyone as a POW to my grandfather's unit in Tours. But, I cautioned myself, there would be hundreds if not thousands of such prisoners.

"Perhaps M. Duprés can help. He is more knowledgeable about the history of Tours than I." She disappeared, to return in a few minutes with the chief records clerk. He carefully inspected the ledger, and then cautiously began to unravel its possible implications.

"Well, you see," he began, "Tours was a transfer center because of the railroads. Few soldiers remained here for any periods of time, except for the air deport and the support depot where your grandfather was stationed. Prisoners would be moved here, processed, and then moved out. Few were ever here permanently. If your "Antoine" was a prisoner here, there would be few traces to find, unless he were assigned to a stationary unit for some reason."

"And if we found one, it would mean a high probability it could be him," I extended the logic. "How can we find the name associated with this number?"

"Hmmm, that I do not know," Monsieur Duprés answered.

The young clerk broke in excitedly.

"But M. Duprés, that would be easy! Come, I will show you!"

She excitedly left the room and headed for the stairs. She descended three flights, M. Duprés and I following, until she unlocked the basement door and entered another storage area.

"I remember moving these records here last spring," she offered.

"Yes!" M. Duprés blurted out. "Yes. I remember. They must be here!"

The two started quickly scanning boxes of stored records, until Mlle Honorée let out a shout.

"Over here! ICI!"

Inside were ledger cards with names, numbers, and duty stations written in neat orderly rows. Each card was for a separate person. Each person had a number, beginning with "P" - prisoners of war.

"Look for any prisoner with the first name, Antoine. If your Antoine is here, he will be in such a group. Also, look for P64335. Since his name is French, there should be only a few, if any." The "only a few" part was encouraging; the "if any" not so.

There were hundreds of cards in last name order, which might as well have been random since we did not know Antoine's last name. With the three of us pouring over them, we were able to get through the box relatively quickly. It was Mlle Honorée who made the discovery.

"Oh, regarder ici! Mon Dieu! Voila!"

She held up a ledger card excitedly. It listed the locations and charge payments for prisoner P64335. Antoine Bouchard.

The three of us started at the ledger, as it stared back at us, incredulously.

"But how do we know it is THE Antoine?

"Come with me," Monsieur Duprés snapped, and he grabbed up the ledger card and headed briskly back upstairs to his office.

He placed a phone call. "Monsieur Richard, s'il vous plâis."

We waited for what seemed an eternity.

"Monsieur. M. Duprés, from the records section, le department d' Indre-et-Loire ... Bien, merci. I have an emergency request. I need a payroll record from the 447 DDE, CO B, AEF, Tours, France, April, 1919 ... oui. Merci."

He placed the phone down.

"It is time to go to lunch."

The time dragged on as M. Duprés and I sat at the bistro across the street and shared a glass of wine.

"We must wait, but hopefully not for long. It has been an exciting morning, n'est pas?"

"Oh, but I simply cannot stand the waiting," I said, and we both laughed, somewhat nervously. We would not have to wait very long.

The young clerk came hurriedly out of the building and down the stairs, crossed the street briskly, and ran up to us waving a plastic-sheathed piece of paper.

"Oh, monsieur. I am, as you say, without a breath! Look," and she placed the FAX on the table.

It was a copy of a payroll record for the 447th Depot Detachment Engineers, Co B, Tours, April 15, 1919, from the French military records archives in Vincennes.

By this time Company B had sent home most of its compliment, so there were only a dozen left in the unit, preparing to be sent home. On the first line was Cpt. Richard Osland. From the diary I knew this was Grandpa Andy's company commander. The names below, and their pay amounts, were in alphabetical order. Listed second from the top, after "Aiken, C.S., Sgt" was,

Anderson, H. W., Cpl 19.30

The same amount listed in his diary pay record for April 1919. The last entry made my heart stop beating.

P64335. Transfer Payment, DPT I-L
16.40

Antoine Bouchard, P64335, was assigned to Grandpa Andy's company, now reduced to only twelve men. In such a small unit, it is inconceivable they would not have known each other. Here was the Antoine of the letters!

"Incroyable! Un autre verre, s'il vous plâit - another glass!" M. Duprés excitedly called to the waiter, who poured a round for the three of us at the table. He stood up and raised his glass.

"To success, to luck, to my tenacious assistant, Mademoiselle Honorée," and he bowed for which she blushed deeply, "and to your Antoine!" he toasted.

I stood up, raised my glass with the others, and smiled. With tears streaming down my face, smiles all around, I looked up to the sky and could barely speak as I choked back the tears.

"Grandpa Andy, I have found Antoine!"

CHAPTER 7 - PONT-AVEN

Again, the kingdom of heaven is like a net that was thrown into
the sea and gathered fish of every kind.
— *Matthew 13:47*

"Allez, Bouchard! Step it up there. I have a schedule to keep."

Antoine Bouchard strained under the heavy weight of the boxes filled with export wines from the valley of the Loire - the Chenin Blanc and Sauvignon Blanc demanded by a resurgent English economy. Spared the ravages of occupation and conquest, France's allies in the Great War quickly became its most important trading partners.

Trade with England from the major ports of Brest, Lorient, and Saint-Nazaire created an increasing demand for fish, wine, and other agricultural products. Although the trade organizations dominated the official trade in imports and exports, the tiny port of Pont-Aven routinely shipped tons of wines and other agricultural products to merchants in Portsmouth across the English Channel eager to bypass more traditional channels.

For a small fishing boat owner, the opportunity to offload a cargo of high-priced goods was too good of a premium to pass up.

Gilles De Rosier owned the fishing vessel St. Justine, one of a small fleet of independent boats that fished the waters of Biscay Bay. The large fishing fleets were required to sell their catch to the association fish processors at Lorient, but small boats generally carried on a local fresh fish industry that bypassed government restrictions and taxes. Monsieur De Rosier was as much a smuggler as a ship's captain. Regular payments to the Pont-Aven harbor master ensured his activities would go unnoticed by French authorities.

Life in the quiet coastal areas of Brittany escaped the chaos and economic hardships of France in the years following the Great War. Manpower was in short supply because of the war dead and influenza that killed as many or more young military-age men as the Germans. Work for the skilled was plentiful but wages were still low and conditions hard. Antoine Bouchard learned to be a master of many trades to survive.

There was work to do. While woodcutting at the chateau he had met Captain De Rosier. Bouchard signed on board for a three-day trip when his mate, a coarse drunk who valued his brandy more than his work, did not show up on the quay. He proved to be a quick study, worked hard, and on their return the captain offered Bouchard the mate's position. As the mate of the St. Justine he often loaded the contraband delivered across the channel.

A local priest showed him a small cottage on the edge of the commune that belonged to a man who had yet to return from the war. The priest had made inquiries concerning his whereabouts, but without success. The local military attaché had simply dismissed his request with "Whereabouts Unknown" and filed it away. In case he did make it back, his file would be changed. There were so many who had been killed in action or died unknown in some temporary field hospital of wounds or the influenza that trying to find anyone was near to impossible. Bouchard could live in this cottage until the owner returned. If he did not, it became the property of the church. If Bouchard agreed to work one day each week for the church he could live there and work the small truck garden.

Bouchard eventually earned the confidence of his captain and although De Rosier always piloted the vessel for late night cargo runs, he often turned the St. Justine over to Bouchard who fished the bay alone, splitting the catch with the captain after expenses.

"Ah, Bouchard. You are going out on a day like this?" the harbor master questioned him. The weather this day was blustery, and the sea was churned into a miserable chop of competing waves as the wind blew incessantly against a strong out-flowing tidal current. It was a day only the most adventurous, or foolish, left port. The harbor master had grown accustomed to Bouchard venturing out at times when the rest of the fleet kept safely tied to the docks. He was often at sea for days at a time.

"The fish don't mind the wind, so neither do I," he called back as he untied the St. Justine from the pier.

He wrote every few months keeping a promise he had made to his only friend, in America.

> 18 May 1922
> Mon ami, Andy
>
> I have found regular work and a place to live. You would like this palace of mine, built of stone on fertile ground. At least the three square meters of ground behind the cottage seems fertile. I have not planted a garden, for I have no time to tend such an extravagance.
>
> I work a few days a month for the commune priest for my rent. The rest of the time I am the mate on the fishing vessel St. Justine. The owner allows me to fish the bay alone most of the time. He is older, and bothered by aches and pains to where he prefers to spend the day before the fire with a bottle of brandy. He is tough, but has taught me much of the fishing trade.

He lost his two sons in the Great War. I suppose I have replaced them in his plans to quit the rigors of the sea.

I hope you are well.

Antoine

It was a precarious life. Profits were hard to earn, the work dangerous. Only by fishing when others chose the comforts of the hearth and wine bottle could he carve out a life working another's boat.

He preferred the solitude.

At night, when he was ashore, he stayed close to the fire inside the small stone cottage. He feared the night above all else. The unsettled weather of spring in Brittany would bring frequent thunderstorms as the winter reluctantly released its tenacious grip. The thunder rolled in, crackling and snapping, as he sought shelter in the cottage. His pulse was already pounding as he closed the shutters tight against the gusting winds. He knew the dreams would return tonight.

The small cottage at night was illuminated only by the faint glow of the embers of the dying fire. The walls closed in around him, and he slept fitfully. Faces appeared, faces of comrades lost, of times past. His brother's face appeared - at first soft and boyish, morphing into a mutilated apparition - silhouetted by the glow of the fires of the bombardments that just as suddenly dissolved into the reddish glow of the hearth. He woke dripping in a cold sweat, screaming out a warning of the impending bombardment.

"Down!" he screamed, and buried into the mean ticking to shield himself from the fragments. There was no use trying to run; there was no place to run to. The trenches were his life, his protection.

To leave meant certain death. So he burrowed ever further into his nightmares, deep into the mud and gore, seeking refuge.

On the sea he felt at peace. The openness of the bay and the rolling of the waves calmed him. Even in the confined space in the ship's forward where he slept, far more closed in than his cottage trenches, the smell of the sea air and the constantly rolling waves eased his fears and calmed his dreams. When his brother spoke to him, it was of gentler times in the hills and rivers of the Alsace, not the battered plains of Poland or the trenches of Flanders. Tonight the terrors returned, and he wept and prayed for dawn to come.

The following day, he wrote to Andy,

> 14 Dec 1923
> Dear Andy,
>
> The terrors return most every night. You have asked me to pray, but I find myself praying not for peace, but for death and release. I finally fell asleep when the thunder passed, but when I awoke my left arm and hand were again numb.
>
> I feel God is mocking me.
>
> The sea is the only place I can feel at peace.
>
> Antoine

Bouchard routinely fished the Brittany Cape. Occasionally he would venture further east, toward the Channel Islands, those bits of rock just off the French coast that were a part of the British Commonwealth. Over time Bouchard discovered the small ports along the northern coast where he could put in to offload his catch, make repairs, or just tie up for a needed night of rest before heading back to the Breton coast.

It was in the tiny port of Pont-Aven on the Biscay Bay that he met Marianne Laroque.

———⊗∞⊗———

Present Day

I began the process of deciphering and cross referencing the letters on the train from Tours back to Caen. The letters read easily enough, and I had a general sense of their perspective, but there were subtle references, responses, and secrets hidden between the lines. They were a puzzle without directions.

I began by creating a table and identifying each letter by date order. In the next column I gave a brief description of the context as I understood it. The third column contained key words or phrases that needed some contextual focus. The last column was reserved for my own comments. I hoped by breaking these down in this manner it would be easier to manage the hidden meanings and agendas.

One of the tasks I had completed before arriving in France was to make a timeline of the places Grandpa Andy had lived throughout this period. As a young divinity student it was difficult to balance schooling and work. Andy held a number of student pastorates between 1922 and 1930, and had to move often. By 1935, when my mother was seven years old, he had joined the Civilian Conservation Corps as a chaplain and was stationed in the Medford District of Oregon. My mother often fondly told stories of living in Roseburg, in southern Oregon's Rogue River region - one of the finest fishing rivers in the west. Fishing was my grandfather's passion.

I was surprised to learn Andy had been recalled to Army service in June 1941, nearly six months before Pearl Harbor and America's entry into the war. He quickly found himself stationed in New Guinea and then the Philippines.

As for Antoine, the few letters I had led me to the Brittany coast. The only actual address was for the chateau where Antoine chopped wood:

> Chateau Domaine de Kerbastic
> 56520 Guidel - Morbihan
> Bretagne Sud, France

A quick check online showed the chateau was still there, and operating as a hotel. Many of the chateaus and shops of the region had stood for centuries. I located the chateau on the mapping program and noted the possible ports nearby. The main district center near the chateau was Lorient - I decided to concentrate my search through the records there. Lorient was a mere 10 minute drive from the chateau according to their e-brochure, so I decided to make a reservation there for my stay in Lorient.

The Chateau Kerbastic is a magnificent 17th century mansion set in stone-walled grounds and beautiful gardens about 10k from Lorient. It was the home of Breton royalty. The grandson of Comte Maxence Melchior Edouard Marie Louis de Polignac, the owner of the estate in the latter 19th century, was the father of Prince Rainier III of Monaco, who married Grace Kelly. Over the centuries it has been host to some of France's most notable writers and artists, such as Jean Cocteau, Marcel Proust, and Sidonie-Gabrielle Colette.

I checked into one of the smaller rooms and took some time to walk the grounds. Antoine lived here, according to his letters, and cut wood during the postwar period. I asked the manager, but there was no such record.

"Casual laborers would not be recorded," was his answer. However, he confirmed such an activity would have been likely. He also confirmed the estate manager of the chateau in 1922 was Amaury Garant, the name mentioned in the letter.

I drove a rented car into Lorient the following morning, and sought help at the hall of records. I was expecting to locate records relating to the birth of the child Ariéle or the marriage between Antoine and Marianne. I was guessing these relationships, but was fairly certain this was the case.

Armed with a research outline I downloaded from the Family History Library of the Mormon church, I began to search the civil records of births, deaths, marriages, and occupations contained in Lorient. It was a short search.

"Do you know the birth date of the father?" - No.

"Do you know his place of birth?" - No

"What about the mother - her maiden name?" - No

"Where did they live?" - Sorry. I don't know that either.

"Do you know what church they were married in?" - No.

"Je suis désolé, monsieur." That was that.

I drove around Lorient and enjoyed the sites of the city, but came away with not much in the way of concrete information. When I got back to my room at the chateau, I went back online and dug deeper into the sources - of records and methodologies that might help unlock the information I sought.

The server at breakfast the following morning gave me the best advice I had since arriving.

"The church was the center of all activity. My grandparents lived in this region, and their parents before them. There are almost no civil records of my family, but we could trace them through the records of the church. You might start there."

Great. Which church? I learned records of activities during and after the war years could be frustratingly erratic and incomplete.

Marriages and births were often held at small churches in the rural areas, and often the records were kept locally. That made them particularly susceptible to being destroyed or lost in the chaos of the war years.

Most of the residents of the Breton Peninsula are Catholic, so it made sense to begin by checking the diocese in the region. I went back to my room and buried myself on the Internet.

I found the Archdiocese of Finistére was the largest organizational unit of the region, and the Diocese Quimper included the region to the west of Lorient. The area to the east is the Diocese of Vannes. Between these two there are hundreds of individual churches, and the number in small ports while less was still intimidating.

I placed a call to the headquarters of the Archdiocese of Finistére and learned, through my increasingly better French, that the records do not include all the churches in the archdiocese; neither did the records at the diocese level, especially during the early war years. I would have to check records at each church if I could not find my information in the civil records.

The task seemed overwhelming, again. I spent hours searching the web for a clue that may lead me to an electronic archive, but eventually gave up.

I turned back to the letters to see if I could find something to help narrow my search.

Pont-Aven, 1924

Pierre Villar walked through the quiet early morning streets of Pont-Aven. Dawn would not come for several hours, but soon the villagers would begin to arrive for their daily breads and cakes. He would only bake what would be sold today, ensuring the bread was always fresh. The local priest would pick up what did not sell - his tithe to the church that kept this little commune church supplied with bread even in the hardest of winters.

The bakery was already warm from the ovens when he opened the door and walked in.

"Bonjour, ma minette," he smiled warmly at the young woman stoking the fires of the bakery. Her long, auburn hair was tied up to keep it away from the fires. Her apron was already covered with white flour, her brow sweating from the hard morning work and the heat of the stoves. Pierre could not help but marvel at her beauty, a face that comforted him in his old age.

"Bonjour, Papa!" she cheerfully replied. His daughter Marianne was his pride, so strong and independent, yet as lovely and slight as her mother who he lost to the influenza these seven years past. She would arrive an hour before her father to light the fires and prepare the dough for the morning baking. By noon they will have sold the day's bakings and closed the shop. In the afternoon she tended the garden plot just outside of town where she grew vegetables and a small crop of grapes to make the annual set of wine.

Pierre Villar was known across the peninsula for his fine brandy, but he refused to make any more than he could drink and share with his family, friends, and his priest.

"One does not sell a gift from God," he would always say when asked why he would not sell his fine brandy.

Villar's bakery shop was a short walk from the quay where the fishing boats unloaded their catch, and from where on this blustery day Antoine Bouchard was preparing for another day at sea. The tide would be turning by early afternoon and the St. Justine was scheduled to clear the harbor by 2:00. Marianne arrived after noon, her hair now falling loosely past her shoulders, blowing in the harbor wind and glistening in the afternoon sun.

Antoine saw her as she rounded the corner and stepped onto the dock. He had watched her from a distance for many months, occasionally stalling leaving the quay just for the oft chance she would come by and deliver packages of breads to one of the boats in the harbor. The ship's owner, Monsieur De Rosier, would often scold him for being so shy.

"You are not fit to be a Frenchman!" he would cry out, waving his arms in disgust. "A beautiful woman walks by every day, and you hide like a schoolboy! Mon Dieu, I am ashamed to share my boat with you."

They were out on the bay hauling in a load of fish one day when he cried out, "Antoine! She is a woman! A woman wants amour, wants to be shown a man has his heart just for her!"

"I cannot. I simply do not know anything to say," he replied.

"Vraiment? Ah, it is easy! You simply look her straight in the eyes, smooth out your voice, and speak slowly and softly, 'tes yeux, j'en rêve jour et nuit' - I dream about your eyes day and night. She will fall over dead for you - I guarantee it!"

His bullying did little to boost Bouchard's confidence. On the days Marianne would walk down the quay, and the older boat captains would politely doff their hats and acknowledge her with an "Allo" or "Bonjour, Marianne" and the deck boys would be gawking or whistling, he would step behind the wheelhouse or go below decks. His heart would be pounding, nonetheless. He was miserable.

"Bonjour, St. Justine!" she called, approaching the boat. "J'ai votre épicerie - I have your groceries," and she stopped alongside the fishing boat, awaiting a response. "Allo! Capitaine?"

Antoine panicked. Why was she here? That rascal, De Rosier. He ordered up some groceries for her to deliver! It is a set up! What shall I do? He was trying to think, when Marianne stepped on board. He was trapped! "Ah, bonjour. I am looking for Capitaine De Rosier," she smiled. She had seen this handsome young man before, but they had never met. That was a little odd, she thought, for the commune was so small. They should have met, if not on the streets or the bakery, at least in church.

"Uhmm, I did not order these," Antoine stammered, afraid to look into her green eyes.

"Oh, really. And just who are you? I have an order here from the captain of the St. Justine, M. De Rosier. It is already paid for, and my instructions are to deliver it before 1:00 this afternoon." She looked at him with amusement, now fully aware he was desperately looking for a way out of this meeting.

"Just put them down," he stumbled, "I will put them away later."

"I will not! I do not know who you are, or why you are on M. De Rosier's boat. Perhaps you are here to steal his provisions," she declared, in a mock serious, teasing voice. "I will wait for le capitaine, if you don't mind. In the meantime, I will put these below decks in the galley," she declared matter-of-factly, and stepped past him to go below. A breeze caught her long, auburn hair and it blew in his face as she moved. He though he was going to faint.

As she stepped back on deck Captain De Rosier appeared on the dock.

"Ah, bonjour Madame. Welcome aboard. I see you have met my mate, Antoine Bouchard."

"Actually, M. De Rosier, he has not so much as bothered to introduce himself. I should be insulted," she teased with a smile aimed in the captain's direction.

"Je suis désolé, madame. Permettez moi de vous présentez Monsieur Antoine Bouchard. Antoine, Madame Marianne Laroque."

De Rosier bowed slightly in an almost mockingly formal introduction, reveling in Bouchard's sheer panicked expression.

"Enchanté, Monsieur Bouchard," she replied, and extended her hand in greeting.

A lump rose in his throat, but he managed to croak a garbled, "Enchanté," himself and reached out to take her hand. It was slight but firm, surprisingly soft for a woman of the working class. His was rough, hardened, and sweaty, but she did not flinch or draw back. She warmly shook his hand, lingering just a little longer than he dared believe she would.

"Monsieur De Rosier, I have put your supplies in the galley. I must be away. I have a delivery to make to the church this afternoon. Antoine, it was a pleasure to meet you," she smiled. With the captain taking her hand, she stepped back onto the quay, and turned back. "Au revoire, Antoine. Good luck on the bay this afternoon. Captain," and she turned away, walking down the quay. Antoine's eyes followed her until at last she reached the side of the net shed where she turned and waved before disappearing down the street.

Antoine sat back on a pile of nets, and was sure he would vomit. De Rosier simply cried, "So! Now you have met!" He laughed heartily as the boat's engine roared to life.

Present Day

The letters were personal, and as such contained customary period pleasantries - what one of Professor Tauscher's students called "real-life-boring." Andy was from a passionately evangelistic family whose father wrote letters almost entirely in the language of the faithful. This style tended to permeate Andy's letters as well.

I browsed the letters looking for keywords. There was a thread that appeared early and seemed to dissipate, then return. The words and phrases kept recurring, "dreams that trouble you", "despair", "the terrors", and so forth. One letter in particular was unusually direct.

> 5 Feb 1924
> My dear Antoine,
>
> I have been blessed with a pastorate in Lafayette, Oregon. This is called the Willamette Valley - the destination of the wagon trains of the old west stories, the Oregon Trail.
>
> This part of Oregon is beautiful, and reminds me of Tours. Some of the farmers here are growing grapes for making wine - which made me think of you. Perhaps they will equal the French grapes one day.
>
> St. Justine be praised! The patron will watch over your labors I am certain. Even a Baptist can appreciate such guidance!
>
> There are two members of the congregation here who fought in France in the Great Offensive of 1918. I have sat with them many times helping them find God's forgiveness. The terror you speak of afflicts them as well. The doctors refuse to help, for there is no medicine that can alleviate such pain.
>
> I think of you when I listen to their fears. One cannot walk, but is confined to a wheel chair even though the doctors cannot find anything wrong. His daughter tells me he walks through the house in his sleep. There is a connection between your arm pain

and his inability to walk during the day. I hope I can find out how to help him, God willing.

You are never alone, my friend.

Trusting in Him,

Andy

I became distracted by the information about the man who could not walk. Professor Douglas had spoken of the "whispers in the winds" - these were the counterpoint to Antoine's "point," and often seemed to be answers to something contained in a previous letter. Since only a precious few of the letters were found from Antoine to Grandpa Andy, I was forced to infer much from these counterpoint comments.

Antoine had some kind of infirmary. Perhaps he had been wounded in battle, but the implication was his issues were psychosomatic, at least as far as a lay interpretation was concerned. I retuned to the Internet and began to research the term to make certain I was not propagating some discredited snake-oil problem.

I came to the conclusion this subject was far too complex to reduce to a simple set of answers. However, the overwhelming body of information diverted my attention to the subject of severe trauma and its effects on the human condition. Even if it did not directly answer any of my questions, I knew it would be important in helping unravel my great mystery.

Pont-Aven

"You called her 'Madame Laroque.' Not 'Mademoiselle,'"
Antoine ventured as they headed out into the stiffening breeze off
the bay.

"So, you think you are going to find some virgin schoolgirl to fall
in love with you, eh, Antoine?" The captain chided him. "You're
not exactly a prime catch yourself! She's a grown woman, Antoine.
And a woman does not need some fresh-faced school boy to dote
after her. She wants a man who will provide for his family, who is
not afraid to work, and work hard."

"But how could she love someone like me? My clothes are dirty.
My hands are rough and calloused. I smell like fish!"

"She does not already know this? Believe me, the entire
commune knows you smell like fish! Mon Dieu, you are impossible.
I give up. Enough teasing. It is no contest anyway.

"Marianne is the daughter of Pierre Villar, the baker. This you
know. What you do not know is while she was a girl in school, at
the beginning of the Great War, she met a young Parisian - Robert
Laroque - and they fell in love. They were married in Paris without
the knowledge of her father and not in the church. As you can
imagine, her father refused to acknowledge the marriage, and it
created a rift with his daughter.

"Within the year, her husband was conscripted into the army, and
was killed after a few months in the northern offensive of 1917.
Marianne was devastated, and hid in Paris, afraid to return home.
Her father went to Paris and found his daughter. Together they
healed the wounds that had separated them, and he brought her, and
the body of her husband, back to Pont-Aven.

"To honor her father, the priest gave a blessing in the church to
the marriage of Marianne and Robert. On the same day, they

blessed his soul to God, and buried him in the church cemetery. It was the saddest day anyone can remember in Pont-Aven.

"Since then she has worked with her father in the bakery. It has been 8 years now, and she has healed her heart of that painful day."

⸗⸗⸗

The Procession was interrupted by the noise of the door opening, spilling the hymn momentarily out into the street. Pierre Villar turned to see who would be so rude as to interrupt the beginning of mass, and saw the mate who works one of the boats in the harbor try to slip unnoticed into church.

"Completement debíle!" he spat, annoyed anyone would be so late to the mass.

"Papa, sssh," Marianne whispered, and tried to see who had so irritated her father. What she saw made her smile discretely, watching the young man in his recently scrubbed but rumpled clothing, black hair combed back, and ill-fitting coat slip into the pew. She turned back and laughed to herself.

So, she thought, the quiet fisherman decided to follow me to mass. At the end of the Procession, she quickly turned to glance back at him, and their eyes met momentarily. Antoine immediately glanced down, pretending to be preoccupied with a rosary he clumsily removed from his coat pocket.

Monsieur Villar looked over quickly at her, annoyed she would bother to turn to look at such a creature. As he watched her face brighten, the little smile turning the corners of her mouth ever so slightly, he frowned deeply. Not with my daughter, he told himself. I will keep my eye on this one, he vowed.

After the priest blessed the congregation at the conclusion of mass, Marianne stood and turned around to watch Antoine. He had risen early and all she saw was the door closing behind him. She shook her head, amused.

"Come, Papa. I have work to do."

"On Sunday? We do not work on Sunday, daughter," he scolded her.

"Oh, really? And just who prepares your supper, and cleans the dishes, and picks up after the mess you leave on your 'day of rest' - hmmm? It is easy for you to rest, you have a slave to do your housework for you!"

He growled at her impudence. No daughter should speak to her father in such a tone. It made him smile, however. She is so much like her mother, he thought. God has blessed me with two such beautiful women in my miserable life.

The quay was quiet as she walked by the next several days. The fishing fleet emptied the harbor early, even before Marianne arrived to tend the stoves, as the winds and the seas quieted. By evening the holds of the boats were filled to capacity. The crews, exhausted from the hard work, stayed on board with just enough sleep to start yet again the following day. The processing house and markets were full but the streets were quiet with the boats out all the time.

As all fishermen have known since boats first plied the Biscay Bay, days of nonstop fishing took their toll on boats, gear, and crew. Even the heartiest of captains would eventually have to put back to port for an extended stay to make repairs, provision, and rest.

On this day, the St. Justine remained in port.

"Bonjour, madame." She was surprised to turn and see him standing in the bakery, without Captain De Rosier egging him on. The good Captain had told her of his mate, the hard working but shy

Antoine Bouchard, and how he had watched him follow her every move like a smitten schoolboy. So they concocted the "chance" meeting on the boat to break the ice. He had fled church in a panic, she laughed, but at last, here he is. What now?

"Bonjour, comment allez-vous, Monsieur Bouchard?" she smiled, deliberately using the more formal greeting. Her formality threw him off balance, and he fumbled for something to say.

"Je vais bien, merci," he replied. "I am fine." His captain had schooled him on how to approach and greet her, and together they had practiced this meeting many times while at sea. At this very moment, Captain De Rosier was sitting with friends at the café with a bottle of wine and a loaf of bread, describing the scene to his friends who roared with laughter at Antoine's predicament.

"I need to get some bread for the boat," he stumbled, knowing that was not at all what he was supposed to say.

"Be direct," De Rosier had told him. "A woman likes a man who is bold, a man with a plan of action to woo her. Not some stumbling imbecile. She may say 'no' to your first advances, but that is like the fish who teases the bait before striking - it is just the first step of the dance."

He was determined to get through this, and not suffer yet another day of insults on the boat or at the café with the other fishermen.

"Very good. What can I get for you?" She could sense his nervousness and knew something was ready to burst forward from him, likely very clumsily, but sweet nonetheless.

"Uhm," he muttered, and looked nervously around the shop.

"Oh, monsieur, we are fresh out of 'Uhm' but perhaps you would like a few croissants," she teased. It was too much for Antoine to take.

"I would be pleased to invite you to lunch this afternoon!" He blurted out. There. He had said it. He was ready to be humiliated, but better to stand up to his captain and the others.

"Déjeuner? Peut-être. Perhaps. But not at that dirty café you men stink up when you come off the boats."

Perhaps. What did she say? Did she say yes?

"I will make a lunch," she stated matter-of-factly. "You bring a bottle of wine, I will bring cheese and bread, and glasses. I suppose the are no clean ones on that smelly boat of yours. I know a nice place we can enjoy the sun of the afternoon."

Antoine stood looking at her, slightly stunned, not certain what had just happened. She was smiling casually at him, still rearranging her breads for sale. Two villagers walked in and she stopped to wait on them. When she finished, she turned back to him.

"So, anything else?" She raised her eyebrows slightly, amused at his obvious discomfort.

"No, no," he stumbled.

"Bien," she replied, "you can meet me here at 1:00 this afternoon after I close the shop. OK?"

"That would be fine," he returned. He had forgotten the closing De Rosier had prepared him to use.

"Merci. I will see you then. And Antoine, I have a name. It is Marianne, not 'madame,'" and she turned back to the ovens. He began to slowly back out towards the doorway.

"Au revoire, Antoine," she turned and called out, smiling sweetly.

He would remember that sweet smile, and this day, for the rest of his life.

The summer of 1925 was a time of release from the dreams that had terrorized Antoine since the end of the war. When he was not at sea he regularly courted Marianne, despite her father's cold reception. It had become somewhat of a joke between them, as Marianne would not bow to her father's demands. She loved her father very much, and worked hard to keep the bakery profitable, but she never could understand his radical politics, nor did she approve of the men he kept company with.

Marianne and Antoine would often return to the field where, under an old maple tree, they had shared their first picnic. Her boldness and strength belied her soft, gentle nature. It lifted him, empowered him, and he began to dream of good times, of family and friends, and a long life with this beautiful woman.

He finally wrote to Andy about Marianne.

> 23 Jly 1925
> Mon ami, Andy
>
> For once I can write to you without complaining of my dreams. You see, my friend, they have been filled with the visage of a beautiful woman. Her name is Marianne.
>
> Marianne is the daughter of the baker. She is more beautiful than I could imagine, and I cannot see what she sees in me. But there it is, as you always say.
>
> When I am with her, I am at peace.
>
> I will ask her to marry me one day, this I know. For now, I must prepare to be worthy of such an angel.
>
> Antoine

Andy Anderson wrote as well. He was working as an Associate Pastor, learning the trade much as an apprentice. He had married, and wrote to tell Antoine of the birth of his first child, a girl named Bonnie, in October 1925. Just why they chose a Scottish name for the daughter of a Swede Bouchard could not understand, but such were the Americans.

As the winds on the Bay turned cold, and the rains returned, the people of Pont-Aven prepared for the long winter. Antoine decided he would not spend this winter alone.

CHAPTER 8 - PARTI NATIONAL BRETON

Patriotism is when love of your own people comes first; nationalism,
when hate for people other than your own comes first.
— *Charles de Gaul*

"He is not one of us!" Pierre Villar slammed his fist down on the table. "I will not agree to this marriage!" Just the thought of this was blasphemy to him, and he spat on the floor.

"Papa! I am not some little girl you can scare with such nonsense! I am a grown woman, and I have my own mind!"

She stood defiantly in the doorway of their cottage. Her father glared back at her from the table.

"What do you know of him? Eh? Where does he come from? What of his family? He is a stinking fisherman who runs contraband wine. What kind of life is that?"

"He is a kind and decent man. He works hard to make a living. That should be good enough!"

"It is not! I forbid it!" he thundered.

Nothing would be settled this day, which was like so many others before. Marianne was set on seeing her Antoine; her father was determined to rid his life of this outsider. They had been through these arguments many times. The old ways are forever gone, she would try to convince him. The Great War had turned everything Villar believed upside down, and scattered the inhabitants of the tiny Breton community to the corners of France - those that did not now lie beneath its cold ground.

He was determined not to lose his daughter again. This is not over, daughter, he muttered to himself. He dared not make such a bold statement out loud. Marianne, like her mother, was a force of nature, not to be trifled with.

Marianne slammed the door after her and headed for the bakery to stoke the morning ovens.

Bouchard was a different matter, he resolved. I will have my moment, rest assured.

The two men sat at the café and looked suspiciously at each other. Léon Vercher was the harbor master of Pont-Aven. Nothing moved through the small port without his knowledge, and the paperwork to clear the port could easily become bogged down. Nothing that a small favor passed quietly at the local café could not resolve. The payments were generally known among the merchants and captains, but it was something that was never spoken. It was in everyone's interest to look away.

Today was different. Pierre Villar had breached the code of silence with Monsieur Vercher and the tension between them spilled out onto the muddy street.

"What is your intent, Monsieur Villar?" He asked suspiciously. Villar was not a wealthy man, but as the only baker in Pont-Aven he knew everybody, and everybody's business. He could make life difficult for him.

"A simple favor, Léon. That is all," he slowly began. His informal tone disarmed M. Vercher somewhat, and he realized he was being manipulated into something, perhaps something he could profit from.

"A simple favor? The bite of a snake is a simple thing, Pierre."

"Now, Léon. There is no need to be so defensive. I am just after some simple information, that is all. Information I am prepared to compensate you for."

"You talk boldly for a miserable baker," he replied.

Villar noticed a change of tone, and knew he had piqued the harbor master's interest.

"Miserable, maybe, but perhaps we can help each other a little. I don't care about your little intrigues on the dock, Léon. I am interested, however, in my daughter's safety. A father must protect his only child, don't you agree?"

"You talk in circles, Villar. What do you want?"

"I would be interested in knowing when the St. Justine leaves port with one of its 'special' cargos."

"What is your interest in such matters? What does it matter to the local baker, so long as they buy their bread from you?"

"I do not want my daughter to marry a smuggler, monsieur."

"That is a strong accusation," Vercher carefully offered, pulling back slightly in his chair.

"Mon Dieu, Léon, I do not care what cargo the St. Justine is carrying, to where or for whom. Nor do I care what they pay you to look away. I cannot sit back and let that bastard fisherman Bouchard steal my daughter. With enough information on him, I can make certain he leaves my Marianne alone. For good. So you see, a little information from time to time, shared over café or wine among friends. It is such a little thing."

"Vraiment. This 'little thing' - how little?"

Villar smiled. The one thing he could count on was the greed of the harbor master. Marianne was wrong - the war had not changed everything after all.

26 Nov 1925
Mon ami, Andy

Marianne has agreed to marry. I am stunned beyond words.

Antoine

"Yes, child, I will bless your union through the church. Your father has told me he does not agree." The priest knew Marianne would have her own way, but he also knew she wanted to respect her father as well.

"I am not a child, Father. As a widow, of a marriage blessed in this very church, you cannot deny me my day before God based on such old traditions."

"The Lord says to honor thy father," he countered, knowing he was on a losing track.

"I will honor my father by asking him to bless our wedding in church. I will honor him by being a dutiful daughter. The Lord does not say I am bound like a maiden to his decree. I am an independent woman of the church, and I will be wed in the church!"

"Antoine is not baptized in the church," the Father remarked, as a last ditch attempt to dissuade her on behalf of her father. He knew her response before he even completed the remark.

The meeting ended as the Father knew it would. He knew Marianne was right, and as a widow was within her rights as a member of the church and the community, despite her father's anger. That night he included Antoine, Marianne, and Pierre Villar in his prayers. The following Sunday Antoine was baptized in the Pont-Aven Catholic church.

Antoine and Marianne were wed in church just after the new year. There were few in attendance because of the foul weather, but as the day had approached the well-wishers who came into the bakery gave their blessings to the union. Pierre Villar refused to attend, and ended the day passed out from too much brandy in his home. He would never forgive Marianne for abandoning him again.

Marianne made the humble cottage she and Antoine shared into a warm and loving home. She planted the garden come the following spring, while she still kept the garden she had worked these past years for her father. She still stoked the fires at the bakery every morning, despite the days her father never arrived. He spent too many days lost in a drunken haze, shut up in his cottage with a bottle of brandy.

When Antoine was out to sea for days at a time, Villar would rise and walk to the bakery in the morning. When the St. Justine was in port, he refused to talk to Marianne, and would not acknowledge Antoine even when passing him on the docks making his rounds.

Marianne reconciled her father's anger, but refused to give in to his rantings. The villagers would talk about them in whispers, but Marianne refused to allow them to anger her.

"The old women love to gossip," she would tell Antoine, sitting by the fire as the summer waned, and the autumn color returned to the land. "But they still need their bread, and who would shun the baker in such a small village?" she would add with a smile.

At night, when the darkness closed in, held back only by the soft glow of the hearth, Marianne's warmth brought peace to him at long last.

Ariéle was born in May 1928. She had her mother's green eyes, and brilliant red hair.

21 Oct 1928
Mon ami, Andy

I cannot describe the joy I feel when I hold Ariéle. I
see her mother in her face, her eyes, and her
stubbornness!

This life could not bring greater happiness. We have
both been blessed.

Your friendship has given me the strength to dare to
live such a life. Such a friend is a rare gift.

Antoine

Pierre Villar refused to accept the Alsatian's child as his
granddaughter.

"He is dangerous. He is interested in revenge against this fisherman
for daring to marry his daughter, for driving her into what he
believes is a sinful pairing and bearing a bastard girl-child. His
emotions are his weakness, but he can be used."

Vercher talked quietly with the two men as they sat in the café.
His comrades were members of the PNB, the Parti National Breton -
a nationalist Breton extremist organization. The PNB saw the
German Nazis as a potential ally in their goal of a fascist Breton, free
of foreigners and Jews. Smuggling had become one of the means by
which the local organization, based in Lorient, funded its activities.
That meant remaining on good terms with the local harbor masters.
Léon Vercher was only too pleased to do their bidding, as long as he
remained in the circle.

"Can he be recruited?"

"I believe so. He is angry about the foreigners in port, especially this Alsatian Bouchard. He is connected with other small shop keepers in Pont-Aven. He thinks the democracy is out to ruin him with its taxes - like they all do."

The men laughed, and poured another glass of wine.

"He also pays me to tell him when the boat St. Justine makes a run with contraband," he chuckled. His two comrades were not as amused.

"Is he working for the police?"

"No, he is not that smart. He is looking for a way to strike at this Bouchard. A modern Madame Defarge!" They all laughed heartily at this reference to the character in Dickens Tale of Two Cities who so passionately seeks revenge she presaged her own destruction.

"Nonetheless," the smaller of the two comrades mused, "he will have to be disposed of at the right time. This information could be used in the wrong places."

Present Day

"OK, OK, let's settle down. We are going to dispense with the usual curriculum today. Instead, I want to discuss the historical context of the 'Juno Letters.' Our friend Mr. Hewitt is away in France tracking down details related to the letters."

Professor Douglas shunned modern electronics for a white board, colored markers, and an old overhead projector.

"We have discovered Antoine!" he announced with a flourish, writing the name "Antoine Bouchard" across the board. "As we suspected, Antoine Bouchard was a French resident of the Alsace-Lorraine at the start of the Great War who was conscripted into the

German army. General practices during the time suggest strongly he was stationed at the Eastern Front."

"How do we know that, Professor?"

"We don't for certain. What we do know is the Germans did not trust the French conscripts. Both records and anecdotal evidence indicate these soldiers served in the fight against Imperial Russia. When Russia abandoned the war after the revolution, these troops were transferred en masse to the Western Front.

"Verifying this, however, is difficult. It is important to realize how incomplete the record is. It is true there are massive amounts of records of troop dispositions, supply records, individual soldier records, and so forth. Much of this information is digitized, but finding that one specific piece of information you need can be a challenge.

"Again, we need to take the broad view. Antoine Bouchard is confirmed to have been working as a POW for the American 447th Depot Detachment Engineers in Tours. This was H.W. Anderson's outfit."

"How was this confirmed?" It was the same student, a small bookish boy of nineteen who liked to interrupt.

"Let me show you." He turned and strode to the white board and began to draw two parallel lines, top to bottom, several feet apart.

"The letters run on two tracks - one just after WWI, the other during WWII. If you plot the dates on a timeline," and he stepped over to the projector and put up an acetate with a graph for display, "you see there are several letters early in the timeline, a cluster around the mid-1920s, then a gap. The letters begin again in 1941 and increase in frequency until the final letter on June 6, 1944.

"We do not know if there are any more letters stashed away somewhere. Given the circumstances behind the letters, I am somewhat amazed they survived at all. Neither do we know if this gap is significant or circumstantial.

"There are some things inferred by this. The first is that the two characters in this puzzle began to write in 1919. We know when Anderson was discharged - it is shown here in the timeline, before the first letter. That is a positive indication the two knew each other at Tours. That is where Mr. Hewitt started.

"What we learned in the process is this," and he approached the white board again. "First, German POWs, especially these of French descent, were assigned to work details inside France. They performed menial work, such as kitchen duty in a headquarters unit." He began to outline the talking points as he spoke.

"Second, such activities involved the transfer of funds. One of the fundamental methods of historical research is what is called forensic document analysis - or simply, 'follow the money!' Where there were fund transfers, there will be records.

"Third - funding records tend to persist. Finding them can be a challenge, as is wading through several million cryptic and rather dry entries. But that's where you have to look.

"What Mr. Hewitt found was a POW assignment based on a serial number, P64335. That serial number was eventually traced to a file on one 'Antoine Bouchard,' and through that information to the payroll records of April 1919 for CO B, 447 DDE. Anderson was paid 19.60f on that record, and a transfer of 16.50f was paid for P64335."

"But Professor, there could be hundreds of people in that unit."

"You are right! Except, by 1919 the unit was demobilizing, and there were only a handful off soldiers left - only 12 were listed on the payroll record. In a unit as small as that the likelihood these two knew each other is high. The fact we have letters between them confirms this, at least within the scope of plausibility. Remember, we are not trying a criminal case here. Our 'burden of proof' is much less."

"OK, Professor, we have found Antoine, and identified him. What do we know about him? Anything?"

"At this point, very little. We know he was a casual laborer at Chateau Kerbastic, which places him in Brittany, then a fisherman on the Breton peninsula. Hewitt is now trying to track this information down.

"We also know he met a woman, married, and had a child. A girl child. Civil records are of course excellent sources, but given the turbulence of the times immediately following, these cannot be a sure thing. Church records may also help, but these were kept at the local church, not in some massive data repository like you are all used to."

"So Hewitt would have to know which church they were married in," one of the students added, "which he would only know if he knew where they lived, which is what he is looking for!"

"Indeed. The proverbial 'tangled web' - and I don't mean the Internet!" Douglas smiled.

That barb started a low chuckle rippling through the room.

"Now, the gap. There may simply be few letters written during the period. Perhaps things are somewhat quiet. Both persons married and had children - certainly a major distraction as many of you know. But here," and he pointed to 1940 on the timeline, "here is where the story begins to intensify."

"The 'peaceful calm' we hope existed here in the gap is now breached by the outbreak of the Second World War. Germany invades Poland, September 1939. France and Britain declare war, much to Hitler's surprise. A period of relative quiet in the West follows, called the 'phony war' in most histories - although you would have a tough time selling that description to the Polish people.

"Then the invasion of the Low Countries. For the second time in the century, Germany invades Belgium, Denmark, and Holland - and then France. In a relatively few weeks, the blitzkrieg routes the French and British armies. British and many French troops evacuate through Dunkirk, Paris is occupied, and Germany extends its grip on the industrial resources of France, nearly doubling its industrial capacity in the process. It is now in command of Europe. The democracies have been knocked to their knees.

"Our task now is to follow the events that surround the letters, to build the scenery that forms the backdrop of this melodrama. Hewitt will remain in France, and is sharing his research regularly with me. We, in turn, will do much of the background work for him."

He stepped forward and handed out stacks of papers to each row in the auditorium.

"Pass these back, if you will. There are research assignments based on your work groups. Please read these through and have an outline ready for next Monday," he concluded as a slight groan arose in the class.

"Aw, come on! Did you really think we were going to study out of that textbook they made you buy? We are not going to read about history. We are going to write it!"

<hr/>

CHAPTER 9 - A SHAMEFUL PEACE

Peace came at a terrible cost. France abandoned its principles, its honor, and its people. The promise of the Enlightenment collapsed under the Nazi boot. People began to disappear without a trace. It was then that France raised its fist - not as a nation, but as individuals determined to not die quietly.

"Antoine!" The pounding continued on his door, and the terror dream returned. Artillery shells began to fall all around him once more. He pressed deeply against the sleeping Marianne, seeking the refuge of her warmth. The pounding continued, and Marianne awoke.

"Antoine. Antoine, wake up," she pressed him. "There is someone at the door. Antoine!" She shook him out of his terror, and as the trenches dissolved from his dreams, he heard the pounding on the door himself for what it was.

He leaped from the bed, and grabbed the axe from near the hearth.

"Who is it?" he demanded, brandishing the axe tightly in his right hand.

"It is De Rosier, you Alsatian moron! Open the door!"

The owner of the St. Justine stepped quickly through the door, and over to the hearth. Even though it was late June, the late night air was cold, the wind brisk.

"Get yourself ready. We have a cargo," he stated brusquely.

"What? At this hour?"

"Now, Antoine! There is no time to waste! The German Panzers will be in Lorient soon. British soldiers are flooding into St. Nazaire and Brest, and the German planes have bombed the cities. Get your things, we have to leave for England, right now!"

Marianne had by now dressed in a warm gown, and began to collect together some things for him to take. Her heart was racing with fear as she looked over at the peacefully sleeping Ariéle.

"What are we transporting? Why can't it wait until the morning?" Bouchard questioned as he pulled on woolen pants and his boots, in protest.

"Not what. Who. Now get going! I will meet you on the boat!"

With that, De Rosier stormed out the door and headed for the quay where the St. Justine's engine was already running. Antoine covered the 3 kilometers quickly, in time to find Léon Vercher standing with a lamp at head of the quay.

"Do not get in my way, Vercher, not on this night!"

"We have an agreement, De Rosier!" he snapped. "I expect my payment!"

"You will get your money," he growled. "On my return. There is no room for negotiation."

"Three times the payment!" Vercher demanded.

"D'accord. Trois fois! Now get out of my way!"

The harbor master withdrew just as a group of four men crossed the dock from a warehouse. One carried a small machine pistol. They moved cautiously, looking around as they crossed the open space for the boat. Vercher withdrew quietly toward his office, keeping a watchful eye.

"Get aboard, quickly!" De Rosier barked, and went to the pilot house to complete preparations. Bouchard appeared at the end of the quay, running toward the boat. The man with the weapon raised it menacingly.

"Non! C'est mon second! - That's my crewman!" De Rosier barked, and the man lowered his weapon, warily.

Bouchard cast off the stern mooring lines, cleared the spring lines, and ran forward. When the bow line was cast off, De Rosier engaged the engine. Bouchard jumped on board as the stern swung in towards the quay, and De Rosier nosed the boat out into narrow inlet leading to the bay. Once clear of the other vessels tied to the dock, he pushed the engine to full throttle.

"Take the helm, Antoine," the captain called out. As the two changed places, De Rosier came down to the deck and ushered the four into the cabin below. The cabin lights were kept off, the only light the glow of a cigarette.

The captain kept his human cargo below decks until they were an hour out into the Bay of Biscay, heading north towards the English coast.

"You may go on deck, until daylight. Then the German planes might spot us - there can be no one on deck but me and my mate," he told the man with the machine gun. The men agreed, and stepped out into the fresh air of the bay.

There were three Englishmen and their French guide, the one with the machine gun. The English spoke perfect French, however, but kept their conversations to a minimum.

The British Expeditionary Force (BEF) had been routed in northern France. While the majority of its men and equipment were in retreat towards the channel, others had fled south toward the Brittany coast. The ports of St. Nazaire and Brest would evacuate nearly 80,000 British troops in a single weekend. French and Dutch citizens fleeing the Germans made do with whatever transport they could find.

Bouchard looked down at the three Englishmen. They were not in uniform, but wore the garb of French middle class businessmen.

One of the men had brought aboard a small dossier. Bouchard had seen enough of war to know these were not regular soldiers. Spies, he thought, or perhaps government attaches fleeing Paris. Whoever they were, his captain's haste underscored their importance.

As dawn broke, the chaos that reigned on the Brittany Peninsula seemed far off. Antoine was still fearful for Marianne and Ariéle, however. He was not there to protect them. Marianne would see to his daughter's safety, this he was confident of, but in such chaos anything could go wrong.

The captain ordered his cargo below decks, but no German planes appeared overhead. The St. Justine pressed ahead on a northerly course, keeping clear of the Channel Islands before turning north by east toward the English shore. Just after midnight, under a cloudy sky as black as Hell, Bouchard spotted a light in the distance. It flashed three times. Then stopped. Then twice. This repeated, two more times. One of the Englishmen appeared on deck.

"That is the signal, Captain. That is the rendezvous."

"Bouchard, change course for that light - half throttle," De Rosier commanded. Antoine Bouchard cut the throttle back and steered east. Before him was a blackened shape lying low in the water, difficult to ascertain. The light flashed again.

"Cut your engines," the Englishman called out. The captain looked at Bouchard and nodded. The St. Justine's engine fell silent, the vessel slowing, then bobbing in the swell of the channel. A powerful searchlight glared ominously from the darkened shape, blinding all on board.

"Captain, thank you for your assistance," the Englishman reached out and shook De Rosier's hand. He passed an envelope to him he had removed from the dossier. "As we agreed, Capitaine."

A small raft appeared out of the night and came alongside. The four men of the human cargo slipped over the side and, crammed in the small raft, began to paddle back towards what Bouchard realized was a British submarine.

⸺∞⸺

By June 21, 1940, Lorient was firmly under the control of the invading army, bolstered by elements of the 5th Panzer Division that occupied Brest. Orders from the French command prohibited armed resistance or escape, and the Lorient garrison was paraded shamefully through the streets heading for POW camps. Few would ever return.

By the following week the Gestapo had located in the commune's administration building and the French police were given instructions under the General Orders of Occupation. Few regular army or secret police would be necessary owing to the complicity of French authorities.

The occupation was formal, almost civil. The population that had been spared the ravages of the first war were hopeful of avoiding such a fate, and cooperated with the occupying powers - the Germans and Italians.

The PNB, however, would suffer a different fate. The cooperation of Vichy France meant the radical counter-democracy elements Germany had supported throughout France were simply no longer necessary. The organizers of the PNB fled for their lives and the local cells went underground. The Gestapo and French Police rounded up known PNB sympathizers, and these disappeared from view before the summer had waned. The nationalist's dream of establishing an independent Breton state with German aid collapsed as quickly as the French army had in Flanders. Breton nationalism had become an obstacle to Franco-German cooperation in the form of the Vichy government.

Lorient was prized as a potential base for German U-boats, along with St. Nazaire and Brest. By the spring of 1941, 15,000 conscripted workers from Holland, France, Belgium, Portugal, Spain, and Morocco were transported to Lorient to begin construction. The base was operational in August. The flurry of activity was good for local business, so the excesses employed by the Germans were tolerated.

The French police and their German overseers were preoccupied with the building of the Lorient submarine base, and the tiny port of Pont-Aven was left largely alone. The local police could be counted on to do their part to maintain order, and to chronicle the activities of those they deemed suspicious. The harbor masters in the small coastal ports were brought under the control of the French police. Despite this, Pont-Aven remained under the official radar screen, and smuggling, both of goods and information, became good business - for both the smugglers and the police.

For the captain of the St. Justine, it remained a dangerous but profitable time - more profitable than selling fish.

The terrible dreams returned. Antoine seethed with terrifying visions of Marianne and Ariéle being torn away from him, spinning out of sight, out of his grasp. The images of war flashed through his mind, the memories of horror replaying like a broken record, back, forth, back again. He screamed aloud, waking Marianne. Antoine was drenched in sweat, shaking uncontrollably, his left arm and hand numb.

"Marianne, you must go! It is not safe here!" he announced in the safety of the dawn. Antoine knew he had to act quickly to protect his family. Marianne was firm in her resolve to stay.

"You don't understand! They will come for you - I have seen it, over and over. They took my brother and shot him, they drove Rachelle and Justin to their deaths. This is real, Marianne. It is not safe here!"

They argued for days, but he made no progress.

The butcher disappeared in the middle of the night, leaving no trace, save for a ransacked cottage and a murdered dog. The townspeople knew it was the French police, acting under the control of the Gestapo in Lorient. Marianne still stood her ground. She would stay with Antoine in Pont-Aven.

———— ∞∞∞ ————

The first raid on the submarine pens at Lorient was launched by the RAF 27 Sep 1940. By the following spring, Lorient had become a prime target of British bombers. The newspaper The Argus published in Melbourne carried the following story:

> Monday, March 24, 1941
> BOMBS ON LORIENT
> R.A.F. Uses Big Aircraft
> LONDON, Sun (A.A.P.)
>
> Some of the latest R.A.F super-bombers dropped
> very heavy bombs on Lorient, the U-boat base on the
> Bay of Biscay, on Friday.
>
> It was the third night in succession Lorient was
> raided.
>
> The Air Ministry states the raid lasted several hours.
> Bombs aimed through gaps in clouds were seen to
> burst around the harbour, the west dock, and the

western bank of the river, where there were violent explosions.

Other planes attacked docks at Ostend.

Two planes are missing from these operations.

———⧉———

Antoine and Marianne heard the explosions even as far away as Pont-Aven. Ariéle, now thirteen years old, hid under the bed, if only to help soothe her fears. The following day people were saying many R.A.F. bombs had missed their targets and fallen all over the area, destroying large sections of the city and killing French civilians. This was the second major raid on Lorient in as many weeks. Marianne knew they were in as much danger from the British bombers as they were from the Germans.

Now that the Battle of France was over, the Battle of the Atlantic was in full force. The British had mounted an extensive campaign to cripple the U-boat fleet destroying so much of its supply lifeline to its colonies and the United States by attempting to destroy the submarine pens and repair facilities on French territory. The concentrated raids began in March and would extend for seven months. Lorient was the largest of these hardened facilities, and a prime target.

The war had come at last with its full fury to the Brittany peninsula.

Marianne had to bury her pride and think only of Ariéle.

"The priest has told me of a monastery near Chantelle in the Lyon region. It is well within Vichy, and he says it would be safe. He has connections in Lorient that can arrange transport for you and Ariéle. He says it is safe."

"When will you join us?" she asked, knowing in advance such a reunion was unlikely, at least for now.

"Soon," he lied. "Soon."

He wrote to his friend in America,

> 8 Apr 1941
> Dear Andy,
>
> The Boche are back and life here is very dangerous. They came with their administrators and police and have occupied the towns. We have been issued identity papers which we must carry everywhere.
>
> I sent Marianne and Ariéle away to safety.
>
> I will still try to write. I do not know when I can post a letter again.
>
> Antoine

"What have you done with my daughter?" he screamed at Bouchard. Antoine was tending gear on board the St. Justine tied up dock side when Pierre Villar, in a brandy-fueled rage, tried to climb on board.

"Back off, Pierre," he warned, and pushed him back onto the quay. He staggered and fell, more from the brandy than the shove.

"My Marianne! Where have you taken her?"

"She is someplace safe. Away from here, from the British bombs and the Germans. I will tell no one where."

"It is that priest, isn't it? Eh? That priest that dishonored me! He did this!"

"Mind your own business, old man," Bouchard warned him menacingly.

"My own business? This is my business! This is my daughter!"

"She is my wife, and my daughter. They are my responsibility, Villar. Not yours!"

Villar glared up from the dock.

"Do not speak to me of your bastard child!"

Antoine jumped down off the boat to the dock and grabbed Villar by the lapels of his coat and lifted him menacingly off the ground.

"I have listened to your filth long enough, Villar. Call my Ariéle a bastard child again and I will break your neck!"

He cast him violently to the ground and stood over him for a long moment before returning to his work. Villar managed to regain his footing.

"You will see, Bouchard. You will pay for stealing my Marianne. You will see!"

In May 1941 the French police in Paris began rounding up nearly 4,000 men, mostly Jewish, in the first of several such "cleansings" supervised by the French police. By the time the news reached the Breton region, the local faction of the Parti National Breton (PNB) had resurfaced and tried to capitalize on the crackdown. Lists of Jews, suspected socialists, communists, and anyone who opposed the fascist splinter group were turned over to the harbor master at Pont-Aven who acted as the de facto police captain under the German occupation.

The third name on the list was Antoine Bouchard.

"I will look into this," he said calmly, and placed the papers in his desk, locking the drawer after him. The harbor master had no intention of turning this information over to the police in Lorient, who were simply the ground troops for the Lorient Gestapo. Payments from the St. Justine and other vessels running illegally out of the harbor were making him quite wealthy. He would, however, use this to his advantage, leveraging the threat of exposure for more payments from local business owners.

The two PNB operatives left the police office, unsure if they were going to get cooperation or not. Pierre Villar met them in the street and ranted.

"That criminal will just blackmail them for more money," he spat. "He is a worthless pig!"

———⊗∞⊂———

Chaplain Anderson left the commandant's office at the Civilian Conservation Corps headquarters for the southern Oregon district in Medford and drove the 90 miles to his home in Roseburg. He had been the chaplain for the CCC in Oregon for the last six years, but that stability had just been shattered. When he finally reached home, he had some unsettling news for his wife Lucile and their daughter, Bonnie. He had been recalled to active duty, and ordered to report to Fort Lewis, Washington.

He was uncertain what the fuss was all about, he would recall later, for the United States was still at peace despite war in Europe and Japanese expansion in China. His uncertainty would be laid to rest in a few short months.

December 14, 1941
Dear Antoine,

The Japanese attack on Pearl Harbor has meant a general mobilization here in America. I cannot go into any more details, except to say I am heading overseas to the Pacific. Once again, we are cast into the pit by man's folly.

I pray for you, and ask Him to deliver your beloved Marianne and Ariéle home safely.

Write to me at my home address. I will ask Lucile to forward your letters to me, if you can post one.

Trust in the Lord, that reward in heaven will be waiting for all.

In God's name,

Andy

———— ⊗⊗⊗ ————

Two men stepped aboard the St. Justine as Antoine finished greasing the turnbuckles on the net gear. He knew one of the men - Maurice Paschal, who worked at the net shed. He had frequent dealings with Maurice, especially while refitting the boat between sailings. The other man was unknown to him, and he had not seen him in Pont-Aven before.

"Bonjour, Antoine!" Maurice called. "Ca va? - How are you?"

"Ca va bien," he replied back, growing slightly suspicious. Antoine did not take quickly to strangers, and the presence of the unknown man was curious, especially in such a small port as Pont-Aven.

"I would like to speak with you, in private. Below deck, if you would oblige me," Maurice said, looking around furtively.

"What for?" Antoine replied.

"Please, Antoine. I would prefer not to talk in public. You have known me a long time, ever since you arrived in Pont-Aven. I have never treated you dishonestly, have I?" he responded.

Antoine nodded his head in agreement, and motioned the two below. He looked over the stranger carefully as he stepped down into the cabin. He was average height, no significant characteristics, somewhat normal in appearance for a French working man. Nothing that would stand out as unusual. I will remain on my guard, however, he reassured himself. He followed the men below deck.

"I have coffee," Antoine motioned to the galley, and the two men seated themselves at the table.

"Oui, merci," the stranger replied.

Bouchard poured three cups of coffee and laid them out on the table, then sat down.

"You must really learn how to make coffee. I will have my Therésa come by and show you," the man named Maurice kidded him. The informality did little to help Antoine relax, however. He took a sip of hot drink.

"I have work to do. We are leaving this afternoon for the Channel Islands, so let's get to it. What do you want?" Bouchard got right to the point.

The stranger spoke first.

"I will be brief, Monsieur Bouchard. My name is Zacharie Senesac. I am from Lorient. I am a butcher there, and own a small shop. We are here because Maurice tells me you are a man who can be trusted. A man who does not collaborate with the Germans like so many do. And a man of honor."

Antoine was not swayed by the flattery. *What does he want? They are up to something, illegal likely, dangerous or seditious, most likely.*

"So, get to the point," he interrupted.

"D'accord - OK," Maurice broke in. "We know you occasionally move certain goods through the port the authorities know nothing about."

At the mention of the smuggling, Bouchard tensed with alertness.

"Relax, we are not here to blackmail you, like that pig Vercher," Maurice returned.

"Monsieur Bouchard, I am part of a group of Bretons who don't trust the Germans or the French authorities that collaborate with them in this occupation. The Germans are taking everything they can from France, and using its people as work slaves for their war effort. The French police are their agents in raping their own country."

This was not news. The people in Pont-Aven had heard of the takeover of industry, the conscription of workers, of people simply disappearing into the "Night and Fog" as it was called. It was clear - even in such a small commune - that the local police were complicit with these activities.

"So? This is not news to me."

"No, I should think not. However, it is just a matter of time before they come to you for something. The harbor master is a part of their conspiracy. He takes bribes from you, pays bribes up the chain - all to keep his little financial empire intact. At some point, someone up the line will get caught, fail to pay a bribe, or have a higher payment demanded of them than they can make. At that point, this little profitable enterprise will collapse. You are exposed in this, just as the harbor master is, and your captain as well."

Bouchard was becoming increasingly alarmed by Monsieur Senesac's frankness.

"We have a network of French nationalists, people inserted in the levels of the bureaucracy throughout Lorient and the surrounding region. They supply us with information so we can stay ahead of the Germans and their French puppets. We have resources at our disposal when needed to help protect those of us who despise the Boche and Vichy as well.

"We are the ones who found the refuge for your wife and daughter, through the priest here in Pont-Aven."

That was the connection. That was the hook they felt they had in him. It now was becoming clear.

"OK, so how much?" Bouchard knew they wanted something, probably payment.

"Antoine, I am not here to collect a bribe, or to solicit payment. No one in our organization is doing this to make money. We may, from time to time, have need of a boat. A way to transport small packages of information or stolen papers offshore, at night. The runs you make with cargo to England - these could be useful to us in arranging the transfer of such packages."

"And why should I help you, and put myself in danger?"

"Such deliveries would be paid for, of course," Senesac stated, carefully avoiding the question.

"Why now? What do you need now?"

"Nothing, I assure you. My objective was to talk with you, to allow you to understand my mission, and my needs. We will use only those who can be trusted to remain quiet, and who will make the sacrifice for us, and for France. My intent is simply to open a dialog with you for the future. If this cannot be, then so be it.

"All I ask is that you think this over. We would like to talk with you again, perhaps bring you an offer at some time, for you to consider."

"An offer?"

"Oui. We would not presume you would risk yourself unnecessarily. If we have a need, I would contact you quietly, through Maurice, and ask if you are interested."

"Antoine," Maurice added, "I am a part of this group. I will know everything there is that is necessary to know. I will talk with you quietly if they need you, and you can agree or not, as you see fit."

The three men sipped their coffee, and the silence grew around them.

"I will think about it," Bouchard stated matter-of-factly. He knew as the entanglements increased he was putting his wife and daughter at a greater and greater risk. The world around him was spinning out of control, and he was powerless to stop it.

"Bon. That is all we ask." The two men slipped out from behind the table, and stepped back on deck.

"I will contact you only through Maurice," Senesac said as he turned to face Antoine once he stepped onto the pier.

"I am making no promises," Bouchard was adamant.

"We understand," he added, and the two turned and strode off down the quay.

None of the men were aware of the pair of eyes that followed them down the pier.

CHAPTER 10 - THE GESTAPO

One year
They sent a million here:
Here men were drunk like water, burnt like wood.
The fat of good
And evil, the breast's star of hope
Were rendered into soap.
— *Randall Jarrell*

Bellenave, France

"Bonjour, madame," the Mother Superior said as she offered her hand to Marianne. "Welcome to our humble monastery." Humble, indeed. The Chantelle Abbey was an impressive fortress of stone, a collection of numerous Romanesque buildings, and run by a community of Benedictine sisters.

"Thank you, Mother. This is my daughter, Ariéle," she responded back, quietly. It had been a longer journey than normal, complicated by security checkpoints along the way that had to be avoided. After three days they had reached the small commune of Bellenave in the interior in the region under the administration of the Vichy government. The sisters of the monastery at Chantelle had agreed to take the two refugees in for protection, after having been contacted by an agent for the Lorient resistance working through the Catholic church.

"Come in, child," she soothingly offered. She led the two through the courtyard and introduced them to one of the nuns working in the garden. Sister Marie-Thérèse was in her late seventies, but stood strong and confidently.

"Come, come with me," she added quickly, and led them into the fortress. As they worked their way through a maze of hallways, the sister explained how they were to spend their confinement.

"Do not speak to anyone of your past lives while you are here. This is for your protection. You will dress in the robes of an initiate and work in the infirmary. This will allow you to blend in and not be noticed."

They turned the corner and the sister opened an ancient wooden door to a small room with two rough beds.

"You will sleep here, eat with the other initiates, and generally follow my orders. We are a simple community. We grow our own food, and make soaps and other goods for sale in town to help pay for what we cannot grow. The infirmary offers help to the poor in the villages we service.

"We have few comforts here," she smiled, "but our life is quiet, and the work is not so hard. Helping others is God's work, and I hope you will find it restful as long as you are here."

"How long must we stay here, mother?" Ariéle asked.

"Oh, my child, we are not a jail! You and your mother are offered sanctuary. You may leave at any time you desire. When it is safe, I presume your father will come for you. In the meantime, please accept our humble sanctuary, and rest in God's hands in these troubled times."

Her warm smile and calm voice soothed their fears.

"Now, you must be tired from your journey. I will leave you. The bell will sound for supper. Tomorrow I will help you settle in to your work routine."

"And my daughter?" Marianne asked.

"There are many children who come to the monastery for school. I hope you will permit the sisters to attend to her schooling as well," she smiled.

The sister retired, and Marianne and Ariéle settled in for a rest after their long journey.

Sister Marie-Thérèse had been correct. Although the life was plain, the work was not any harder than she was used to. The food was plentiful and nourishing, the grounds quiet and secluded. She felt safe here, but continued to worry about her Antoine.

—— ∞ ——

Léon Vercher sat in his office and listened to an agitated Pierre Villar ramble on about that damned Alsatian pig Bouchard sending his daughter away - to protect his bastard child! The smell of brandy filled the small room on the edge of the quay and the putrid mix of brandy, fish, oil, and an unwashed Pierre Villar repulsed him. You need to clean up and get back to your bakery, he thought to himself, but the story Pierre Villar was telling alarmed him, and he put up with the rancid smell.

Vercher was especially interested in the part about the meeting Villar had witnessed on the St. Justine. He had been keeping an eye on Bouchard that day when he learned the St. Justine was getting ready to leave port. From a small room in a nearby warehouse he could watch the goods and supplies being brought aboard. Whenever any unusual looking cargo was spied, he kept notes of the times and dates.

"Tell me of these men," Vercher replied to his rantings. "Do you know their names?"

"One was Maurice, who works in the net shed. The other was a stranger. They boarded the boat, then went below deck. I followed them as best I could, but lost contact at the edge of town."

"What did he look like?"

"My height. A clean face. Nothing special, nothing that stands out."

"Pierre, you are imagining things. What is so strange about two men joining Bouchard aboard the vessel? Perhaps they simply had business - he does almost all the fishing now."

"Well, you would know if they had some special cargo, now wouldn't you," he sneered. Vercher bristled. This was not the first time Villar had implied a threat. He knew too much, or thought he did in any event. He was becoming dangerous.

"I will look into the matter, Pierre. In the meantime, I suggest you go back to your bakery. You are seeing shadows, my old friend." He ushered Pierre Villar out of his office, and closed the door behind them. "By the way, do you know where they were sent to."

"She told me they were going to a monastery near Bellenave. Her and that bastard child of his. He stole her from me, and I will kill him for it!"

Villar stormed off in a rage, back to his bottle of brandy, I suppose, thought Vercher. Interesting information, he thought. This could be profitable for me.

When Villar was out of sight, he opened his top drawer and removed a file. Inside was the dossier on a suspected conspirator the Lorient police were investigating - Luc Brodeur, who often used the name "Senesac" as a cover. The picture showed a man of average build, and nothing unusual to distinguish him.

As the defacto police representative, he now had a telephone installed in his office that rang at police headquarters in Lorient. He picked up the phone.

∞∞∞

The knock on the door of his cabin was loud and demanding.

"What is it? Who is there?" Antoine demanded. As he opened the door two men appeared before him - one in the uniform of the French police, the second in a gray trench coat. The man in the trench coat stepped inside before Bouchard could respond. The policeman followed.

"So come in," he replied sarcastically.

"You are Antoine Bouchard?" asked the man in the trench coat.

"Oui, I am Bouchard. Who are you?"

"I am Capitaine Foucault, Department Morbihan, Lorien," the policeman stated curtly. "That is all you need to know." He stepped around the room looking inquisitively.

"We have some questions to ask of you."

The police captain opened a folder and laid some documents on Antoine's table. The top one was a single page report typed in letters too small to read from where Bouchard stood, but the letterhead was clear - Geheime Staatspolizei. Gestapo. The report was entitled "Bouchard, Antoine - Alsace."

"You are a German citizen with French nationality. A veteran of the Great War."

"I am a French citizen."

"Monsieur, you are Antoine Bouchard. Your discharge and naturalization papers were located in the civil records of Strasbourg. You were born in the Alsace region under the administration of Imperial Germany. Your naturalization as a result of the illegal

Versailles Treaty does not invalidate your German citizenship. You and your family are therefore under the command of the German Reich, regardless of your current residence. You are expected to serve your homeland, monsieur."

The second report was obscured by a photograph of the man known to Bouchard as "Senesac." Bouchard stiffened.

"You know this man?" Speak carefully, Bouchard thought. They would not be here if they did not already know the answer to that question.

"I have met him. Once. He came to my boat a few weeks ago."

"What did he want?" asked the man in the trench coat, in a perfect French accent, not making eye contact.

They know the answer to this as well. I am certain of it.

"He wanted me to run some goods to the Channel Islands - without notifying the harbor master." It was a lie, but a plausible one.

"Your answer is remarkably frank, monsieur," stated the Gestapo agent. "Did you report him to the harbor master?"

"I told him to leave me alone. I was not interested in his intrigues. I have a family to support."

"Yes. So you do," the man in the trench coat responded, in a slow, deliberate tone. "A wife, and a young daughter, I believe?"

At this, Antoine became alarmed, and struggled to maintain his composure.

"Where are they now, Monsieur Bouchard?" he asked, again, not making eye contact.

He refused to fall into the trap that was set. Instead, he tried to turn the conversation away.

"I asked before, what is your purpose?"

"We are just trying to maintain order in these very difficult times, monsieur. There are many people who seek to profit from the, shall we say, unusual circumstances. I hope you are not one of them, monsieur."

"I am just a fisherman. I only wish to be left alone," Bouchard answered back.

"Ah, yes. So you do. But then again, there are others who think you might be helpful to them as well. That would not be a good thing, for either you ... or your family."

The threat was very clear. Bouchard began to panic.

"What do you want?" he snapped.

"Ah, monsieur, again the mistrust," the trench coated man said as he stepped around the room slowly, menacingly. "We just want to impress upon you how important it is to maintain a good relationship with Monsieur Vercher, the harbor master. As the local police representative, he wants to help maintain order. I presume you do as well?"

The question was a trap he could not escape.

"We know that, occasionally, we may need some assistance from the loyal German citizens, even those living in France. I am sure you are one of those."

Bouchard waited for the trap to close.

"Do not be alarmed, monsieur, for you are too old for conscription in the German armed forces. However, you can still serve your homeland in other ways. Monsieur Vercher will be calling on you occasionally, for information and assistance, for the benefit of France, monsieur, and of your homeland, the German Reich. I am told we can count on your cooperation. That is all."

The captain collected the documents from the table and returned them to his valise. The two turned and walked towards the door.

"By the way, monsieur. I hope all is well with your wife and child. When a woman and a young girl child seek the refuge of the Benedictines, it is generally from a man of violence, or heavy drink. I pray that is not the case here. I hope you understand how important it is to cooperate."

The threat could not have been more clear.

That night he slept fitfully thinking of his Marianne and baby girl. Finally, he rose and under the light of a single candle, wrote to his friend in America.

> 10 Jly 1941
> Dear Andy,
>
> The Boche have found me again! I was visited by the police. They told me I would be expected to do my duty to Germany - once a Boche always a Boche!
>
> They know where I sent Marianne and Ariéle! I am afraid for them. I do not know what they want me to do.
>
> They stole my youth. They will steal from me no more.
>
> Antoine

<hr/>

A black Mercedes sedan pulled into the courtyard of the monastery, and two dark suited men and two uniformed German soldiers exited the doors quickly. The soldiers ran toward the infirmary. Shortly there were screams, and they returned dragging a woman and a young girl, dressed in initiate robes, out into the courtyard.

One of the sisters ran screaming after them, and grabbed one of the soldiers by the arm, trying to hold him back. One of the men in civilian clothing raised his pistol and struck her across the forehead. She fell to the ground and lay very still. The two who were dragged from the infirmary were pushed roughly into the sedan, and it turned quickly, spewing gravel in the courtyard as it sped off into the late afternoon.

Over the next several months, Harbor Master Vercher occasionally asked Antoine Bouchard for a small favor - a little information about this person, some background on another. Each time a request was made, it seemed the requests were becoming more complex, more involved. The escalation of his informing was placing him at risk of being discovered by anti-German cells operating in the area. His was a dangerous tightrope.

He knew the Gestapo were watching Marianne and Ariéle. They knew where they were hiding, or at least had enough information to bluff him into compliance. The threats were obvious, the risks great. He was spiraling downward into an abyss he could not control. He began to panic.

He needed to break the spiral.

"Vercher, un moment," he interrupted the harbor master one morning as he walked to his office. Bouchard desperately wanted to contact the man they called Senesac, but he knew he was being watched as well. So he concocted a scheme to meet with this man from the conspiracy cell with the foreknowledge of the Gestapo and the police.

"What is it, Bouchard?" he asked.

"I have heard of something - a shipment coming in from England. I do not know when or where, just a rumor. I thought you should know."

"Is that all you know? A shipment of what? Can you find out more?"

"That is all I know. If I ask too many questions, I would raise suspicions, I fear."

"We need more information, Bouchard. I expect you to find it," Vercher snapped.

"OK, I will try. I suppose I could try to meet with this Senesac again. He wanted my boat - maybe he needs a boat to make this delivery. You could get your information from that."

"How do you know to contact him?" Vercher asked suspiciously.

"I don't, but Maurice Paschal would. You probably are watching him, but I can get to him quietly."

"I will have to check in. Do nothing until I talk to you."

Bouchard left, knowing he had planted a seed that would take root quickly. Even so, he was surprised at just how quickly it happened.

Vercher met him at his boat that afternoon.

"Make your contact. Try to find out when and where this shipment is due. It will go well for you if you do."

Present Day

One of the letters, what I called the "July Letter," haunted me. Something had gone terribly wrong.

I was visited by the police ... They know where I
sent Marianne and Ariéle!

Throughout my research and travels, I had maintained an active
email correspondence with Professor Douglas. He provided me
with criticism, advice, and historical notes - suggestions, really - to
help guide me in my search. This letter was the topic of several
emails. He had given me a clue I needed to follow while here on the
coast of Brittany:

> The French police collaborated with the Germans
> under the terms of the General Occupation Order.
> What we generically call the "Gestapo" were mostly
> French secret police working for their Nazi masters.
> Although the letter does not indicate the police were
> Gestapo I would presume for the sake of research
> that such was the case.

> Try to locate records for the sub-camps of
> Natzweiler-Struthof, a concentration camp in the
> Alsace region, a few miles from Strasbourg. This was
> where most French deportees were interred. I have
> attached a list of the sub-camps in the French system
> and a map showing the network, most of which fed
> Natzweiler-Struthof.

The very subject caught me completely off guard. I had not
considered Antoine's family may have been sent off to a
concentration camp. As I looked over the list of sub-camps I felt a
cold chill creep over me. The systematic map of sub-camps showed
the scope of the receiving and forwarding stations that supplied an
increasing number of French citizens to the camps.

I searched for more information on the deportations in France. I
found a web site that documented the commemoration of the 70th

anniversary of the Vel d' Hiv roundup. On July 16 and 17, 1942 more than 13,000 Parisian Jews were arrested. During what was the largest roundup of Jews in occupied France, 8,152 people, including 3,000 children, were locked up for 4 days in the Vélodrome d' Hiver in Paris under inhumane conditions, before being sent to the death camps. Between 1942 and 1944 almost 12,000 Jewish children were deported from France, 2,000 of whom were less than 6 years old. Only 200 returned alive.

The Vel' d' Hiv Roundup was not the first such action. Nearly 4,000 Jewish men were arrested on 14 May 1941 and taken to the Gare d'Austerlitz and then to camps at Pithiviers and Beaune-La-Rolande. There were several camps in the general vicinity of the Brittany coast, the most likely one, according to a note scrawled on Dr. Douglas' scanned map, was called Choiseul, in Chateaubriant. It operated from 1941 to 1942. Clearly the camp system was operating with its terrible efficiency at the time of the "July Letter."

The three met in a farmhouse halfway between Lorient and Pont-Aven, away from prying eyes.

"The Gestapo knows who you are," Bouchard explained. "Both of you. I saw a file with your photograph."

"Why are you telling us this?"

"Because they have my wife and daughter under watch. I thought I had removed them to safety, but they know. I don't know how, but they are blackmailing me to help them. I have been feeding them false little bits of information, but they are demanding more and more."

"What do you want from us?"

"I will give you my boat if you need it, but I need you first to find out about my wife and child. If they are safe. Find that out for me, and I will work for you. I told Vercher there were rumors of a shipment coming into the peninsula, as a pretext for meeting with you. I have to report back something, Senesac."

"The Lorient police captain is greedy, and desperate for something to show off to his Gestapo handlers. We can give him his 'shipment,' in exchange for information about your family and the use of the boat to bring in a real shipment," Senesac replied.

They concocted a plan. Under cover of a rainy night, a few boxes of explosives and blasting caps taken from one of the cell's safe houses was left in an abandoned shed at the head of one of the small inlets along the coast between Lorient and Pont-Aven. The land had been abandoned for many years, so it would be impossible to trace who was responsible. Bouchard would alert the Lorient police who, in turn, would alert the Gestapo. A raid would find the stash, just as the real shipment - considerably larger in size - was arriving aboard the St. Justine and offloaded through the port as Vercher was away - clearly, he would want to be at the phony shipment for the credit as well.

If the deception was successful, it would build credibility for Bouchard with the Lorient police, and set the stage for larger and more successful interactions and counterintelligence operations in the future.

On the night of August 12, 1942 the Gestapo raided a small shed in an isolated inlet and seized a small cache of explosives, as planned. In Pont-Aven, a small crew unloaded boxes of ammunition, weapons, and explosives from the hold of the St. Justine, and carried them away to a safe house while the harbor master was off taking the take credit for the cache seizure.

The Gestapo report filed the next morning wrote of the cooperation of Antoine Bouchard and Harbor Master Vercher. Captain Foucault was pleased he had Bouchard right where he needed him. As long as he did not know what had happened to his family - if so, he would have to disappear.

Present Day

Rabbi Bernheim welcomed me into his office, a beautiful walnut paneled study next to the synagogue in Lorient. On his desk were several old ledgers. He bade me to have a seat.

The rabbi was a generation younger than I, and when I had asked him by phone about the possibility of records still existing for deportees out of the Lorient area during the war, he immediately requested I visit him.

"Such a conversation requires a face-to-face meeting," he insisted. I remember thinking at the time I had struck a sensitive nerve.

"I am quite comfortable discussing this in English," he started. "I studied in New York and lived for almost ten years in the United States before returning to Lorient."

"I must admit I was a little surprised you would not talk on the phone, pleasantly so. I usually have to recant my entire journey before convincing someone to meet with me. At times I sound like a broken record."

He smiled, and added, "Well, Americans are not always known for their patience."

"A well deserved criticism, I am certain."

We both laughed at the inside joke, then he became serious.

"You see, Jewish deportation and French collaboration during the occupation is a subject the French would rather see kept buried away from public view. It is complex, socially and politically. Over the years, the synagogue has worked with others, especially in Israel, who have toiled to collect and preserve records of the Holocaust. My predecessor was particularly - shall I say, obsessed - with documenting the activities here in Brittany that led to the deaths of so many. It made his life here difficult, but he persisted, nonetheless.

"Perhaps you have heard the term 'Nacht und Nebel' - Night and Fog. That is the phrase the Germans and their French collaborators used to describe the disappearance of people without trial or official action. It was used as a weapon against the resistance, and anyone who was seen as a threat. Since Lorient was the location of the largest U-boat base during the war, the Gestapo had a major presence here."

He rose and began to slowly pace around the room as he spoke.

"You mentioned the sub-camps. They were often rather crude facilities, not much more than weigh stations, to use an analogy. They, in turn, were supported by locations within the cities and communes where people would be brought, processed, and passed on. The network was much larger than anyone would have believed, and involved far more local people than one might think. Some are still alive today, and certainly they have relatives here. So you can understand the topic is very sensitive.

"As the Germans retreated following the Allied assault on France, most of the official records - the records kept at the major sub-camps and those at Natzweiler-Struthof itself - were destroyed. Those people still in the camps were moved quickly, often with terrible losses of life, to camps in Germany and Poland. Most of the inmates of Natzweiler-Struthof were force-matched to Dachau."

"So the odds of finding records would be slim," I remarked, displaying a slight despair borne out of experience.

"Ah, Mr. Hewitt, the capacity of man to create order in the face of chaos, even with the terrible ferocity of the Nazis, is irresistible."

He turned back to his desk, and opened one of the leather journals.

"A clerk in Lorient kept a secret copy of transfer records during the entire period of the German occupation. When the Allies arrived, he bartered these handwritten journals for his safe passage to Spain. They eventually were given to the synagogue when it first reformed here - a time of considerable resistance, as you might expect. Few know they exist, outside of an organization of the Elie Wiesel Foundation research group.

"I have some latex gloves, and must insist you wear them. I will leave you alone while you search the journals. Some things are best left to a single man, and God."

As he moved to the door, he turned.

"You may record the information for your research, but I cannot allow you to copy anything. And no one is to know these archives exist. Those are my conditions."

"Agreed," I replied quietly, rising to my feet. He turned back to the door, and quietly left, closing the door behind him. I looked at the journals, and my hands began to shake. I was suddenly overwhelmed by the awful reality contained within those pages.

The handwriting was flawless, meticulous, a metaphor for the terrible contradiction of order to such hideous chaos. Page after page listed people, activities, rumors, and comments of persons identified only by initials. The second of the two journals was where I found the beginning of the list, in careful column order. A date, a name and gender, known residence, and camp. It was the start of their terrible journey to where, only God knows.

In the entries for the month of April 1942, my worst fears were realized. I managed to write the entries down in longhand and carefully closed the journal before I collapsed into the chair, sobbing. What had begun as a journey to reunite the memories of two old friends had taken a dark, evil turn. I sat for several minutes, unable to breathe, unable to think.

I removed the gloves and threw them into the waste basket next to the desk, then left the study. Rabbi Bernheim was in the anteroom, and upon seeing my expression, simply extended his hand. We acknowledged our goodbyes without speaking.

Later that evening in my room at the chateau I sent an email to Professor Douglas.

I found this entry in private records at a synagogue in Lorient:

> 18 Apr 1942
> M, Bouchard, Female, Pont-Aven, La Guiche
>
> 18 Apr 1942
> A, Bouchard, Female Child, Pont-Aven, La Guiche

La Guiche is a sub-camp of Natzweiler.

Because of the time difference, the email would have arrived just before the start of Dr. Douglas' morning class. He wrote back to me,

> I am so sorry. Will cancel class today.

———∞———

Chapter 11 - The Stuff of History

Let us be silent, that we may hear the whispers of the gods.
— *Ralph Waldo Emerson*

The word from Lorient dropped him to his knees in despair.

"No, no! Not my Marianne, my Ariéle!" he cried. In a panic he paced quickly around the room, unable to breathe, unable to speak any further.

"Je suis désolé, Antoine - I am sorry, but we have confirmed it. The Gestapo arrested Marianne and Ariéle three weeks ago. They were taken from the monastery by force. We cannot determine where they are being held or what has happened to them since."

"Those Hun bastards, they promised they would be safe if I cooperated!" he screamed. "How did they know they were there?"

"There is more, Antoine. One of the sisters who tried to stop them was beaten badly and has died. I do not know who."

Antoine knew his Marianne would not have gone without a fight, and knew she was in terrible danger.

"No! Marianne!" He fell to the floor and wept uncontrollably.

The men passed around a bottle of brandy to ease the edge, but Antoine refused.

"Our contact in the police department says a man from Pont-Aven she could not name implicated you with smuggling, and told of your family going to Bellenave."

His breathing stopped again, and he felt the weight of truth pressing down on him. He knew it could have been only one person. Pierre Villar!

———∞∞∞———

Present Day

I boarded the train again for Paris. In my research I found a series of articles on trauma and its manifestations in survivors of the world wars, especially Holocaust victims, even some 70 years after. The author was Dr. Simone Severin who had an office in the Pigalle district within walking distance of the Paris train station. I phoned and after an extended conversation, she invited me to meet with her and have lunch to discuss my project. I emailed her a copy of the letters and my notes for her to review.

The receptionist ushered me into a modern, slightly spartan meeting room. Water and a glass of wine were waiting on the table. Dr. Severin joined me shortly.

"Ah, bonjour, Monsieur Hewitt. I am delighted to meet you. I hope you had a pleasant trip. Is this your first time in Paris?"

"No, my second visit. It is such a beautiful city. I need to spend more time exploring Paris when I am not so preoccupied."

"Bon! I have read your narratives and notes, especially your correspondence with Professor Douglas. Your research has been thoughtful and very thorough, although I am sure you are frustrated by the numerous dead ends."

"Yes. Many records, especially those from Natzweiler-Struthof, were destroyed as the Allies advanced. Many others are buried away so deeply they are difficult to find."

"Yes, and you will find many have been destroyed by French authorities as well. The extent of French cooperation with the Germans throughout France is a closely guarded secret. Many wish that period could be simply swept away and forgotten. Such will not be the case, I am certain.

"As you know, I specialize in trauma. I began my interest in the subject because of the neglect in the field of rape and child molestation I felt paralyzed the world of psychotherapy when I began in the 1970s. The more I worked with victims of violent personal trauma, I realized how similar symptoms existed in survivors of wartime violence, political repression, terrorism, and especially the Holocaust.

"I am especially interested in the developing profiles of the key players in your drama. Your grandfather's reaction to his World War I experiences is not so unusual. He did not serve in the front lines, but it is a mistake to assume trauma in war is manifest only in combatants. His move into the clergy and his subsequent work during WWII are likely extensions of his conscious reality coming to grips with his experiences in France. He was able to create what we call a narrative out of the conflicting and traumatic events. As a consequence - unlike so many others - he was able to turn that experience into a positive mission in his life."

"One thing Professor Douglas did not know is Grandpa Andy earned his doctoral degree in theology when he was 82," I added. "The title of his thesis was 'The Abnormal Symptoms of Religious Manifestations Resulting from Extended Confinement in Japanese Prisoner of War Camps.'"

"Vraiment! Oh, my. I would love the opportunity to review his work."

"I have scanned the original. I would be pleased to email you a copy when I return to the States."

"Your grandfather sounds like an extraordinary man. Now, what I wanted to discuss with you. Working with the university over the years I am quite familiar with the process historians go through in their research. I have some additional ideas for you to consider.

"One of the fundamental elements of historical research, indeed any form of empirical research, is to verify specific aspects of an event, or testimony to an event. In many ways, it is like psychotherapy - the gathering of narratives to recreate events of the recent past.

"In therapy, however, especially in cases of trauma, such a narrative may not exist in the minds of the victims. The memories of a traumatic event are not encoded like normal memories of day-to-day activities. Recurring trauma, such as confinement in a concentration camp or violence associated with war, results in an even more dissociated array of encodings. It can take years of therapy for the truth to become known, at least the truth as best a victim can recover it. One learns to take a very broad view."

I thought of Professor Douglas' lecture on the Uncertainty Principle and the similarity to her perspective.

"You can usually rely on a reasonable degree of legitimacy in the narrative of a witness to historical events. Different accounts may surface of the same event through witness testimony, but they are still somewhat similar as to form and circumstance. Details will differ as people see and remember the same event differently. However, the individuals are still able to complete a narrative of the event despite the different perspectives."

Again, there were parallels with the Douglas lecture.

"When a person is a victim of trauma, especially repeated trauma, their ability to narrate the experience is often incomplete, or even nonexistent. Memories of the traumatic events can be encoded in disjointed means that are not rational as one might expect. Denial is commonplace. Events that may seem real to the victim may not have occurred in the manner they remember - although assuming the trauma did not occur and is just a manifestation of their imagination, what was once termed hysteria, is a mistake. The trauma itself has caused the memories to be disjointed, obscured, malformed, or worse yet, recurring.

"Outside pressures from society, family, and friends can lead to a suppression of the reality of the trauma, and it can resurface sometimes years later. No one is immune from the pressure of peers. Even Freud, with as great an effect as he had in the origins of psychotherapy, could not rationalize the society he had encoded in his own intellect could produce the kind of monsters he found within all the recollections of his trauma victims. He ended up disputing his own work and denying the reality of his victims' experiences.

"It is true there are disagreements among academics why Freud disputed his own research. It is generally known, however, that under the pressure of his peers he rejected years of his own work and the emerging science of trauma therapy evaporated into the ether.

"It was not until my generation, who saw this as much of a feminist issue over rape and child abuse and therefore refused to be cowed by peer pressure, that trauma therapy began to make legitimate strides.

"I would be cautious either taking too much of what you are told at face value or of denying an atrocity occurred. Neither bias is valid. Under protracted therapy some atrocities are often revealed, pieced together and altered as additional components of the atrocity are recalled, the likes of which seem incredible to the listener. We know from experience such events actually did and continue to occur, however difficult they are to reconstruct.

"I would also caution you to be a 'disinterested listener' as difficult as that is. Empathizing with your subject who is recounting images of traumatic suffering, such as surviving the death camps, can trigger deep rooted traumatic memories in the narrator that are not yet resolved."

She took a sip of water, and looked closely at me.

"It can also effect you. One thing we have learned is trauma is contagious. It is all too easy for a therapist to internalize the terror and trauma, often triggering hidden memories and fears. In my own work I keep close observations on myself as well as my patients. In one case, a patient who had been continually bound and forced to commit sexual acts with a relative had repeated visions of this relative emerging through a wall in her bedroom at night, much like a ghost, even long after the relative had died. She fantasized that the only way to stop the ongoing rape was to drive a stake through the dead relative's heart - even though rationally she knew the relative had been cremated. After months of therapy with her, I began to have a similar nightmare. It was terrifying despite my rational ability to resolve the source of the fears.

"In therapy we develop a peer support group to help guard against such encoding of the patient's traumatic experiences. My writings are peer reviewed regularly, especially the section of my personal reactions."

"How can you know when a person is not recounting their story accurately?"

"I would suggest if one of these victims wishes to recount their story you try to team with a therapist skilled in trauma therapy who leads the discussion - if and only if the victim agrees willingly to have you as an observer. You are playing with potentially volatile areas of a person's psyche, and you may trigger reactions that may be harmful to your story teller."

"But it has been over seventy years since these events occurred."

"Yes, that is so, but where these memories have not been reprocessed into the cognitive state, time has no basis. I have often worked with patients who are victims of PTSD from Korea and Vietnam for whom the memories are as vivid and active as if they occurred yesterday.

"I appreciate it may not be possible to arrange such a collaboration. I have some advice. If your storyteller can recount their story in discrete terms and form together a story that seems reasonably sequential - regardless of how incredulous it may seem - you are more likely to be talking with someone who has come to grips, at least in part, with the trauma of their past.

"If, however, their story rambles, shows signs of the sequence of events being jumbled or confused, or if such significant traumatic events such as internment or killing are spoken of in sanitized terms, I would urge extreme caution. Now, these are generalizations, of course, and as a layman you should not try to act the role of a therapist, just an observer."

"Sanitized terms? Just what do you mean?"

"Well, for example. I treated an especially troubled Holocaust survivor in his late 80s who still had horrible nightmares of his captivity. He used such phrases as 'housed' to describe being confined in the barracks, eight to a wooden bunk. He 'lost' family and friends in the camp. He did not harbor any surface resentment towards the guards, and spoke of them almost in a friendly and familiar tone. And yet in therapy, the visions and experiences he revealed were terrifying. It was my first experience with a survivor of a death camp, and the difference between his waking state recollections and those under hypnotherapy disturbed me greatly.

"I eventually learned these atrocities were quite real. As he slowly was able to bring these memories out and associate them with his current life, he began to talk of being 'locked away' by the 'butchers' in the camp. Quite a different perspective, but a very common response."

She got out of her chair, went to a filing cabinet, and pulled out a report.

"This is a case study that has been widely circulated as part of a learning packet for those of us who do severe trauma therapy. This has been carefully edited to avoid any way to identify the patient so it can be shared as an example.

"I have to meet with a patient briefly, so if you do not mind, my receptionist has arranged for lunch in the café downstairs. Take a few moments and read through it, then let's talk about its implications after I join you. D'accord?"

Pont-Aven, 1942

He stormed out of the cottage and ran down the road toward the edge of town where Pierre Villar lived, and where he had wooed his lovely Marianne. Maurice and Senesac chased after him. He broke through the door, and found Villar alone inside, overcome by drink.

"What have you done! You stupid bastard! They arrested Marianne and Ariéle! They have taken them away! Your own daughter!" he grabbed Villar by the throat and tried to squeeze the life from him. He violently pushed him back against the fireplace as Villar gasped for breath, too drunk to effectively resist. Senesac and Maurice ran through the door and knocked Bouchard hard against the wall, and he lost his grip on Villar's throat.

"No, Antoine! You cannot kill him. Not yet, anyway. They will arrest us all. We have to get out of here!"

They grabbed Antoine and forced him out of the door and back down the street, half carrying him as he collapsed in exhaustion and desperation.

Villar recovered from the attack and rose to his feet trying to understand what happened. Marianne is arrested? How can this be? They promised they would just watch her! That they would help me get Bouchard, but that she was safe! That Vercher - he lied! He lied to me, just as sure as the Germans had!

He stumbled outside and headed as fast as he could towards the harbor master's office. He found Vercher inside, on the telephone.

"You pig!" he screamed. "You arrested my daughter. You took my Marianne! I will kill you, you money-grubbing bastard!"

With that he lunged at Vercher, and the two fell to the floor. Pierre Villar was too drunk to put up a decent fight, and Vercher was able to push him aside, and ran out of his office. He would deal with Villar. This was one step too far.

The next morning, the bakery did not open. Pierre Villar was not seen in Pont-Aven again.

Present Day

I took a seat in the café and ordered a glass of wine. While I waited, I took the report in hand and looked at the cover. It was an abstract of a patient's narrative of an event in eastern Poland in 1941 by the Einsatzgruppen, the SS killing squads.

> I watched as the guards selected 12 inmates and
> brought them out of the group standing together. To
> each was sent 10 inmates. The 12 were instructed to
> herd them toward a pit and make them line up in a
> row. This they did without objection. The guard

then gave each of the 12, one by one, a pistol and ordered them to shoot each of the 10 in their section in the back of the head. They complied, and one by one I watched the bodies fall into the pit. No one even bothered to see if they were dead, and by the cries coming up I knew they were not all killed immediately.

When the inmate had finished killing his 10, the guard ordered him to stand and face the pit. The next of the 12 brought his 10 to the pit and they stood alongside the first inmate. He then shot each of his 10 including the first of the 12, and they fell into the pit. They then repeated the same thing with each of the 10s. When the last of the 12 was left standing by himself, the guard took his pistol, ordered him to face the pit, and shot him in the back of the head. He fell forward into the pit.

Those of us who stood and watched this then took shovels and filled in the pit, even though they were not all dead. We buried these alive.

I thought, you have a pistol. Shoot the guard! By the time I had witnessed this each day for several days, I no longer had such thoughts.

I looked up at as Dr. Severin joined me at the table. The waiter brought her what I assumed was her customary glass of wine.

"By the look on your face I can see you were moved by the report. You can imagine recounting such terror could invoke trauma itself. A rational mind could easily bury such detail deep within their subconsciousness. The therapist who recorded this narrative at first discounted its credibility. We now know this activity to be an accurate retelling - we have had independent verification. Later, the therapist became a leading expert on Holocaust survivors after first having to reconcile his own sense of perspective with reality.

"Yet notice how this survivor refers to the groups of inmates. They are the '12' and the '10'. They cease to be people, but are relegated to anonymous groups, what the Nazis saw as subhuman. This was a conscious objective of the camps, part of the process.

"I once read an account from survivors of the camp at Dachau. The interviewer asked each survivor what could have happened if all the inmates simply rushed the gate at once. We know from historical analysis there were simply not enough bullets in the machine guns on the towers to kill them all. They could have pushed through, although of course hundreds if not thousands would have died. They were going to die anyway. So why not?

"The answer was universal. 'Where could we have gone? How could we have lived? It was futile.' Futility is a powerful opiate."

"I can see it would be suicidal," I replied.

"Suicide is an interesting subject in this respect. A unique perspective on suicide was presented by Jacobo Timerman, a publisher and a man of letters who was imprisoned and tortured for political dissent in Argentina in the late 1970s. He wrote of suicide as placing one on par with the violence of the perpetrators, of making an active attempt to preserve control by making a defiant stand to end one's life. To deny the devil his due, which is not to kill you - which is of itself a small act - but to dehumanized you to where death has no meaning.

"There were inmates at Dachau who threw themselves on the electric fencing, knowing it would kill them. There is a story told by the children of a man who was caught sleeping when he was supposed to be in a work group, and how the Nazis beat him to death in front of his children. His dying breath was to recite Psalm

22 - 'Eli, Eli, lama azavtanu? - Oh, God, my God, why have Thou forsaken me?'; a symbolic reaffirmation of his faith. Under such extreme conditions, an act of individual defiance can be ultimately empowering, even if it means your death."

On the train trip back to Tours, I carefully reviewed my notes of the conversation with Doctor Severin. I thought of Marianne, and pondered her fate in the Natzweiler-Struthof camp system. My attempts to find out had so far ended in failure.

It had taken me awhile to reread the notes I took in Lorient. Antoine lived in Pont-Aven - the evidence from the Lorient ledgers confirmed that. I looked on the map, and found Pont-Aven at the head of a long finger channel coming off the Bay of Biscay not far from the chateau. That was my next stop. After the flood of emotions I experienced discovering this piece of information, I renewed my commitment to find out everything I could about Antoine Bouchard.

Église Paroissiale Saint-Joseph-St Joseph's Church-on Place d'Englise in Pont-Aven was built in 1872. More of a chapel than a church, the beautiful granite architecture is classically Breton. I spoke with the priest who gives the Sunday service, and he was kind enough to let me look through the book of birth, marriage, and death records. It took a while, pouring over dutifully inscribed and beautifully penned entries, but I eventually found the following:

> 8 May 1928
> Baptism, Ariéle Lysette Bouchard

5 May 1928
Birth, Ariéle Lysette Bouchard,
Antoine Bouchard, w. Marianne

15 Jan 1926
M. Antoine Bouchard, fisherman
Mme Marianne Laroque, baker

10 Jan 1926
Baptism, Antoine Bouchard

The entries forced a smile, long missing since my trip to Lorient.
I can just imagine Antoine asking Marianne to marry, only to be told
in no uncertain terms he would have to be baptized in the church
before the wedding. The birth of Ariéle shortly thereafter confirms
the period of happiness referenced in the letters.

I was curious, however, at the entry for the marriage of Antoine
and Marianne, and asked the priest for a clarification.

"She is listed as Madame Laroque. A wedding following a divorce
would not be permitted in the church, n'est ce pas?"

"Vraiment, monsieur. In those days, yes. She would have to
have been a widow."

I looked back through the records further, on a hunch, and
discovered the answer.

Apr 23 1917
Blessed unto God
M, Robert Laroque, Marianne Villar

and the same day,

Apr 23 1917
Blessed unto God
Robert Laroque
S, Marianne Laroque

"Father, can you explain these entries to me?"

"'Blessed unto God, the Marriage of Robert Laroque and Marianne Villar' - this means they were married, or more correctly, their marriage was blessed in the church. The other entry - a burial, Marianne Laroque, survivor."

"Robert Laroque and Marianne Villar were wed, the same day Robert was buried?"

"Oui, this is an interesting entry. Un moment, s'il vois plâis," and he left by the side door into the small room where the archives were kept. After a few minutes, he returned.

"Monsieur, the priest blessed the union of Robert and Marianne as an honorarium, not an official marriage. According to the papers, they were married in Paris in a Protestant church. Robert was killed in the Great War in 1917, and re-interned here on that day in April. To be buried in the cemetery, he had to have been blessed by the church - and that was the honorarium ceremony, making their marriage sanctified in the Catholic church."

"So they were married, and he was buried, on the same day."

"In the eyes of the church, God rest his soul, yes. That is correct."

"And the name, Villar?"

"The records show Pierre Villar was the baker in the commune who requested the honorarium. However, there is nothing listed in his tithe account after June 1942."

The empty tithe account could mean only one thing - Pierre Villar had left Pont-Aven, one way or another.

"One more thing, Father. Saint Justine. Is that one of the patron saints of this chapel?"

"Non, monsieur. Why do you ask?"

"One of my grandfather's letters to Antoine includes the phrase, 'St. Justine be praised!'"

"Saint Justine?" He paused. "This Antoine you speak of. What was his profession?"

"He was a fisherman."

"A fisherman?"

The priest wrinkled his brow, thought for a moment, then his eyes lit up.

"Follow me, my son."

We walked out of the chapel to an old garden on the side, now mostly encroached upon by a parking lot. In the center of the garden was a monument with an inscription.

"It translates roughly, 'To those who gave their lives to the sea'," the priest remarked.

The monument had been erected in 1972 as a part of a centennial celebration. One of the entries chiseled into the granite edifice read:

> June 1942
> Saint Justine
> A. Bouchard, Mate - lost to God

But I knew he had not been lost!

"You're kidding!"

Professor Douglas was practically giddy when I spoke to him on the phone that evening.

"I cannot believe it. What a find! Amazing! The odds against finding such a piece of information are enormous! And sitting out in plain sight all along. The class will be very interested in hearing this news. Take a break - on me! You deserve it!"

"You buying dinner?"

He laughed, and promised a lunch when I returned.

"One more thing, Professor. I called my rabbi contact in Lorient on a hunch. Pierre Villar is listed in the transfer registry. He was arrested June 1, 1942, and transferred to Choiseul sub-camp. He most likely ended up in Natzweiler-Struthof."

"Or he was shot," Douglas offered. "Sounds to me like you have stumbled upon a resistance cell, or people suspected of resistance activity. The Natzweiler-Struthof camp system was where Maquis arrests were sent."

He paused momentarily, then added, "But there is something about the date of the St. Justine's disappearance that strikes a chord with me. I'm just not sure what it means. Let me get back to you."

I hung up the phone and sat back on the bed in my room at the chateau. The day had been a revelation. It felt good, like the day I found Antoine in Tours.

I thought of Antoine and Marianne, and little Ariéle, and remembered what Professor Douglas had boomed out to his class - "This is the stuff of history!"

CHAPTER 12 - ATLANTIKWALL

Fixed fortifications are a monument to the stupidity of man.
— *General George S. Patton*

The Normandy Coast, 1941

The waiter looked up from wiping the small table as the German officer stepped into the restaurant.

"Bonjour, Oberleutnant Reiner. Déjeuner d'aujourd'hui?" The captain looked disdainfully in his direction, and sat down. Each day that the captain was in the small French commune of Bruneval on the channel coast he took lunch at Domaine St-Clair. Each day the waiter would ask the same question, "Lunch today?" The young officer was annoyed.

Oberleutnant Reiner, a company adjutant with the equivalent rank of lieutenant, wore the insignia of the coastal defense communications company. On a junior officer's pay he could not afford the luxury of eating in a local restaurant every day, but he let it be known he would "favor" an establishment that accommodated a German army officer. So the owner of Domaine St. Clair kept a running tab for the German officer who promised to pay at some future date or otherwise reward the owner in some manner.

The tab conveniently formed a record of when Oberleutnant Reiner's commander was in the area. Whenever the regional commander Hauptmann (Captain) Fleischer was at the reserve headquarters, located about an hours deployment northeast of Bruneval, Reiner would be called to headquarters. He would take his lunch at the headquarters mess. A lunch at Domaine St-Clair meant his commanding officer was away on routine business and

Reiner was back on duty at a nearby villa. This was useful information to the local resistance.

Bruneval was a small village that sat on a bluff overlooking the English Channel, just north of the port of Le Havre. A routine British reconnaissance flight had photographed an oddly shaped but distinct German installation near a villa that sat prominently isolated on the broad Norman plain. Air Intelligence suspected it was a new form of German radar.

On December 5, 1941, a lone Spitfire piloted by Flight Lieutenant Tony Hill flew towards the French coast some 100 km north of Bruneval, along a line where previous reconnaissance and pathfinder aircraft had been mapping German coastal defenses. German ME 109 fighters would routinely rise to intercept these flights from a base just north of the point of coastal interception. Anticipating just such a reaction, the pilot entered German-controlled airspace at 35,000 feet, nearly its service ceiling, and abruptly banked his fighter to the right. He powered at a shallow angle down and away to gain maximum speed to elude any pursuing fighters, flying along the coast. The maneuver caught the German coastal defense by surprise, delaying a reaction just long enough to permit Hill to photograph the obvious shape of a large radar array at Bruneval.

It was a Würzburg radar, the cornerstone of the German early defense system. It had a shorter wavelength than earlier German radar systems. Intelligence decryption had revealed to the British that the new radar was less effective at long distances, but more precise for short range detection and control, especially of gun positioning. Analysis by intelligence back in Britain confirmed it was a new radar system, called the FuMG 65 Würzburg-Riese.

It was placed strategically at the northern approach to the Normandy coast, one of the primary coastlines being considered by the Allies for the inevitable invasion of Europe. Its location on the coast, while making it convenient for directing fire against an invasion fleet, also placed it within reach of British forces. Most of the other main German radar systems were landlocked, deep inside German territory.

The discovery set in motion a bold plan. It would have been relatively easy to mount a bombing raid on the installation, but British intelligence wanted to examine the new radar. It was essential that it be recovered, relatively intact, to assess its capabilities to detect ships, planes, and direct coastal gunfire. German defenses in and around Bruneval had to be ascertained. It fell to the French resistance to provide the details.

———∞∞∞———

The meeting was held in a small office deep within the Air Intelligence headquarters at Adastral House in the Kingsway area of London. Three officers stood around a large scale model of the Bruneval plain with distinct German positions clearly identified.

"Gentlemen, it is clear that a frontal assault would be ill-advised," the senior officer said, pointing to the landing beach directly in front of the radar location. Major John Frost, who led C Company of the 2nd Battalion of the 1st Parachute Brigade, had meticulously reviewed the intelligence gathered by members of a local resistance cell and provided by an operative known to the British as "Colonel Remy."

"The installation is composed of two areas. The villa is approximately 90 meters from the edge of the cliff, and the Würzburg apparatus is here between the villa and the cliff," Frost said pointing to a location approximately midway between the cliff and the villa. "These smaller buildings house a small garrison of coastal infantry - about 100 soldiers. Guard posts ... here, and here, and ... here," as he pointed out the positions on the model, "are manned by approximately thirty guards, making a total force of about 130. The installation is operated by a detachment of signalers.

"North of the village is a platoon of infantry guarding the beach approaches. A fortified strong point ... here ... is supported by pillboxes and machine-gun nests on the top of the cliff overlooking the beach. The beach is not mined and as you can see has only sporadic barbed-wire. However, it is patrolled regularly, and a mobile reserve of infantry is believed to be available at one hour's notice, stationed some distance inland.

"Our contacts in the area have been monitoring the mobile reserves for some time. The unit is responsible for a number of support areas along the coast. The command unit routinely reviews the general preparedness of all these units. Communication while in transit between response areas can be easily disrupted. We will plan our attack when the commandant of the mobile reserves will be off on one of his routine inspections."

"How will we know he will be out of position?" asked one of the contingency planners.

Major Frost looked up and acknowledged the planning officer, a man known for his meticulous attention to detail that others might overlook.

"The local resistance has the routines of the German officers clearly defined. The regional commander's movements are predictable based on the locations and movements of his subordinates."

Frost continued his briefing as the planner made a series of notes.

"The mission, gentlemen, is to drop a team of paratroopers here," pointing to an area marked with a large red circle, "and photograph the radar in detail. We will have a technical specialist on the drop team, and he will oversee the dismantling of the radar. They will bring back whatever components they can move to the beach for analysis. A small naval task force will rendezvous here," he finished, "and remove the drop team."

"And what of these coastal defense gun positions?"

"No. 12 Commando will provide covering fire against German coastal positions. As long as we can execute the attack and removal before the mobile reserves can act, losses should be at a minimum. The operation is set for a window between February 25 and 28, and will be referenced by the code name BITING."

In Le Havre a shop owner had just closed up for the evening. After locking the doors, and securing the back supply entrance, he slipped into a small room behind a movable wall. Inside the room, lined with old mattress stuffing to muffle any sound, was a small radio. He tuned every night to the BBC, listening for a message that would be coded in the regular broadcast. He waited every night for an hour, one-half hour after closing. He had repeated this every night for several weeks. Tonight he would be rewarded for his efforts.

It was a routine report, news about a football player, that caught his attention.

> In football news, Chelsea reported today that
> midfielder Angus Herbert would not play in this
> week's match at Stamford Bridge due to a sore knee.
> He would be out of action at least through the end of
> February.

A SORE KNEE. That was the code word. The raid at Bruneval was on, set for the end of February. He shut off the radio, secured the door, and quietly, routinely, left the shop for the short walk home. He stopped for a glass of white wine at the corner bistro. He usually ordered the local merlot.

"How is your sister, Jean?"

"She is well. She writes that she will be visiting us at the end of February for a week. It will be good to see her again. It has been too long."

With that, he read the newspaper and relaxed after the days work. A routine evening, or so it appeared. He would never know what plans would be set in motion by the glass of white wine, and all the better.

———⊶⊷———

On the afternoon of February 27, 1942, Oberleutnant Reiner had lunch at Domaine St-Clair. As midnight approached, the resistance group Le Confrérie Notre-Dame (CND) was ready. Paratroopers executed a low-level drop at a series of locations and quickly formed to advance on the villa. On a whistle they attacked, catching the Germans by surprise. At the same time, some distance away, communication lines leading from the villa to the headquarters of the mobile reserve had been cut by members of CND. Two small bridges between the reserve units and Bruneval were also destroyed.

German troops reformed and began to lay heavy fire on the commandos, now quickly disassembling the radar unit. Vehicles carrying a mortar unit arrived and began to assemble for a counterattack. Other paratroop units engaged the German pillbox and secured the beach after a brief encounter with a patrol. The commandos set up a defensive position, awaiting the navy to pull them off the beach, as the German infantry units began their counterattack. The navy, however, was nowhere to be seen.

By now radio communication had been established with the mobile reserve commander Hauptmann Fleischer who was further north along the coast. It took him almost an hour to establish contact with his reserve unit company commanders and order them to counterattack. By the time they detoured around the two destroyed bridges, it was too late. The presence of a German destroyer and two E-boats that coincidentally crossed their path had delayed but failed to spot the small support force. Despite the delay, three LCAs (Landing Craft) supported by three gunboats arrived offshore in time to evacuate the men and the components of the Würzburg radar unit. By the time the mobile reserves arrived, the fighting was over.

The raid was an unqualified success. The British lost two men killed, six wounded, and six missing, however these men would survive the war. They also brought back two prisoners, including one of the radar operators. The Germans suffered five killed and three missing. The loss of the radar installation was a serious blow to the German command in the area.

Oberleutnant Reiner would never pay his tab. He was shot by his own headquarters firing squad two days after the raid. Colonel Remy had passed information on to the Germans through a trusted village official, himself a member of CND, that he had overheard several locals discussing the radar installation at a corner restaurant. The Gestapo rounded up several of these suspected resistance and they disappeared without a trace. They were known collaborators - a 'fait accompli.'

Colonel Remy met with two of his most trusted operatives in the root cellar of a small abandoned cottage on the outskirts of Cordemais, a village on the Loire near Nantes. The cottage was strategically isolated, near where the Loire enters into the Bay of Biscay. The lands around the small stone cottage were worked to benefit the priests of the Temple de Bretagne, so it was normal for an irregular assortment of people to be seen occasionally in the area. The Gestapo kept a keen eye for irregularity as an indicator of suspicious activity. However, irregularity at the farm was a normal occurrence that could be easily overlooked.

"This is the next target," he explained as he rolled out a small map. "Saint-Nazaire."

"Mon Dieu," exclaimed the taller of the two, codenamed "Gapeau." "It is one thing to attack a relatively undefended coast like Bruneval, but a major port?"

"There will not be a major assault, at least not like one would expect. I have been briefed on a small part of the plan, but the details will not be sent to anyone on French soil. Surprise and deception are necessary."

The resistance was a loose confederation of French nationalists, some of whom could operate with military precision, most whom could not be counted on to follow directions, and others who were simply not to be trusted. The Gestapo was ruthless in rooting out resistance members and sympathizers, and would attempt to infiltrate the cells wherever possible. Plans were seldom shared with more than a critical few. Colonel Remy was one of those few.

"The target is the dry dock. It is the only facility on the coast of France where large ships such as the Tirpitz can be docked for repairs. It cannot be seized, but it can be damaged and put out of action. That is all you need to know."

These were the words communicated to Remy by British intelligence operatives who comprised the Jedburgh team - code named "Harry" - who would organize the maquis for the mission against Saint-Nazaire. The Jedburgh was the British code name for a three-man intelligence team used to coordinate activities of the French resistance, or Maquis. "Harry" had been flown to coastal France by glider, then disappeared into the French countryside, only to reappear for strategic meetings with Remy when necessary. Harry would eventually make its way back to England if successful.

Nothing was on paper, and nothing but the capture of Remy and his torture could reveal the objective. That is how it would remain. Harry would wait in France long enough to ensure that the operation remained undetected. Remy knew all too well that if he were captured, Harry would stop at nothing to ensure he were not interrogated. Remy knew that meant killing him.

Remy continued with the briefing.

"Our role is twofold. First, we will gather intelligence on the disposition of German forces defending Saint-Nazaire. Specifically, the routines of the reserve garrison located here," as he pointed to a spot marked in blue on the map. "Just before the raid, we will sever the communication lines and try to delay communication between the port garrison and reserve forces dispersed in the villages spread between St. Nazaire and Lorient."

"We could help in the attack, Colonel," the smaller of the men remarked. He was always itching for a fight with the Germans, and a bit of a "loose cannon" as British intelligence officers would characterize him. "If we move in along this road, we can blow up this bridge and attack the guard posts here at the entrance of the dry dock. That would give us a commanding attack point to disrupt a German counterattack."

Remy did not like improvising, but he all too keenly understood the man's hatred of the Germans, and his penchant for action. His son had become a victim of "Nacht und Nebel" - and simply disappeared into the "night and fog" of occupied Europe. By war's end as many as 7,000 French citizens ended up as such in concentration camps, like Natzweiler-Struthof.

Remy reluctantly agreed to consider a diversionary attack against the guard houses as a part of the operation, but would not divulge this information to Harry. The relationship between Britain's

Special Operations Executive (SOE) and the French resistance was at best strained, at times downright distrustful.

———— ∞ ————

Combined Operations Executive Headquarters (COE) reviewed the report based on intelligence gathered from numerous sources, including MI6, air and naval intelligence, and Harry, prior to the operation.

> Germans troops in the immediate vicinity - 5,000
>
> The port is defended by the 280th Naval Artillery Battalion under the command of Kapitän zur See Edo Dieckmann. The battalion is composed of 28 guns of various calibres from 75 mm to 280 mm railway guns. These are positioned to guard the coastal approaches.
>
> These heavy guns are supplemented by the guns and searchlights of the 22nd Naval Flak Brigade under the command of Kapitän zur See Karl-Konrad Mecke.
>
> The brigade is equipped with 43 anti-aircraft guns ranging in calibre from 20 to 40 mm, performing both anti-aircraft and coastal defense duty.
>
> Concrete emplacements on top of the submarine pens and other dockside installations provide defensive cover for these guns.
>
> Local defense and the security of the ships and submarines moored in the harbour are under the command of Harbour Commander Korvettenkapitän Kellerman. The 333rd Infantry Division is responsible for the defense of the coast between St

Nazaire and Lorient. Troops are based in the town itself as well as dispersed in villages nearby. Estimated deployment times are between 30 and 60 minutes.

The German Navy has at least 3 surface ships in the Loire estuary: a destroyer, an armed trawler, and a minesweeper, the latter being the guard ship for the port. We can expect a high probability of additional vessels in port.

The 6th and 7th U-boat flotillas are permanently based in harbor. They are commanded by Kapitänleutnant Georg-Wilhelm Schulz and Korvettenkapitän Herbert Sohler respectively.

After reviewing the operation plans, COE approved the raid. It was codenamed "Operation Chariot."

Vice Admiral Louis Mountbatten, chief of Combined Operations, addressed the raid's co-commander, Lieutenant Colonel A.C. Newman.

"I'm confident that you can get in and do the job, but we cannot hold out much hope of you getting out again. Even if you are all lost, the results of the operation will have been worth it. For that reason I want to tell you to tell all the men who have family responsibilities, or who think they should stand down for any reason, that they are free to do so, and nobody will think any worse of them."

Newman passed on Mountbatten's offer to his commandos, but not a single man backed away.

March 27, 1942

The port of Saint-Nazaire was buzzing with activity. Vice Admiral Karl Dönitz, commander of the German U-boat offensive, had arrived to conduct a surprise inspection of the base that controlled the entrance to the Bay of Biscay and the southern approaches to the English Channel. He walked the quay of the massive Normandie dock with Korvettenkapitän Herbert Sohler, in command of the 7th U-boat flotilla.

"We have made extensive preparations in the event of an attack. Our air defenses are the finest on the coast. We have sufficient heavy guns and infantry reserves to repel any significant force." Sohler walked stiffly upright, seeking to convey an air of supreme confidence and superiority. Dönitz was not so certain.

"The British are like fleas on a hound," he chided Sohler. "They have been pricking us at strategic points all along the coast. The rumors you have heard of our successful defense at Bruneval are just so much nonsense, Sohler. I cannot protect my U-boats from the British commandos with empty boasts and hyperbole."

Sohler considered a commando attack an absurdity.

"Herr Vizeadmiral, with all due respect, an attack on the base would be hazardous and highly improbable. We will be prepared for any commando attack."

"I hope you are right, Sohler."

———

March 28, 1942; 01:20 hours

The British convey approached the Biscay coast, 21 vessels strong, carrying 246 commandos among a force of 611 soldiers and sailors. The commandos disembarked and stole across the sandy shallows until challenged by German call signs. The attack force had pretended to be a German convoy returning to port using call signs provided by decrypted German Ultra intercepts, and was able to approach close to the port before the ruse was discovered.

German shore batteries opened up, raining murderous fire on the flotilla. The HMS Campbeltown, an obsolete destroyer modified to float high in the water to navigate the shallows, was packed with high explosives in its bow. Despite blistering fire and mounting casualties, the suicide ship ran full at 19 knots and rammed headlong through the protective submarine net into the massive gates of the Normandie dock, driving her explosive-filled bow 30 feet into the dry dock.

Commandos scrambled off the destroyer and attacked pump houses and dock equipment to complete the attack. The retrieval boats had mostly been destroyed by German fire, so the commandos had to fight their way inland, seeking safety. Few survived. A small group fought their way past the guardhouse near the main entrance of the port, and were immediately swept up by a small force of French resistance fighters that had staged an attack on the guard house. Only 242 of the attacking force of 611 returned to Britain after the raid.

The Germans believed they had successfully repulsed the attack. While the lock gates were heavily damaged, repairs began immediately. Cleanup was underway just before noon when a party of 40 senior German officers boarded the ship to inspect the damage. Delayed action fuses suddenly ignited the explosives packed into the old destroyer's bow. The massive explosion killed them all, along with almost 300 others in the vicinity. The explosion destroyed the dock gates and swept the Campbeltown into the dock, sinking two tankers that were there under repair.

Saint-Nazaire was out of action, and would not resume normal operations under well after the war. Deprived of a defensible repair and supply facility, the battleship Tirpitz, the sister ship of the famed Bismarck, spent the rest of the war hiding in Norwegian fiords. It was finally capsized by a massive 22,000 lb. 'tallboy' bomb delivered by an RAF Lancaster of the 617 'dam Buster' squadron, having failed to be the destroyer of British commerce that the Kreigsmarine had dreamed.

———— ∞∞∞ ————

Commando raids continued along the French coast. The following August combined forces of Britain and Canada attacked the northern coastal port of Dieppe, across the English Channel, in what would be an exploratory attack to help prepare the Allies for the eventual cross-channel invasion. Intelligence reports had indicated Dieppe was not heavily defended. That intelligence would prove to be false.

The raid was a disaster. No major objectives of the raid were accomplished. A total of 3,623 of the 6,086 men who made it ashore were either killed, wounded, or captured. The Royal Air Force failed to lure the Luftwaffe into open battle, and lost 96 aircraft, compared to 48 lost by the Luftwaffe. The Royal Navy lost 33 landing craft and one destroyer.

Combined Operations Executive (COE) learned a terrible lesson. COE would escalate intelligence operations throughout France to learn the full extent of German preparations. A failure of information for a larger invasion could mean disaster for Allied forces of an unprecedented scope.

German propaganda described the Dieppe raid as a military joke, noting that the amount of time needed to design such an attack, combined with the incredible losses suffered by the Allies, pointed only to incompetence. Hitler, however, had been provoked into making one of the fatal decisions of the war. The attacks along the coast persuaded him to commit scarce resources to build massive defensive fortifications and fortresses stretching from the border with Spain, along the French coast to Denmark, and extending north along the shores of Norway.

Adolf Hitler issued Führer Directive 40. Unbeknownst to the Allies, Hitler had almost clairvoyantly predicted the operational directives of the invasion of Fortress Europe when he wrote:

In the days to come the coasts of Europe will be seriously exposed to the danger of enemy landings. The enemy's choice of time and place for landing operations will not be based solely on strategic considerations. Reverses in other theaters of operations, obligations toward his allies, and political motives may prompt the enemy to arrive at decisions that would be unlikely to result from purely military deliberations.

The German paramilitary engineering group, Organization Todt, began construction of what would become known as the Atlantic Wall. The mighty Wehrmacht that employed blitzkrieg to annihilate the armies of Europe turned to largely static defenses to protect Fortress Europe, draining critical resources from the defense of the Eastern Front. Even before the opening of a second front, Germany was paying a terrible price for a two-front war.

Colonel Remy and the CND grew in importance, size, and audacity. Compiling information on the defense of France became an all-consuming mission. At Führer headquarters, the raids on St. Nazaire, Bruneval, and Dieppe only served to invigorate Hitler in his struggle for military dominance over his generals.

René Duchez was well known to the Gestapo in Caen. The unimpressive-looking Duchez was a housepainter who excelled at taunting the secret police, only to fall into feigned seizures when

confronted. The Gestapo thought he was an imbecile, although of
no threat to the Reich.

What they did not realize was that Duchez had been a courier for
the organization Century, and his more public antics aimed at the
Gestapo worried his resistance comrades.

The town hall in Caen had a bulletin board with a notice pinned
on it seeking vendors to provide remodeling services for
Organization Todt, in charge of building fortifications along the
Atlantic coast for the defense of France. The bulletin was read by
the imbecile painter, Duchez. He decided it would be an
opportunity to look around the headquarters just to see what he
could see - a little fun that the Germans would pay for, literally.

"I would like to speak to Faultier Schnedderer," he announced as
he entered Todt headquarters, his pattern book in hand.

"On what business?" the young clerk who manned the office
demanded. He wore the silver encrusted uniform of a Todt
employee, but looked more Wehrmacht than Todt.

"Your bulletin - asking for wallpaper renovation. I am a master
painter. I have come to discuss the project with the Faultier."

Duchez was shown into the site manager's office where he met
with Herr Schnedderer, who expounded at length about the kinds of
wallpaper that were befitting of such an important man. He fancied
silver cannons on a navy blue background, he said, but there were no
such patterns in the book.

The two men poured over the patterns looking for a suitable
alternative.

"Come back tomorrow morning," Schnedderer announced. "I
will have made my decision."

The following morning, Duchez returned, and met Schnedderer in his office once again. His desk was covered with papers and maps that he could not make out from a distance.

"This one," he announced, opening the pattern book. "What is your price?"

"12,000 francs, Herr Schnedderer," Duchez replied, an offer deliberately lowered to ensure he received the award.

"Good! When can you begin?"

"At your convenience, Herr Schnedderer," he replied.

"Wait here. I will make the arrangements," and Schnedderer left the room. Left alone, Duchez quickly examined the maps on the desk, and to his astonishment, he saw words such as "Blockhaus" and "Sofortprogramms" - highest priority construction. The map was a blueprint of the fortifications along the Normandy coast.

Duchez carefully folded the map, and quickly hid it behind a 2-foot-square mirror in Schnedderer's office. As soon as he stepped away from the mirror, Schnedderer strode back in.

"You will start Monday," he announced, and dismissed Duchez from the office.

Herr Schnedderer was away on business Monday morning when Duchez arrived with paper, pails, and brushes to begin the work. However, the clerk at the front desk said he knew nothing about the job, and refused him entry.

"Impossible!" he shouted. "Herr Schnedderer insisted I begin work today. I demand you contact him immediately," he shouted, getting louder with every moment. He had to at the very least gain entry to the office to retrieve the map.

"Do not presume to order me," the clerk replied haughtily.

"I demand to be allowed to do my work!" he was almost screaming.

"What is this?" Another uniformed Faultier entered the foyer to see what was the commotion.

"Faultier Keller," the clerk responded. "This man says he is to begin work in Faultier Schnedderer's office, but I have no order to allow him entry."

"Herr Keller," Duchez began, lowering his voice. "Herr Schnedderer was insistent. I wish to be in his good graces, to get more work, you see? If you permit me to work today, I will paper your office for free."

"Very well, I like that idea!" Keller agreed. "He has permission, and will do my office first!" he snapped at the clerk, and returned to clear his office of papers. "I will prepare my office for you."

By day's end both offices were completed, and the map had been carefully removed from behind the mirror and rolled up inside one of the unused rolls of wallpaper.

Duchez met Girard at the popular Café des Touristes in Caen on May 13, 1942. The room was filled with German soldiers and several suspected Gestapo agents. A casual Duchez handed Girard a large envelope.

"So, what is this, Duchez? Another of your taunts or intrigues?" he asked, skeptically.

"Oh, nothing much. Just the blueprint for the fortifications in Normandy. That's all," he added matter-of-factly.

Girard was not convinced, but whispered, "Where did you get this?"

"I stole it," he said, smiling and sitting back in his chair, "from the Todt Organization." He nodded in acknowledgement to a German soldier sitting nearby who dutifully ignored the "Caen imbecile."

Girard quickly stashed the envelop inside his coat, shook hands with Duchez, and strolled as casually as he could from the bar.

"If this is another one of his jokes," he told himself, "I will personally strangle him."

Safe within his home, he opened the envelope and spread the document out across the table. Across the top the document said, "Atlantikwall." The map covered the area from Le Havre to Cherbourg, the exact location where the Allies would land the following spring, although neither Duchez or Girard knew at his juncture that this would be the invasion zone.

Present Day

"There are at least two versions of the story," Professor Douglas confided by phone as he checked his notes. "One is that the map ended up in Paris and was secreted to London through the north coast by the resistance network. This version is largely undocumented and very generalized, and appeared in the very early accounts of the clandestine war right after the declassification of the Ultra secret.

"The other story is that Colonel Remy, the operative name used by Marcel Girard, felt the heat of the Gestapo closing in on him, and took the map and his family to London by boat. Duchez remained in France and coordinated resistance activities throughout the war. His wife was arrested by the Gestapo, questioned, then sent to Ravensbruk. She survived, although more than half of the Century resistance members were killed.

"What is most interesting … ."

He stopped for a moment, and the weight of his next statement could be felt in the coming.

"Marcel Girard is reputed to have left France in June 1942 … aboard a fishing boat … from Pont-Aven!"

"Incredible," I gasped. "What are the odds - lost in the same month? And we know that Bouchard left Pont-Aven and ended up in Normandy, even though there is no record of him there. If he was the one who transported Girard, perhaps he arrived under an assumed name. If so, where did he get his papers, and what happened to the St. Justine?"

"More puzzles, my friend. More puzzles."

—⚬⚬⚬—

"I am sorry for the rough treatment," Antoine Bouchard apologized as he stuffed Girard holding his infant daughter into a forward locker. "You will have to keep the child quiet. We will go through inspection first."

Girard nodded his head, and pulled out some small chocolates, putting one into the baby's mouth. Moments later Harbor Master Vercher stepped aboard for the cursory inspection required before any vessel could leave port.

"Fishing alone again, Bouchard?" He asked nonchalantly. He knew there would be no cargo on this trip, and no payment either, for Captain De Rosier personally piloted the frequent contraband runs. He did not bother to look below, but signed the security pass and ushered Bouchard on his way. A warm fire and a bottle of brandy were awaiting him at home.

The St. Justine pulled away from the quay and navigated down the narrow passage leading to the Bay of Biscay. Bouchard turned north, and refused to look back as the boat and its mate disappeared from Pont-Aven forever.

He grasped the gold cross he wore around his neck as a tear rolled down his cheek, and thought of Marianne, Ariéle, and his friend Andy Anderson - somewhere in the Pacific.

Captain DeRosier stormed into the office of the harbor master with a fire in his eyes, interrupting the meeting with the Prefect of Police from Lorient, Captain Foucault.

"He stole my boat! That Alsatian dog stole my boat!" He screamed. "And you let him out of the harbor!"

Vercher looked at him incredulously as the Prefect broke in.

"What are you ranting about?"

"That bastard, Bouchard! I came down to work on the St. Justine, and it is gone!"

"But Monsieur De Rosier, Bouchard often fishes alone."

"He may fish alone, but he does not leave port without my permission. Never! My boat is gone! I tell you, it is stolen!" He slammed his fist down on the table in disgust.

"Who checked him through the port security?" the Prefect asked curtly.

"I did, Capitaine. Personally. There was nothing unusual, and he talked of fishing to the south of the harbor entrance." Vercher was scrambling, knowing he was lying.

"He is usually gone this long?"

"No, he is not!" snapped De Rosier. "For all I know he is mixed up with some nonsense or another. But I want my boat back, do you hear! You are responsible!" He was pointing an accusing finger at Vercher.

The Prefect picked up the phone and placed a call to his headquarters in Lorient.

"OK, monsieur. I have reported your vessel as stolen. We will find this Bouchard and arrest him, I assure you." As he spoke, Vercher paled with fright.

"You had better!" De Rosier stormed out of the office and defiantly walked back towards the center of the commune.

"Inform the Gestapo, Vercher. I smell a rotten fish here, and I will not be embarrassed by such a problem in my district!"

"Right away, Capitaine," he choked the words out with difficulty.

De Rosier emptied the wine bottle, and took a deep drink from his glass as he sat at the café with an old friend.

"Ah, Gilbert," he mused. "These Germans are like the big fish. Easy to catch, even easier to fillet!"

The two men laughed, and ordered another bottle of wine. His boat would be declared lost at sea, along with its mate, Antoine Bouchard. The Gestapo would never find a shred of evidence that Bouchard had escaped Brittany.

Captain De Rosier would live quite comfortably on the payment made by British intelligence for the St. Justine and its precious cargo.

> 3 Jly 1942
> Dear Andy,
>
> My life has turned upside down. I have fallen into things I cannot control, but cannot tell you about. Even you, my best friend. It is too dangerous.
>
> I do not know what will come of me, or where I will end up. For now, the police think I am a thief.

If I am lucky, they will think I am dead. That is the only way I can escape the grasp of the Gestapo once and for all.

This letter will be postmarked from London, I am told. But that is not where I am headed.

I will write when I can.

Your friend,
Antoine

CHAPTER 13 - THE SAINTE MARIANNE

People trust their eyes above all else - but most people see what they wish to see,
or what they believe they should see; not what is really there.
— *Zoë Marriott*

The car rattled along the dirt roads as it sped through the countryside heading east. Marianne and Ariéle were gagged, their hands tied behind their backs, and jammed into the back seat with one of the uniformed French policemen and a plainclothes security officer. One of the Vichy policemen was driving, and the other sat in the front. The second car containing the other security officers had followed them for a while, but turned south a short time before, heading for Lyon. Ariéle was crying at first, but soon just burrowed against her mother for comfort.

In less than two hours they entered the small village of La Guiche and finally stopped before an imposing looking building situated on a terraced hillside overlooking the small valley. As they entered the courtyard, Marianne could see the sign, "Le Sanatorium de La Guiche." It sent a chill of horror down her spine, but she tried to not show her fear in front of Ariéle.

The car came to a stop beside a stone wall below the main building complex, and the passenger in the front seat got out, moved to the door, and opened it.

"Sortir maintenant! - Get out, now!" he demanded. As Marianne tried to slide over to the door she was grabbed by the arm and dragged out, stumbling as she exited the car. Ariéle was pulled out as well and told to stand still.

These men are not Germans, Marianne kept replaying over in her head, even though they spoke little on the drive from Chantelle. She had heard the stories of French collaborators, but it was all too difficult to accept that her own countrymen would be doing the bidding of the Germans so easily.

"De cette façon! - That way!" the smaller of the two policemen demanded, and shoved them in the direction of a flight of stairs to the left of the courtyard leading up to the building. The taller man led the way up the stairs, walking with a slight limp. Marianne could see he was missing a small piece of his right ear lobe. Funny, she thought to herself, that such a thing would catch her attention at a time like this. The short one prodded her in the back with a small baton as she walked, and she felt her anger rise. Keep calm, she told herself, keep calm.

At the top of the stairs they were met by a uniformed attendant who turned and spoke to the taller man in a low tone Marianne could not hear. The policeman began to speak in an angry voice, and became very animated although still she could not make out the conversation. The attendant appeared to acquiesce, and turned, walking back into the building. They were prodded by the short one to follow.

Once inside, they were led down a long hall. It was cold and damp in the building, the walls a dirty painted plaster. It smelled of alcohol, urine, and harsh cleaning chemicals. The air was rancid and foul, and Ariéle began to cough as she struggled to breath with the gag still in place. At the end of the hall, they were pushed into a small anteroom, and told to sit on the wooden bench against the wall.

No sooner had the door closed behind them, with the one-eared French policeman standing guard, then a side door opened and a tall man in a white coat and thin-rimmed glasses entered the room, agitated.

"What is this? Who are these women, and why are you here at my office?" he demanded. "If these two are infected, they should be taken through the ward entrance."

"Docteur Gerard," the one-eared man began, "I have orders to detain these two women until further notice at your facility."

"Orders? Under what authority?" he snapped back.

One-Ear produced a document and handed it to the man in the white coat, what Marianne perceived was likely the medical supervisor. He examined the paper, and obviously unhappy with what he read, simply spat, "Incroyable! - Incredible!" and turned and strode back through the door, slamming it behind him.

Shortly, two small rude-looking attendants showed up with the short policeman and moved Marianne and Ariéle out of the foyer and back up the hall. They were ushered up a staircase, through a barred doorway, and finally shoved into a room that looked more like a barracks, with rude beds along the windowed side. The windows were barred. Seven inmates were housed in the barracks, bedridden. Several were obviously ill, and the acrid smell of urine and vomit permeated the room. It was hard for the two of them not to wretch from the smell.

The policeman untied the gags from their mouths and removed the handcuffs. Ariéle grabbed onto her mother for safety.

"You," one of the attendants gave Marianne a shove in the back, "this is your bunk. You will stay here until I come back for you. You," and he motioned to Ariéle who instinctively drew back from him even closer toward her mother, "you will come with me," and he grabbed her by the arm and began to pull her away.

"Momma!" She cried out and grabbed for Marianne. Marianne reached out for her, and demanded, "You leave her alone. She will stay with me!" She tried to push her way between the small attendant and Ariéle. At that moment, she was struck violently in the side of the head by the one-eared policeman, and fell to the floor, unconscious.

"Momma - non, momma!" Ariéle cried out as she was grabbed and dragged out of the room, fighting as she was led away. It was a harsh blessing that Marianne, lying bleeding and unconscious on the floor, could not hear the fearful cries of her daughter.

She would never see her beautiful Ariéle again.

Present Day

I checked into Hotel de Paris on the quay at Courseulles. I planned to make this my base of operations as I expanded my research, and made a point of talking up my project to anyone and everyone in the commune, hoping to get some sort of break in my search for Antoine Bouchard.

"Pardon, monsieur. Et vu l'Americain, M. Hewitt?" The older gentleman had entered the restaurant and spoken briefly with the owner who had pointed him in my direction. He carried a plain vanilla envelope.

"Oui, C'est moi," I replied.

"Monsieur, my name is Gaston Marklin, I am the harbor master of Courseulles. I may have some information for you. May I join you?"

"Please. Asseyes vous." He sat in the opposite chair and signaled to the waiter who promptly brought a glass of wine.

"You are researching activity here in Courseulles during the invasion. The mayor says you are looking for a specific person, a person who he says has no records here at all, yet appears to have been here during that time."

"Yes, that is so. I am afraid I am having little luck trying to connect a certain Antoine Bouchard with Courseulles, even though a packet of letters between him and my grandfather were found here not long ago that contains quite specific references to this village, and especially the port. They indicate he operated a fishing boat." I kept other details to myself, at least for the moment.

"Perhaps I may have a clue for you. In 1994 we celebrated the 50th anniversary of the D-Day landings. I had just taken the position of harbor master. The village was crowded with hundreds of Canadian and British soldiers and their families, many of whom fought here in 1944."

He settled back and took a deep sip of his wine.

"I was approached by a man who as a young seaman had served aboard a British submarine. He said his submarine had routinely rendezvoused with a small fishing boat in the English Channel between November 1943 and May 1944 to collect information from the resistance on German installations and troop dispositions in the Normandy area. Once he was allowed on deck to help collect a packet, and he saw the name on the boat. It was called the 'Marianne.'"

Marianne! That name jumped out at me from across the decades. Marianne - Antoine's wife, who he sent away to safety with their daughter, Ariéle. Whom he married in the chapel at Pont-Aven.

Normandy, 1942

Monsieur Le Collette noticed the vessel tied to the quay outside of the lock. Before the occupation, vessels routinely changed ports following the schools of fish from the Bay of Biscay around the peninsula to the Bay of the Seine. With tightened security checks the arrival of a new vessel in Courseulles-sur-Mer was becoming rare.

He opened the office of the harbor master late this morning. The tides were not favorable to early departures so the boats heading for the fishing grounds offshore left the harbor the night before. Courseulles-sur-Mer sits at the mouth of the Seulles River. Where the river enters the Bay of the Seine it falls over a rocky reach that is exposed at low tide. A lock had been built that holds the high water level within an estuary that extends south of the river mouth. Around this artificial harbor was the commune of Courseulles. The top of the lock forms a bridge from one side of the narrow harbor to the other. At high tide, fishing boats could simply tie up along the eastern edge of the quay and offload their catch. At low tide they could be stranded in the mud unless they traversed the lock into the basin.

However, once inside they were at the whim of the rising and falling tides and had to carefully time their arrivals and departures to maximize their time at sea. Along the Norman coast tides could often rise over 10 meters (32 feet) and piloting a vessel in these waters, with their high winds and strong currents, taxed the skill of many a sailor.

The harbor master controlled the locks. Le Collette therefore controlled the livelihood of Courseulles.

Antoine Bouchard had crossed the English Channel at night without lights and at half-throttle to avoid detection by the German E-boats that patrolled the coastline operating out of Cherbourg and Le Havre. The reduced speed made for a slow and uncomfortable crossing as the St. Marianne rolled in the heavy cross swell without the added power to push through the waves. By morning he was exhausted, and glad for the low tide that allowed him time to sleep before the harbor master came on duty.

Antoine rose, prepared coffee, and sat back to await the arrival of the harbor master. He remained on board, as was the custom when arriving in a new port.

Le Collette approached the St. Marianne just after 8:00 a.m. The authority of the harbor master extended to any vessel registered in port, or tied up within the lock. By custom, he would not approach a vessel unless the captain or crew indicated they wanted to offload cargo or catch or enter the port, or just before the locks were to open. Despite the occupation, the country was still largely administered by the French and subject to French law and customs.

"Bonjour, Capitaine," he called out as he stepped to the edge of the quay. He remained dockside, also the custom. Despite his quasi-police powers granted by the new "enlightened administration" of France that permitted him to board and search at his discretion, this was still a small port. He knew his position, and perhaps his life, could be at risk by displaying too heavy a hand unless backed by the Gestapo in Caen. Courseulles was a mere 18 kilometers from Caen, and the Gestapo could be called upon for assistance in relatively short order if necessary. So far he had not needed them, much to his relief.

"Bonjour. Je suis Capitaine Charbonneau of the fishing vessel St. Marianne. I request permission to enter the harbor."

The routine was somewhat formal, oddly so given the strong working class nature of the fishing fleet. The custom had survived unchanged for centuries. The difference - now a vessel's registration papers and the crew's identity papers were required to be available at all times. To be caught without papers could mean an immediate arrest. A boat without proper documentation could be confiscated.

This was the first time Bouchard had used his assumed name, given to him along with a forged set of identity and vessel papers by British Intelligence in Portsmouth. In exchange for Colonel Remy and the stolen map of the Atlantic Wall, SIS had purchased and repainted the St. Justine, giving the vessel the new name, St. Marianne. They gave the boat to Bouchard in exchange for "certain favors" in the coming months. To further complete the ruse, the deck gear had been completely changed. Even De Rosier would have a hard time identifying the St. Marianne as his former boat.

"Permission to come aboard?" the harbor master answered back.

"Granted." With that Bouchard braced for his first security check with the forged papers. He knew that if the harbor master saw anything unusual he had nowhere to hide. His fate rested on the quality of those forgeries.

"Everything is in order, Capitaine. Consider yourself registered," Le Collette answered as he wrote the pertinent information in a small notebook. He did not have to ask for the St. Marianne's port of debarkation. Under the occupation, a vessel's owner had to be cleared at his previous anchorage by the local harbor master, his papers stamped, and his subsequent destination recorded at the port of origin. Communication between the small ports was marginal at best, and immediate verification was next to impossible. This method ensured a clear administrative path for a vessel to change ports, or put into a 'foreign' port while at sea for repair, rest, or to offload a catch. It also allowed the forger's craft to bypass the security apparatus. It worked.

"I have repairs to make, and need to lay up for a few days." This was a lie, but a realistic one that would allow Bouchard time to familiarize himself with the surrounding countryside, contact the SIS operative in Caen, and not draw any unwanted attention to himself for remaining in port.

"The lock will be open until 10:00, Capitaine. There is room alongside the quay behind the trawler Remage. I will register you there. It is close to both the chandlery and bakery."

With that the harbor master turned and stepped back on the quay.

"Will you be of any further need for my services, Capitaine?"

"Non, c'est tout - that is all."

"Welcome to Courseulles, Capitaine. Je suis á votre service - I am at your service."

Antoine Bouchard finished securing the St. Marianne to the quay and went below deck and poured himself a cup of very bad coffee. Marianne made the best coffee he had ever tasted, he thought to himself, and he could feel the anger within well up again. He needed to keep himself under control, he reminded himself repeatedly, if not for him, for his family. If they are still alive.

At the same time a worker from the construction regiment Todt was setting up a camera and tripod across the road in front of the bakery. His assignment was to photograph the entire Courseulles port area as a part their preliminary assessment of risk and defensive position suitability for this section of the Atlantic Wall. One of the photographs showed the lock bridge in a closed position, with a row of fish vendors in the foreground. Behind one of the vendor tents one could just make out the name on the bow of a fishing vessel - St. Marianne.

The Courseulles harbor master continued with his narrative.

"The man was asking if I knew the name of the captain of the Marianne, and if he was still alive. When I asked why he thought he would be from Courseulles, he told me that they routinely met offshore, with Courseulles the closest port. He could not be certain.

"I went back through the harbor records of the period and found no mention of such a vessel. If there had been a 'Marianne,' it would have been recorded when first registered in harbor, when hauled for repairs, or when requesting access through the locks for any unscheduled opening. The fact that there was no such records at all, no mention whatsoever, means likely one of two things.

"The obvious one, of course, is that the young sailor heard incorrectly, or was mistaken to think the vessel was from here. The other ... well, it was war and anything can be bought for the right price, even anonymity.

"When His Honor Monsieur Pouille told me of your inquiries, I started looking through the photo archives, and, well, look here."

He pulled an old black and white photo from the envelope and laid it on the table. It was a picture taken of one of the fish markets set up on the quay. It was labeled in white, meaning the negative had been written on by dark ink. The label read,

Todt Reconnaissance Photo, June 1942

Behind the vendor's canopy, tied to the quay, was a fishing boat. The name was clearly visible on the bow of the boat - the St. Marianne.

"OK. Who was Saint Marianne?"

"That is just the point. There is no saint named Marianne."

But there was a missing wife named Marianne who would have held such position, at least in the heart of Antoine Bouchard.

"I went back and checked. There is no corresponding entry in the port registry receipts."

"Meaning what? What are the registry receipts?"

"When a vessel was first registered in the port, a docking certificate was issued and signed by the harbor master and filed by registry number. The log book of various activities then simply listed the registry number - much like a license plate. For some unknown reason there was no record of that vessel's presence in port."

"Perhaps the registry document was later destroyed, maybe on purpose," I added, thinking through the possibilities.

"I thought of that. If so, there would be log entries for a vessel whose registry document was not on file. So I cross-referenced a number of registry certificates with the log, but found too great a number of irregular entries to be meaningful. My guess is that some records may have been lost or destroyed at some point.

"The intelligence submarine, by the way, operated out of the port of Portsmouth, just across the channel. Portsmouth was the location of a naval intelligence department during the war."

We chatted for a while longer, and I briefed him on what I knew about Antoine Bouchard, and what I did not know. There was still nothing to directly connect him to Courseulles. However, the St. Marianne as the name of the boat was too close to be a coincidence. Much of the details of naval intelligence I knew were still classified, even after all these years.

As usual, I had more questions than answers.

I boarded the ferry in Caen that routinely sailed to Portsmouth on the south coast of England. On the voyage, I reflected on what I had learned, and what I still did not know. One thing that haunted me more than anything else - what happened to Marianne and Ariéle? The trail of information went cold just as the story of Antoine began to take on new life. Where would all this end?

Chapter 14 - La Guiche

*If Tyranny and Oppression come to this land, it will be in
the guise of fighting a foreign enemy.*
— *James Madison*

Marianne's life at La Guiche was hell. She had awakened still on the
floor where the police had struck her, covered in blood. The
inmates in the ward were all quite ill, many with tuberculosis. They
would be treated until well enough to return to the work camps, or
were sent to their deaths in Naztweiler, Dachau, or Auschwitz.
There was no one to dress her wounds, so she fashioned a dressing
herself and slipped into the filthy bed to try to rest. Her head ached
from the blow, and the loss of Ariéle left her dazed and confused.

The following morning, she was roused out of bed by an orderly,
and prodded with a long stick along with those from her ward who
could walk to the morning meal. Then she was escorted to the
laundry where she toiled throughout the day, under constant guard,
until taken back to the ward to sleep.

Each day was the same. Each day brought her less and less hope
of learning about Ariéle. Questions to anyone who could hear went
unanswered, and sometimes were met with a blow across the back
with the prodding stick.

The weather in late October 1942 was colder than usual. The
sanitarium was a dismal place, with water seeping down the sides of
the walls and dripping through the faulty roof in many places. It was
cold and damp, the heating mostly nonexistent. The patients in the
tuberculosis ward died at high rates. The coughing and misery was
enough to drive even the hardest heart to insanity.

Marianne was confronted by one of the guards who masqueraded as an orderly at the beginning of her laundry shift.

"PP378. Commandant's office. Immediately."

He barked the order, and stood ready with a small wooden baton to enforce the command if need be. Marianne's rough tunic was stenciled "PP" - a designation reserved for political prisoners held in the sanitarium as a cover for their political incarceration. The institution held about 30 such prisoners at any time before they disappeared without notice, to where only God knew.

Marianne left her station and walked slowly down the hall. She knew the way to the Commandant's office all too well. Twice weekly since she arrived midsummer she was interrogated in the "office" by men she only could guess were French collaborators of the Gestapo. They had so far only threatened her, but the intensity of their questioning began to grow in weeks past. She expected the worst, and prepared herself mentally as she walked.

"Good morning, madame," the Commandant addressed her as she entered. "Please, have a seat."

Marianne was immediately suspicious. The usual chair with its restraints was not there. In its place was a simple ladder back wooden chair. She sat carefully, slowly, gauging the intent of the men in the room. Unlike each time before, the "orderly" left, closing the door behind her.

The commandant was a gaunt-looking man who spoke an odd dialect of French that was at times difficult to understand. Today he was reviewing a file of papers on his desk as she walked in.

"I have been reading in your file, madame, that your husband is suspected of smuggling, of stealing taxes and duties from the lawful administrators of France."

She did not respond, but looked stonily ahead.

"Now, that is not such a crime. Certainly not one that cannot be rectified, with certain considerations."

He hung for a while on that last phrase, and Marianne stiffened at the implications.

"Madame, I am offended. I would not suggest favors of … of a sexual nature. I am sure you have heard such rumors, but I can assure you they are just the complaints of malcontents." He refused to look at her as he continued the dialog.

"It seems, madame, that your husband has gone missing. He has been accused by a certain Captain De Rosier of stealing his boat, the St. Justine." He carefully looked up at her after that accusation.

"My husband is no thief!" Marianne shot back, unable to control her anger and disgust.

"No. When I read the report, based on what we know about you, I thought not."

What do you mean, what you know about me? I have been very careful not to reveal anything.

"So he is not a thief. Thank you for confirming this. One can only assume, therefore, that he is indeed, involved in other clandestine activities. Perhaps those who would seek to undermine the lawful authority?"

He looked intently at her. He has trapped me, she realized.

"Such activity would require severe consequences, madame." He began to browse through the file some more. Marianne simply grit her teeth and resolved not to panic.

"It says here that you were separated from your daughter," he began to take another tack.

"What have you done with Ariéle?" she spat, angry at being manipulated.

"Oh, madame. We have no interest in your innocent daughter. The child was returned to Pont-Aven some time ago, which is why we learned of your husband's disappearance. The child was left with the local priest," he said, not looking up, then added, as he slowly raised his head, "It would be a shame if these stories of your husband were true. Perhaps if we knew his whereabouts, we could dispel any questions about his loyalty."

Was Ariéle really safe? Is he lying? What is he really after? The questions swirled around her mind, confusing images, confounded by lack of sleep and hunger. How can I protect my Ariéle? What is Antoine doing? She knew of the payments to Harbor Master Vercher. Was this what they were after? Were they using her, threatening Ariéle through her, to get information on the corruption of this petty official? Was Vercher involved in something else, something more dangerous?

I will not let Antoine or Ariéle suffer because of that puissant Vercher.

"So, is this about the harbor master, Vercher?" She tried to ask, to turn the conversation back to something she could manage, or manipulate.

"Why would you ask that, madame?" He looked up slowly.

He is trying to trap me, she thought. Should I give him something to use as leverage?

"That man, Vercher, he has been accepting bribes for some time. Long before the current situation."

"And what situation is that, madame?"

"Since the German occupation," she stated slowly, carefully.

"You mean the cooperative administration," he corrected.

"Yes, the cooperative administration," she echoed, with a hint of sarcasm.

"And your husband, he has paid these bribes?"

"My husband is the mate on his boat, not the captain."

"Then how would you know of these illegal payments, madame?"

"Everyone in the commune knows of this. It is something not spoken of, but well known."

"Why have you not reported this to the police?"

"You think the police do not know? That they do not profit from this?" Marianne let her anger spill out, and immediately realized she had said too much. Her interrogator simply looked back down at his papers and made some notes.

"Are you accusing the prefect of the district of accepting bribes, madame?" She knew she stumbled, letting her anger get the better of her.

"No, monsieur. I have no such knowledge. I am simply angry about being away from my family." Her attempt to recover from this mistake sounded feeble, she knew.

"Yes, well I am sure with your cooperation that matter can be resolved quickly. Now, again. The whereabouts of your husband?"

"He is a fisherman. He goes out for extended periods of time. It is what fishermen do."

"Ah, so it is. But it has been several months since he cleared the harbor, madame," and he again slowly raised his head and stared intently at her. "The ship's owner has reported the vessel as stolen."

What? He is lying again, he must be, she thought. Antoine would never steal De Rosier's boat, no matter what the circumstances.

"The authorities have been searching for him, as have his fellow fishermen. There has been no sighting of the St. Justine or Monsieur Bouchard. We are all quite concerned."

She tried to not let her panic show, and replied in as composed a voice as she could.

"He often travels to the Channel Islands, or the Cherbourg peninsula … wherever the fish are being caught. He would not steal the St. Justine."

"Apparently, the ship's owner does not share your opinion, madame."

He pulled two files out from his stack of documents and opened them for Marianne to see.

"Do you know either of these men?"

There were dossiers of two men on official stationary. She did not know either of these men, but quickly realized that the police believed she did. Perhaps, she thought, I can play this fish.

"Yes, I have seen them. I do not know their names, but they came to our home one night."

"And for what purpose, madame?" She knew she had caught his attention, although now it was the interrogator who tried to appear calmly disinterested.

"I do not know. My husband did not know them. I was asked to leave the room, but listened as best I could from the bedroom. They spoke quietly, but I heard my husband tell them to leave and not return. He came to bed angry, and said they were looking for a charter, but he told them he was only the mate, and to leave him alone."

"And when was this, madame?"

"Several months ago. Perhaps February, or early March."

"And your husband has not seen them again?"

She guessed correctly this was the trap. She would not be caught again.

"Yes, they came to the boat, but he again told them to leave us alone." She remembered a night in March when Antoine returned from the harbor upset, and could not sleep. She would play out her suspicions. "This was late March. He had not seen them since."

"I see. And did he speak to Harbor Master Vercher about these men?"

"I do not know, monsieur."

He paused for a moment, then closed the files, rearranging them neatly on the desk. He called out for the orderly who immediately reentered the room.

"That will be all, madame. The government thanks you for your cooperation in this matter. I am certain we can resolve the rest of this unpleasantness soon."

With that, Marianne was led back to her barracks. A glimmer of hope filled her thoughts, of seeing Antoine and Ariéle soon. It made the cold and damp night more bearable.

The commandant placed a phone call.

"She knows nothing that can help us. But she knows of Vercher and Captain Foucault ... Too much ... I agree."

He hung up the phone, and reached for a stamp from his desk. On top of the cover report on Marianne Bouchard he stamped, "Stateless Person of Jewish Descent."

The following morning Marianne was roused early and told to shower. She would be leaving, and would be returned to Pont-Aven. She could scarcely believe what she heard. She quickly showered, dressed, and eagerly followed the orderly down the hall out into the courtyard of the sanitarium, eager to leave this dreadful place behind.

A black police vehicle was waiting. She was ushered into the back seat, and this time there was no guard, no reason to fear. The driver was handed a paper that gave him his instructions, and he drove off.

At the road junction in the commune of La Guiche Marianne saw that the sign pointed left towards Lorient. The car turned right.

"This is the wrong way!" She called to the driver. There was a grate between her and the driver, common in police cars. She banged on the grate to get the driver's attention. "The wrong way! You are going the wrong way!"

She reached for the door handle as the car slowed to make the turn. The handle would not work, the door would not open. She pounded her fists on the window in desperation. She was wearing only the soft slippers of her captivity, so had no hard shoes she could use to break the windows. So she turned on her back and tried to kick out the window. It was no use. She was trapped, and realized she was destined to not see her Antoine or Ariéle, perhaps never.

CHAPTER 15 - THE TURNING POINT

The control we believe we have is purely illusory, and ...
every moment we teeter on chaos and oblivion.
— *Clive Barker*

Police Captain Charest looked her over carefully. She is thirteen, he made mental notes to himself. Hair, brilliant red. Long and well kempt. A slight figure, not yet fully developed, but promising, nonetheless. Green eyes, a very pretty face. Yes, she will do, I am sure.

"Elle est acceptable pour moi, Docteur - she will do fine," he said in perfect French. He signed a form that the orderly handed him, and barked an order to the common German soldier that accompanied him. With that, Ariéle was led out of the sanitarium and was placed in the back seat of a waiting car. The soldier closed the door, then took the driver's seat. The police captain took the back seat next to her. Ariéle was frightened and panicking.

"Do not fear, mademoiselle. You will not be harmed."

"Where is my mother? What have you done with her?"

The captain refused to answer her, and simply stared out at the countryside passing by.

Ariéle awoke hours later when the car was brought to a stop in front of a nondescript warehouse. She was roughly dragged into a small holding room, bare with a simple light bulb hanging from a wire in the center, and a small barred window looking out to the alley below. She could hear unfamiliar noises - the noises of a city. The door was slammed behind her, and the light went out. It was cold, and she curled up in the corner, drawing her knees up to her chest to maintain as much warmth as she could. Ariéle began to rock back and forth, quietly crying, fearing for her life, and fearing for her mother. It was late at night before she slept again out of sheer exhaustion.

Ariéle was wakened in the morning by another German soldier. They barked at her in German, which she did not understand, and was rudely dragged to her feet. Again, she was pushed into a car, and they drove off through the streets. She had never seen such a place - each street was like a tunnel with buildings reaching uniformly high on each side, a turn, then more streets the same. The streets were busy with people, and German soldiers were everywhere. She could only guess this strange place was Paris. There was no green grass anywhere, no smell of the sea, and the streets were dirty with trash. It was a frightening place.

The car came to a stop in front of a building that looked on the outside like all the others. The street in front was busy with soldiers and what looked like solder's vehicles parked all around. She was escorted into the entrance. When the soldier-driver displayed a paper document, she was ushered through a side elevator past a German sentry, through a private guarded entrance, and into an office where she was told to stand and wait.

Ariéle stood alone in the office, an ornate suite above what appeared to be some sort of German army command in the center of Paris. She had never seen such a room. It could only be described as opulent, although the finery displayed everywhere bewildered her. Where was she? What was she doing here? She had been warned by the captain who transported her not to ask about her mother again, or she and her mother would be severely punished. So Ariéle kept quiet, and kept her fear to herself. Her mother would want her to be brave, despite how hard it was.

She was alone in the room for several minutes when a side door opened and a German officer, obviously of a high rank, briskly strode in followed by a beautiful, well dressed woman. The woman walked with a fine graceful movement, Ariéle noticed, and appeared to dote over the officer. They both approached her.

"So, this is the one," he smiled at her. "Yes, very pretty - very pretty, indeed!" he commented as he walked slowly around Ariéle, looking her up and down. His gaze alarmed and frightened her. The woman followed closely behind, and she too looked at her closely, although Ariéle felt almost drawn to her gaze, almost comforted by it, a feeling quite different from the officer.

"Get her cleaned up, and into something ... suitable," he added, with a disdained stare at the rough garment she was still wearing from the convent.

The woman spoke for the first time.

"Oh, Colonel, she will do very well, I am certain. So young, and fresh. Just ready to be properly taught," she added as she took his arm and steered him away toward the entrance, almost pushing him away from her, Ariéle thought. "I will take very good care of her."

"I will be away in Berlin for the next several weeks. I expect some results when I return," he said as he turned back to look at Ariéle again.

The woman gave him a studied, beguiling look, and then, turning him around once more, almost like managing a puppet, Ariéle thought, walked him back through the door and down the hallway. She could no longer see them, but could hear more conversation, which the woman clearly controlled.

Shortly, she returned.

"Come my dear," she said gently. "We need to get you a bath, and some decent clothing. Do not speak, child. We will talk when we are in private."

And with that, the woman guided her down the hall and up some stairs to the apartments on the top floor of the suite. She was taken into a private area at the far end of the complex, and into what appeared to be the woman's bedroom. A maid was waiting in attendance for orders from the woman.

"Draw her a bath, get her cleaned up, and I will find some suitable clothing. And bring some bread and cheese. I am certain those German dogs did not feed her," she said quietly, almost under her breath.

"Oui, madame," the maid answered, and with a soft and reassuring smile led Ariéle into the bathing area.

———⁂———

"Child, please sit here. Share the bread and cheese with me, and let's get acquainted."

"Where is my mother?" Ariéle asked, and tears quickly filled her eyes, the pent up emotions finally loosening in a flood of tears and terror.

"Oh, child, I do not know. I am so sorry. I know you are frightened," and she stood and walked over to Ariéle, giving her a reassuring embrace. Her gentle nature disarmed Ariéle, and she let her emotions go.

"That's OK, child. Let it out. It is OK to cry here. You are safe here with me."

When she regained her composure, the woman directed her to eat.

"You need your strength, child. Please, tell me your name."

"Je m'appelle Ariéle, madame," she responded politely. It had been yesterday morning since she had eaten, and she felt weak, her hands shaking.

"I am Madame Bourait, the mistress of the house. I am also your governess from now on."

"What am I doing here, madame?" she asked, choking back tears as she tried to eat a little.

"Ariéle, my poor child. You are a prisoner here, as we all are. It is a prison without bars, with good food, and fine clothes, but a prison nonetheless. Do not be afraid, child. I will protect you, and soon you will learn to trust me. Now, I know how frightened you are, and that is understandable. Together, we will last out the German occupation, you will see. For now, you need to eat, and get some sleep. We will talk more tomorrow."

Ariéle soon learned the routine of the house, as Madame Bourait called it. The suite was the home of the commander of the Pigalle district of Paris, Colonel Reiniger, and was located on the top two floors of the command center which had requisitioned the rest of the building. The command headquarters were near the center of the old city at Place des Victoires.

The Colonel had lavish tastes, and kept fine food, wine, and brandy on hand. He excelled at throwing lavish parties for Nazi dignitaries and army officers, and used his command staff to requisition whatever was necessary from "cooperative" local shops and businesses that could use the protection of the area commandant. He kept a mistress, Madame Bourait, who served as his hostess at these parties and managed the household servants.

Ariéle also learned soon enough why she was here. Ariéle had been purchased by the Colonel from the French police who were known to kidnap young French girls and provide them as mistresses to German officers. His orders had been quite specific - he wanted a very young girl, a country maiden - fresh and virgin - that he could "train" in the proper way to serve a German officer. This would be the task that fell to Madame Bourait. He had several women who served as his sexual partners when he had need, or needed to provide entertainment for one of his guests, including Madame Bourait. This new one, he boasted to one of the officers in his command, he would keep to himself - and save for when she was just ripe enough.

In the meantime, she was to have training in manners, etiquette, and schooling so that when he was ready for her, she could assume the role of the head of the house - and replace Madame Bourait at his pleasure.

When Madame Bourait revealed all of this to Ariéle, she was despondent, and wanted to run away.

"No, child, that would be suicide. I cannot allow you to do that. Believe me, Ariéle, I will keep you safe from that German pig. The Colonel is fond - too fond - of his brandy, and his ready women. He is like putty in my hands. I will keep him from you, I promise."

She took Ariéle under her guidance, and trained her in the manners and arts of a woman of the city. True to her word, she kept her away from Colonel Reiniger.

———— ∞ ————

The priest stepped through the doorway first. He had not been inside this old stone cottage for years, ever since its owner had died during the influenza outbreak following the Great War. The cottage had become the property of the church as was the custom, but it was in such disrepair now it was difficult to find an occupant. Many of the rural poor believed the pandemic was a curse from God and refused to enter any cottage where someone had died of the influenza.

Antoine Bouchard had benefitted from this reluctance once before, after his release from custody in 1920, and sought out such a place intentionally. He would have no visitors here.

"It is a humble cottage, my son. Humble as our Lord, Jesus," he declared. The priest had negotiated well, however, and Antoine had agreed to provide the parish with scrap bottom fish and unsold shellfish as his payment for rent. This suited him fine. Payment by SIS for the Atlantic Wall map would provide a nice cushion, and the British would pay for even more information.

"Thank you, Father. It will serve me fine," he assured the old priest, and he escorted him to the door.

"Those in need will give their thanks in ways known only to God, my son," he concluded, and slowly began the long walk back to town.

Antoine surveyed his surroundings. The cottage had a single room with a stone fireplace and a metal hook for hanging a steel pot. The room had no stove, and the fireplace was the only source of heating or cooking. Along the far side was a crude wooden bed - smaller than the bunk on the St. Marianne. He inspected the mattress. The ticking was coarse but sound, the stuffing old and worn. It had molded out years ago and he immediately emptied it in the truck garden out behind the cottage. He could get new straw easily enough.

There was a heavy coating of dust and fine dirt on everything. He began to sweep the dirt off of the rough interior walls, and he thought how Marianne could turn such a pig sty into a warm and comfortable home. As he thought of Marianne, his knees felt weak and he had to sit on the empty bed frame for support. Since he arrived in Courseulles he had thought of her often, wondering how she would do this, take care of that, wondering if she were still alive, and what had become of their little Ariéle.

The terrors at night returned. Antoine was wracked by guilt for sending his family away to what turned out to be an uncertain fate. Was he wrong to help the British escape from Pont-Aven? How could Marianne be betrayed by her own father? Was her father's hatred of him so deep it meant she was now lost to him? Was he wrong to play the Lorient police for fools? Did this lead to Marianne and Ariéle's arrest? The sequence of events became confused, the facts distorted by fear for their safety. He slept little, and grew increasingly angry and bitter.

He finally turned to his friend Andy for help, knowing he could not send his letters, but took comfort in writing out his fears, as if in confession. He trusted no one else, not even the priest.

> 14 Oct 1942
> Dear Andy,
>
> I cannot post this letter, I am certain of that. But it helps me to write to you.
>
> I have to take extraordinary measures to protect myself here, although I cannot tell you where I am.
>
> I fear my own foolish actions have endangered Marianne and Ariéle. I cannot sleep, and my anger towards the Germans and their French puppets grows every day. I feel it consuming me.

I think of you and our talks, and it helps calm my terrors. But they return every night.

Pray for me, Andy. This world is collapsing into chaos.

Antoine

In the corner of his small cottage, Antoine began to dig what would normally be a small root cellar. He stole boards from the back of the dockyard at night, and shored up the sides to prevent them from caving in. He cut the floor boards to make a trap door. It was barely deep enough to stand upright in. He chiseled out several stone bricks that formed the bottom of the foundation and cut a space just large enough to hold a tin box he confiscated from the chandlery garbage pile. It was this box that held the letters, paper, and pen that he used to write to Andy Anderson. He intended to someday send these letters when they could be safely posted. For now, once he replaced the bricks the box was safely away from prying eyes.

Antoine kept to himself. The men in the commune would stare at him from their tables at the café, mistrusting this stranger. The women would gossip among themselves. Where once not so long ago the port was filled in the summer with rich Parisians on holiday, now under the occupation strangers were scrutinized and mistrusted.

The Todt Organization commandeered a building at the end of the harbor to serve as a staging and design headquarters when they began to build the series of hard fortifications along the beach frontage to repel any possible attack. Normandy was one of the main potential landing areas, and with the port of Le Havre to the east and Cherbourg to the west, and Carpiquet airfield just outside of Caen, there were major strategic objectives the Germans rightfully knew the Allies coveted.

Construction of the Atlantic Wall began in earnest in 1943, and Antoine Bouchard was in a perfect position to monitor and report on its construction in Normandy. At the same time, forced labor conscription drove many otherwise neutral French citizens to form loosely organized and independent resistance cells. The battle for France was beginning, again.

CHAPTER 16 - A BODYGUARD OF LIES

In wartime, truth is so precious that she should always be
attended by a bodyguard of lies.
— *Winston Churchill*

Present Day

I made an unannounced visit to the Portsmouth Dockyards supervisor. After waiting patiently for over an hour he agreed to meet with me. His response was less than helpful.

"In 2008 we worked with Highbury College here in Portsmouth to archive the records of the dockyards as a part of a historical data project sponsored by the city. The data is extensive. The physical records have been stored away for posterity, and are not available, but the electronic records are searchable. However, one must make a formal request for access."

My request for access to the records was refused. The information itself was declassified in 1996, but the records system that held the information was behind a secure firewall, and access was restricted to authorized personnel only.

I contacted Highbury College and spoke with Professor Hugh Howden. I briefed him on my suspicions about the Sainte Justine, Colonel Remy, and the tale of the Atlantik Wall map. To resolve this, I needed access to the closed data.

"Yes, I believe we have the data sets. Those records were declassified before the project began, and when we had completed the compilation, we gave the government a data set that was then added to their system. The original data set, however, is still somewhere here in the archives."

This was more encouraging. I returned to Courseulles via Caen by ferry and had to wait three excruciating days for the results. I had a bit of luck, finally. I recrossed the channel and returned to the college where I was ushered into a computer lab by Professor Howden. There I met one of his master's candidates, a data specialist named Jimmy Sinclair.

"We have a massive amount of raw data available," he began. "Perhaps if we sit and talk over exactly what you are after, and how such information might be recorded, if at all, we can look for ways to crack open this little puzzle."

This guy knew his stuff. Inside of minute bits of raw data our lives lie splayed open. Reading the data, and determining what is relevant and what is not, however, can be almost impossible. It is a concept called "hiding in plain sight," the notion that you can become lost in a sea of seemingly irrelevant information. If you know what data bits to seek, you might just unlock quite a compelling story.

"I am looking for a boat called the Sainte Marianne, based in Courseulles-sur-Mer, maybe. It possibly called in port sometime between, say, 1940 and 1944."

He ran a search correlating Courseulles-sur-Mer and the vessel, with no results.

"I didn't really expect to find a match there, but we had to start somewhere. How about the Saint Justine? That was the name of the boat allegedly lost at sea by Antoine Bouchard in June 1942."

Again, no results.

"Try under 'Port' - Pont-Aven, 1942."

There was one entry, but it was a barge decommissioned and cut up for salvage. No fishing boats, and nothing closely related to my search.

We went through various kinds of searches, types of services, types of activities, length of vessel, types of vessel, names of vessels, variants on names … nothing. Hours passed, and we were nowhere.

The professor stopped in to see how we were progressing.

"Look at it this way. You have simply narrowed your search," he smiled. "If what you say is true, there is a key somewhere. Think of what you have not thought about."

The white board in the computer lab was filled with scribbles, all leading nowhere.

"Was the boat ever hauled out?"

The question was simple. We had not checked it before, assuming that if the boat was on a clandestine mission it would not have remained in port long. "What if that is a false assumption? Try it."

A search of the haul out records for the St. Marianne yielded no results. We were brainstorming, throwing about seemingly odd combinations of facts and circumstances and getting nowhere.

I sat back and looked again at a schematic of the data model.

"What if the name 'Marianne' was not in a primary field, but somewhere else. There are a couple of large text fields where miscellaneous data could be stored."

"I can create a 'fuzzy' search routine against those fields, but given that the fields are not indexed, the search will take a while. Likely several hours or so. We have to share server processing time."

He wrote the query, set the processing parameters, and submitted it to the database. We agreed to return in the morning and see what, if anything, came back.

I arranged for a room nearby, and ate in a nearby pub. That night, as I lay awake trying to think of what we may have neglected, what other possibilities there may be, I began to worry I was losing my own personal sense of perspective. Perhaps I was chasing a phantom that simply left no trail, because there was really nothing to leave in the first place.

Professor Howden joined us in the morning as we examined the results of the text search. There were 33 records in the record set, displayed 10 per page. I looked at the indexed fields that displayed on screen.

"I need to examine the text fields of this data set."

The search took some rather broad interpretations of the word "Marianne." The first two pages of records were mostly irrelevant, with some foreign names thrown in as well as a few obvious typographical errors that matched close enough to be included.

On record 28 we found the word "Marianne." It was in a set of instructions to the yard crew entered into the text field since there was no other place to put the information. The entry read,

> Date: 28/6/42
> Vessel: unregistered
> Port: unknown
> Misc. directive.
> Repaint name, S. Justine to S. Marianne.
> Auth ASIS6774578

"This is a very odd entry. There is a boat - but the name is not under the 'vessel' field; and no port of origin. Both 'unregistered' or 'unknown.' Yet there is the name 'St. Justine' in the directive field."

"This is interesting - the authorization number. I don't suppose either of you know what the 'ASIs' in the authorization number stands for?" the professor asked.

"No, but I suppose it is some boat yard charge code. 'As-is' - whatever that stands for," his student answered.

I looked at the professor, and he smiled. We both knew at once what it meant - one over on the bright student data keeper! "A-SIS. Category A, meaning highest priority; SIS - Secret Intelligence Service, the British intelligence corps, often referred to as MI6. Strictly James Bond stuff here. Voucher 6774578." The professor practically exploded with giddy satisfaction.

"Find that voucher, Jimmy!"

Sinclair logged into a new window and selected another one of the primary databases. After negotiating a security clearance routine, he requested Voucher 6774578. In an instant the data was displayed on the screen.

"OK - let's see. Yes, this confirms the payment charged to British Intelligence for the work listed in the dockyard record. This also has a reference to a General Order 6-998GH. There is nothing in our data system that this points to, I'm afraid," Jimmy answered.

"That is why you are the student, and I am the professor," Professor Howden joked. "Print me a copy of that screen, Jimmy," he added, and grabbed me by the arm. "Come with me. I think we can resolve this very easily."

We went back upstairs to the professor's office where he ordered tea from his secretary, and settled into a large overstuffed leather office chair behind his opulent desk. He picked up the telephone, and placed a call. After the usual pleasantries, he looked up at me and asked, "Would you mind waiting outside for a few minutes, Mr. Hewitt?"

I backed out of the room, my curiosity piqued, as he left his chair and closed the office door behind him. After about ten minutes he returned, and invited me in.

"So sorry for the cloak and dagger, old boy, but some things are best done privately. I am sure you can appreciate that." He had a big schoolboy smile on his face. "I think this may help you."

He passed an email to me which had the return email address redacted. I sat back into his visitor's chair and read through the text of the message.

> Hugh,
> Data declassified, 2/15/98
> GO 6-998GH
>
> 15 Jun 42
> Payment authorized; 2525 ps; in francs. Transfer G. De Rosier; SW account #847599HG9909409.
>
> Payment for S JustinePayment authorized, notes; 100 ps; francs; J. Charbonneau
>
> 6774578; payment for misc. refurbishing services, S. Marianne
>
> 6748922; payment for issuance identity papers, J. Charbonneau

"What am I looking at?" I was excited, but not quite certain what I was seeing.

"Well, I had some time to decipher it, you see, while I kept you waiting, with the help of its author. Basically, the SIS authorized the payment of 2,500 Pound Sterling - something like $10,000 U.S. during its time - quite a nice sum, too, by the way - paid to a Swiss bank account for G. De Rosier ... ."

"The owner of the Saint Justine," I interrupted, "who reported the vessel lost!"

"It seems it was lost ... to the British Intelligence Service! The second payment was cash - 100 pounds, paid in francs, to a 'J. Charbonneau.' The voucher we originally found for miscellaneous refurbishing services - including the name change ... ."

I could not hold back my excitement, and added, "And payment for new identity papers in the name of J. Charbonneau!"

I looked at the professor, and we both knew the answer simultaneously.

"Antoine Bouchard took the Saint Justine to Portsmouth, unloaded Colonel Remy and his family with the Atlantic Wall map. It was purchased by the SIS in exchange for the map, refurbished ... ."

The professor finished the narrative, "And Antoine under the false name of 'J. Charbonneau' was issued new forged identity papers. He then took the Sainte Marianne, as it is now called, to Courseulles-sur-Mer where the harbor master was probably paid off to look the other way. From there he routinely met with British Intelligence. He was working for the British - and the St. Marianne was his payment. The St. Marianne that was photographed in the harbor at Courseulles-sur-Mer in June 1942, apparently under the command of J. Charbonneau, aka Antoine Bouchard."

CHAPTER 17 - THE DEVIL'S DANCE

Vengeance is a dish best served cold.
— *Thanatos*

February 1943

Antoine cautiously approached the German officer sitting at the café reading. He was Hauptmann Gerhardt, one of the officers coordinating Wehrmacht defensive interests with the Todt Organization.

Gerhardt appeared in his mid-thirties and carried the stiff and deceptively polite bearing of Prussian military tradition, but was ruthless in his execution of duty. Rumor had it he had commanded a mechanized infantry company that had been badly mauled in the Battle of Kursk. This disgrace could have ended his career, possibly before a regimental firing squad. However, his career was salvaged by the intervention of his wife's uncle, a major general on the Atlantic Wall military command. It was a reversal of his fortunes career wise, but he understood the importance of his benefactor in rebuilding his career reputation.

"Herr Hauptmann," Antoine began. "May I have a moment of your time?"

The officer looked up from his reading and eyed Bouchard warily. Local French citizens seldom simply engaged a German officer in casual conversation.

"Who are you, and what do you want? I am not part of the local administration, so if you have a complaint, you must take it to the regional commandant." He was annoyed that the locals of this tiny village seemed to complain about everything, as if they were not proper channels for such things. These French are like disobedient children, he thought to himself.

"I am not here to complain, Herr Hauptmann, but to speak with you about a sensitive issue regarding the beach construction." Antoine was referring to the installation of concrete bunkers and field cannon at the mouth of the Seulles River. This caught Hauptmann Gerhardt's attention.

"Then speak, man, and be quick about it!" Hauptmann Gerhardt did not invite Antoine Bouchard to sit.

"I am a fisherman, Herr Hauptmann. Jacques Charbonneau." Why does this concern me? Gerhardt thought dismissively. "One hears things, sees things. Especially along the quay and in the warehouses. Things that might be of value, especially for someone involved in building such an ambitious project."

"And what do you know of this project?" he snapped.

"I have eyes, Herr Hauptmann. Everyone in the commune talks of the gun emplacements. How could they not, they are being built in plain sight?"

The low dunes along the coast line were but a short walk away from the center of the commune, and the construction work and supply convoys were notoriously exposed to view. Security was nearly impossible.

Hauptmann Gerhardt carefully eyed this insolent French fisherman. He watched his eyes carefully. These French seldom looked you straight in the eyes, and certainly could not be trusted. This one has an intense stare, he thought. Unusual.

"So, what do you want?" I should have this man arrested. I don't trust him. He wants something, probably trying to sell some irrelevant nonsensical information. He will be sorely disappointed.

"As I said, Herr Hauptmann, a man sees things, and hears things. Possibly even learns of people who might want to disrupt your construction plans."

Gerhardt's interest piqued instantly, but he remained stoic, not wanting to appear too interested. The Gestapo in Caen was obsessed with routing out resistance elements. He distrusted the Gestapo even more than he distrusted these dirty French peasants, but he could see an opportunity to make some strategic career headway if he could expose one of these irritating resistance cells.

Bouchard, who had been studying the German's facial reactions carefully, noticed his eyes momentarily dilate. He had hit a nerve.

The officer proceeded carefully.

"So tell me, fisherman, what is your interest in this?"

"I do not care about politics, Herr Hauptmann. Or your occupation, either." With that backhanded slap Hauptmann Gerhardt bristled slightly. "I catch fish, and sell fish. That is all I am interested in," he continued. A typical Frenchman - no education, no culture, no manners. "The buyers give special treatment to certain boats, and try to block me out of the market. They like to think they control Courseulles. They despise you Germans, that is an easy thing to see. If you can - disrupt - their little cooperations, I stand to benefit."

"And you do not hate the Germans, I suppose," he added scornfully.

Antoine reached into his pocket and withdrew a folded paper. He laid it on the table in front of the officer.

"And what is this?" he asked, feigning disinterest.

"My discharge papers. I was a soldier in the German army in the Great War. I was taken prisoner during the Spring Offensive and held captive by these French bastards."

Gerhardt unfolded the paper and read it carefully. It confirmed the fisherman's story - Jacques Charbonneau, P68219, was discharged from French custody 12/3/1920. Antoine could easily recount experiences in graphic detail of his service on the Eastern Front, in Flanders, and in the prisoner system, even if his papers belonged to another Jacques Charbonneau, of Salzburg in the Alsace. Charbonneau actually died while in French custody. Any check by the German authorities would verify his story, however, for the records had been carefully doctored to provide Bouchard with this cover. SIS had made certain of that.

Hauptmann Gerhardt refolded the paper and unbuttoned his tunic pocket, and slipped the document inside. The ruse had worked.

"I will check on this, Jacques Fisherman," he answered carefully. "I will return your papers if they are verified. If not, I will have you arrested and shot."

He dismissed Bouchard rudely. His heart was pounding, however, and he knew he had stumbled upon an opportunity to help erase the stain on his career record. If this Jacques Charbonneau checked out, he could plant him deeply inside the community and leverage him for useful information about the local resistance.

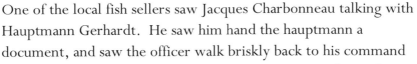

One of the local fish sellers saw Jacques Charbonneau talking with Hauptmann Gerhardt. He saw him hand the hauptmann a document, and saw the officer walk briskly back to his command office at the head of the harbor. Le Organisation Civil et Militaire (OCM) would keep a close eye on this fisherman.

Antoine wrote his friend.

14 Feb 1943
Dear Andy,

I fear I have lost Marianne and Ariéle. I can find no
information about them. The terrors grow every
night, as is the hatred growing deep within me for
these Germans. Forgive me, my friend, but I wish
them all dead.

I am playing a dangerous game. The German
commander thinks I am a loyal ex-soldier. They are
desperate to uncover the local resistance fighters, and
need someone local as an informant. This gives me
the chance to learn information that my Anglo friends
will pay for.

Antoine

———⊗⊗⊗———

Hauptmann Gerhardt sat at his favorite table at the Hotel de Paris
sipping a glass of the local wine. On the table was a report he had
just finished reading detailing the service record and history of one
Jacques Charbonneau, discharged soldier and POW. Sitting across
from him was the harbor master, Monsieur Le Collette. He did not
have a glass of wine.

"Monsieur, as you know I am most interested in routing out some
of the unsavory elements that could disrupt my orders here in your
dreadful little port," he started with an air of superiority. His tone
and the gist of this conversation alarmed Le Collette. "I think you
can be of help to me and, I am certain I can reciprocate, in time."

What is he after?, Le Collette asked himself.

German officers all liked to think they were all-powerful, and pretended to command extraordinary resources. In reality, the command structure was so rigid that a successful officer learned to bluff and extort his way to influence over the locals.

Did he know of any of my activities? Le Collette began to sweat and fidget in his seat. Gerhardt was too self-absorbed to notice.

"This fisherman, Charbonneau. He is of some use to me. He served Germany after all, in the Great War. He was taken prisoner, you know, and has no love for you French," he added with a smirk. "I understand he has some difficulty in getting a good price for his smelly fish. I believe you have some influence in this regard, do you not?"

Le Collette did not answer, for he knew that Gerhardt already knew the answer to that question, or he would not have asked. The look on his face gave this away, and Gerhardt simply placed his wine glass on the table.

"I thought so," he replied curtly, answering his own question. "I would consider it a personal favor if you were to … intercede … on his behalf in this manner." The phony Prussian mannerisms made Le Collete cringe inside, knowing it was more than an implied threat.

"I will look into it," Le Collete answered carefully.

"Good! And on another point, one less complicated … ."

The harbor master knew he was being watched, and the longer he remained at the table with the German officer the more suspicious others became of his actions.

"It would be helpful," Hauptmann Gerhardt continued, "if the activities of this vessel were not recorded, monsieur. Prying eyes need not know of its comings and goings. How do you record such activity?"

Le Collette was suspicious of the officer's intentions, and was careful and measured in his response.

"I keep a log, Herr Hauptmann. It lists the date, activity, and the registry number of a vessel's activity."

"This registry number. Explain it to me."

"When a vessel is registered, I issue a certificate to the captain. I then simply record the number of that certificate when an activity occurs."

"And you have such a document on this fisherman's boat?"

"Oui, Herr Hauptmann."

"And if that document disappeared, how would anyone know of the boat's information?"

"They would not, Herr Hauptmann."

"Good. There are those working against the Reich here in Courseulles who could disrupt my plans if they were to trace this boat's activities. I want you to destroy that certificate, monsieur. Immediately!"

Le Collette saw this unexpected turn of events as an insurance policy in his game of double-hand.

"Oui, Herr Hauptmann. Consider it done!" Le Collette felt like he had just been given a reprieve from a probable death sentence.

With that, the anonymity of the St. Marianne was guaranteed.

Graye-sur-Mer is a tiny village nearly near Courseulles on the other side of the River Seulles. It is a short walk to the port, and the priest who gave the mass routinely walked the river bank path to the shore bridge and into Courseulles collecting unsold fish for the poor serviced by the church. He would then walk the back roads, giving blessings to the old and the ill who could not travel easily to the church for mass. His walks were routine, and went unnoticed. He tended to the spiritual needs of the outlying peasants and the Catholic conscripts who managed to sneak away occasionally for confession.

Every so often he stopped by Antoine Bouchard's cottage when he saw the St. Marianne in port. Antoine was not a regular at mass, but welcomed the priest when he made his rounds. He arrived at the usual time this morning.

"Good morning, my son," he offered quietly.

"Welcome, Father, come in," and he swung the cottage door open. The priest entered and looked around the small cottage. It was neat and orderly, save for the rude bed coverings that were in a scattered disarray. The terrors are back, he thought to himself. God has made a rough road for this child of His. To what end he could only guess. "Sit and share a glass of wine with me."

As the old priest took a slow sip from the wooden mug, he began to speak.

"God has plans for each of us, Jacques," he began. The priest knew him only as Jacques Charbonneau. No one would ever know his real name - he guarded it with his life. "And only through giving our life to Him can we find salvation."

Antoine had heard this story many times, but wondered why the priest was bringing this up now.

"It is not a coincidence that you are a fisherman, Jacques. God has had a special role for the fisherman in his work on earth, witnessed by the Great Fisherman, Jesus. Traversing the turbulent waters, one must rely on faith or be wrecked on the shores of sin."

"Sometimes, a messenger arrives to spread God's news, to help in the fulfillment of His will. It is our duty before Him to listen with an open heart, and steel ourselves to life's travails in fulfilling our task for God."

OK, old man, just what do you want. He could sense there was more than a sermon behind this priest's remarks.

"There are many here who are willing to work against the forces of Satan that occupy France. They are called to do many tasks, separate tasks. The purposes of these are known only to Him."

The priest reached into his cassock and removed a sealed letter.

"Even an old priest is called to deliver God's message," he added with a slight smile, sensing the air of suspicion growing in Antoine. He handed Bouchard the envelope, and turned to leave. "I will return each week at this time, on those days when the St. Marianne is in port, for those times when God calls. Even the Germans are blind to the pandering of a silly old priest."

With that the priest left, and continued on his humble rounds.

Bouchard locked the door, and closed the window shutters as well. Under the light of a small oil lantern, he opened the envelope.

He recognized the code name on the top of the letter - Absinthe. He was told when he first left Portsmouth that he would be contacted and given further instructions by Absinthe, and only him. He read the letter carefully.

Absinthe

This is the only written communication you will receive. The courier who delivered this is to be trusted. He will deliver instructions to you, but you are to have no additional communication with him at any time. Your actions must remain secret to all others.

You will rendezvous at 01:30, 14/3/1944. Same
manner and location as last delivery. Below is a list
of needs. Please advise on conditions as detailed,
verbal only.

Destroy this document once read.

Below this was a checklist of local facilities of the Atlantic Wall
with questions about their status, troop assignments, and resource
availability.

CHAPTER 18 - THE STORY OF MARIANNE

I thought brave was not being afraid. Bravery is being
terrified and doing it anyway.
— *Laurell K. Hamilton*

Marianne soon grew too exhausted to try to escape. She slumped back down in the seat and eventually slipped into a semiconscious state. The black Mercedes wound its way through the French countryside on the mean dirt roads, heading towards the Alsace region.

After several hours the car began to climb through the Vosges Mountains on crude winding roads. The temperature in the car began to fall as the temperature outside became colder and colder. The trees had already begun to change color and the grasses had turned brown.

The car slowing caused Marianne to awaken. She wiped the moisture away from the side window and could see a crude wooden gate, barbed wire stretched in three stands across the top extending along the fence, and a small shack and tower on the right. Above the gate was a small sign, "Konsentrationslager Natzweiler-Struthof."

The car slowed to a stop and a uniformed guard came from the shack and confronted the driver. After a short conversation in German, of which she could understand little, the gate opened and the Mercedes drove inside. As it turned to the right, she could see the imposing sight of a single gallows in the center of the courtyard.

When the car stopped, the door was opened by another guard and she was grabbed and dragged roughly out of the car. The air was crisp and cold, the wind penetrating the thin sanitarium tunic. Marianne looked around in a panic, but saw no one save for her guard. The Mercedes drove away through the opened gate, and it was closed tight behind. No one spoke to her. The guard prodded her with a large wooden stick, sharpened at the end, towards a small building.

Once inside, she was confronted by a guard who had the task of registering her.

"Your name?" he demanded. She refused to answer, and was struck across the top of her shoulders by the guard with the stick.

"Answer, Jewess," he demanded, and struck her a second time.

"Bouchard," she spit out. "Marianne Bouchard."

"Where were you illegally living?" What did he mean, illegally living?

"I am a citizen of France … ."

She was again struck even harder across the back of her shoulders.

"Shut up, Jewess, and answer the question! I will ask you only one more time. Where were you illegally living?"

"Pont-Aven," she spit out.

"So you admit that you were illegally living in France. As a Jew, according to Le Statut des Juifs of 1940, all Jewish immigrants were ordered to leave France or face arrest."

"I am not Jewish. And I am no immigrant!" she spat, and was again rewarded with a sharp crack across the back.

The clerk finished his accounting, and stated nonchalantly, "Send her along."

She was again prodded in the back by the guard with the sharp stick even harder than before. Shoved into a cold room with a long table on the side, she was ordered to strip off her clothes by another guard - this one with a menacing staff with a barbed steel end that looked more like a mace. She knew that a strike by this monster could be fatal, so she stripped and threw her rude tunic on the table.

The guard with the mace prodded her into the shower, which was cold. A caustic chemical was poured over her head to kill any lice, and she was then pushed through to the next room. There, another guard waited with shears, and her beautiful auburn hair was clipped rudely from her head. She was given a striped dress of thin cotton, wooden sandals, and a triangular black head cloth. She was then ushered outside into the cold wind and marched along down the hill to one of several barracks stretching below her.

The guard opened the door and shoved her inside without so much as a word, and she stood staring into hundreds of pairs of eyes peering from gaunt, skeleton-like faces. The smell inside made her wretch, but she managed to keep from vomiting. She stared in horror at this incredible sight, until another woman inmate slowly approached her. She grabbed her by the arm and said quietly, "Come with me. Do not look at them."

She was pulled through the tightly packed barracks into an anteroom where the only inmates were eight women. While it was not as crowded as the main room, with its four tiers of wooden bunks, it was crude nonetheless, and there was no door to separate them from the men on the other side.

"Stay here," the woman said. "My name is Gela. Listen to me carefully, and do as I do, or they will simply kill you."

<hr>

Winter in the Vosges Mountains was brutal. Marianne would huddle close together with the other women inmates for warmth, and the small group would help rouse each other when the waking hour came. The penalty for not rising in time could be a severe beating, or worse. A survivor's account written after the war recounted the morning routine.

During summer, we get up at four o'clock in the morning; during winter, when days are the shortest, we get up at six. We go to the washrooms where, half naked, we have to wash ourselves with freezing water, we dress, then we receive a pint of infusion or of a beverage they call coffee. Then we go, five abreast, to the roll-call place ... The roll-calls often go on for hours, and there we stand still, in the snow during winter, under the rain during summer, without any coat of course.

———— ⌒⌒⌒ ————

Today the daily roll call lasted longer than usual. The count was short and the guards were furious. They hit one inmate with a baton and demanded to know where the missing prisoner was. The inmate fell to the round and was kicked repeatedly in the stomach until he lapsed into unconsciousness.

They found the missing inmate in the barracks, still stiff from his death rigor. Two inmates were pulled out of the line and had to carry the corpse from the barracks to the crematorium on top of the hill while the rest stood in line, forced to watch. The scene was repeated so often it scarcely was even noticed by the long-term inmates.

Marianne watched everything, unwilling to spend even a single moment passively in this evil place.

Eventually, the line of inmates was ordered to Platform I where the daily work squads were formed. The inmates had to labor for the Third Reich to stay alive. Once they could not produce more than their cost to maintain, they would be eliminated, and replaced by others capable of work. The Thousand-Year Reich would survive only through slave labor.

Marianne had been lucky. Most of the prisoners who were sent to the French camp at Natzweiler-Struthof were transported by train to the nearest station at Rothau, 5 miles from the camp. From there, they had to walk up the 2,500 foot mountain to the camp. Le Struthof, as the French called it, was located about 20 kilometers from Strasbourg on a bald mountaintop, a former ski area for Strasbourg residents.

Prisoners entering the camp were marched past a large farmhouse with many annexes that held the gas chambers and the workshops used for medical experiments. A small villa with an oddly out-of-place swimming pool was on the left a few hundred yards from the gate - the dwelling of the commandant, a sinister man named Kramer.

As the days rolled into early December, the scene was an imposing spectacle, the snow covering everything from the living blocks, observation posts, and electrified wire fences. All this whiteness was violently lighted in the dark night by powerful searchlights. Compared to this man-made hell, God's creation - the moon - looked pale.

Approximately 7,000 prisoners in the concentration camp system were in the Nacht und Nebel category - people who simply disappeared into the 'Night and Fog' as they called it - and most of them were French resistance fighters. The majority were sent to Natzweiler-Struthof. The camp, however, was not built by the Germans, but by the French and was administered by France before the collapse of the Vichy Regime in 1943. Inmates were isolated from the entire world and forced to work to survive in the nearby rock quarry.

"Stay clear of that one," Gela told her, pointing to room number 1 in block number 5. "It is the 'shot room' where the sick and the

wounded are taken for injections. No one ever comes out of that
one alive."

Blocks number 1, 10, 11, 12, 13, and 14 were for the prisoners
who were healthy. The work in the camp was supervised by kapos,
who were prisoners themselves. They were usually criminals who
had the power of life and death over the prisoners. Marianne was
housed in Block 14 with the few women who remained alive, and
who managed to avoid being raped to death by the guards or the
kapos.

———⬣———

It was April and in the valleys the spring rains warmed the earth and
green returned to the fields. On the mountain top, however, the
wind was still as cold as it was in January, and the snow clung
tenaciously to the ground. The morning work crews formed after
roll call each day, and trod off in groups of 80 or so looking like
skeletons.

Marianne worked in the infirmary, among inmates suffering from
typhus, dysentery, and a host of other diseases. She would watch
helplessly while they were taken to Room #1 for shots, knowing
they would simply be put to death.

The guards routinely beat and raped the women assigned to the
infirmary. Marianne steeled herself to this abuse as best she could.
Death awaited any inmate who became pregnant for it reduced their
capacity to work - an instant death sentence at Natzweiler.

Prisoners who were not contagious would often be carried off to
the medical annex. Rumors about human experiments abounded,
told in secret whispers among the inmates, but anyone caught
voicing such a thought out loud would be hung in the courtyard
gallows.

She was weakened by hunger, and always cold. There was no heat, she had no coat, and she wondered how she had managed to survive the past winter. She knew she probably would not survive another.

While the weather moderated as the months dragged on through summer, they were forced to rise two hours earlier, and the work became harder. Inmates died by the scores each week, only to be replaced by more sorry souls forced to march up the 2,500 foot mountain. The supply of labor never dwindled.

Neither did the supply of subjects for the experiments. Dr. August Hirt, a Professor at the University of Strasbourg, was conducting research on racial characteristics. When he requested Jewish skeletons that were undamaged by bullet holes or body blows, Heinrich Himmler ordered that Jews should be brought from Auschwitz to Natzweiler so that they could be killed in the camp's gas chamber and stripped of their flesh.

───◦◦◦───

October 8, 1943

The inmates filed into the mess hall, exhausted from the hard day's labors. Even though it was still early in the autumn, the mountain cold permeated everything, and Marianne struggled just to sit on the hard wooden benches. She had a terrible secret kept from the other women, but knew she could hide it for only so long.

The women whispered among themselves that today was the beginning of Yom Kippur. To keep the tradition, they should fast.

"We cannot fast. The kapos would punish us for that."

Marianne heard them, and knew that today her journey into submission and humiliation was over. She had made a decision that she would not be broken, would not give them the pleasure of watching her dance on the gallows or of stripping her body of flesh for the mad doctor's exhibits.

"They will kill me," she told Gela, "but they will not break me."

Her Ariéle had been taken from her. Antoine probably killed. She could feel the abomination growing inside her, impregnated by one of the kapos who routinely raped her - her death sentence. She would take not a single step further into the abyss.

When the meal was brought, as meager as it was, she pushed the bowl away. The guard struck her with his stick.

"Eat," he ordered. Instead, she stood and faced him. An officer immediately stepped forward and unsnapped the cover of his pistol holster.

"It is Yom Kippur, and today I choose to fast."

Gela cried out, "Marianne, you are not Jewish. Do not do this."

She looked at Gela, and a quite resolve settled over her.

"The Boche says I am a Jew. They treat me like a Jew. Today, I will fast like a Jew."

The officer drew his service pistol and placed it against her temple.

"You will eat, or you will die like a Jew."

Marianne Bouchard closed her eyes and remembered the beautiful smile of her Ariéle, and a warm spring day when a shy fisherman entered her bakery and the picnic they shared on the grass.

She spit in the German's face.

He pulled the trigger, and shot her in the forehead.

Her journey through Hell was over.

Chapter 19 - A Tightening Noose

The supreme art of war is to subdue the enemy without fighting ...
appear weak when you are strong, and strong when you are weak.
— *Sun Tzu*

The storms along the coast of Normandy in the winter of 1943-1944 kept the fishing fleet in harbor for most of December. Antoine was one of the few hardy souls who dared venture out, challenging the rocky shoals just offshore. But the damage to gear and body made him reconsider, and like most of the other boats the St. Marianne mostly remained dockside. Bouchard took whatever jobs he could to help buy bread, wine, and cheese.

Construction activity in the area had slowed. The fortunes of the Nazi war machine had taken a terrible turn when the largest tank battle in history erupted in unspeakable violence near Kursk on the Russian plains. The Wehrmacht was reeling from its greatest defeat following on the heels of the disastrous Stalingrad campaign, and retreated in force back toward Poland. Even in defeat, however, the German army was a formidable opponent. Resources had been diverted to the Eastern Front, drawing both raw materials and manpower from nearly every sector of occupied Europe.

By November, 1943 Hitler issued Führer Directive 51, declaring that all resources now had to be directed toward fortifying the western defenses against an anticipated invasion. In January he appointed Field Marshall Erwin Rommel to lead the reorganization of the Atlantic Wall defenses. In Normandy, rumors of new orders began to circulate. Bouchard took advantage of the foul weather to learn more about what was planned, and pocket some extra money in the process.

The owner of a large warehouse on the edge of the harbor hired him to help move building supplies from the railhead at Caen. On their return, the lorries took a turn off the main Caen-Courseulles road and stopped at an open field back away from the beach several kilometers.

"Stack the lumber over there," the yard foreman barked. There were piles of rock and brick, lumber, and boxes of unmarked materials staged all over the field alongside the road. Bouchard thought it strange that so much material would be dropped off this far from anything, and when he finished his work that day he made a crude map of the area indicating the location of the stockpile. Over the next several weeks he had added several other locations to his supply station map. The Germans were planning new construction when the weather broke.

It was late January when he learned the true nature of the projects. The warehouse foreman had summoned Bouchard and about a dozen other local workers to help him clear space at the warehouse. It took several days, and it was obvious that something large was arriving.

He was not disappointed. Under cover of darkness to avoid the scrutiny of RAF reconnaissance flights, German transports moved slowly along the main road hauling a large cargo. It was easy for Bouchard to hide behind one of the outbuildings at the yard and spy on the delivery of four 100mm field guns that were stored in the warehouse and covered with large tarps to avoid detection. These were joined by other smaller field guns shortly thereafter. The Germans were building new hardened defense placements for mobile artillery that could withstand bombardment, yet be moved once an invasion came with relative ease. SIS planners in Britain would pay dearly for this new information.

By mid February Antoine had completed his map detailing the new construction, the locations of the inland strong points, and the new barracks and command posts built or commandeered in the immediate area. He was careful not to venture too far towards Caen. The active presence of the Gestapo in the city and the added security at the Carpiquet airfield made these areas more dangerous. He could walk the backroads of rural Calvados with relative impunity, but wandering around Caen could easily draw unwanted attention.

On the afternoon of February 20 he boarded the St. Marianne as the tide began to rise and the winds that had pummeled the coast abated, preparing for a run up the coast. The fresh fish markets had been nearly empty these past few weeks, and the demand for product was high. All the local boats were busy preparing for what was forecasted to be moderate weather for the next week or so, and the locks would open for the fleet at 5:00 PM. It was a general opening, so no record of the vessels leaving would be made this night. Harbor Master Le Collette strolled along the docks and the quay side chatting with the boat captains as they made their preparations, as was his custom.

"Ah, hello, Jacques," he called out as he approached the St. Marianne.

"Monsieur Harbor Master," Antoine acknowledged, politely but cautiously. Rumors that Le Collette played all sides against each other in the deadly game of survival in occupied France made Bouchard suspicious. For his part, Le Collette was certain that Bouchard, as Jacques Charbonneau, was spying for the German authorities. Wasn't it Gerhardt who told him that Charbonneau had been a soldier in the German army in 1918, and a prisoner of the French army? Gerhardt talks too much, he would tell his circle of friends, those who kept a close eye on anyone suspected of collaboration. It was not a coincidence, he would remind them, that the warehouse owner Touland would hire Charbonneau to haul supplies between Courseulles and Caen when needed, and employ him in the warehouse. The Germans paid dearly to stage war material and supplies at his warehouse, and the profits Touland was making marked him as dangerous.

"Where are you off to?" he asked, knowing no fisherman would give him a straight answer, but this casual banter always preceded a general fleet sailing.

"The Channel Islands, most likely," he replied back. Antoine knew that Le Collette would not believe him, but he was not going to follow the fleet despite reports of a large run in the island waters. Instead, he was setting the stage for an absence of several days. He also suspected that if Le Collette was selling or trading information to the Germans, they would want to know if he were going to the Channel Islands. German preparations to hold these strategic islands at the entrance to the English Channel had been extensive, and E-boats from Cherbourg and Brest routinely patrolled the waters. Fishing boats were stopped and searched on a regular basis, and the German command was especially interested in any notice of boats leaving for these waters.

Antoine had been warned to stay away from the Channel Islands by SIS. Operatives planted by the British in the nearby ports provided a steady stream of information on German dispositions in the islands, and they did not want to alert German authorities unnecessarily by expanding observation beyond SIS local control.

"The lock will be open at the evening high tide," he advised, mindful that his own unique position between the local fisherman, merchants, and business owners, the local resistance, and the Germans required him to maintain an apparent good working relationship with all parties.

"What about the morning tide?" Bouchard asked, not really interested in the answer so much as clearing him for being absent until morning.

"I like my sleep, Captain," he laughed. "If you need to offload, you will have to tie off bayside." With that, Le Collette moved on down the line, stopping and chatting with each boat captain in their turn. When he finished his rounds, Le Collette returned to the Harbor office, and picked up the phone.

"Yes. Several boats are planning to head toward the islands," he spoke cautiously, certain that the information was not accurate but was always of interest to the German officials. He knew the E-boat patrols would be alerted, and his job was complete. It was useless information, save for maintaining his credibility.

When the locks opened, the St. Marianne followed the small parade of boats up the narrow channel that led past the shallow beaches and turned west at the marker buoy. When dusk finally gave way to the blackness of night, helped by a cloudy sky that eliminated any moonlight, he slowly moved out of sight of any of the other boats and turned off his running lights. Safely out of range of prying eyes, he turned north and headed for the open channel.

The channel that night was black and deathly still. The St. Marianne motored at half throttle with its running lights off, crisscrossing the rendezvous area in the dead calm sea. Antoine kept looking at his watch as the hands slowly, maddeningly crept toward the half-hour mark. He was exposed out here in the channel, but he knew the German E-boats seldom ventured this far on a routine patrol. Even if they did, they always ran with their searchlights on and their engines could be heard at a great distance, especially on such a quiet night. He had been boarded and searched numerous times and was generally known by the boat commanders as just a local fisherman.

Shortly after 3:30 in the morning, the stillness of the night was broken by the sudden rush of water flowing off of the conning tower and deck of the submarine as it broke the surface - a familiar routine he had reenacted almost monthly since last summer. This time was different, however. Before he had carried only information in his head, never documents.

A powerful searchlight quickly bathed the St. Marianne in its stabbing light, and Antoine knew the submarine's gun was manned and readied for action just in case. He steered toward the sub and throttled back just off the starboard beam as a life raft slid off the side and the men inside began to paddle towards him.

As the small boat came alongside, Antoine tossed the two-man crew a line and snugged the raft close to the hull. One clamored aboard, sidearm at his waist. The second waited in the raft, a young midshipman manning the oars. Antoine and the boarder went below deck.

The cabin was barely illuminated and curtains covered the small cabin windows, keeping the St. Marianne nearly invisible on the dark sea. The two men sat at the galley table and the boarder unfolded a small map of the port of Courseulles. In muted tones, Antoine quickly updated his contact on the status of the gun emplacements at the mouth of the port, the locations of the infantry bivouacs in Graye-sur-Mer, and the critical supply choke points for the movement of munitions and men to the beach defenses - all the locations he had meticulously drawn on his crude map.

The contact refolded the map, slipped it in a waterproof pouch, and returned on deck. He flashed a light in the direction of the submarine, and returned to talk to Antoine.

"E-boat patrols are reported to have been increased, and two new boats were recently added to the patrol out of Le Havre," he explained.

This information alarmed Bouchard, and his contact acknowledged it quickly.

"Hold your position, captain. You will be joined shortly by a tender, and your hold filled with catch … if you are boarded on your return, you will have your proof that you were busy fishing, too busy to bother with the annoying British."

With that he slipped over the side into the raft, and returned to the submarine. As it stood guard, a fishing tender powered through the still night and came alongside the St. Marianne. Bouchard secured the lines, and several deck hands scurried aboard. One opened the hatch as a net full of fish was hoisted out of the tender's hold and moved into position over the St. Marianne. Two more hands guided the net into the vessel's hold and released the load. With a hold full of fish, the illusion was complete. It all seemed a little comical to Bouchard, however necessary.

The tender backed away as its crew released the mooring lines and scrambled back aboard. Once safely away, the ship turned north at full throttle for England. The St. Marianne throttled up its engine and headed south by southwest. Once within two kilometers of the shore, it would turn to traverse the coastline simulating its return from the fishing beds.

Antoine breathed a sigh of relief as he switched the running lights back on. A quick glance back at the empty channel verified the submersion of the sub and the disappearance of the tender, signaling that it was safe to resume normal operations. The curtains were withdrawn and the cabin lights brought back to half-lit, the customary lighting for a vessel underway at night.

As expected, the Le Havre E-boats intercepted him at first light. The boat's captain sounded a loud horn demanding he heave to, and two sailors boarded the St. Marianne. All they found was some bitter coffee on the stove, a smelly French fisherman, and a hold full of fish. Had they been experienced with the fishing trade, they would have seen the net marks on the fish, something that a trawler like the St. Marianne would not have done. But the German navy was full of conscripts from the nearly landlocked Germany, and the inexperienced crew noticed none of these subtle signs.

Come early afternoon, the harbor master simply noticed the St. Marianne tied to the outer quay waiting for the rising tide. The captain was sound asleep on board. Nothing unusual, nothing to note in his security log book.

That night, Antoine wrote his American friend.

> 22 Feb 1944
> Dear Andy,
>
> The meetings at sea are becoming routine. The harbor master suspects nothing, for the tides favor coming and going at night, as does the fishing. The Germans patrol in their E-boats, but the patrols are ineffective.
>
> The E-boat commanders are lazy, and the crews stupid, for there is little to do besides boarding smelly fishing boats.
>
> Everyone knows an invasion is imminent. No one believes it will happen here. I do not think so, either, but I pay for my boat by passing information and filling my hold with British fish.
>
> It is a lot of fuss over nothing, I am certain.
>
> Antoine

The coast of Normandy was cold and blustery that February. The outdoor garden was closed at the Hotel de Paris, and Hauptmann Gerhardt took his afternoon glass of wine and cheese inside the restaurant. Today he was joined by a dour looking police detective from Caen, one of the French police who fronted for the Gestapo coordinating anti-resistance activities throughout the region. The two had a muted conversation at the officer's favorite table, safe from prying ears - or so they thought. Monsieur Racine, the owner of the hotel, made a point of doting over the German colonel to catch as much of the conversation as he could.

"Monsieur Marchand, we have checked out this fisherman carefully. He was a German soldier in 1918 on the Western Front, and served as a prisoner of the French. All these details have been verified."

"So why is he still here in France?" The policeman was naturally suspicious, and doubted the efficacy of the German intelligence.

"He could not return to his home in the Alsace because of French recriminations. The illegal Treaty of Versailles granted him French citizenship, where he would have been driven east out of the Alsace as so many were. This works for our advantage - he appears French, but hates the French, and has allegiances to the Reich. This makes him very useful, in a limited manner."

"I do not trust this double game, and I do not trust this fisherman."

This policeman is a fool, Gerhardt thought to himself. I can use this fool to misdirect attention and take credit for clearing the resistance out of this sector.

"Here he is now. I sent my aide to bring him here."

Antoine entered the Hotel de Paris feeling somewhat uneasy at being seen in such a public place with Gerhardt again.

"Come on over, fisherman. This is Police Lieutenant Marchand of the Calvados department. I want him to hear your report." Gerhardt never referred to Antoine by name, even in his presence.

"I am uncomfortable talking in such a public place, Herr Hauptmann. One never knows who is listening."

"Nonsense, fisherman. We are the only ones here. This is my personal table, and M. Racine is most accommodating to me. You are to make your report, immediately."

"As you wish, Herr Hauptmann."

Gerhardt could not help but think these French are like small children. Show them the rod of authority, and they break to your will so easily.

"There is a cottage on the Caen-Bayeux road, just a kilometer east of the small cemetery. The cottage has a stone chimney in disrepair, and a small barn behind with a portion of the roof gone. The cottage has been abandoned since the last war, but three men meet there once a week. I have been watching them from behind a stone wall."

"And what of their meeting?"

"I have not been able to get close enough to overhear their conversations, and they keep a lookout posted near the door in case anyone approaches. But they meet regularly for about an hour, then leave - each leaving at different times, and each going a different direction.

"So I followed each one separately over three weeks. One man is from Lorient. I verified this from the inn keeper where he is staying. The other is from St. Nazaire, according to the local priest. I provide fish to the church for the poor, and the priest is willing to help me in exchange for the authorities overlooking his trade in brandy."

"Ah, the work of the pious," Gerhardt smirked.

"The other man is local, but I do not know him. I will continue to try to determine his family."

"Is that all, fisherman?"

"Yes, Herr Hauptmann."

"Then you may go."

Antoine quickly left the restaurant, stopping to make sure the way was clear before crossing over to the quay and stepping aboard his boat.

"I will set a team in place to watch this cottage," the policeman offered. He was intrigued most by the where these men came from - ports on the Bay of Biscay with major submarine pens - too convenient to be a coincidence, considering submarine ordinance was routed through Caen by train.

"I will report this to Oberst Deptolla at the Château de Tailleville. I have been ordered to keep him informed of the anti-resistance activities in this area."

This was a lie. Gerhardt actively pursued Oberst Deptolla's favors to feather his own nest even though Deptolla was mostly annoyed by his attentions. When the invasion came, he wanted out of this backwater command, and hoped to leverage his way into a fighting command with information. Having contacts in the Caen Gestapo headquarters could not hurt his chances of securing a front line assignment, he figured.

Aboard the St. Marianne, Antoine wrote another of his letters to Andy Anderson.

> 4 Mar 1944
> Dear Andy,
>
> I have been providing the Germans with false
> information on local resistance activity to learn as
> much as I can about their activities. Hauptmann
> Gerhardt is a fool who is so anxious for a transfer to a
> fighting unit he will believe most anything.

The police in Caen are greedy bastards who wish to please their Gestapo masters - so much so that their reports are exaggerated beyond belief.

Greed and self-interest will be the downfall these arrogant Germans and their accomplices. I am fearful, however, that there are those here who believe I am helping the Germans.

I must remain cautious and diligent.

Keep me in your prayers.

Antoine

"I understand, General. I can make the arrangements immediately," Hauptmann Gerhart promised, and hung up the phone. He barked a command to his orderly, "Get me that fisherman, the one who likes to interrupt my afternoon meal. Quickly!"

In a few minutes the orderly returned with "Jacques Charbonneau" in tow.

"Ah, fisherman," Gerhardt started. "I have need of your boat, right away. You will be compensated, of course. And you fuel tanks filled courtesy of the German army."

"Oui, Herr Hauptmann," he responded. This will be a good opportunity to do some close quarters spying, he thought.

"Good. Be ready to depart within the hour," he demanded.

"But Herr Hauptmann, the tide is low, and the lock is closed. My boat is inside the lock tied to the quay. We must wait until high tide to get the lock opened."

"Leave that to me, fisherman. You be ready to depart as ordered!"

"As you wish, Herr Hauptmann," Bouchard acquiesced, laughing to himself at the German officer's insistence despite the absurdity of it all.

The harbor master was not so accommodating.

"Herr Hauptmann, this is not possible!"

"You wish me to tell General Marcks that you will not cooperate, Harbor Master?" The threat was obvious. General Erich Marcks commanded the LXXXIV Corps. A veteran of many campaigns, he had been instrumental in sparing Paris from bombardment. Unlike many Generals, he believed Normandy would be the primary invasion zone selected by the Allies.

"But to lower the water in the harbor, it is not good. The deep draft boats will mire in the mud. The boats along the quay will all have to be floated free of the pier or their mooring cleats will pull off. This will be sheer chaos, Herr Hauptmann, and the captains will object."

"And I care about that why?" Gerhardt shot back. "You have your orders, Harbor Master, and I suggest you get busy. We leave within the hour," and he dismissed Le Collette by simply ignoring he was even there.

The harbor exploded with frantic activity as water was released through large valves at the bottom of the lock bridge and the level inside the harbor began to drop. Crews swarmed over the boats tied to the quay as mooring lines strained under the unexpected drop in water level, and many were simply cut against the strain. A large fishing schooner listed seriously as its keel went to ground, its hapless crew sitting helplessly by as the mast tangled with the rigging of nearby boats. Angry ships' captains were met by armed German soldiers that streamed into the harbor and took up defensive positions at key points along the docks.

The St. Marianne had been moved to one of the floating piers, and sat with its engine running awaiting Hauptmann Gerhardt. All of this activity was dutifully noted by the friends of the harbor master, who began to doubt his role in all this activity.

After an hour, right on schedule as warned, a German staff officer's car followed by a truck carrying troops pulled alongside the dock. After the soldiers exited and took up their own defensive positions, the doors to the staff car opened and four officers exited, stopping to look around momentarily. They then moved openly and arrogantly down the gang to the dock. The officer in the lead was wearing the heavy cloak and red-striped formal trousers of a German general. The other officers followed attentively. They were met at the St. Marianne by Hauptmann Gerhardt who stood at rigid attention.

"Heil Hitler!" he responded when General Marcks turned toward him.

"Ya, ya," he responded with an indifferent salute and an immediate dismissal. "Is everything ready?"

"Yes, Herr General."

"Good. I wish to depart immediately."

With that the officers who had arrived by car boarded, along with two armed soldiers, and finally Hauptmann Gerhardt. One soldier took a position on the bow, machine gun at the ready, while the other hovered near Bouchard as he backed the St. Marianne from the slip and navigated the shallow harbor and the harbor channel out to the Bay of the Seine. Boat crews and locals simply glared at them as they departed, no one daring to say anything.

"Head two kilometers to sea, then turn east," the General's attaché commanded Bouchard. Antoine simply followed orders, but kept his attention riveted on the casual talk around him. They paralleled the shoreline just beyond the reefs for a while, passing Bernières-sur-Mer and past the opening of the Caen Canal. Bouchard was then ordered to reverse course. The St. Marianne passed the channel entrance to Courseulles and continued west. All the while, the officers were busy pointing out features, especially gun positions. The general questioned them extensively on their preparations.

As the wind increased and the temperature dropped, the officers retired below deck for the trip back to port. Bouchard moved to the inside steering position, and was generally ignored by the party. As a bottle of brandy was opened, the officers examined a large map that one had unfolded for the General, who stood commandingly at the head of the small galley table.

"The enemy will have to bring their tanks and mobile guns ashore using large landing craft. These will be vulnerable to the heavy guns … here, here, and those inland as well. They will never get close to the beach."

"So, Hauptmann Grote, you have been remarkably quiet," the general stated. "What is your opinion?"

Hauptmann Grote commanded the hardened bunkers overlooking the beach at Courseulles and had been invited on the boat trip at the last minute.

"General, I have included in my reports my objection to the installation of the guns. The attitude of fire of the shoreside cannons is too high to allow them to fire on the beach itself."

"General," one of the officers countered, "the attitude of fire has been maximized to destroy the landing craft that will be bringing tanks to the beach while still offshore. That is where they will be most vulnerable. A single direct hit will destroy one of those craft and sink many tanks at once."

"But General," Grote objected, "if the tanks come ashore, both the command bunkers and hardened gun positions will be vulnerable."

The general chuckled. "So, Hauptmann Grote. What do you think the Allies will do? Launch their tanks into the water? Perhaps they will just swim their tanks to the shore? Do you have secret intelligence on a new class of Allied 'U-Panzers?'"

The officers all laughed together at General Marcks' joke at the expense of the embarrassed Grote.

"I have seen enough, gentlemen. This is an unlikely location for heavy armor to be brought ashore in any event. These reefs will make it difficult for large landing craft to operate under heavy fire. You may have many targets to shoot at, but I agree they will remain offshore. We have a shortage of heavy guns, and I won't waste any more here. We have the 21st Panzer Division available to repel any successful shore incursion, and mobile artillery to break up any inland movement. There will be ample mobile reserves if the Allies are foolish enough to invade on this beach."

With that, the inspection party headed back to port. The general's attaché unfolded the map and in the confusion of preparing to disembark, left it momentarily on the steering station console. Antoine quickly stashed it under the galley lazarette. Out of site, it was forgotten, and the officers disembarked the St. Marianne leaving the defensive disposition map behind.

Both Harbor Master Le Collette and Captain Jacques Carbonneau were viewed with an even greater degree of suspicion than ever before by the citizens of Courseulles.

Three men met in the wine cellar of the old chateau. They arrived at different times, from different directions, each stopping to make certain no prying eyes were watching them as they descended the steps and tapped in code on the door. Inside the dark cellar was illuminated by a small oil lantern. The men spread a hand-drawn map out across the floor.

"Here are the choke points," the one with the large mustache said as he marked in pencil on the map. "You can see the telephone wires they have run between the gun emplacements and the command center. They converge at this point," and he made a large circle where the lines converged near a small house next to the bridge linking Graye-sur-Mer with the Caen-Courseulles road. "Blowing this bridge and cutting these lines will isolate the garrison from the command center and prevent its deployment to the east. The reserve mobile guns in Caen and in the new encasements will be stuck on this side of the river."

One of the men with long gray hair had a list of things to check off. The last on the list was a name ... Jacques Charbonneau.

"This one needs to be silenced as soon as the signal is given. I have been watching him. I have personally seen him meeting with Hauptmann Gerhardt at the Hotel de Paris. And yesterday Charbonneau took a small group of officers including General Marcks and Gerhardt out on his boat for the afternoon. He is very friendly with Harbor Master Le Collette as well."

"What do you think he is giving the Germans?"

"He listens to everything, and asks too many questions. His boat comes and goes at odd hours, and none of the local fisherman know anything about him. They do not trust him."

"What do you suggest?"

"André will kill him and Le Collette as soon as the signal is given."

The two others stared intently at the gray haired man.

"Killing men from the commune ... this is serious business."

"It can be done, and appear to be the work of the Germans. Besides, what will it matter? If the invasion fails, all of our lives will be worth nothing."

The man in the mustache nodded his head solemnly.

"If André can do this thing, so be it. But we cannot acknowledge it, or lend support for this. We cannot speak of this again."

The meeting broke up, and the three disappeared into the dark of the Calvados hedgerows.

Police Lieutenant Marchand spent the next several weeks watching the empty cottage on the Caen-Bayeux road with no results. He submitted a report to the head of the Caen Gestapo questioning the motives of Hauptmann Gerhardt and the legitimacy of his informant, a Courseulles fisherman named Jacques Charbonneau.

Gerhardt was transferred to a supply headquarters near Cherbourg, his plans for a fighting command derailed.

The Gestapo made plans to arrest the fisherman.

CHAPTER 20 - THE FINAL MEETING

I would rather walk with a friend in the dark, than alone in the light.
— *Helen Keller*

Joseph Graumann pedaled his bicycle through a hard rain heading westward from the village of Tailleville. Gale force finds pummeled the coast making the ride difficult, wet, and cold. Each morning he would leave the Gefechtsstand, or division command post, at Château de Tailleville and deliver mail and orders. He would pick up routine correspondence from three of the company command posts in this area - Courseulles-sur-Mer, the regular post at Graye-sur-Mer, and the Ost Battalion command post nearby - and return. Other dispatch riders served the company strongpoints at Bernières-sur-Mer, St. Aubin, and other fortified defensive positions in this area.

The Normandy coast was dark at this early hour, an hour before dawn. The moon this morning was obscured by the thick cloud cover and the waves crashed on the beach in a fury. It had been the worst weather this late in the season in recent memory and was not forecasted to improve any time soon.

As the courier pedaled through the port, he could smell the aroma of estuary mud. It was low tide, and where the river flowed into the harbor seaside of the lock it exposed a small falls. Small boats lay stranded on the mud waiting for the next tide to float.

The fishing boats had unloaded their catch and the fresh fish vendors were setting up their tents along the quay. Reefs offshore provided a wide variety of fish and shellfish for the local industry, especially scallops and oysters. German troops, used to meager war rations, would frequent the fish market with what little script they could scrape together. A clandestine system of price fixing ensured they paid a higher price than the residents of the village.

The system of couriers that bicycled between the defensive positions were crucial to the local commanders' communication plans. Because of its small harbor and central location just north and slightly west of Caen and the nearby airfield at Carpiquet, Rommel considered Courseulles a critical defensive position even though Wehrmacht analysts discounted the likelihood of a major assault taking place here. Planners thought the reefs that supported the local fishery would discourage the Allies from landing large ships capable of carrying armor. Nevertheless, it was still a heavily defended position on the northern parts of the Normandy coast. Although the harbor was insufficient for large scale movement of troops, stores, and vehicles, its loss would allow the Allies to secure a stable foothold from which to launch attacks against Caen and Carpiquet, quickly reinforcing troops in a rapidly evolving front.

The Widerstandsnest, strongpoint WN29, overlooked the harbor at Courseulles-sur-Mer. It consisted of three heavily reinforced casements. The H677 enfilade (overlapping chain of fire) bunker was a heavily reinforced concrete cannon position with a protruding fire wall that restricted the exposure to enemy fire coming from anywhere except virtually head on. Limited to a 58 degree field of fire, the formidable 88mm cannon could easily attack any enemy forces offshore that could direct a frontal assault against it. The bunker complex included machine gun nests to sweep the beaches of infantry and vehicles that might be placed ashore.

Two 612 style casements housed 75mm cannons, each with a 60 degree field of fire. Another strong point, designated WN31, contained another 75mm cannon and machine guns as well as two 50mm cannons. The third strongpoint, WN30, was located south of Courseulles near the cemetery and protected the approaches to Graye-sur-Mer immediately inland up the river.

Additional Widerstandsnests were built stretching along both sides of the coast, towards Arromanches to the west, and St. Aubin and Bernières to the east, as well as inland at Beny and Graye. At Mare, a kilometer south of Ver-sur-Mer, the Germans had built four casements with horse-drawn 100mm long range cannons to support the beach defenses. With overlapping fields of fire, any invasion fleet would come under a considerable threat from these hardened defenses, and the beaches would become kill zones for approaching infantry. The key to these formidable defenses would be coordination. Their Achilles heel was the ill-trained, inexperienced static infantry composed largely of Eastern European conscripts, Hitler Jugend, and old soldiers - many compromised by injuries received in battle.

The courier arrived every morning at the same time, just before dawn, and reported to Hauptmann Grote, the company commander at Courseulles. Grote took the dispatch and read it dispassionately.

"More paperwork, Joseph?" he asked the courier, who stood shivering in the early morning dampness of the command bunker. "If only we could fight the war with paperwork, we would defeat the Allies with ease," he remarked, sarcastically. "Ah, something different today, eh, Joseph? A meeting at the chateau. Now that's original."

Joseph Graumann, a mere boy conscripted into service in the Hitler Jugend just after his fourteenth birthday, stood respectfully at attention, grimacing at this backhanded slap at the German command. He still had the spirit of youth, and the full effect of Nazi propaganda fueled a fire of National Socialist zeal. He chafed at the thought of his local commander making fun of command.

After reading the dispatch, he initialed the courier's log book.

Joseph would then wait for dawn, warming himself by the small coal-fired stove, then at the same time every day would continue on his way south of the village to the command headquarters of the Ost Battalion 441, or east battalion, composed mainly of Ukrainian conscripts from the Eastern Front.

Joseph hated this leg of his morning dispatch rounds. The strange language and uncouth demeanor of the foreigners made him nervous. One in particular, wearing the uniform of an Unteroffizier (American sergeant or British corporal), frightened him. He was rumored to have committed unspeakable atrocities towards locals that the German authorities considered partisan. This was a man to fear, a man who craved violence. At age 14, he had sworn to do his duty for the Fatherland, swearing personal allegiance to the Führer, but he could not understand why the great German army needed such trash to do its work. A least he didn't have to go there in the dark.

He was glad to be in and out of the foreign command post at Graye-sur-Mer just south of the port. The ride along the Seulles River had been easier, with the fresh wind coming off the bay and across the open beaches at his back, shielding him from the rain. He cycled back to regimental headquarters at Château de Tailleville and reported to the commandant, Oberst Deptolla.

The strongpoints in and around Courseulles were connected to headquarters by telephones. Wires were strung on temporary poles, trees, and buildings. They were, however, vulnerable to the ever-present Maquissard so were intended mainly for short, emergency communications. Routine communications and written dispatches were always delivered by cycle riders. Radio communications were scarce in this part of the Atlantic Wall, limited to headquarter companies and their command centers, and easy to jam by enemy invaders.

"Do you think it is a good day for an invasion, Joseph?" Deptolla joked easily with his dispatch rider and asked him the same question almost every day. Why do they ask me such things? Joseph asked himself, uneasy at being drawn into such a conversation. "The generals say that Churchill will be visiting us at Calais. I am not so sure. But it would be just my luck if they attacked there, and I spent the rest of the war stuck here, out of the action."

Oberst Deptolla had spent the past winter on the Eastern Front - the "real war" as he called it. The son of a Prussian officer, the men of his family had served Imperial Germany with distinction for generations. Unlike the young officers now transferring into his command, he was classically trained in the arts of warfare. Enthralled by the swift victories in the west, especially the victory over Germany's traditional enemies France and Great Britain, he was equally alarmed by the attack on Russia. A two front war was not winnable. This the general staff officers of OKW understood all too well. But who was there to stand against Hitler? And besides, the Western Front had as of yet failed to materialize. If the East could be stabilized before the allies invaded, perhaps there was hope yet. A stable Eastern Front might open the door to negotiate with the West. After all, was not the Communist menace the real enemy?

In the meantime, he had his duty to perform. If the invasion happened here in Normandy, he would be prepared even if his fellow Wehrmacht officers were not. He commanded a well designed and fortified defensive position, but had limited access to the mobile power of the Panzers. His infantry units were static, and expected to hold their positions at all cost.

He had been seriously wounded by shrapnel in the leg, and walked with a pronounced limp. He could easily serve in this command center where there was little chance of action, so he had been transferred here to command a mix of Hitler Jugend, old and wounded soldiers, fresh trainees, and the Ukrainians. He had dreams of achieving a great battle victory, and wearing the Iron

Cross, but those dreams had faded into obscurity at this post. "My God," he had written to his wife, "I have been relegated to Hell."

He was, nonetheless, a German officer. Despite his sarcasm, he would continue to do his duty. Today was just another day - check the duty rotation roster and review the dispatch orders. After review, they were placed in a dossier under the appropriate heading. At the back of the dossier was a folder with the simple title - Standing Orders Invasion.

Rumors had persisted for many months that the Army Group B commanding general, Field Marshall Rommel himself, had openly quarreled with OberGeneral Von Runstedt over tactics and preparations in case of an attack in the Normandy area. Rommel believed that a quick counterattack to hold the landing force on the beaches in conjunction with massed artillery was the key to defeating the invasion. Von Runstedt, however, favored a more deliberate approach - letting the Allies form on the beach, exposing their heavy equipment and infantry divisions, then defeating them in a broad frontal assault. He had fought with Keitel over the reserve Panzers, now under the direct command of the Führer himself. Unless otherwise ordered, the Panzers would be held for the anticipated assault at Pas de Calais in northern France.

The 21st SS Panzer Division, however, was a different story. Stationed to the north of Caen on a strategic crossroads, the 21st had been moved under Rommel's orders to holding positions near the beach. One of the most important regimental commanders, and an officer Deptolla had served with in Russia, was SS Colonel Kurt Meyer. Meyer was selected to command the young Grenadiers of SS-Panzergrenadier-Regiment 25-personally selected by Hitler to show the success of the Hitler Jugend corps.

Under a general standing order, long forgotten by most front unit commanders, this position meant that individual commanders could order elements of the 21st to assist enemy repulsion efforts in the event of an invasion. Only the SS elements of the 21st were part of the strategic reserves held back by Hitler. To Rommel's thinking, this allowed him to act at least partially to achieve his direct and early assault planning in case the invasion occurred at Normandy. If the main assault did take place at Calais, the 21st would be in position to attack the southern flank of a successful incursion, or repulse an Allied assault on the port of Cherbourg.

Mobility was the key, as Oberst Deptolla knew too well from his experience on the Eastern Front. In the monotonous days and months manning this backwater post he had concocted various scenarios where he was the victor, boldly executing the standing orders while his fellow commanders waited for higher orders, unleashing the firepower of the Panzers, saving the day. Rommel himself would award him the Iron Cross. He had planned his counter strike a thousand times over. I will not fail to act, he boasted, if only to himself.

Today he had ordered his sub-commanders in the area to a meeting at headquarters where he would outline, once again, his tactical plan for the invasion that he hoped would come to Normandy.

Commanding the eastern edge of his command zone at St. Albin and Bernières-sur-Mer was Hauptmann Rudolf Gruter. Like him, Gruter had served in the East, and was experienced. From his gun positions, he could establish overlapping fields of fire with the main gun battery at Courseulles - Hauptmann Grote's position.

To the west was the command center at Tailleville-Tombette. Hauptmann Johann Grzeski was relatively inexperienced, but seemed a capable officer. He had only recently arrived in the battle sector and had yet to take part in Deptolla's regular planning sessions.

South of the seaport was the strongpoint of Graye-sur-Mer/La Rivière under the command of Hauptmann Gustav-Adolf Lutz. Lutz was a competent officer, but like many assigned to the Atlantic Wall defenses he was untrained and untested. Experienced battle veterans were needed on the Eastern Front. The coast defensive fortifications, designed by Albert Speer and implemented by Rommel, would multiply the fighting strength of the ill-trained and inexperienced field soldiers, at least until reinforcements could arrive. At least that was what these officers thought was the general command imperative.

And, of course, there were the Ukrainians from Ost Battalion … the bane of his existence. The presence of non-Aryan soldiers in his command was an insult, and it made him question the very fiber of the OKW command. They were only marginally trained, undisciplined, and a constant source of trouble. I'll send them against the first wave, he chuckled to himself, and be done with them.

They met in the dining room of the chateau that had been converted into a command center with maps of the Courseulles area on every available empty wall space. Daily changes in troop dispositions were recorded and redrawn, along with planned routes of counterattack. As Deptolla reviewed the maps before the briefing he knew despite the bold planning there were no definitive plans for retreat. Such a contingency if even discussed could have resulted in his immediate arrest and execution. So he kept his strategic withdrawal plans to himself, leaving no telltale paper trail to indict him.

His aide ushered his sub-commanders into the room. He invited them to take tea - a small luxury in the middle of this chaos he allowed himself.

"Good morning, gentlemen. Please be seated," he began, standing up before the east wall maps. "For the benefit of Herr

Grzeski, we will review the counter-invasion troop dispositions and counterattack options. It is clear that a high invasion risk period is imminent, so I wish to review and adjust defensive plans as needed while we have the time." He could sense an air of apathy in the room.

Bouchard took advantage of the numerous small jobs that could be found while the fishing boats remained in harbor to move throughput the countryside keeping a close eye on the German preparations. He maintained a low profile, and was seen so often simply ambling along the dirt roads and the hedgerows that few paid him any heed. He was very thorough in tracking the routines of the officers and especially the dispatch couriers. These were the key to disrupting communications should an invasion occur. So he made a point of being seen, and ignored, every day when Josepf Graumann completed his route back from the coast command post to the communications post at Château de Tailleville.

On this day, the weather began to moderate, and Bouchard had received the clandestine signal from the local priest that the British wanted to meet with him again. The submarine meetings had increased in number, so much so that Bouchard was anxious lest he be boarded again.

"This will be the last contact," the young officer told him in the galley of the St. Marianne that evening. "The patrols are increasing, and we have orders to stand down for the time being."

Bouchard gave him the latest defensive updates, including the stolen map left on board earlier, and was preparing to finish the meeting, when the officer laid down a packet wrapped in a brown package. It was heavy, as indicated by the sound it made when hitting the galley table.

"This package has instructions for you. Open these as soon as you move away. Commit the contents to memory then toss the package overboard. It is weighted so it will sink immediately." With that, he slipped back over the gunwale and retreated to the sub. The St. Marianne motored away, the last time he would meet the submarine.

Bouchard set course back towards Courseulles and went below. Under the glow of the cabin lights he read and reread the contents of the package. It told of a British operative who has parachuted into Normandy with sets of false battlefield reports intended to be replaced on the morning of the invasion to disrupt German counterattacks. The operative will contact Bouchard the morning of the invasion if, and only if, the invasion occurred in Normandy. He was to look for the code words 'Little Fish' for verification.

He tossed the package overboard. What absurd nonsense, he thought. A suicide mission if ever there was one. These British are stretching the line very thin.

2 May 1944
Dear Andy,

Am I the only sane person in the world? Or am I insane and falling into Hell?

There will be something happening all around me very soon. Forces are lining up that will upset the very fabric of life itself. I am drawn into it and cannot escape.

I wonder where you are and what your life's challenges are. Am I so bound up in my own troubles that I have forsaken my only friend.

I cannot mail these letters, nor receive any from you. I can only hope all is well.

I hope we can meet again someday, and this chaos will be over. Or perhaps we have to die to achieve peace.

Go with God, my friend.

Antoine

The priest called on Antoine Bouchard on the morning of May 26.

"My son, I have not seen you at mass these many weeks. This distresses me. I expect to see you for confession tomorrow."

"See you for confession." That was the signal. By a prior arrangement, if there was a critical reason why the priest needed to see him, or pass sensitive information, he would chastise Bouchard for not having confession - an innocent admonition in most cases that would go unnoticed in the parish where few of the working rural men attended mass on a regular basis.

At mid-morning the next day, Bouchard entered the small chapel cautiously. Mass had already begun and the rough pews held a few matronly women with small children in tow and a handful of men. Several German soldiers sat off to one side, their usual air of arrogance stifled by the somber atmosphere of the church and the stares from the locals. One of the soldiers was the young Hitler Jugend courier, Joseph. Bouchard slipped into a pew in the back as quietly as he could. It was well known that he provided fish for the priest's sustenance rounds, so no one wondered why he would be attending mass today.

The old priest began by announcing that a visiting priest from Toulon would be helping him with mass and confessions as, he said, "The Lord has blessed me with the infirmities of an old man." Bouchard suspected this was a lie, and chuckled to himself that the old priest would tell a lie in church, even under the circumstances.

As the mass continued, the Toulon priest, a man in his late 30's, quietly moved in the background lighting candles and assisting some of the older worshippers as they came forward for the sacrament. As mass ended, the worshippers milled around in the courtyard waiting for the opportunity to complete their confession. Getting time away from the rigors of rural life was difficult, and many would combine mass and confession on the same day.

Bouchard waited until all the others had completed their confessions, then entered the confessional. He was not surprised to hear the voice of the younger priest on the other side of the screen.

"You received a document recently, with the code 'Little Fish.'" He waited for a reply.

"Yes, I am to assist you, I assume."

"I will remain here at the church during this mission, then return to the coast for extraction."

"What do you want me to do?"

"We know from your reports that a courier carries operational dispatches between Château de Tailleville and the fortified strong points along the coast, especially the forward command post. My assignment is to intercept any dispatch on a specific day, soon, and replace it with a forgery. The purpose is to relay a false set of battlefield conditions if the invasion occurs here."

The invasion … here? He would not be here on such risky mission unless the invasion were imminent. He dared not discuss such a possibility, and he knew he would not get an honest answer anyway, but this was a confirmation. The invasion would be in Normandy, and very soon.

"What do you need me to do?"

"I will accompany you on your rounds for the next several days as we distribute food to the needy. You will show me the routes, the timing, and the individuals I can expect to encounter. If the invasion comes, I will intercept and substitute the fake dispatch. You will not be involved. Nor will you assist in my evacuation, for your own safety. It is best you know as little as possible."

Bouchard knew he had heard enough already. If he were caught, the Gestapo would make quick work of him, to be certain. Showing the young 'priest' around at this time would arouse suspicion, from both the Gestapo and the local maquis. This was a deadly game, which further reinforced his belief that the invasion was imminent.

The following day, Sunday, May 28, Bouchard and the operative masquerading as a priest ambled slowly through the hedgerows of the Normandy coast, talking with the locals, the old men and women who had difficulty making it to church, and recording for the priest the routes. On Monday, May 29, they were walking the road at the junction of the Caen-Bayeux road when the courier Joseph came into view. He stopped his bicycle when he approached the two.

"Good morning, Father," he said, respectfully. Like many Germans, he was raised in a Catholic family, but the teachings of the church conflicted with the Führer ideology. Once removed from the confines of the military training inside Germany, doubt began to creep in as Joseph confronted the brutality of his commanders. Maintaining his tie to the church helped him hold onto some semblance of his humility.

"Good morning, my son," the priest responded in German laced with a heavy French accent. "I saw you at mass. It is good to see that even soldiers have not forgotten God."

The two chatted briefly, then Joseph bade him farewell, feeling better for this chance meeting. But he had a schedule to keep, and promised to see the priest again, soon. The priest decided this junction was where he would set up his ambush. By creating a relationship with the young German courier, he might more easily intercept him without having to kill him first.

On each successive day, the priest made a point of appearing on the road at slightly different locations, and always stopped for a brief hello, regardless of the weather. On Saturday, June 3, the priest took Joseph's confession.

In Caen, the Gestapo chief signed an order calling for the immediate arrest and execution of a suspected Maquisard, Jacques Charbonneau of Courseulles.

That evening, Antoine wrote a letter to his American friend.

> 26 May 1944
> Dear Andy,
>
> I am playing a dangerous game of deception, something much more involved than what I had agreed to. I am certain that an invasion is imminent, and will happen here in Normandy.
>
> I have met with a British agent who is masquerading as a priest. He is part of a plan to disrupt invasion day communications between the beach and headquarters with false battle reports.
>
> This "Little Fish" has a nasty bite.

I am very afraid. I feel like I am being watched, both by the Gestapo and the Maquis. It makes little difference. I have promised to help, to make a stand for Marianne and Ariéle, but I am afraid.

It is so quite here. The weather is terrible, and no one expects any kind of activity at all. The stillness is frightening. It reminds me of the moments before the artillery barrage in the last war, when the only sound was the singing of a lone thrush, just before Hell arrived.

I will continue to write, and I hope someday these letters find their way to you.

Antoine

Present Day

The reporter met me at the Hotel de Paris. She was young and energetic, a common condition among reporters just beginning their careers in small newspapers. The editor of the Caen newspaper, a friend of the mayor of Courseulles, had sent her to talk to me about my investigation. I was not certain that my story had sufficient detail to warrant much consideration, but her enthusiasm was disarming.

"Ah, monsieur, it is a wonderful story! I am certain my editor will agree when he sees the complete outline!"

I had shown her the letters and the outline of the sequence of events I had created so far.

"I am afraid there are more questions here than answers," I apologized. "I have checked all the cemeteries in the area looking for

Antoine's grave, or Jacques Charbonneau, but with no success. I even checked the German cemetery at La Cambe. And I do not know what happened to either Marianne or Arièle. I am currently stuck, going nowhere."

The reporter in her went into high gear.

"But this … this is very compelling. The intrigue, the deception, the danger. It is all folded neatly between the lines of these letters, and it is waiting to be told!"

I gave her a conditional release for the use of the letters, and bade her good luck. I honestly did not expect the meeting to bear fruit.

The following week M. Racine, the proprietor, greeted me with a paper in hand as I arrived for breakfast.

"Monsieur, voila! You have made the newspaper!"

On the front page was a small headline in the lower right corner, "D-Day Deception."

> Courseulles-sur-Mer - A French fisherman and British agents conspired in the final moments before the D-Day invasion to dupe the Germans into believing they had stopped the Canadians on Juno Beach. According to an American researcher, letters written to his grandfather but never mailed were uncovered recently in Courseulles. The Juno Letters tell a story of heroism and intrigue that is unfolding in and around this small seaport.

The story went on to tell of Antoine Bouchard, who lived under an assumed name with false identity papers, and how he led a double life deceiving the Germans and assisting the Allies. It revealed his fear that the resistance might think he was a collaborator, and the resolve he felt to avenge his wife and child, who fell victim to German atrocities.

"The Juno Letters?" M. Racine smiled. "Has a nice ring to it. It sounds good for business!"

The week following, the story appeared in the Paris newspaper, Le Monde, and subsequently in the British tabloids who added their own unique brand of sensationalism to the story. It began to spread on social media.

In Winnipeg, the publisher of The Winnipeg Guardian received an email from one of his associates with the simple subject, "You need to read this ... ."

CHAPTER 21 - JUNE 6, 1944

The art of war is simple enough. Find out where your enemy is. Get at him as soon as you can. Strike him as hard as you can, and keep moving on.
— *Ulysses S. Grant*

"Tell me, Joseph. Do you think the Allies would invade in such a storm?"

The young courier simply stood at attention, and hoped he would not have to respond. The days of June 5, 6, and 7 had been identified by Field Marshall Erwin Rommel as a high invasion-risk period, having the right combination of moon and tides. For weeks the front line units and strong points had prepared for an imminent attack, but with this massive storm there was little chance of an invasion. German weather forecasters predicted no relief for weeks.

Joseph had arrived before daybreak in a driving rain, and huddled close around the small cast iron stove listening to Hauptmann Grote droll on. He was bored, tired of being wet and cold, and hadn't eaten yet. The war seemed far away this stormy morning.

Rommel had returned to Berlin to attend his wife's birthday - and secretly meet with General von Runstedt to urge him to release the Panzers contrary to Hitler's orders if there were an invasion. Even the naval situation report showed a relaxed posture - E-boat patrols would be curtailed during this storm. OKW determined that an invasion would not be feasible until July at the earliest. For now, it was a rare chance to relax.

Grote reached for a cup of hot coffee. Coffee was hard to come by in this remote backwater command. The wine was no better. He knew the French kept the better wine and cheese hidden away, and surrendered a vile swill to the Germans.

"You can relax, Joseph. Even those crazy Americans would not attack from the sea in this storm."

The command area of Widerstandsnest 29 was buffeted by the high winds that whipped through the open gun ports facing the sea and the open entry doorways facing inland. It was nearly impossible to shield oneself from the weather. Hauptmann Grote, Joseph, a communications soldier who manned the phones, and the gun crew spent the dark early morning hours trying to stay dry.

Thunder resonated from the channel and broke over the beaches as the first grays of dawn began to dissolve the darkness.

"That's quite a storm, Joseph," Grote commented. "Look at the flashes of lightening!" He stepped outside for a better look, and found he was almost mesmerized by the incredible flashes of light reflecting under and through the clouds over the horizon. The flashes were followed by rolling thunder. It looked surreal, with the dark gray sea blending seamlessly into the same gray sky. As the squalls abated, and the dawn brightened slightly, a strange silhouette seemed to stretch clear across where the horizon should have been.

Grote stood transfixed, unsure of what he was seeing. The lightening flashed again, this time closer, and in a moment he heard the sound ... a sound he had not heard since leaving the Russian front. It was the unmistakable sound of shells flying nearly as fast as sound, tearing at the air, ripping it apart.

Grote could not believe his own ears, and stared out to sea. The shell screamed overhead, and in an instant a massive explosion rocked the earth on the far side of Graye. Then another, and another. Grote was shocked back to reality, and realized only now that the silhouette shape on the sea was a fleet ... a massive fleet of ships. So many ships that the sea disappeared completely.

The communication officer had thrown himself on the floor at the first explosion.

"Get up!" Grote screamed. "Get up, stupid! Get me headquarters on the phone! Now!"

Shells continued to scream overhead, but landed too far inland to have any effect on the beach. The flashes of heavy naval gunfire continued, unabated, unending. It was like Hell was unleashed.

"I have headquarters!" The communications officer practically threw the receiver at Hauptmann Grote, and retreated back to a corner of the casement for protection.

"Hello, hello! This is Hauptmann Grote, WN29. We are under attack! Repeat, we are under attack!"

Joseph listened in a panic to the one-sided conversation, and could not believe what he was hearing.

"Naval fire! Ships! Hundreds of them! ... It's not thunder, you fool! ... I don't know how many! I can't count them all, you idiot! We are taking heavy fire ... hello? Hello?"

The lines went dead. Smaller shells began exploding all around the casement, and the crew inside sought what little cover they could. The bombardment kept coming, and coming ... then fell silent. Grote took a quick count of his men, then ordered them to their positions.

"Gun crew, prepare to return fire! Joseph, go to the other positions and see if anyone is still alive. If so, tell them to open fire!"

The courier scrambled out of the shelter of the casement. In a few minutes the heavy guns of the shore batteries opened fire on the invasion fleet. The crews had survived the initial bombardment.

Joseph ran back into the command center, breathless.

"Landing craft approaching the beaches!" was all he could gasp out. Almost immediately, the overlapping fields of machine guns and mortars began to belch fire down the beaches. Screaming human voices could be heard over the appalling explosions and machine gun fire. The noise was frightful.

Suddenly, the face of the gunworks was blasted head on by a tank round. It was a sound and explosion Grote had heard a thousand times, but one he was not expecting. Then two more, in quick succession. The last explosion opened a large gap in the front of the gun position and spewed concrete throughout the casement.

"Tank fire!" the gun crews echoed, almost in unison.

"Tanks? That's impossible!" Grote screamed over the din. Large landing craft were still not visible, so there was no way tanks could be ashore.

"Look! There!" The lookout pointed directly in front of their position. On the beach was a tank, one that Grote recognized as an American Sherman. It was preparing to fire on the adjacent casement. In the water, rolling heavily in the swell, was an oddly shaped craft coming ashore, but he could not see what it was. A covering of some type, like a canvas skirting, appeared as the craft rolled ashore. When the canvas dropped, Grote was staring down the muzzle of a Sherman tank's 75mm gun. The tank had swam ashore ... as impossible as that seemed. Grote flashed back on the joke at his expense in the galley of the fishing boat, "You think they will swim them ashore?"

"Do we have phones? Or radio?"

"No! Communications are down!"

"Joseph! Come here!"

Hauptmann Grote hurriedly wrote an urgent dispatch. It read:

Initial bombardment ineffective
Enemy tanks ashore. American Shermans
Some kind of skirt allows them to swim ashore
independently
WN30 out of action. We are taking heavy fire
Requesting 21 P counterattack immediately.

"Take this to headquarters. And hurry! Tell them you have seen these floating tanks. They are real. And they are taking us apart!"

Joseph grabbed the dispatch and stuffed it quickly in his pouch. He ran out of the bunker, ducking at each explosion, and grabbed his bicycle. I will never make it, he feared, but he promised he would die trying.

The bunker was rocked by another blast that ripped apart the protective concrete in front of them. The sound echoed through the casement, a deafening sound. Grote scrambled back to his feet, and screamed, "The telephone ... the telephone!"

Then all was quiet.

It was 4:00 am on June 6. Antoine Bouchard was wakened by a pounding on his door.

"It is Little Fish. Open up!"

Bouchard had spent a long night convulsed in his nightmares, and was slow to rouse. He stumbled to the door, and unlatched it. The British agent pushed his way inside and slammed the door behind him.

"It's beginning!" he gasped, out of breath.

"What's beginning? What are you talking about, man?" Bouchard responded, still half asleep.

"The invasion! Now!"

It was still eerily quiet, as the bombardment had yet to begin. But the agent had received the coded message by radio and was moving into position.

"A bombardment will begin shortly. We need to get into your cellar until it is over, just to be safe!"

The two men squeezed into the small root cellar Antoine had dug in the floor. There was barely room to breathe. It was a short wait. Shells tore overhead as the naval gunfire landed long, and the fields behind the German positions were blasted apart by the explosions. Shrapnel ripped the windows out of the cottage, and nearby concussions blew down the door. Had they been sitting at the cottage table they would have been torn to bits. Then the bombardment stopped.

"Time for me to go!" the agent blurted out, and threw open the crude hatchway, revealing the damaged cottage interior.

Bouchard looked around the remains of his home and cried out, "I am coming with you!"

The agent did not protest, and the two slipped quickly up the small lane and into position near the Caen-Bayeux crossroads, and waited. They could hear the roar of battle on the nearby beaches, the sounds of aircraft overhead, the blasts of heavy guns. Hell had erupted in Normandy.

Shells from the giant armada offshore screamed over the rooftops of Courseulles, landing past their intended targets, destroying civilian homes, and killing French residents of the Calvados. When the Canadian troops finally hit the beach, they had to face murderous fire from the intact hardened defensive positions that should have been destroyed by the naval fire.

Two shells smashed into the local Catholic church. The priest, Antoine's contact with British intelligence and the only person in Courseulles who knew his true allegiance, was killed in the blast.

Joseph managed to get free of the machine guns, mortars, and small arms fire on the beach without incident, and frantically pedaled his bicycle down the road heading for the headquarters unit at Chäteau de Tailleville. As he passed the cutoff to Graye, another boy he knew, another of the Hitler Jugend assigned to courier duty, appeared on his right. He was carrying a small machine pistol, which Joseph did not have.

"I have orders to deliver my satchel to Chäteau de Tailleville, and to shoot anyone trying to stop me!" he gasped, breathless. Joseph decided to join him for protection.

As the two couriers rounded the corner, they approached the crossroads to Tailleville. Bouchard remained on the other side of the hedgerow while the agent jumped out to stop Joseph.

"Joseph, wait," he cried! He was certain that Joseph would stop for him, but was not prepared for the second armed courier. The two boys stopped, and before Joseph could tell his partner this was the priest, the second courier unshouldered the machine pistol and opened fire, following his instructions to shoot anyone that tried to stop him.

The agent was hit immediately with a spray of bullets that ripped into his chest, and threw him back against the hedgerow directly in front of Bouchard. Joseph ran up to him, screaming "He's the priest. Conrad, he's the priest!" It was too late.

The two boys stood over the agent's bloody body. Neither had ever fired at a person before, and they stood shaking in disbelief.

"Conrad, you have killed the priest!"

Conrad looked at Joseph, and threw the machine pistol to the ground, his hands still shaking. Seeing this, Antoine sprang from his hiding place on the other side of the hedgerow and pounced on the gun. With a short burst of fire, both boys fell to the ground. Bouchard grabbed the dispatch parcel from Joseph, struggling to continue breathing, then reached inside the coat of the agent and took out the envelope that held the forged document. He grabbed the three bodies one by one and dumped them on the other side of the hedgerow. He then threw the bicycles into the ditch and headed back to his cottage, his heart pounding.

What should he do now? The agent was dead, the courier dead. How important is this thing anyway? He decided to look at what was in the dead courier's packet before he decided what to do.

The second courier's bag contained some battlefield intelligence and a status report but nothing that appeared important. He pulled the papers from the other bag and found what he was seeking - the situation report from WN29, the forward command bunker. As he read the request for the 21st Panzer counterattack, he knew he had to act. On behalf of his France, his Marianne and Ariéle, he had to make one last sacrifice. The original situation report was thrown into the fire and he placed the dead agent's forgery, still in its sealed envelope, into the bag.

He wrote one last letter to his friend, Andy. He knew this could very well be his last letter. He wrote in a hurry, in a shaky hand, realizing he had little time:

6 Jun 1944
My Dear Andy,

This will be my last letter, for I will die this day, I am
certain of it. I wish only to be remembered as a
patriot, but that cannot be.

Pray for me. You are my only friend.

Antoine

He opened the lid to the tin box that held his precious letters, and
placed this last one inside carefully before closing the lid. He slipped
the box back into its hiding place and replaced the brick covering it.
He then backtracked to the spot where he had stashed the bicycles
and climbed aboard, pedaling furiously towards the Chateau,
uncertain just what he would do once he arrived.

The ground was flat and at this early stage relatively
unencumbered. As he hurried through the bocage, he could hear
scattered gun fire all around him as paratroopers that dropped into
the region at dawn engaged scattered German units.

Finally, the chateau came into view. He heard "Halt!" and was
stopped immediately by two German soldiers standing sentry duty.

"I am Jacques Charbonneau, a soldier of the Great War for
Germany. I have a dispatch from the beach!"

"And how did you get this?" one soldier demanded.

"The courier, he was killed by a shell blast just outside my home.
I grabbed the bag and came here with it."

The sentry saw that the courier bag was official, and pointed his
rifle at Bouchard, motioning him toward the door of the chateau.
Inside was a scene of complete chaos.

"Who is this?" an officer demanded. "What is he doing here?"

"He has the courier bag from WN29. He says the courier was killed by a shell blast," the sentry reported standing at attention.

"Do I know you?" the officer asked, staring intently at Antoine.

"No, Herr Oberst. But I often assisted Hauptmann Gerhardt in certain … matters of interest," Bouchard was careful to not elaborate.

"Ah, yes, I remember him speaking of you. A fisherman, and a former German soldier as I remember the conversation. How did you come by this, fisherman?"

"The courier would pedal past by my cottage every day. He and I became friends. This morning as he passed by there was a shell that hit near the road, and Joseph was hit. I came out to see what had happened, and he told me this had to be taken to the chateau, that it was urgent."

"Did you read the dispatch?" The colonel began to open the bag and saw that the situation dispatch was in a sealed envelope.

"No, Herr Oberst. I simply grabbed the bag and hurried here."

"And what of the courier?"

"He did not live very long after, Herr Oberst."

"I see. Well, it looks like everything is in order. The Fatherland thanks you again for your service, fisherman. I suggest you find a safe hole to crawl into until we repel these invaders. Dismissed."

With that Antoine was ushered back outside and warned again to take refuge. The officer opened the satchel and unsealed the envelope. His face brightened as he read the dispatch.

"Get me WN29 on the phone to confirm!" he ordered.

"I am sorry, Herr Oberst, the phone communications are still disrupted."

"Radio, then!"

"We have no radio contact with the beaches, Herr Oberst."

"Damn Maquis! If I were running the security here, things would be different! Get me Caen headquarters, immediately!"

A call was placed to the battalion headquarters at Caen where telephone communications were still open.

"Yes, this is Oberst Deptolla. I have a report from the beach at Courseulles ... yes, General. It says,

> Initial naval bombardment ineffective.
> Taking small arms and mortar fire.
> Successfully repelled armor carrying landing craft.
> Casualties light.
> Enemy casualties heavy.
> Evacuations from the beach beginning."

Oberst Deptolla waited for instructions from headquarters.

"Yes, sir, we will be ready."

As the Canadian Royal Winnipeg Rifles and Regina Rifles overran the beach defenses and swept through Courseulles, and the Canadian Scottish secured Bernières-sur-Mer just to the east opening the harbor to Allied transports, General Richter at his Caen headquarters was reviewing the situation map.

"Reports indicate that the center of this sector at Courseulles is holding, and has inflicted heavy casualties. The invasion there has faltered. Here to the east, paratroopers have taken the bridge over the Caen Canal, and threaten our flank. We cannot mount a counterattack towards Arromanches until that threat is cleared. I am ordering the 21st Panzer Division to proceed here, towards Haut Lion. Once the flanking threat is passed, we will advance on Arromanches and destroy the Allied invasion on the beaches."

By afternoon, Colonel Kurt Meyer had ordered his armor forward into a hornet's nest of paratroopers, but found few hard targets to engage. Stymied, he eventually withdrew to prepare for the westward counterattack that never came.

By this time, Canadian forces had landed more than 3,200 vehicles and 21,500 troops on Juno Beach, and had established the largest bridgehead of the invasion. By nightfall the Canadians held positions near Carpiquet on the Caen-Bayeux road, and the Germans had lost the opportunity to counterattack.

A man in a rumpled coat and a scarf pulled up over his face burst into the office of the harbor master as Le Collette was frantically trying to make contact with the local military command headquarters. Shots rang out, and Le Collette fell to the floor. In the chaos of the bombardment, no one noticed the rumpled man hurrying through the streets away from the port.

Antoine Bouchard was not certain if his efforts had succeeded, if the ruse was complete. He moved carefully back down the narrow road toward the safety of his cottage root cellar, watching for any sign of danger. Scattered firefights erupted all around him, although he had yet to see any of the combatants.

As he approached a sharp turn in the road, two men stepped out from behind the trees and leveled their weapons at him.

"Halt!" was all he heard, and his world went spinning. What had happened? Had he been shot? His senses were blurring. He could see the faces of the two men standing over him as one reached down and snatched the gold cross from around his neck.

The last thing he saw was the face of his beautiful Marianne, calling to him.

"Come back to me, Antoine. Come back to me."

CHAPTER 22 - THE GUARDIAN

In a time of deceit telling the truth is a revolutionary act.
— *George Orwell*

Present Day

The story in the Caen newspaper started the emails and letters flowing. Most were from people curious for more information. Since I had reached somewhat of a roadblock in my investigation, I took the time to answer as many as I could. After a morning of email writing, a tedious and repetitive task that was yielding no new information at all, I gave up in exasperation and decided to take a stroll down the beach toward Bernières to clear my thinking.

The small package was waiting at the front desk of my hotel when I returned. Monsieur Racine, the hotel manager, called to me as I passed by the concierge desk to bring it to my attention. It was addressed only as "M. Hewitt," and there was no indication who left it.

"I do not know, monsieur. It was left at the front door when I arrived. I am sorry, but I have no idea where it came from."

"Merci, monsieur," I remarked.

"You would like café, monsieur?"

"Oui. That would be fine. May I take it in the dining room?"

"Of course, monsieur. Lunch will not be for an hour or more, so you will not be disturbed."

Monsieur Racine was, above all, a strident advocate of his guests' privacy. I took a seat at my table near the window. The waitress brought me coffee and a croissant.

"Are you enjoying your notoriety, monsieur?" she asked, teasingly.

"Ah, Monique, I am! I love the senseless busy work! Especially when it gives me a reason to stay here and visit with you!"

She smiled, accustomed by now to my harmless flirting, and left me to my mysterious package.

I opened the mailing packet and withdrew two envelopes. The first was unsealed, and contained a handwritten note. It simply read,

R 1278; La Cambe

La Cambe was the German cemetery near Bayeux, just a few kilometers west. Initially, many American soldiers killed in Normandy were interred there, but these had mostly been removed and returned to the states or reinterred in the American Cemetery at Colleville-sur-Mer overlooking Omaha Beach. La Cambe became the official German cemetery after the war.

I had already searched the grave registration for La Cambe with no results. The number of "unknowns" buried on the grounds, however, meant that my search was incomplete. Was this a grave registry number? I wondered just what it meant. Another misdirection?

I took a long draw from the coffee cup, and set the cup back on the saucer.

The second envelope was sealed. I opened it and removed a small gold cross and chain. I turned the cross over in my hands, and read an inscription on the back side:

To Henry from Father

I stood and stared at the inscription. Henry - Henry Anderson. To my grandfather from his father. I was stunned, and simply stared at the cross, rolling it so slightly between my fingers. This was the cross mentioned in the letters!

The sounds of the dining room, of the busy dock outside, of the traffic passing by - all melted away into a faint haze. Monique returned to refresh my coffee and broke the spell it had cast.

"Monsieur, are you all right?" she asked, her voice questioning.

"Oh, yes. Yes," I stumbled. "Je régrete, mademoiselle. I was just a little distracted."

She refilled the cup, and walked away. She stopped and turned, and looked inquisitively at me. I just smiled and nodded a "thank you," and she left for the kitchen.

I was unsure what this meant. What was Grandpa Andy's cross doing here?

My head was spinning. Someone had this cross. No, someone had taken this cross. That someone was returning the cross. Had they seen the news stories? Did they know something? A secret they did not want revealed, perhaps, but wanted to be rid of?

Registry #1278, La Cambe. A grave this person knows about. Who is buried in grave 1278? The person who owned this cross? Antoine Bouchard? Could it be?

I gathered up my things and left in a hurry. I knew Monsieur Racine would simply charge the coffee to my room.

I took the car and drove to La Cambe Cemetery - a short drive away. The cemetery office was still open, and the administrator, whom I had visited before, was eager to help me.

"So, monsieur, you have more information?"

"Oui. I have a very strong reason to believe that the person I am searching for is buried in grave number 1278."

"Vraiment? Let's see," and he took me back into the archives. In a catalog file, he pulled out the drawer "1001-1499" and sought out record 1278.

"Voila!" he called out, and removed a 3X5 card. "Let's see, there are six soldiers buried in grave number 1278 - this was the custom, you see, to place many bodies in a single grave. There were so many, and frankly, not a great deal of sympathy for laying the German dead. Many at the time felt they were lucky to be buried at all."

Six? My heart stopped a little at that piece of information. He continued.

"Let's see. Five of the bodies are clearly identified by their Wehrmacht registry numbers. Each will have an identification tag attached to the shroud, in case there was an opportunity to reinter them later. The last one, the top one in the grave, is unidentified. It simply says, "1278-1; Identification-Unknown, C-F.""

"What does that mean? "Unknown, C-F?"

"Why, monsieur. An unknown civilian - French, of course!"

"A French civilian - in the German soldier's cemetery?"

"That would be very odd, monsieur, given the sentiment at the time."

"I don't think so. Frankly, that explains a lot."

"Good morning, Larry. I am so glad to meet you!" The voice boomed over the din of the busy bistro.

"Angus McDonough," I responded as I rose and shook his hand. "My pleasure. What can I order for you?"

"Oh, a pint of that ale you have would do just fine!"

Angus McDonough looked every bit the part of a slightly eccentric Scot, complete with his kilt, a long twisted mustache, and plaid cap. The cap had a pin slightly off center - the official insignia of the Winnipeg Rifles. He walked with a swagger that was as loud as his hello. I motioned to the waiter for another glass of beer that arrived quickly as we completed the small talk.

"Ah, that is better," he sighed after taking in a deep drink. "The swill they sell you on the airplane is enough to make a good Scot turn to tea!" He reached down and lifted up a small valise, dropped it on the table, and unsnapped the latches.

I had received a phone call from the secretary of the Royal Winnipeg Rifles Association after the first newspaper story was published in Canada. The association suggested a meeting with Angus McDonough, the group's official historian who had a wealth of information on the Juno Beach story. He was already on a plane to France and would contact me on his arrival.

He listened intently to my narrative on a preliminary phone call, and promised to share some of his research at our meeting.

"Now, let me show you what I have, and what is more important what I have found since reading *The Juno Letters* story." He pulled a stack of papers from the briefcase and dropped them with a thud on the table top.

"As I explained on the phone, I have been the official historian of the Winnipeg Rifles for about twenty years now. I have collected reams of documents, recollections, and various memorabilia over the years. My passion had been to recreate the stories of the Juno invasion, to preserve for posterity the sacrifice made by my brothers in arms on that magnificent day. You have provided me with an interesting solution to one of my biggest mysteries."

He turned to a photograph of Kurt Meyer, the infamous division commander of the 21st Panzers, and the architect of the notorious killing of Canadian POWs at Abbey Ardennes near Caen just after D-Day.

"The big question was always why Kurt Meyer, one of Hitler's most feared and capable panzer commanders, sent his advance mobile elements into the hornet's nest of paratroopers east of Bernières-sur-Mer instead of Courseulles where the armor came ashore. The panzers certainly crated havoc for the paratroopers, but in a swarm of bees, even the biggest fly swatter is the wrong tool.

"We know that Allied planners developed the most complex system of subterfuge ever devised to precede D-Day and disguise Allied intentions. The goal was to convince the German high command that the main attack would come at the Pas de Calais. This is well known, of course. Keeping the main body of panzers out of action during the critical first days was paramount. But the 21st was already in Caen, and it was not hamstrung by requiring Hitler's personal order before engaging. It was late in mobilizing and even then was sent into a sector where it had little effect the afternoon of the invasion. It then retreated and set up a defensive position near Caen where it created a formidable barrier to taking the city.

"The question has always been why it was not sent against the main body and the armor coming ashore."

Angus McDonough grew more excited as he continued his story.

"I've never been able to piece the entire picture together. So I have never published this. What I have always wondered is why no one ever came forward to claim responsibility - and credit - for a masterful bit of subterfuge."

He turned the photo of Meyer over, and underneath lay an old and faded document in German.

"Look here," he said, and passed the document to me to examine. "This is the German dispatch that I found in a collection of documents that Canadian infantry recovered from the Abbey Ardennes, the area headquarters. It is this document that kindled my search these past years for an answer to this puzzle."

I examined the dispatch. It was dated 6/6/1944. 0800 hours. The paper was yellowed, and it had been folded several times, indicating it likely was read and changed hands with each new fold. I could not read the German, so I turned to the translation that Angus pushed toward me as I read.

> Initial naval bombardment ineffective.
> Taking small arms and mortar fire.
> Successfully repelled armor carrying landing craft.
> Casualties light.
> Enemy casualties heavy.
> Evacuations from the beach beginning.

"But this is nonsense. The initial bombardment was relatively ineffective, that is true. But the rest ... why would they send such a dispatch?"

"Indeed, why? It is signed by the Widerstandsnest 29 commander, Hauptmann Grote. This is his signature. Or so I thought, all these years."

"What do you mean, so you thought?"

Angus took another deep drink from the glass and motioned to the waiter for another round.

"I never found anything to dispute the authenticity of this document. The paper was right, the dating was correct, the signature looked authentic. It was found among an entire trove of documents by the infantry on D-Day plus 5, not supplied at some future date by an impostor - which happens often by the way. But it made no sense. German commanders often falsified reports that would have otherwise brought bad news, and exaggerated good news. But something so desperate as the invasion, what use would it have been to misrepresent such an obvious and dangerous situation?

"Something in the newspaper story struck a chord. When I read the part how Antoine talked about misleading the Germans on D-Day, as alluded to in the 'Letters,' I was stunned. I went back through pages and pages of my notes, and stumbled across a notation I had made a long time ago ..." and he stopped to pull out a journal with a page bookmarked. It read in large almost doodling script: "Was this a hoax?"

"Here was confirmation that an 'intelligence operative' was serving at the direction of SIS, something that had never been postulated before. We of course knew there was resistance activity - the OCM had a cell in Caen. That was well known, but no one who survived the war had any knowledge of such an operative. It was not until I read the part of the submariner that it made sense, but just had to be proven. This document was a carefully planned forgery, planted somehow on D-Day to mislead the German command and send the 21st somewhere else, anywhere else, but to the landing beaches at Courseulles. But how to prove it?"

The second beer arrived, and just as quickly disappeared during a long pause in his story.

"I began to dig. I had made a mistake - a big one. As a historian I always believe the truth lived in the details. But I was mislead, because this detail, this 'obvious' original document was, in fact, a forgery. Look what I found."

He opened a file folder that he had deliberately left closed until now. On the top of the file sat a photocopy, marked "TOP SECRET - SIS EYES ONLY." It was an exact duplicate of the original dispatch, except the signature, although the same name and scrawl, was slightly different from the original - different because this was a second original dispatch, complete with its own forged signature.

"My God," I gasped. "It was a fake all along!"

"Planted by SIS. And this copy was suitable for distribution if the original fell afoul of circumstances. And there is more … ."

Attached to the photocopy of the second dispatch was an operational report of "Little Fish," the code name for an operation where a fake battle dispatch was to be delivered to an operative parachuted into Normandy. The operative, code named "Little Fish," would attempt to meet with "AB" and with his help intercept the ground delivered dispatch, made necessary by the communication disruption on the morning of the invasion by the OCM, and substitute this fake dispatch. The intent was to provide false battlefield intelligence, and permit German headquarters to release elements of the 21st to attack - but not at Courseulles, where the battle was reported to have gone as planned for the Germans.

"AB" was the same designation SIS used for Antoine Bouchard when they requisitioned his false identity papers! It was safe to use his real initials because no one knew an Antoine Bouchard - as far as the Germans and the French knew, Antoine Bouchard had been lost at sea.

In a letter to Andy Anderson, Antoine had referred to the operative as this "Little Fish" with a nasty bite.

"There's more," Angus continued. "With the help of friends in the British press, we were able to uncover the identity of the British operative 'Little Fish.' He was Leftenant Robert Carlson, who parachuted into Normandy in late May. He made contact with the resistance cell in Caen, then nothing else was heard from him. His body was recovered June 7 alongside a back road outside of Graye-sur-Mer. His death was attributed to enemy action."

I stared at the report, trying to absorb the implications held between the lines - for Antoine, and for the Canadians coming ashore that terrible morning.

"We don't know exactly what happened, except that the phony dispatch was delivered to the German commander in the area. Look at his situation report for the afternoon of June 6."

Angus laid down another photocopy of a memo, this one indicating the enemy had been repulsed at Courseulles, securing the sector center, and calling for armored reserves to be sent towards the canal bridge to the east to prevent an encirclement by airborne troops in the area, ultimately allowing a counterattack in force toward Arromanches once the east flank was secured.

"The ruse worked! This is the proof! You have solved my twenty-year puzzle, my American friend!" I looked up at a broad smile on Angus' face, his eyes bristling with excitement.

"Angus, you have solved the puzzle for me as well. I have proof now that Antoine was a hero for France - the patriot as he desperately wanted to be remembered."

I told him of the gold cross, the grave at Le Combe, and what I suspected.

"He was not a collaborator. But he was dumped into a common German grave by those who believed he was, and whose most treasured keepsake - my grandfather's gold cross - was stolen from him in death."

Angus scribbled some notes as I spoke, then continued with his narrative.

"The critical period was the first hour or two after the end of the naval bombardment. As you know, the naval bombardment was ineffective. The shells fell mostly long or short and failed to destroy the hardened strongpoints. They killed a large number of civilians and destroyed many homes and buildings in the area, but did disrupt communications and infrastructure. The shore guns remained operational, however, and opened fire on the naval armada. The hardened caseworks provided sufficient protection for the guns and their crews. "When the infantry hit the beach they were met with a murderous crossfire. Units were broken up and reformed in an ad hoc manner as soldiers improvised and fought their way inland. Stories from survivors retell the individual acts of bravery as men rushed the machine gun nests and strongpoints to neutralize the fire.

"The infantry was to have also been helped by close air support. This did not materialize. The third leg of the support triad was armor - the amphibious or duplex tanks.

"The Germans did not know about the amphibious tanks, and never considered that individual tanks could make it ashore but would have to be offloaded from large landing craft. Their casework guns were built for long range and could not lower their attitude of fire sufficiently to hit the tanks once on shore.

"Of the nineteen duplex drive tanks that headed towards the shore at Courseulles, only fourteen made it to the beach. The others sank because of heavy swell or succumbed to fire offshore. Those tanks, however, immediately opened fire - destroying machine gun nests and the remaining large guns.

"No one knows when the information about the amphibious tanks reached headquarters or how high up the chain of command the information went. But two things are clear - the standing orders of the day permitted the commander to order a counterattack by elements of the 21st Panzers, but the German command did not respond to the tanks on shore. They missed the opportunity to repel the invasion.

"Had the 21st Panzer division attacked the beaches on the morning of D-Day at Courseulles, the two amphibious Shermans that made it ashore would have been easily destroyed. The hardened positions and the big guns would have remained operational, and the invasion here might have collapsed. Even assuming that the soldiers on the beach could carry out their destruction alone, hundreds more

Canadians, perhaps thousands, would have died on the beaches and the carnage at sea could have been catastrophic.

"As it was, by the time the 21st began to move back from the aborted eastern attack, we had landed some 3,200 vehicles and 21,500 troops on Juno Beach, liberated Courseulles and Bernières-sur-Mer, and secured the port as the first major beachhead on D-Day."

I sat back and took a deep breath. This chance meeting, triggered by the junior reporter's story, had turned the corner of the investigation in a whirlwind of information.

"The Winnipeg Rifles, indeed all of Canada, owe a debt of gratitude to Antoine Bouchard for the part he played and his sacrifice on D-Day. He helped buy critical time that closed the window of opportunity for the German counterattack. We lost 349 brothers on Juno Beach that morning - it could have been a lot worse.

"You have a marvelous ending to your story, my friend. And I have the missing piece that will allow me to publish this story after all these years. What do you plan to do now?"

"I am not sure," I replied, still trying to bring all this into focus. "I still do not know what happened to Marianne or Ariéle. But I know one thing. Antoine deserves a better legacy, and a better burial, than what he was given."

"I can guarantee you," Angus replied, looking intently at me, "this will resonate among the survivors of Juno Beach, their families, and the families of those who died at Courseulles. We are well connected politically and can move obstacles for you if we need to. What do you need from me?"

The outer lobby of the editor of The Winnipeg Free Guardian intimidated me slightly as I sat waiting for my appointment. I was not clear about why the editor of Winnipeg's largest newspaper wanted to meet with me, but I had a hunch Angus McDonough had something to do with it. So I arranged to fly to Winnipeg as the first leg of my return home. I had been away a long time and had business that needed attending.

I had walked the short distance from my hotel to the newspaper offices and arrived early, which is my habit, and now sat fidgeting wondering just why I was here. The editor's receptionist was very professional and avoided any small talk, so I just sat, waiting. My appointment had been for 11:00. It was now past 11:30.

The door to a side conference room finally opened and Thomas Clarendon, the paper's editor, strode briskly out into the lobby and extended his hand.

"Larry, welcome. I am so sorry to keep you waiting." He grasped my hand firmly and literally pulled me in close, a little closer than my American sense of personal space liked. But after spending as much time in Paris as I had where there is no personal space to speak of, I took this all in stride.

"My staff and I wanted to have this whole project all spec'd out before we met, but the news is a demanding mistress! I hope you will bear with us on this."

"Certainly, Mr. Clarendon."

"Call me Tom," he boomed out. He was a large man, and I can imagine a young reporter would be very intimidated by his commanding presence. "No formalities here! Come in, please." As I entered the conference room, the table was filled with staff, files, and iPads. The staff was here to work.

"Everyone, this is Larry Hewitt. Let me go around the table briefly ..." and he went through a series of introductions. When he got to the end of the table, I was looking into the broadly smiling face of Angus McDonough. He was dressed in a tailored suit and tie, what appeared to be an expensive one at that - quite a different look than I was used to.

"And you know Angus McDonough, of course."

"Yes, I just don't recognize him in a suit!"

The little joke just fell on the floor and sat there - the staff looked at each other nervously. It was Tom who broke the spell.

"Hah!" he boomed out. "So I suspect you've seen him in his kilt? Not the best legs in town, to be sure."

Angus smiled and chuckled to himself, obviously pleased that the staff was unsettled on his account.

"Please, you sit here, and we'll get under way."

"Thomas, I think I need to bring my friend Larry up to speed with what we've been up to. He has been traveling, and I have been moving a little faster than my ability to communicate with these new gizmos," he added as he pushed his iPad away.

"Very well, Angus. You take the lead."

As he stood up, Angus McDonough showed very quickly he was used to commanding such a gathering. He spoke in a clear and forceful manner, unlike the Angus who engaged in such lively give-and-take with me before. The staff was riveted on his presentation, and I wondered what his relationship with the paper was. There was much of this man I did not know, obviously.

"You have all read the briefs, so I will not elaborate on the details except to say that the story of *The Juno Letters* is a compelling one that reaches out across several generations of Canadians spotlighting one of our country's most important moments - the invasion of Juno Beach on D-Day."

"The Juno Letters?" I interjected. Again, the staff reacted like this was someone who you did not interrupt.

"That's what we're calling the piece," the editor chimed in.

The blank look on my face gave away my confusion.

"Larry, lad. You obviously haven't got a clue what I'm talking about," Angus laughed, and the tension among the staff began to wane slightly. He continued.

"We're going to do a series of articles on the story of Antoine Bouchard, the letters, and what happened on D-Day. I am setting up a nonprofit to raise the funds to reinter Bouchard in an appropriate place, and we can leverage the publicity to pressure the local French officials to approve the reinterment. I am calling the piece *The Juno Letters*. It will be written by Shelly and Mark over there, and they will collaborate with you on content. We have the contract all ready - we can go over it when we break for lunch."

Tom Clarendon joined the conversation.

"We will be asking for the copy rights, of course, and will compensate you accordingly. You will still have publishing rights under the agreement if you choose to produce a book on the subject. It's all spelled out in the agreement, and I think you will be pleased with how Angus put this together."

Things were moving very quickly, and Angus could sense I was still a little unclear what was happening.

"Tom, perhaps we should go to lunch and let these people finish their preliminary work for the afternoon session. I need to bring my friend up to speed on a few things anyway."

"Fine. Why don't you and Larry head to lunch and I will join you in a few minutes?"

In the elevator, Angus began to fill in some details.

"You have some questions, I am certain."

"Just a couple, Angus. You kept referring to 'we' in there. Do you work for the newspaper? I thought you said you were a businessman."

"And a newspaper is not a business?" he laughed. "No, I don't work for the paper." He looked intently at me and his eyes narrowed. "I own the newspaper!"

That little piece of news left me speechless. Angus just laughed.

"I told you I was connected," he teased.

"Well, that explains why the staff looked like they were sitting on corncobs," I added.

"Hah, that's a good one!" he laughed. "These people I want you to work with. They are the best we have. I know we can put out a story that will be read throughout Canada, and will carry over to the world press as well. This paper is connected to all the major services, and I have already spoken with our representatives on the continent about getting collateral coverage in the major newspapers in our service group."

The elevator stopped and we strode out of the lobby and into the street.

"My favorite restaurant is just around the corner," he said, and took off at a brisk pace. "Tom is a good man, and I have made it very clear to him that this project is important. I generally don't interfere much in the editorial side of the paper, but this one is near and dear to me."

"Here we are," he announced, and we entered a small pub just around the corner. I was expecting something a lot fancier, and told him so.

"No, not for me," Angus explained. "I came from a working family, not some fancy highbrows. I get enough of that crap as it is. It's a pint and fish and chips for me any day!"

The Winnipeg Guardian would publish the first installment of *The Juno Letters*, a six-part feature, in early spring, Angus explained. The political leverage would be strongest immediately afterwards, but would fade with time. Everything needed to be coordinated to come together by June 6 - the day he planned to have a memorial service in Courseulles-sur-Mer for Antoine Bouchard.

"The project plan is quite specific. The paper will also staff the nonprofit and we will use the Guardian's resources to help with the fundraising. Tom has assigned Jennifer Sinclair to lead the project team - she is a powerhouse player, and I have special access to her. She is joining us for lunch ... in fact, here's Tom and Jenny now."

A very professional and attractive woman walked through the door with Tom Clarendon and strode confidently up to Angus. He gave her a big hug and a kiss.

"Hi, dad," she beamed, and turned to me. "You must be dad's friend, Larry. I'm Jenny."

This man Angus McDonough was full of surprises.

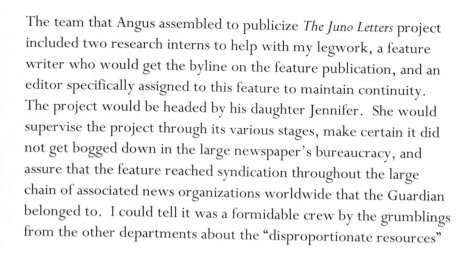

The team that Angus assembled to publicize *The Juno Letters* project included two research interns to help with my legwork, a feature writer who would get the byline on the feature publication, and an editor specifically assigned to this feature to maintain continuity. The project would be headed by his daughter Jennifer. She would supervise the project through its various stages, make certain it did not get bogged down in the large newspaper's bureaucracy, and assure that the feature reached syndication throughout the large chain of associated news organizations worldwide that the Guardian belonged to. I could tell it was a formidable crew by the grumblings from the other departments about the "disproportionate resources"

assigned to the story. Having the owner as your patron had its advantages.

Jennifer opened the first of the editorial meetings with an enthusiastic promise.

"*The Juno Letters* story will create its own traction to help the research assistants wrap up some of the loose ends, this we can be certain of. As long as we can get the French affiliates to participate."

"What are some of the challenges to getting their cooperation?" Tom Phillips, the project editor, brought up a critical point in the politics of historical exposure - some things are better left buried, according to those most affected through history or culture.

"I have experienced many levels of resistance during the research, mostly at the bureaucratic level, but sometimes among the locals in and around the Calvados region. The entire issue of French collaboration and cooperation with the German occupation is still very sensitive. For some it was simply an issue of practical survival. The French army had been routed, Paris declared an open city to avoid its destruction, and the countryside occupied very quickly. Despite the limited troop presence in police and administrative positions, one cannot dismiss the strong likelihood of military reprisals, and extreme ones at that. Despite this, it is also clear that people took advantage of the oppressive administration to settle old scores, and ramp up secular nationalism, such as the resurgence of Breton independence that sided with the Germans, only to be shunted aside when Vichy proved to be a valuable ally to Germany in the occupation."

"How organized was the resistance in the Normandy area?"

"That's a difficult topic to distill down to a simple answer. It is true that resistance organizations sprang up almost as soon as the country signed the armistice, but they were not well coordinated. It was not until later in the war that they began to work in any form or organized fashion. Most of the people who joined the resistance did so in an independent manner, often local cells operating alone, and these after the Germans implemented a policy of forced labor conscription. The popular notion of a general organized uprising is a myth.

"The British secret service created special teams, called Jedburgs, to help organized resistance cells in various areas of occupied France, with varying degrees of success. And we know that Antoine Bouchard almost accidentally became involved with the resistance when he transported the infamous Colonel Remy, Michel Gireau, to England with the map of the Atlantic Wall.

"We also know that Antoine, running the St. Marianne as the boat was now called, regularly passed information to the British via submarine rendezvous in the channel. The is no indication anywhere, however, that this was a coordinated operation with other resistance units. Quite the opposite. I believe that Antoine, as Jacques Charbonneau, operated completely independent of the Caen resistance cells and may, in fact, been targeted by them as a suspected collaborator."

"Why do you think that?" Janey, one of the interns, asked.

"There are repeated references in the letters to acting alone, walking a thin line, having to be careful of locals, and so forth. When the invasion began we know anecdotally that reprisals against collaborators and others with whom resistance members had personal grudges were often carried out. There is an entire story here of a large transfer of assets illegally during the invasion and after from certain French civilians to others through violence."

"Sounds like a witch hunt mentality."

"Very much the same thing. If you had a grudge, or suspected anything of another you did not like, the chaos during the invasion would be a great opportunity to seek retribution. You can imagine that any of these people still alive as well as their descendants might not want this information made public."

"So, the moral is we can expect opposition from many levels. We need to anticipate and outflank the opposition, and create an immovable force through careful and strategic positioning. We will use frontal assault marketing to break through the obstacles," Jennifer left as the standing marching orders.

"We need an objective, something to highlight early on as the goal of the feature. I propose that we leverage funding to pay for the exhumation and reburial of Antoine Bouchard in a more fitting place. The reburial can take place on the next June 6 anniversary date. That gives us six months. That should be plenty of time to pull this together."

The Juno Letters opened on April 15 with a large headline on the front page of The Winnipeg Guardian - "Sacrifice on D-Day Saves Canadians." I was back in France when the first story appeared. Angus sent me an email with a link to the electronic version.

The introduction began with an explanation:

> A stash of letters never mailed but recently found on the Normandy coast tells of intrigue, heroism, and sacrifice that saved the lives of hundreds if not thousands of Canadian soldiers on D-Day. The unlikely friendship between a French fisherman and an American chaplain reveals the truth behind a series of incredible events that preceded the invasion of Juno Beach. The Winnipeg Guardian will publish a series of six feature stories telling of Antoine and Marianne Bouchard, and the Reverend H.W. "Andy" Anderson. It is a tale of subterfuge, deception,

heroism, and finally an act of terrible injustice that cries out for righting.

The first obstacle came from the French government's Foreign Combatant Grave Registry.

Mme Jennifer Sinclair
Winnipeg Guardian

Dear Mme Sinclair,

The ministry regrets to inform you that your request for approval to exhume the remains of internment #1278-1 has been denied.

At this time there is insufficient documentation to establish a reasonable identity for the deceased.

The response became a part of the second installment of *The Juno Letters*, and caused a flood of letters and emails in support of *The Juno Letters* project and the reburial. It accomplished exactly what Jennifer Sinclair had wanted - it spotlighted the source of the official opposition and created a newsworthy event to parallel the feature story to help catch the attention of the world media, especially in France.

The administer of the Calvados Department looked at me and simply shook his head.

"Monsieur, what you are asking is very unusual. I simply do not have the authority to allow you to disinter one of the bodies at La Cambe. Not based on such a request. You are not family. Even if you were, I do not know under what authority I could grant such a request."

"I have proof that the person buried in Grave 1278 is Antoine Bouchard, who was wrongfully branded a collaborator when, in reality, he performed a sacrifice for France that got him killed. I am seeking justice, monsieur, for my grandfather's friend, for the memory of his wife and daughter who disappeared during the war, and for the citizens of Courseulles who deserve to know this man helped liberate their commune."

"Ah, monsieur, I sympathize with you. I must admit your motives are very compelling. I simply have no authority in this matter. I am sorry. I suggest you contact the Ministry of History and Antiquities in Paris, monsieur."

I was not surprised by his refusal. I had already placed a call to the regional historical officer, who referred me up the maddening French bureaucratic chain. It was a process that could take months. I called Jennifer who promised to rally some support.

A week later the Paris newspaper Le Monde carried a story it had picked up on the national wire from a follow-up story by my reporter friend in Caen.

Patriot or Traitor?

Caen. The mysterious Antoine Bouchard was a patriot of France whose heroic action saved hundreds of Canadian soldiers landing on Juno Beach on June 6, 1944. His body was dumped in a common grave in the German cemetery at La Cambe as a traitor - an injustice that must be undone. This is the claim made by the American researcher, M. L.W. Hewitt, who has unravelled a tale of intrigue and heroism from the so-called Juno Letters.

"Antoine Bouchard was a hero. I have a duty, as do the people of France, to right the terrible injustice that has branded him a traitor," M. Hewitt told a group of reporters before the Prefecture in Caen on Wednesday. He was joined by a representative of the Winnipeg Rifles Juno Beach Association, a group of D-Day veterans, and their offspring.

Albert Devlin was a survivor of the D-Day assault on Juno Beach.

"M. Bouchard's sacrifice meant that hundreds, if not thousands of Canadian soldiers - including myself - survived the assault and were able to help liberate France. We owe Antoine Bouchard our lives," M. Devlin insisted.

Authorities in Calvados have refused to allow the inspection of the body known only as a "French Civilian - Unknown." Unless authorized by the Ministry of History and Archeology, only a family member can request the exhumation of the body buried in grave 1278. Calls to the Paris office of the Ministry have not been returned.

The story of *The Juno Letters* continued its way through Internet blogs and social media to all corners of the world much faster than I could have hoped. Messages and emails began to arrive from former combatants, people who had survived the German occupation, history buffs, ancestry researchers, and students. I made a commitment when the first correspondence began to arrive some time ago that I would answer every letter. There were so many that my own research began to bog down, and I seriously considered giving up that promise.

Until I met Gela.

I received a video in an email. It was sent from Haifa on the coast of Israel by a college student who explained that the video was of her grandmother, a woman named Gela, who had survived the French concentration camp at Natzweiler. Gela was too frail to travel, so her granddaughter filmed her story and narrated the translation.

> I was an inmate at the work camp called Natzweiler near Strasbourg. We were worked very hard, and it was always so cold. The conditions in the camp were brutal, and many died from starvation and disease.
>
> One day a woman arrived in camp. Her name was Marianne. She was the bravest woman I ever knew. Marianne was my friend.

CHAPTER 23 - MADAME SOULLANT

When I despair, I remember that all through history the way of
truth and love have always won.
— *Mahatma Gandhi*

"The Story of Marianne" video went viral on the Internet and
generated a new flood of correspondence. Most contained stories of
survivors or the stories survivors had told to their children or
friends. A few helped fill in details here and there. The more
information I gathered, the more I realized a serious publication
would have to come from all of this investigation.

Various holocaust survivor groups donated funds to help build a
memorial for Marianne at Natzweiler and to help reinter Antoine. I
was going through some of the stories when a knock at the door to
my hotel broke my concentration.

"Monsieur Hewitt? Special delivery," M. Racine politely replied.
I signed for the envelope and went back to my desk. I quickly
opened the envelope. It contained a note and a train ticket from
Caen to Paris for the following morning. The letter was polite and
to the point.

> Madame Soullant wishes the pleasure of your
> company at her residence in Paris Tuesday, April 6,
> at 1:00 PM. This matter will be of utmost interest to
> you. A car will be waiting at the train station in Paris
> for your convenience.

It was signed, Me. A. Lenoir. I had to ask at the front desk what
the "Me" stood for, and the clerk replied "solicitor" - or attorney.

I boarded the morning train to Paris in the downtown station in Caen, and settled back for the two-hour ride. My curiosity was running high. Just what information would Madame Soullant have that would encourage her to send me the train tickets sight unseen?

As expected, a driver was waiting for me as I stepped off the train. We drove through the streets of downtown Paris a short distance, then disappeared in an underground private parking entrance. A few minutes later I was ushered through an elegant rooftop home to a beautiful garden, awash in the soft spring sunlight of Paris.

Tea was waiting as I arrived.

"Bonjour, M. Hewitt. I am so glad to have the opportunity to meet with you."

Madame Soullant presented a gracious and well-mannered appearance. She was in her eighties, and obviously used to the finer aspects of life. She motioned for me to join her at the tea table. She offered me her hand, and I kissed it in the formal manner. I saw a tell tale tattoo of a red-orange comet on the inside of her wrist.

"Oh, my, you have been studying your French manners!" she exclaimed, displaying a playful nature I found wonderfully disarming.

"Please, sit and enjoy tea with me this afternoon."

"Forgive me, madame, but I am curious about the tattoo. Is there a significance to the comet?"

"We are all foolish sometimes in our youth, monsieur," and she smiled. Then she got straight to the point.

"I have read with a great deal of interest the stories in the newspapers about your so-called Juno Letters - I believe that is how they are called. I must congratulate you on unraveling such a mystery, and on documenting the stories of so many whose voices were left silent by the horror of the war. I myself have such a story you may find enlightening."

"May I take notes, madame?" I carefully asked. I had found that many survivors of the Nazi horror would speak to me, but were reluctant to allow me to take notes as they spoke or record their conversations.

"Oh, but of course. You see, much like your elusive Ariéle, I was a young girl when the Nazis invaded France. I never knew what happened to my father. My mother was arrested by the French police and we were hauled off in the middle of the night. I was separated from my mother and never saw her again.

"I was sold to be servant and a concubine, and was moved to Paris. The German officer who bought me was a part of the northern defense control headquarters which were on the first floor of the chateau where I was imprisoned. The officer had a mistress. She was kind to me, and worked very hard to keep me away from the Colonel when he drank, which was often. As a result of her efforts, I survived the war still a maiden, a feat uncommon among the young girls taken by the French police for the Nazis."

As I kept notes, I marveled at the lack of ambiguity in her descriptions. Most of the survivors I had documented had obscured much of the harshness of their treatment, using such benign words as "passing" and "housed" instead of murdered or imprisoned.

"Your recollections are especially vivid, madame. That is something I do not usually encounter."

"I have had a lifetime to reconcile my feelings, monsieur. For years I refused to grieve for my mother or father. I would not give the Boche the victory of a single tear. Eventually I learned that to grieve for my lost family was a victory over my perpetrators for I have survived - and they have not."

I could not help but admire this woman who had endured so much at such a young age, yet had triumphed over the terror. She continued her narrative.

"When the Allies invaded France, there was much frantic activity in the headquarters. The mistress of the house hid me away in a small anteroom in an office, and told me to stay very quiet, no matter what I heard. I lay very still, and in a few minutes I heard footsteps, then gunshots.

"I found out later that she was an informant in the resistance, spying on the headquarters unit, and passing information through the resistance to England. On that day, she hid me then opened a back door that was usually guarded - she had seduced the guard, and he was preoccupied elsewhere sleeping off a bottle of the colonel's best commandeered cognac.

"Members of the resistance entered the headquarters through the abandoned back door and opened fire, killing the colonel and many others. They then fled out the back and into the streets of Paris.

"We fled the chateau, seeking refuge in a safe house. The drunken guard was shot in the chateau courtyard for his misconduct."

She stopped and took a sip of tea, and chuckled slightly when she placed her cup down.

"Forgive me, for I know that God would disapprove of me showing amusement at another's violent fate, but I could not help myself."

I had to laugh at her obvious delight in telling of the guard's execution. She composed herself and continued.

"We moved from house to house to hide from the police. We used assumed names and managed to avoid capture by the time the Americans and Free French liberated the city.

"After the war I stayed in Paris. I had the opportunity to attend a real school for the first time. A few years later, I met a beautiful young Frenchman who had a head for business, as you say in America. He built several successful businesses during the postwar period. We were married, and I became pregnant with the first of our three children. After my children were grown, I began to spend more time in his business offices and learned all I could about their operations.

"My love passed away thirty years ago, and I assumed control over his holdings. I found I had learned quite a lot more from him than I thought, and have been very successful in my own right."

Her housekeeper came back to refill the tea cups, and she stopped to take a sip, then pushed an envelope across the tea table to me.

"I am most impressed by your efforts to raise the funds to re-inter your Antoine in a more fitting cemetery. Please accept this check for your organization. It should provide sufficient funds to guarantee a decent burial for your patriot."

I was stunned by the unexpected offer, and stammered, "Thank you, madame. Your generosity is most appreciated." I dared not look at the check.

"My motivations are not charitable, monsieur. On the contrary, they are quite personal. You see ..."

She stopped to take a deep breath, her eyes starting to tear up slightly.

"My christened name was Bouchard."

I looked at her in amazement, stunned, unable to speak for what seemed an eternity. I looked into her green eyes, and saw Marianne and Antoine smiling back at me. I drew back in my chair and whispered softly, "Ariéle."

She smiled.

"As his daughter I will claim his grave and authorize his exhumation, monsieur. I have already made a contact in the government at the highest level to ensure you will have their cooperation."

She handed me a second envelope.

"Inside you will find the contact information you will need to receive your authorization. The gentleman listed is expecting your call, and I can guarantee you will have his cooperation."

I reached into my valise and pulled out the small gold cross. Mme Soullant let out a soft gasp as I extended my hand to her. She gently, reverently, took the cross in her hands.

"This was my father's, and he wore it every day of his life. I used to play with it on his neck as a little girl."

"Please accept this, with my gratitude."

Ariéle smiled as a tear ran down her cheek. She reached forward and grasped my hands firmly.

"Thank you for finding my mother and father."

CHAPTER 24 - A PATRIOT OF FRANCE

*War may sometimes be a necessary evil. But no matter how necessary,
it is always an evil, never a good. We will not learn how to live
together in peace by killing each other's children.*
— *Jimmy Carter*

My flight back to Paris from Portland was scheduled for later that evening, so I was in no hurry. The cemetery in Salem, Oregon was lit by a brilliant Willamette Valley sun this early morning as I walked up the lane. I had a small map with a location marked on it, the final resting place of my grandparents.

I stopped and stood quietly, reverently, before the marker for Henry W.

"Andy" Anderson and Lucile Anderson. I felt a sense of connection after this long journey that amplified fond memories of my childhood, and filled me with a wonderful sense of pride.

I had donated the original letters to the Canadian museum at Juno Beach. They made museum-quality copies for me to take home.

"Hi, Grandpa Andy. It was a long journey, but I fulfilled my promise to Antoine to deliver these."

I placed the small package with the Juno Letters on Grandpa Andy's grave.

It was a small moment in the scheme of things. It was a moment I will remember always.

———

June 6, Present Day

The fish market on the quay at Courseulles-sur-Mer was filled with tourists enjoying the warming summer sun as the fresh coastal breeze began to wan and weaken. It would be a beautiful day along the Normandy shore. Visitors from around the world had convened throughout Normandy to celebrate this anniversary of the Allied landings of D-Day, and the publicity surrounding the memorial service for Antoine Bouchard took center stage. Courseulles had never seen such a crowd, dominated by young families with children, an entire generation that rose to honor the hero of *The Juno Letters*.

The hustle and bustle of the busy seaside morning was broken by the sound of gun fire, multiple rifles in unison, first once, then twice, then a third volley - a stylized, ritual sound, followed by the strain of bagpipes.

Monsieur Racine, the owner of the Hotel de Paris, interrupted his guests in the outside courtyard, asking, "Un moment, s'il vous plâit - one moment, please" - and bowed his head. People all over the commune stopped what they were doing in silent reverence.

In the local cemetery, seven soldiers stood at attention, rifles at parade rest, dressed in the uniforms of the Canadian Royal Winnipeg Rifles and First Canadian Scottish Regiment. Two pipers in traditional kilt played a haunting tribute - "Amazing Grace" - a song of honor. A crowd gathered around the fresh earthen mound bedecked with flowers, and the French Tricolor was folded over the simple grave. A magnificently kilted Angus McDonough stood among them with tears in his eyes.

The pipers' strains ended. M. Racine quietly said, "Merci" to his guests, and they resumed their conversations.

A priest blessed the grave, and the large crowd began to disburse.

Angus McDonough took the arm of his daughter Jenny and they walked happily back towards town for a long-awaited stroll on Juno Beach.

A young girl stayed behind, and placed a small bouquet of flowers on the grave. She wore a gold cross around her neck.

"Voilá, grandmama! Les fluers sont tres belle! - The flowers are so beautiful!"

Ariéle smiled, watching the girl play in the soft sunlight.

"Yes, they are, child. They certainly are!" She looked up at me and smiled, nodding her head quietly.

The little girl joined her mother and her great grandmother Ariéle, and they quietly walked back toward town hand-in-hand.

The white cross at the head of the grave bore a simple message.

Antoine Bouchard
1898 - June 6, 1944
A Patriot of France

L.W. HEWITT

THE JUNO LETTERS SERIES

BY L.W. HEWITT

The Juno Letters reveal a web of intrigue, love, tragedy, and heroism that reminds us how the two devastating world wars that defined the Twentieth Century changed the lives of its children, and their children's children, forever.

The Juno Letters - Book 1

Letters discovered in a tin box hidden in the foundation of a small cottage in Normandy reveal a terrible secret. Antoine's world is in chaos. His beautiful Marianne, his precious daughter Ariéle, missing. The lives of hundreds - perhaps thousands - of Allied soldiers preparing to storm Juno Beach on D-Day literally are in his hands. The Gestapo hunt him as a traitor - the French resistance as a collaborator. As the invasion erupts all around him, Antoine must choose - to find Marianne and Ariéle, or face Hell even if it means he could lose his family, his only friend, and his life.

Cross of Fire - Book 2

Gela Pientka defiantly kept a bloody truth that could topple governments and destabilize world currencies. To protect her family, she took the secret to her grave. Gala's journal, however, exposes a stunning discovery - a corrupt "Money Train," supported by murder and slavery, fueled by the foul stench of greed. Truth is fighting back - fighting to reunite a family ripped apart by the Holocaust, to restore honor - with the Cross of Fire as a weapon against the forces of evil.

Clan of the Black Sun - Book 3

A mysterious stone of black obsidian holds a magical grip over a rural French clan ripped apart by an ancient curse. The Nazis covet the relic as a weapon of immense power that will lead their armies to victory in the West. The Allies fear rumors of the stone mask a deadly weapon that threatens the invasion of Fortress Europe. The resistance risks annihilation to recover it. The French police and the Gestapo will destroy all in their path to possess it.

Print edition available at Amazon and CreateSpace
E-book editions at all major e-book retailers and services
Audio editions exclusively at Audible.com
junoletters.com

ABOUT THE JUNO LETTERS

My grandfather, Grandpa "Andy," was a great fisherman. My brothers and I used to visit him in Vancouver, Washington. I remember him teaching us how to catch fish in Angle Lake, and the giant steelhead he caught on the Lewis River that was flopping around in the laundry tub on the back porch. He was the chaplain of the Veterans Hospital and remained active his entire life - earning his doctorate degree at age 82.

When I developed an interest in the history of the wars of the twentieth century, I rediscovered the man Henry W. Anderson as a soldier in the Great War and an Army chaplain in the Pacific during World War II. In 2012 I visited the locations in Paris where he stayed in 1918. It was while touring the Normandy coast the idea for The Juno Letters took seed. This was a labor of love and deep respect dedicated to the man known to most as just "Andy" - chaplain, grandfather, a great fisherman, and a powerful force in my life.

The story takes place primarily in France and during some dialog I use French phrases or individual words. In some cases an English translation immediately follows. I use the inverted question and exclamation marks (¿, ¡) in writing French dialog despite its discontinued use in some informal writing.

The names of books and articles are listed in italics as are the book series. When using French proper names, I record the first instance with a written out salutation; subsequently I only use the abbreviation: M. - monsieur, Mme - madame, and Mlle - mademoiselle. Note that only the "M." uses a period after the letter, since the others contain the final letter of the abbreviation - a common form.

Corps d'Autoprotection français [sic] is the name of the French auxiliary of the Gestapo. It was also known as the Carlingue. For convenience, I will refer to the various forms of the security organizations as the French Gestapo, and often just as the Gestapo. The Gestapo in The Juno Letters have French surnames, consistent with the Corps d'Autoprotection français.

Organizational structures within the French police, the security police, and local governments were very complex and overlapping. I refer to these organizations collectively as the Police Nacionale.

ABOUT THE AUTHOR

I have coffee most every morning at my "office" - a small table in a 1920s style restaurant and hotel called the Olympic Club in Centralia, Washington. Visitors assume I work there, some think I am the manager. I direct people to the bathrooms - the urinals in this place are a tourist attraction all by themselves. This is where I write. The chaos and atmosphere prep me for the day, and everyone in town knows if you need to talk to me, just drop by the "Oly Club."

Most don't know that I have a master's degree in business, and have run my own technology company for nearly twenty of my last forty working years. I won a national championship on horseback, raced sailboats, wrestled octopus, baby-sat a killer whale, and once was a cook on a salmon purse seiner.

I have led an interesting life - married thirty-plus years, have three children, six grandchildren, and twenty-five foster children. I am now free to pursue my passion for writing - especially about the two great wars of the twentieth century. So I cherish my role as "author-in-residence," or that crazy guy at the table by the urinals - it depends on your perspective.

Made in the USA
San Bernardino, CA
15 September 2014